BRANTFORD PUBLIC LIBRARY
39154900528084

D0291923

DUST UP

FORGE BOOKS BY JON MCGORAN

Drift
Deadout
Dust Up

DUST UP

Jon McGoran

A Tom Doherty Associates Book
New York

This is a work of fiction. All of the characters, organizations, and events portrayed in this novel are either products of the author's imagination or are used fictitiously.

DUST UP

Copyright © 2016 by Jon McGoran

All rights reserved.

A Forge Book
Published by Tom Doherty Associates, LLC
175 Fifth Avenue
New York, NY 10010

www.tor-forge.com

Forge® is a registered trademark of Tom Doherty Associates, LLC.

The Library of Congress Cataloging-in-Publication Data is available upon request.

ISBN 978-0-7653-8030-2 (hardcover)
ISBN 978-1-4668-7308-7 (e-book)

Our books may be purchased in bulk for promotional, educational, or business use. Please contact your local bookseller or the Macmillan Corporate and Premium Sales Department at 1-800-221-7945, extension 5442, or by e-mail at MacmillanSpecialMarkets@macmillan.com.

First Edition: April 2016

Printed in the United States of America

0   9   8   7   6   5   4   3   2   1

For the people of Haiti
and all those working to create a bright,
sustainable Haitian future

DUST UP

1

At the first knock, I was fully awake. It was that kind of sound—hard, sharp, urgent. Loud. I pulled on my pants and grabbed my gun. There was the tiniest pause, and for a moment I wondered if it was a cop. It was an almost perfect cop knock—*bang, bang, bang*. Maybe it was Danny and something was wrong. Or one of my other fellow public guardians got drunk and thought it would be a hoot to "cop knock" my door in the middle of the night. Or maybe I was in trouble.

Then it kept going. *Bang bang bang bang bang bang bang bang.*

That was no cop.

The pounding grew faster, from urgent to frantic. I was halfway down the stairs when it changed again, from a fist against a door to an explosive report. A gunshot. Then another and another. The sounds didn't overlap—when one started, the other one stopped.

Bang bang bang bang bang—BANG BANG BANG.

I skipped the last few steps, but by the time I jerked open the door, both sounds were gone, replaced by the squeal of tires and the engine roar of a black Toyota Corolla speeding away. Just before it disappeared, the driver looked right at me. She was Asian, young, maybe pretty, but her face was contorted. Anguish, sorrow, fear. Then she was gone.

I looked down.

"What is it?" Nola asked, coming down the stairs behind me.

"Stay back!"

She stopped, halfway down. "What is it?" she asked again, quieter, sadder. Like somehow she knew.

"Just . . . stay back, okay?"

The red blossom on his chest was still growing, but his eyes were glassy and gone. Nothing was pumping that blood. He let out a soft sigh. His last breath.

I wanted to close the door, go back to bed and pretend it hadn't happened. Maybe I would have, but he was slumped across the threshold. I knew it would be a while before I closed that door again.

"Doyle?" Nola called, still standing on the steps, sounding small and far away.

I looked out the doorway, up and down the deserted street.

"It's okay," I told her.

That's what you have to say. What I meant was, *I* was okay, although that wasn't true, either. I came back to the bottom of the stairs. "Someone's been shot."

She nodded because she already knew it. Tears were rolling down her cheeks. "Who is it?"

"I don't know."

2

"Ronald Hartwell," Detective Mike Warren announced, reading it off his notepad like it was the result of some impressive feat of detective work. As if finding the guy's wallet and copying the name off his driver's license made Warren a hotshot.

Danny Tennison caught my eye and smiled.

The homicide unit was packed with guys like Warren. He looked good in a nice suit, I'd give him credit for that. Not much else.

We were leaning against one of the parked cars in front of my Fishtown row home while Warren impressed us with his deductive reasoning. Danny was my partner, at least for the time being. After five years, he was considering an assignment with a joint DEA task force. It was a good move career-wise, but I was feeling a bit hard done by.

He was off duty, but he'd come over as soon as he'd heard. His wife Laura had come with him. I'd thought that was strange at first, but now that she was upstairs comforting Nola, I was glad.

"So who is he?"

"Some dead guy," Warren said with a snort, laughing as though he was unaware he was doing it alone. "Seriously, though . . ." His head snapped around. "Maybe you should be telling me."

Mike Warren was a bit of a dick.

"Well, maybe you could look through his wallet a little more," Danny said. "You know, find some more 'clues.'"

Across the street, two pairs of uniforms were working their way down the block, door to door, asking if anyone had seen anything. The guys from the medical examiner's office had already taken away the body.

I pointed toward Albert's, the darkened deli on the corner. "The deli might have surveillance video."

Warren ignored that, looking at me sideways. "You're saying you don't know the man, but I find it interesting he decides to get himself killed on your front doorstep. Weird, ain't it?"

I shrugged. I had told him what happened several times already.

He nodded sagely, as if something would come to him.

"Could be coincidence," Danny said. "Guy sees someone coming up on him, starts pounding on the nearest doorway."

Warren kept nodding, then turned to me. "But you saw the girl who did it, right?" He looked at his notepad. "Isn't that what you said? Fleeing the scene of the crime."

That was not what I had said.

"I don't know who did it. I saw a woman driving away fast. She looked upset."

"So, what," he said, "you don't think she was fleeing the scene of the crime?"

"Pretty rough thing to witness. She might have just wanted to get away before she was next."

"But you didn't see anybody else out here, right?"

I shook my head. I knew she was the main suspect, and she should be, but the look on her face said she wasn't trying to get away with murder; she was trying to get away *from* murder.

Warren shrugged. "Maybe she wasn't running away at all. Maybe she was in a hurry to go kill someone else."

He had a laugh at that, then he held out a business card. "Call me if you remember anything else."

I left his hand hanging there. "I know where to reach you."

He nodded smugly as he put the card away, like he'd heard I was an asshole and I had just confirmed it. "Let me know if you leave town."

I nodded.

"From what I hear, you leave town a lot."

I turned to go inside but was confronted with the blood that drenched the front steps. There was a dense circle of spatter on the front door, too, and a hole where one of the bullets had lodged after it shredded Ron Hartwell's heart.

I stopped and sighed. I thought about going around to the back, but I didn't want Nola to ever see our home looking like this.

Danny clapped a hand on my shoulder. "I'll take care of that."

3

Nola and Laura were talking quietly on the sofa when Danny and I walked in. They had become pretty close friends since Nola had moved in with me a year earlier. Laura had always been fond of me in a disapproving way, but she adored Nola. That had earned me some points.

Laura got up and went to Danny, patting my arm on the way. I took her place on the sofa and put my arm around Nola, kissing her head. Her face was pink and wet.

Danny spoke quietly to Laura, went into the kitchen and found a bucket under the sink, and started filling it from the tap.

Laura whispered to Danny, but he shook his head and slipped out the door with the bucket of hot water in one hand and a roll of paper towels in the other.

Nola opened her eyes and watched him go, then squeezed her eyes against her tears. I understood. The blood being rinsed off our steps was the last of Ron Hartwell. Dead is dead, but when your blood has been washed off the sidewalk and down into the sewer, you were erased. Dead and gone.

I held Nola tight and closed my eyes. Her breathing grew softer.

Danny came back inside to refill his bucket a few times. At some point, I guess when the worst of it was gone, Laura went outside with him. Finally, I heard Danny putting the bucket back into the cabinet under the sink. Nola was asleep. I might have been, as well. I opened my eyes and smiled at Danny.

He gave me a questioning look and a thumbs-up, asking if we were okay. I nodded, and then he was gone.

It was four A.M.

Nola stirred when the door clicked shut. Without a word, she slid off the sofa, grabbed my hand, and pulled me to my feet, into the bedroom, onto the bed. She didn't get undressed, didn't let go of my hand the entire time. She rolled up against my arm until her back was firmly pressed against my front. Then she fell back to sleep.

I had bad dreams. Imagine that.

Ron Hartwell was looking up at me, his body dissolving as it was rinsed down the steps, into the gutter, down the sewer, the whole time his dead eyes somehow protesting, saying this wasn't how it was supposed to be.

I had the same dream several times. The only thing that saved me was Nola, thrashing around from bad dreams of her own.

I had decided early that regardless of how little sleep I got, I was still going into work in the morning. I had rehearsed in my mind what I was going to say to Nola, how I would explain that I had to go in—I had work to do, and I needed to find out what the hell had happened last night. I'd kiss her sleepy head, tell her that she needed to rest and I'd check in on her later.

She was up before I was.

"Good morning," I said, sitting up in bed.

She gave me a tight smile, not quite ready to commit to that yet.

She brought me coffee and sat next to me on the bed.

"What happened last night, Doyle?"

I put my arm around her and pulled her tight. "I don't know, baby. But I'm going to find out."

Three coffees later, I was still sleepwalking, but I was walking.

Nola wasn't much better, but when I suggested she take the day off, she shook her head.

"And hang around here all day? No thanks. Not yet."

We walked out together through the front door. I had considered using the back door, through the basement, but that would have been almost as strange. As it was, I tried not to notice how the sidewalk was still damp in places, tried not to look around for evidence of the killing, or at least not to get caught looking. Nola made no secret about it, scanning the steps, the sidewalk. Danny had done a great job. There wasn't a trace of blood, not even in the gutter. I kept walking—casual, like nothing was out of the ordinary—and Nola kept up, looking back over her shoulder as we walked to the car. I hurried us along, trying to get away before she noticed the splintered hole where they'd pulled the slug out of the front door.

4

Danny looked like hell. He tried to raise an eyebrow at me but could only manage halfway. "You're here," he said.

"More or less. You, too." I plopped into my chair at the desk facing his. "Thanks for last night. For the cleanup and bringing Laura and everything."

He nodded. "You sure you want to be here?"

"Never been sure about that. You seen Warren?"

"He was in with IAD."

My stomach soured. "Internal affairs?" I laughed. "What, do they think I did it?"

Danny yawned and gave a halfhearted, "Probably not."

"How long's he been in there?"

Before Danny could answer, Warren came through the door. "How long has who been in where?" He grinned like he had caught me doing something.

"Any news on the Hartwell thing?" I asked.

Warren didn't look tired. I got the feeling he hadn't been up all night working the case.

He put a photo on my desk. "Recognize her?"

I shrugged. "Looks like the woman I saw driving away last night." In the picture, she was smiling, a big carefree grin with laughter right behind it. Hard to reconcile with the tortured expression I'd seen the night before.

"Miriam Hartwell," he said. "The vic's wife."

I nodded. So she wasn't just a bystander. I felt sad. Whatever her involvement, she wouldn't be laughing like that again for a while. "Did you talk to her?"

He shook his head. "Nope. She hasn't been home. Not answering her phone, neither." He said it ominously, as if it proved she was guilty. To be fair, it was pretty damning, but I thought back to the pain on the face driving away, and I looked at the smile in the photo on my desk. Even squinting, I didn't see a murderer.

"So why was he on my doorstep?"

"You don't have any ideas?"

I shook my head.

"You've never met either of them?"

I shook my head again. "Never."

"Your address was in his phone's GPS."

"So it wasn't a coincidence."

"He had also Googled you. You got no idea why?" He leaned forward. "You sure he didn't find out you were banging her, he comes to confront you, she decides to kill him first? Or you do?"

I laughed, first time that day. I'm pretty sure Danny did too. "Yeah, that's what happened."

"Fuck you, Carrick. That shit happens. You'd be surprised."

He said it in that patronizing way homicide dicks do sometimes: *You wouldn't understand because you haven't seen what we've seen . . . You aren't privy to the dark secrets of the human soul.*

I used to want to work homicide. Thought it was the major leagues. Then I got to know the guys there. Major-league assholes was more like it. I laughed again.

Warren shook his head, pitying me.

"Did you get the video from the deli across the street?" I asked.

He waved a hand dismissively. "Nothing there, just a blank file. No surprise they had an equipment malfunction at a dive like that. Anyway, we put out a BOLO—her and the car. We've got someone on their apartment. We'll have her in custody soon enough. She didn't show up for work today, didn't call in." He laughed. "He didn't, either, but he's got a better excuse."

I looked up at him as he turned to go. "Did they work together?"

"Yup," he said, bored. "Maybe they were up for the same promotion or something."

"Where did they work?"

"Energene Corporation. Some kind of big biotech company."

5

I decided to surprise Nola for lunch. She worked at GreensGrow, an urban farm a couple miles from our house. It was a tangle of hoses and planting tables, sheds, and gardening tools, all strewn around a big former industrial lot. I hadn't found it all that impressive when she first started working there, but it was a hell of a lot of green in the middle of all that gray.

"Doyle!" she said, standing behind a plywood counter. Her hands hovered in front of an ancient fax machine, waiting to catch the paper slowly squeezing out of it. Her face brightened when she saw me, but I could see it had been dark to start with. "I'm just waiting for this order, then I'm taking lunch. Want to go out?"

We sought refuge in the dark interior of The Abbaye, a local favorite a couple miles away. We small-talked around an appetizer, but in the lull while we waited for our sandwiches, she let out a deep, sad sigh.

"So do they know anything about him? About what happened last night?"

I told her what I'd learned from Warren. She listened with her head down until I got to the part about the biotech company.

"Energene?" she said, her head whipping up.

I nodded.

"Both of them?"

I nodded again.

"Hmm." She thought for a second. "What do you think that means?"

I shook my head. "I've been wondering. What do you know about them?"

Nola was a bit of a food activist. She had a degree in horticulture and used to own an organic farm. "One of their main offices is in Philly. They're big. International. Not as big as Stoma Corporation, but they'd like to be. They're into a lot of the same things—chemicals, genetically modified crops, industrial agriculture."

I'd had a couple of run-ins with biotech companies in the year or so since I'd met Nola. We'd met amid the first of them. Big run-ins, including one with Stoma that damn near killed us both.

"So why was he coming to our house?"

"I don't know."

She looked suddenly upset, the conversation bringing it all back to her. I reached across the table and held her hand, squeezing it.

"So the guy who's working the case . . ." she said.

"Mike Warren."

"Right. Is that the same Mike Warren you told me about who botched the investigation into the Kelly Drive shooting last spring?"

I nodded.

"Wait, is he the one who messed up the evidence on that South Street stabbing?"

"That's him."

She stared at me for a moment, thinking about what that meant and what she thought about it. The waiter brought our sandwiches.

"Well," she said, picking up a fry. "Try not to get into too much trouble, okay?"

6

"Of course, he's an idiot," Danny said, sipping his coffee. "We all know that. But so what, Doyle? It's his case."

"Right, and if a guy bled out on your front steps, in front of Laura, you'd be okay with Mike Warren on the case?"

He looked away from me, out the window, then turned back. "Nola saw him?"

"She heard it. She was there. She's freaked out, and I totally get it."

We were working surveillance in South Philly, parked across from the Oregon Diner. Some up-and-comer named Derek Hoyt was taking meetings, trying to expand his network. We were there to take a photographic record of the attendees.

"I hear you," Danny said, raising the camera and snapping a dozen quick photos as two knuckleheads walked up to the front door. "Maurice Blaylock and Tonio Pesker," he said, naming them. I wrote them down. Half a dozen names so far.

I laughed. "So I tell her who pulled the case, and she says, 'Mike Warren, you mean the guy who botched the Kelly Drive shooting and the South Street stabbing?'"

We both laughed at that.

"So what are you going to do?"

I shrugged. "Depends on when we wrap up here."

He nodded.

Five minutes later, the door opened and Blaylock, Pesker, and Hoyt walked out, grinning like they're best friends on Christmas morning. Chances were good that by the end of the year, one of them would be dead and one or both of the others would have killed him.

Danny clicked another series of pictures as they shook hands and separated. Then he looked at me, cocking an eyebrow. "We're done here. What's your plan?"

I shrugged and looked at my watch. "I'm going to go to Energene, ask a few questions."

He sighed. "Of course you are. I'm not going with you."

"Perish the thought."

He looked at his watch. "It's two thirty. I'm going to log these in. Then I have a meeting with Cory Rogers at DEA about the task force."

I nodded but didn't say anything. Danny was excited about working with DEA, and I couldn't blame him. But it meant he was leaving me all alone in the land of the assholes for two months, maybe longer. He knew I was annoyed.

He gave me a big fake smile and punched my shoulder. "So are you planning on getting screamed at right away or not till later?"

"Suarez is in a budget meeting, so I guess not until later."

"Perfect," Danny said, shaking his head. "Budget meeting. He'll be in just the right mood for you."

Suarez was our lieutenant. He and I were not besties.

Danny dropped me at my car, and I drove over to Energene's North American headquarters in University City. It was a strangely likable twist of angled glass and steel, one of the newer buildings on the Philadelphia skyline, poking up into the airspace over the tracks around grand old Thirtieth Street Station.

The guy behind the desk was fifty, African American, with sharp eyes. He was friendly in a customer-servicey kind of way, but with an edge, like if he didn't want me getting past him, I wasn't getting past him. His name tag read BRYANT. I didn't know if that was his first name or his last name.

I put my badge and ID flat on the desk so it wasn't obvious to the people coming and going behind me. "I'm here to talk to Ron Hartwell's supervisor," I said. I had no idea who that was, but I was confident Bryant could figure it out for me.

He studied the ID intently for a moment. "Certainly," he said. "Just a second."

He tapped at the computer then picked up the phone. "Yes, this is the front desk. I have a Detective Carrick here who would like to speak to Mr. Vinson . . . I believe it has to do with Ron Hartwell."

7

Two minutes later, a guy who was not Ron Hartwell's superior stepped off one of the elevators and walked toward me. He was obviously ex-military, and I don't think his hair knew he was out yet, cut close to the sides and a tiny bit longer on top.

"Detective Carrick?" he said as he walked up, extending his hand in a gesture that seemed a lot friendlier than the expression on his face. Luckily, before I shook his hand, I realized what he wanted and handed him my ID to study.

He looked back and forth between my face and the ID. Then he handed it back to me. "Okay," he said. "Can't be too sure these days. What can I do for you?"

"I came to speak to Ron Hartwell's superior. Is that you?"

"I'm Tom Royce, head of security. I liaise with police. Try to make sure there's a minimum of disruption to our operations here."

He clasped his hands in front of him and leaned back, like he was thinking of all the ways I could disrupt their operations.

"Ron Hartwell is dead," I told him, lowering my voice, figuring he didn't know—otherwise, he wouldn't be acting like such a prick.

"I know," he said. "It's very sad. But I'm wondering what it has to do with Energene."

"He was murdered," I said, loudly enough that several of the people walking by stopped or at least slowed down to look. Royce winced. I lowered my voice and leaned closer. "The police investigate these things."

He looked around at the residual attention people were still paying us. Then he looked back at me, squinting to let me know he didn't like me. "One moment," he said, turning away and placing a call on his mobile phone. A few seconds later, he turned back around. "Okay. Come this way."

I followed him to the elevators, where he placed his palm against a glass panel on the wall. A matrix of circles lit up, and he casually scrolled them down with his fingertips until he got to the top of the list. He tapped one of the circles on the top row.

We didn't talk much on the way up or after we got off on the twenty-sixth floor.

I followed him down a carpeted hallway. After a maze of hushed cubicles, there was a series of heavy wooden doors. We passed one that read RON HARTWELL. It was closed. Three doors down, we came to one that read SPENCER VINSON.

Royce gave me an annoyed look as he knocked on the door with the back of his hand.

A voice on the other side said, "Come in."

Royce opened the door enough to poke his head inside, and the voice followed it up with, "Busy, Royce. What is it?"

"Sorry, sir," he said without entering. "That detective is here to talk to Mr. Vinson about Ron Hartwell."

There was a pause, as if they were sharing some nonverbal communication. Then Royce stepped aside for me to edge past him. Up close, he was shorter than I had thought.

Inside the office, a heavyset man in his late forties was sitting behind a desk. His pale face had a glow of perspiration.

In the chair pulled up next to him was a slender man in his fifties who was clearly in charge. He wore a sour expression that probably had a lot to do with the other man's sweat. It made me feel a little more charitably toward Royce.

"Mr. Vinson?" I said to the man behind the desk.

"Yes, that's right." His face remained oddly blank, like he didn't know what expression he should be wearing.

"I'm Detective Carrick."

I turned to the other man, letting him know it was his turn.

"Bradley Bourden," he said. "I'm the CEO."

Yes, you are, I thought. "I just want to ask a few questions about Ron Hartwell." The man behind the desk almost jumped when I looked at him. "You know he's been murdered."

Bourden closed his eyes for a moment. "Won't you sit down?" he said, waving me to the chair still facing the desk. He sent a dull glare in Royce's direction.

I ignored the chair.

"It's very sad," Vinson said. "He was one of our brightest."

"Any idea who might have done it?"

Vinson's face went blank again, like he couldn't imagine the question was for him.

Bourden glanced at Royce again, then at me. "I would hate to speculate."

"Speculation is exactly what I'm looking for, Mr. Bourden. We're trying to develop as many theories as possible. Then we'll see which ones we can rule out."

"Have you ruled out simple robbery?" Royce asked, still in the doorway.

"His wallet was untouched."

Vinson shifted in his seat. It was almost a squirm.

Bourden let out a sigh. "This is a very competitive industry."

I nodded, waiting for him to continue. In the silent pause, I heard a faint buzzing sound behind me and realized it was Royce's phone.

Bourden lowered his voice. "We had recently begun to suspect Hartwell of industrial espionage."

"Really?"

He nodded.

"What do you think he stole?"

Bourden shrugged, suddenly more relaxed, like a weight had been lifted off his shoulders. "Secrets. Who knows? It was just a vague suspicion."

"Based on what?"

He gestured to Royce. When I turned to look at him, he was typing into his phone.

He looked up. "Oh, um, not much. Guilty behavior, I guess."

"Do you have any evidence?" I asked.

Bourden shook his head. "Nothing."

"Who do you think he was selling secrets to?"

Bourden glanced at Royce again, distracted. "Maybe the Chinese. Maybe one of our competitors."

He was so distracted, I turned to follow his gaze just as he snapped, "Royce, what is it?"

Royce's face was twisted in a grimace of awkwardness. "I . . . something came up. They need me at the front desk. I have to go."

Bourden's eyes flared. "Now?"

He seemed frustrated and annoyed. But there was something else in his voice as he said that one word. Nervousness, maybe, or even fear.

"I'll be right back," Royce said. Then he disappeared.

Bourden swiveled his eyes at me and shrugged, as if that was the end of the story.

"Do you think that may have something to do with why he was killed?"

"You want me to speculate?"

"Sure."

"It's a nasty business, industrial espionage. Very unsavory, as I'm sure you can imagine. Frankly, I have a hard time picturing Hartwell getting himself involved in something like that. But if he did, I could see him getting in over his head."

I turned to Vinson. "What's your impression of Miriam?"

He shrugged. "Seems nice."

Bourden sat back, as if he was relieved to be talking about something else. I was surprised he thought it *was* something else.

"She wasn't in today," Vinson added.

"I'm sure she's distraught," Bourden said.

"I don't know her as well," Vinson said. "She's a few levels below Ron in the company. She's a nurse with our on-site health clinic, so it's a different department, too. Human resources."

"She seems perfectly nice," Bourden said. "Of course, we've been looking into her, as well."

"You think she's involved?" I asked.

Bourden smiled, but he wasn't very good at it. "If I had to speculate, I'd say she knew about it but wasn't involved. But who knows, she could have been the mastermind."

I nodded, studying him.

"Did they search his apartment?" he asked. "We'd be very interested in any intellectual property that he might have had there. Or anything to incriminate Ms. Hartwell. Or exonerate her, of course."

"I'm not at liberty to discuss that," I said. Truth was, I didn't know if they had or hadn't. It should have been a no-brainer, but this was Mike Warren we were talking about. It was practically criminal negligence he wasn't right there, asking Bourden and Vinson these annoying questions.

Then a voice in the hallway said, "Carrick? What the hell are you doing here?"

And there he was.

8

Warren looked annoyed and even more confused than usual. Royce was practically glowing with red anger. The muscles in his jaw were bulging, like he had a gerbil tucked in the back of each cheek.

"Hey, Detective Warren. Just asking some preliminary questions about the Hartwell case."

"You mean *my* Hartwell case?"

I smiled. Then I turned to Bourden, whose mouth had fallen slightly open. "My colleague Detective Warren is here to ask some follow-up questions."

As I squeezed past Warren, he grabbed my elbow. "I got this, Carrick," he said through gritted teeth.

"Oh, sure," I said, smiling. "Just trying to help."

Bourden let out a quiet, aggravated huff. "And what can I do for *you*, Detective Warren?"

I turned to Royce, who seemed redder and shorter. "I'll see myself out, thanks."

I slipped past him and started walking down the hallway. I stopped when I heard Warren say, "Miriam Hartwell has gone missing. We think she might have killed her husband."

I wanted to smack him in the head for giving away a detail like that. When I looked around, Royce was standing in the doorway looking back and forth between Warren inside the office and me outside.

When I turned toward the elevators, he was still there. But when I peeked back two seconds later, he was gone, and the door to Bourden's office was closed.

Peering out over the maze of cubicles, I got the distinct impression they were all populated, but I couldn't see anyone. The background hum of quietly clicking keys and human breathing was barely as loud as the ventilation system and the overhead lights.

As I approached the nearest cubicle, I could see a woman in her early sixties typing on her computer keyboard—old school, perfect hand positioning, never looking at the keyboard. She glanced up as I got nearer, startled but recovering quickly with a confused smile.

"Can I help you?" she asked in a hushed voice.

A younger woman popped her head over the cubicle divider, met my eyes, then looked back down.

"Hi." I smiled, gentle and reassuring, as I showed her my badge. "I'm here because of what happened to Ron Hartwell."

She stopped typing, and her face pinched into a sad grimace. "Oh my. Such a tragedy."

"Did you know him well?"

"Not too well, really. He seems really nice. I know his wife better."

"Miriam?"

She nodded. "I used to work with her in the HR department. They're a really cute couple. They were."

"Have you heard from her?"

She shook her head. "No, we're not that close. I'm sure she's devastated."

"Had either of them been acting unusual lately?"

She cocked her head. "Unusual how?"

"Anything, really. Nervous or worried or angry or sad. Anything that sticks out?"

She shrugged. "They might have seemed a little more stressed than usual." She leaned forward. "The scientists are always kind of stressed around here."

"Did they seem happy? Together, I mean."

"Oh, yes. Absolutely. If anything, they seemed closer than ever just lately."

"How do you mean?"

She shrugged. "I don't know really, just a sense."

The head in the next cubicle popped up again. "Sorry, I couldn't help overhearing. You're talking about Ron and Miriam, right?"

The woman I'd been talking to rolled her eyes. "Yes, Sheila, we were."

"They did seem happy. Or closer or whatever. I noticed it too."

"In what way?" I asked.

"I don't know. They seemed to be walking closer whenever I saw them together. And they were always whispering to each other, like they were in on this big secret no one else knew about."

I smiled. "They seemed happy?"

She screwed up her face. "Kind of. More it was just like they were closer, like Lorraine said. Like it was them against the world."

9

When I walked into the squad room, Danny was sitting at his desk. He looked up and opened his mouth, but I held up a hand.

"Me first," I said, and I told him what happened at Energene. He listened, vaguely amused, as I told him the whole thing. "So I'm sitting there, talking to this jerk, and who do you think walks in behind me?"

"Mike Warren," he says, like he wasn't just guessing.

My shit-storm sensors started blinking. "How'd you know?"

"He asked me if that's where you had gone. Someone saw you going in there. I said I didn't know."

"I was wondering what gave him the idea to go there. It seems kind of higher-level thinking for him."

He shrugged.

"Come on, he's an idiot," I said.

He shrugged again. I knew he agreed with me. It annoyed me that he wasn't conceding the point.

"Okay," I said. "So he comes in all, 'I got this, Carrick,' and as soon as I walk out of the office, he tells these guys the wife disappeared and she's the suspect. Didn't ask them any questions, didn't play them at all. Just gave it away."

"So what are you saying?"

"I'm saying Warren's a dumbass."

He laughed and shook his head. "It's not like you have to convince anybody of that."

"Plus, I'm telling you, they were ready with the whole 'industrial espionage' thing. Be interesting to see if they keep going that way or if they drop it now that Warren told them the wife is his suspect."

That's when the door to the squad room swung open and Mike Warren stormed in. He didn't look over at us—just stomped up to Lieutenant Suarez's door and started knocking.

I looked at Danny and smiled. Danny opened his mouth, but I cut him off. "He's not here," I called out, trying not to laugh.

Then from inside the office, Suarez's voice called out, "Come in."

Warren flashed me an evil grin. Then he went inside and closed the door.

I looked at Danny.

He shrugged. "Budget meeting got rescheduled."

"Why didn't you tell me?"

"I tried to tell you."

I scratched the back of my neck. "You could have tried harder."

"You know," Danny said, "this task force thing could happen any day. It's not like we don't have our own cases you could be working on instead of spending time trying to get into trouble or out of it."

Suarez's door opened, and he leaned out, glaring and beckoning me with one finger.

I got up and headed over.

Danny laughed and shook his head. "Tell Mike I said hi. And call me when you get out. I'll be out there doing what all the other narcotics detectives do."

I flipped him off jokingly as I went to accept my fate. Warren was sitting in one of the chairs facing Suarez's desk. He looked away from me, his jaw set, breathing heavily through his nose.

Suarez grunted as he sat behind his desk.

"Carrick," he said. "What the fuck?"

Warren turned to look at me, his head at an angle as he waited for my response.

I shrugged. "Danny and I finished surveilling Derek Hoyt, so I decided to stop by Energene and ask a few questions, see if anybody might have some idea why Hartwell was shot down on my front steps."

"It's not your investigation."

"It was my front steps."

"You're interfering in a homicide investigation."

"What homicide investigation? As far as I can tell, Warren already has it solved—domestic dispute, case closed."

"Bullshit, Carrick," Warren cut in. "I never said that. Besides, if that was the case, why was I there at Energene?"

I snorted. "From what I heard, someone told you I was there, and you didn't want it getting out that you were neglecting such a basic part of the investigation. But once you got there, it seemed like your purpose was to tip everyone at Energene off to the fact that you already had a hard-on for the widow as a suspect." I laughed. "I couldn't believe you told them that, right off the bat."

Suarez's head whipped around. "You told them that?"

"Before he asked a single question," I added.

Suarez looked down and shook his head. "It doesn't matter. You're a witness on this, Carrick, not an investigator. If you had a lead or an angle or something, you should have told Detective Warren so he could follow it up."

"Right," I said. "I'm sure he'd love to hear my ideas, and he'll get right on it when I tell him."

Warren snorted and looked away. Even he knew that was ridiculous.

"Just keep out of his way, all right?" Suarez turned to Warren. "Are we done here?"

Warren let out a disgusted sigh and stood up. "Next time, I'm not going to let it slide."

I watched him storm out the door, then I turned back to Suarez. "The guy's an idiot."

"Yes, but he's not my idiot. You are. And if you get in his way again, I'm coming down on you."

I nodded. Whatever. "I'm telling you, though, you should have heard these guys spinning all this stuff about corporate espionage and stolen secrets, and then he comes in and gives it all away."

Suarez let out a long breath. "Look, I know he's a stiff. Frankly, if he was one of my guys, you wouldn't be my worst. But he's not my guy; this is not your case. Leave it alone. Besides, Warren's keeping an open mind about things."

"How so?"

"Combined the two angles, figures maybe the happy couple were in on it together, but she decides she doesn't want to split the money."

"Actually, makes sense," I said.

"See? You're not the only smart guy out there."

"Fact remains, the only reason Warren went there was because he knew I had."

"You don't know that."

"Does the wife have any priors?"

"No."

"And his theory still doesn't explain why Hartwell was coming to my house."

10

I met Nola after work.

We were both still kind of freaked out about walking up to the front door. She, because of what had happened there. Me, because of the effect it was having on her. As we approached the front steps, I was relieved to see that the bullet hole had been patched and the center panel of the door freshly painted. We stood on the sidewalk, solemnly looking up at it for a moment. I couldn't shake the sense that the life of Ron Hartwell was getting further and further away as the traces of his death were eradicated.

Still, it was nice to have the door fixed and not to be looking at the bullet hole every time we came home.

I was quiet when we got inside. Sometimes Nola likes to hear about my day. Sometimes, she really, really doesn't. I wondered if news about the Ron Hartwell case would hit too close to home, so to speak.

"Any news on . . ." She nodded toward the front door, which now stood as some sort of icon for the nameless thing that had occurred there the night before.

We were standing in the kitchen. She was pouring the wine. She hadn't asked if I'd wanted a drink, but she had guessed correctly.

I told her about going to Energene, about what they'd said, and about Mike Warren showing up. The grief I caught afterward.

"Can't we request someone else?" she asked, which was a delightful thought.

I shook my head. "If you could choose your own cop, everyone would want someone else."

She put down her wine and came up close to me. "Not me," she said, so close I could feel her breath.

"I'm not that hungry," I said. "Are you?"

She shook her head and grabbed my hand, pulling me out of the kitchen and toward the stairs.

So there's hungry and there's *hungry*. Neither of us had been in the mood for dinner, but judging from the next forty minutes or so, I'd say we both had pretty healthy appetites.

And when we were done, we were starving.

The house felt different, like we had taken a big step toward reclaiming it. I was glad. In the back of my mind, I'd been concerned that the place was somehow haunted now. But it wasn't. It was a house of the living.

Nola had been planning on trying some elaborate recipe she'd read, but we ended up sautéing everything and eating it over pasta. It was delicious.

Afterward, we sipped wine and talked about the Hartwell case, about my conversation with Bradley Bourden. I told her about the industrial espionage angle and how Warren thought that could still fit in with Miriam as the killer.

She nodded thoughtfully. "But that still doesn't explain why they were here."

"No, it doesn't. And also, I only saw her for an instant, but she didn't seem like a killer. She definitely didn't seem like someone who had just killed. I guess there's all different kinds of killers, but what I saw was terror and pain." I told her what the women in the office had said, about how they seemed nervous but still very close.

"So maybe they were up to something," Nola said. "Together."

I nodded. "So why were they coming to me?"

"Maybe they weren't selling information; maybe they were just trying to share it. Expose it."

I looked at her. "You mean like whistle-blowers?"

"Maybe."

I laughed. "I'm sure there's all sorts of proper channels for anything they might have found. Why come to me?"

"You know how powerful and connected these companies can be. Maybe the proper channels didn't seem safe."

Twice, I'd tangled with big biotech companies outside of the normal course of my job. I'd seen how the pressure not to mess with them rolled downhill with a vengeance.

I thought about that for a long moment. "But why me?" Both my altercations with big biotech had been declared secret, non-events, kept quiet ostensibly for national security and because I didn't like talking about them.

When I looked up, Nola shrugged. "You've got history in that area. You've taken them on and won. And I know it's supposed to be secret or whatever, but people talk. Word gets around."

Seemed like a bit of a stretch to me. "Maybe. Meanwhile, if she didn't kill her husband, she might have seen who did."

"She could be an important witness."

"Meaning whoever did it is probably looking harder for her than Mike Warren is. She could be out there on the run, terrified. Not just the police after her but whoever killed her husband, too."

Nola looked at me for several seconds, solemn, maybe picturing herself with me murdered and the whole world coming after her. "Are you going to find her?"

"I'm going to try."

The next day was a bad one for Miriam Hartwell, wherever she was.

"They found a gun," Suarez said when I walked in.

"What are you talking about?"

"SIG Sauer P223. Looks like a match for the gun that killed Ron Hartwell. It's down in ballistics. Prints all over it. Preliminary match for Miriam Hartwell. Warren wanted me to tell you. I'm not going to say what else he wanted me to tell you."

"Where'd they find it?"

"Laundry room of their apartment building. Under the change machine."

"Anonymous tip?"

He shook his head. "Landlord called it in."

"Hmm."

He nodded and slapped a hand on my shoulder as he turned to go. It was an uncharacteristically affectionate gesture between us. "I know Warren's a bonehead, but it looks like this time he's right. I hope you and Nora can take comfort at least now we know who did it."

He always referred to her as Nora. I corrected him the first ten times, but now I let it serve as a reminder, if ever I forgot, that I really didn't like the guy.

He went back into his office and closed the door. I dropped into the chair behind my desk.

I still didn't see it, still didn't think it was the wife. Partly it was a hunch, naïve assumptions based on Miriam Hartwell's photo, her expression as she drove away. Part of it might have been because I really didn't want Warren to be right. But there was no explanation as to why he was on my front doorstep, why he'd been coming to see me. From my point of view, that was the most important part.

Danny was out of town meeting with the DEA. I was supposed to be chasing down leads on our favorite new drug kingpin, but I'd gotten a head start—a productive midmorning that netted me three more names on Derek Hoyt's growing Christmas card list.

The way I looked at it, I was ahead of the game.

It wouldn't take long to match the gun to the bullet that killed Ron Hartwell and to match the prints to Miriam. I suspected both would come back as positive matches, and I also suspected I wouldn't accept it when they did. But if I was going to pursue this any further, I needed more to go on, more to confirm my suspicions.

That's what I told myself as I pulled up in front of the large stone house owned by Dorothy Hartwell, Ron's mother. Miriam didn't seem to have any family of her own, so I figured I would start with Ron's.

I walked up the long slate path, past a painfully manicured lawn and onto the cavernous porch, where I rang the bell. Mrs. Hartwell might have been hurting, but not for money.

The woman who came to the door was in her seventies, handsome and polished even though she had obviously just been crying.

"Can I help you?" she asked, poised despite her sorrow.

I showed her my badge. "I'm with the Philadelphia Police Department. I'd like to ask you a few questions about Ron."

She glanced at the badge. "Of course," she said, sad and weary, stepping back and motioning me to come inside.

"I've already spoken to the other detectives. You know that, right?"

"Yes," I said. "And forgive me if any of this is repetitious . . ."

"I understand," she said, waving off my apology.

She offered me a beverage as she led me to the dining room. I politely declined, and we sat at the table.

"I'm very sorry for your loss," I said.

She closed her eyes and gave me a brief nod, swallowing hard against the screaming anguish that churned below the surface. Then she opened her eyes, once again composed. "What would you like to know?"

"Do you have any idea of anyone who might have wanted your son dead?"

A tiny fraction of a smile tugged at her mouth. "None at all. I mean, apparently my daughter-in-law, but I don't see that happening."

"You don't?"

"I wasn't crazy about Ron and Miriam getting married. When Ron's brother Brian introduced them, I thought she was a little . . . young . . . a little childlike. Too much like Brian, in a way. But by the time they got married, I realized she was the sweetest young woman I've ever known and that they were very much in love. They remained so. The detective I spoke to earlier, he was very nice, but he kept saying how surprising it can be when something like this happens, and I know that. Half the time those who do terrible things are said to be the nicest people, of whom you would least expect it. Even so, I can't accept it. Ron and Miriam were very happy together, happier than I ever thought he would be. But apart from that, Miriam wasn't the type to swat a fly. Literally, she would be the one coaxing it out the window." She laughed wistfully. "I thought it was ridiculous at first. I mean, a fly? But that's how she is. Even if she hated my son, I couldn't see her . . . doing what they say. And especially not now."

"Why not now?"

Barely moving, she somehow shrugged, rolled her eyes, shook her head, and looked away, all at the same time, then looked at me with the resignation of a very private person who had already revealed personal information way beyond her comfort level and was about take another step down that road.

"They'd been trying to have a baby," she said, lowering her voice as if we weren't the only ones there. "They'd been going to doctors, having procedures."

"Infertility treatments?"

She nodded.

"When was that?"

"They were still going, as far as I know."

Not exactly what you'd expect in advance of a double cross and a murder. Her eyes teared up and I gave her a moment.

"You say they met through Ron's brother?"

"Yes, Brian. His younger brother."

"How do they get along?"

She smiled bitterly. "Surely you don't think his brother killed him."

I smiled gently back. "Not at all. I'm just trying to gather some background. See what other leads might be out there. You never know what little bit of information might end up being crucial."

"He was here Sunday night, as I told the other detective. He came over for dinner and stayed."

"Where does Brian live?"

She let out a sigh. "He lives in Torresdale, near the river. But he's out of town."

"Oh. Does he know about . . ."

"Yes, he knows. It crushed him. Devastated him. He said he needed to go away, to process it."

"He left you here on your own?" I had a hard time hiding my surprise.

Her left eyebrow twitched the tiniest bit, like she was having a hard time hiding her reaction, as well, but that was as far as she allowed herself to show what she thought. "Just for a day or two. We all deal with tragedy in different ways, Detective."

I hadn't been the best son in the world, but I couldn't conceive of pulling something like that.

"Ron and Brian were seven years apart," she said. "They'd always been quite close, but they used to butt heads a lot too. The last few years, though, perhaps due to Miriam, the political differences that used to antagonize them seemed to fade, or maybe they just realized those things aren't important enough to get between brothers. Anyway, this past year, I'd seen them become closer. Brian is devastated."

"Do you know when he'll be back?"

She sighed again, smoothing a wrinkle from her skirt, trying not to look annoyed. "In a day or two."

"Could you give me his address and phone number? I'd like to talk to him as soon as possible."

She paused for a moment, then sighed. "If you must." She got up and went to a small sideboard, wrote his information on a pad of paper, and tore off the top sheet. Before she handed me the paper, she put her other hand on my arm. "Promise me you'll be gentle with him."

I nodded, and she handed me the paper.

12

A block away from Dorothy Hartwell's house, I pulled over and called Brian Hartwell. His voice mail picked up, and I left a message asking him to call me back. I was just merging onto the Schuylkill Expressway, headed back into the city, when he did.

"Is this Detective Carrick?" he asked, his voice tense, like a piece of wood bent to the breaking point.

"Yes. Is this Brian Hartwell?"

"Yeah. Sorry I missed you earlier. Reception's not so good up here. I seem to be in a good spot now, though."

"Where are you?"

"Lebanon. Just hiking a couple miles of the Appalachian Trail. Clearing my head, you know?"

An asshole in a BMW zipped around me doing ninety, cutting me off and flipping me off at the same time, somehow without putting down his phone. "I'm actually on the highway. Do you mind if I call you back in twenty minutes?"

"You can try, but I doubt you'll get me. I could try you back tonight maybe or tomorrow. I'll be home in a day or two."

I didn't want to put off the conversation, but I needed to take notes. "I can't get to my pen and paper. Do you mind if I record our conversation?" I had an app on my phone that let me record phone interviews onto a cloud server. It had become increasingly handy for long interviews with witnesses.

"Um . . . no, I guess not."

"Hold on one second," I said. I opened the app and began recording. Not the best behavior on the road, but I felt better knowing I wouldn't miss anything. "Okay, still there?"

"Yup."

"So tell me about Ron and Miriam. Were they happy?"

He sighed. "Yeah, they were happy. As happy as anyone is happy. I'll tell you one thing—Miriam absolutely, one-hundred-percent certain, guaranteed did not kill my brother. And no offense, but from what my mom tells me, your pal Detective Warren is a bit of a dumbass if he doesn't understand that."

I checked the phone to make sure that was recorded. "I see. You introduced Ron and Miriam, is that right?"

"Yeah. Ron got me a job at Energene a few years ago. It didn't last long, but that's where I met Miriam. Ron's a bit of a bigwig there. Miriam and I were peons."

"Are you two still close?"

"Pretty close, yeah."

"Has she called you?"

"No. I wish she would."

"Why's that?"

"So I could tell her we know she didn't do it, that we'll help her any way we can." He sniffed, and I realized he was crying.

I gave him a few moments to get himself together. We talked a little more after that, but I didn't get anything much more out of him. When we were done, he said, "If you see her, tell her we love her, okay? And that we're here for her, that we're all mourning together."

By the time I got off the phone with Brian Hartwell, I had an absolute certainty of Miriam's innocence. It lasted the whole way back to the Roundhouse.

"The gun's a match," Suarez said as I walked in. He was standing outside his office, talking to Mike Warren, who was leaning—practically sitting—on my desk. Suarez held up a sheaf of papers. "The prints are a match, too."

Warren gave me the finger but quickly pulled it down as Suarez looked back at him. As I approached, he pushed himself off my desk.

"There's another match, too, Carrick," he said, snapping his fingers as he walked past me. "My ass and your face."

"Hey, Lieutenant," I called out as I sat in my chair. "Someone got stupid all over my desk!"

"It was already there, Carrick," Warren called over his shoulder.

Suarez laughed, then his face turned serious. "Both matches. It's definitely the murder weapon, and her prints are all over it. She did it. Now we just need to find her. Can you let it go now?"

"Nothing to let go, Lieutenant."

"It wouldn't be so bad if some other fool was out there obsessed with doing *your* job the way you're so obsessed with doing Warren's. But there isn't. So you need to let Mike Warren do his job, and you need to focus on your job. Okay?"

"Like a laser beam, sir."

He took a deep breath and shook his head. Then he turned and went back into his office.

Ten minutes later, I was in the basement with Bernie Lawrence, one of our ballistics experts.

"Definitely a match," he said. "You can see for yourself if you'd like." The two slugs were still mounted on the comparison microscope.

"No, that's okay."

"Not what you were expecting?"

I shook my head. "What type of gun was it?"

He reached behind him and handed me a gun in a sealed plastic evidence bag. "SIG Sauer P223."

I smoothed out the plastic so I could see it clearly. I was familiar with the SIG P223, but I wasn't familiar with this one.

"Standard?"

He shook his head. "Not even close. Combat grip, custom rail, night sight. And the numbers have been removed. And not half-assed filed off, they're *gone* gone."

"Really?"

"Yeah. Looks like a pro. Why?"

"This is from the shooting on my front steps a couple nights ago."

"Oh yeah, right. Sorry to hear about that. But it seems like Mike Warren wrapped it up pretty quick for you. Probably a record for him. That's got to be a relief."

"Kind of, I guess."

"Something bothering you about it?"

"A couple things. He's saying the wife did it and her prints are on the gun. But this looks like something a pro would use, not a five-foot-tall, hundred-pound nurse with no priors."

He grunted at that.

I held up my hands. "I'm not saying a woman can't be a gun nut or an assassin or anything, but it doesn't seem to fit, you know?"

"No, I hear you. Actually, the rounds were special, too. Jacketed, custom made."

"Right. Okay, well, thanks. Good information."

The prints and ballistics were pretty damning, but I couldn't reconcile the petite nurse with the souped-up SIG P223 and the custom rounds. And I was having a hard time believing that she would kill her husband in the midst of ongoing fertility treatments. Not impossible, but unlikely.

And none of it explained why Ron Hartwell had my address in his GPS.

13

I'd said I was going to leave it alone, but Suarez had said Warren had the case under control. I guess we both lied.

Ron and Miriam Hartwell had lived in a rehabbed brick warehouse on South Street, west of Broad. Not too many years ago, the neighborhood had been crime-ridden and decrepit. Now the street was lined with expensive townhomes and high-end apartments filled with well-paid young professionals. I still couldn't get used to it, even though the sidewalk trees planted by the developers were almost fully grown.

It wasn't on my way home, but I stopped on my way home, anyway.

I pressed the button for the building super, and two minutes later, a short, stressed-out Hispanic-looking guy in his fifties appeared, flashing a polite smile that almost hid his annoyance at the interruption.

"Can I help you?" he asked.

I held up my badge, and he let out a sigh. The smile went away.

"Are you the super?"

He nodded. "Gonzalez."

"I'm Detective Carrick. Just a few questions."

"Happy to help," he said, "but I'm really busy, man."

"I'll be quick."

"Okay. You mind walking?"

"No problem."

He turned, and I followed, up a short stairway and down a first-floor hallway. It was an effort keeping up with him.

"You found the gun this morning?"

"Yeah, in the laundry room, under the change machine."

"Can you show me?"

He closed his eyes, summoning patience. "Yeah, sure. First, I have to check on something—in the Hartwells' apartment, actually. You want to wait here, or you want to come with me?"

"Um . . . I'll come with you."

The apartment was small but nice. "I just need to check the faucet, make sure it's not dripping again," he said. Then he paused. "The other police said not to touch anything."

I couldn't tell if he was asking for permission to stop the drip or reminding me not to disturb anything. "It's fine," I said, giving us both a pass.

I didn't know what I was looking for, because I hadn't intended to be looking. But I didn't want to waste the opportunity. I scanned the bookcases. On the table by the door was a carved wooden bowl with some mail, a set of keys, three twenty-dollar bills, and some loose change.

In the bathroom, both toothbrushes were in their holders. I peeked in the cabinet but didn't touch anything. The usual variety of tweezers, old razors, first-aid supplies, and several prescriptions—Lipitor for Ron, Xanax for Miriam. Anxiety medication. If I was going on the lam, I wouldn't leave that behind.

When I closed the cabinet door, Gonzalez was standing in the door looking at me. "You ready?"

I followed him down the first-floor hallway.

"Have you seen any sign of her in the last couple days? Miriam Hartwell, I mean."

He shook his head and looked over his shoulder as he walked. "Nah. I saw her a few hours before it happened, though. Kind of creepy, you know? You see the guy, the two of them, walking along, alive and well, a few hours later, he's dead."

"How did they seem?"

He shrugged as he opened the door to the basement steps. "I don't know. Not dead, you know? I mean, they seemed all right. Kind of stressed out."

"Angry at each other?"

"No, nothing like that. Maybe worried or something. Anyway, here's the laundry room." He pointed at the far corner. "There's the change machine."

The laundry room was small, not terrible but nothing fancy. Three washers, three dryers, one change machine. Linoleum and cinder block under fluorescent lights. The change machine sat on legs maybe two inches off the floor.

I got on my hands and knees. Even with my head near the floor, it was hard to see more than a few inches back.

"So, what, you were cleaning back there or something?"

He laughed. "No, man. One of the tenants called and told me it was there."

I looked up at him. "Which tenant was that?"

"Don't know. They didn't want to say."

"How do you know it was a tenant?"

He shrugged. "They said it was. Who else is gonna call about it?"

14

When I got home, Nola was getting dinner ready. She smiled when I walked in, and she came toward me, drying her hands on a dish towel. She took two steps and paused, studying my face.

"What is it?" she said.

"Weird day." I told her about the gun, about the prints and ballistics.

It seemed to deflate her. "Wow," she said sadly, her eyes darting over my shoulder at the front door. The scene of the crime. "So Miriam did it?"

I was struck by the way she called her by name, like she knew her. She'd never laid eyes on the woman. I'd barely seen her myself—a second or two at most—but it seemed like I was so determined to figure out how she could be innocent, I'd not only talked myself into it, I'd convinced Nola, as well.

"I don't know," I said, pulling her toward me. "I don't think so."

I told her about how the gun and the rounds were customized. About the fertility treatments. About the anonymous tip. "And no one can say why they were coming to our place."

"But the gun had her fingerprints on it, right?" she said. "And they found it at their building, right?"

"That's another thing." I told her about going to the apartment, about the cash by the front door, Miriam's anxiety meds left behind. "If she's going on the lam and she goes home first—and for some reason she hides her gun there—why doesn't she grab her cash? Why doesn't she grab her anxiety pills? If she suffers from anxiety, now would be the time she'd need them most."

"Maybe she wasn't thinking straight."

"Yeah, maybe."

I couldn't sleep that night, thinking about all the ways the case was going wrong, all the ways it was tricky, all the ways Mike Warren was trying to keep it simple.

All the ways I was getting myself in trouble over it.

I'd said I was dropping it, and maybe that was what I needed to do. Sometimes things were that simple. You hear doctors talking about looking for horses before zebras. Maybe this was a horse. A wife killed her husband. It happened all the time. Maybe Warren was right. Yes, there were loose ends, coincidences, but maybe there were explanations for all of them. Explanations that had nothing to do with anything other than the fact that a woman murdered her husband. Maybe he was banging on my door because that's just where it happened. Maybe he had my address by accident. As I finally drifted off to sleep, I convinced myself that maybe if Nola and I were going to get over it, maybe I needed to drop it like I'd said I would and let Mike Warren work his case.

First thing the next day, I went into Suarez's office and closed the door. "I'm letting it go," I said.

He looked up at me from behind his desk. "The Hartwell thing?"

I nodded.

"It's a pretty tight case," he said.

"Not my case. I'm letting it go."

"Good," he said, as if the constant burning sensation I provoked in his chest had cooled a half a degree.

"But," I said, and he grimaced. "I just want to tell you a couple things. You can decide what to do with them."

He raised one eyebrow, waiting.

I told him about the custom gun and ammo, about the fertility treatments, about what the coworkers had said about Ron and Miriam, how close they seemed. "And I haven't looked into the angles or anything, the bullet trajectories and where the Hartwell woman was when I saw her, compared to where the bullet came from. Presumably, Mike Warren is all over that, right?"

He didn't move a muscle, staring at me stone-faced.

"And the gun they found," I said. "Remember I asked Warren if it had been an anonymous tip?"

"The landlord found it, right?"

I nodded. "The landlord found it. After he got an anonymous tip. Caller said he was a tenant but wouldn't give a name."

His eyes slowly closed, and he winced before he opened them. "But you're leaving it alone, right?"

"That's what I'm supposed to do, right? Isn't that what you're telling me?"

He let out a sigh. "That's what I'm telling you."

I nodded and got up to go.

As I walked out of his office, he called after me, "I'll talk to Myerson, Warren's lieutenant. Make sure he follows up on that other stuff."

I walked out of his office, past my desk, out of the squad room, and down the steps and onto the street. Part of me was proud of myself, of my maturity, of my willingness to let it go, to get past the stubbornness that I usually allowed to ruin my life and my career. But mostly, I felt like I was giving up when I knew something was wrong, when I knew someone bad was getting away with something, someone good was going down for it, and someone stupid was having their way with how the world should be.

I wanted alcohol, not for its intoxicating qualities but as a disinfectant, to cleanse myself of the slime that seemed to cover me. Okay, maybe not just for the cleansing properties. But it was nine thirty in the morning—getting loaded might have made more of a statement than I was really intending to make.

Instead, I got coffee.

The Roundhouse is on the eastern edge of Chinatown, hemmed in by the Vine Street Expressway to the north and a caffeine desert of museums, monuments, and parks to the south and east. I headed west to Ray's Café, a Taiwanese teahouse with good, strong coffee made with a strange siphon contraption that one of these years I was going to ask about.

The girl behind the counter asked me if I wanted one of their little cookies to go with my coffee. I said no. They didn't seem to match my mood, and I didn't feel like I deserved a cookie, walking away from a botched case like that. But I regretted it the whole time I sat at the counter drinking my coffee.

When I was finished, I ordered a coffee to go. And a cookie.

Stepping back outside, I felt better. The caffeine helped. So did the cookie. My insides were still churning over walking away from the case, basically acknowledging that it would probably never be solved, and we would never learn who killed a stranger on our doorstep.

I put the last of the cookie in my mouth, trying not to let those thoughts sour the taste of it, when I noticed a black Toyota Corolla pacing me down Ninth Street.

The driver was wearing a wig and shades, and as she pulled up next to me, she lowered her window.

"You're looking for me. You found me. Get in."

It was Miriam Hartwell.

15

We stared at each other through the car window for a couple of seconds. I'm not easily surprised, but this caught me off guard. I didn't know whether to turn around and keep walking or arrest her on the spot.

"Okay, never mind," she said, putting the window back up.

"Hold on," I said, getting in.

Even through her disguise, I could tell she was terrified.

"You know the police are looking for you?" I asked.

She laughed, a ragged bark. "Aren't you the police? Besides, there's a lot of people looking for me." Her voice sounded like a poorly played violin.

We zigzagged up to Eleventh Street, then north into Fairmount. She turned and looked at me, her bottom lip trembling.

"Are you going to kill me?"

"What?"

"Ron and I were going to trust our lives with you. He didn't get to. If I'm making a mistake by talking to you, I'd just as soon know now."

"I'm not going to kill you," I said. "I'm just trying to figure out what happened. Why your husband was shot dead on my front steps."

She looked back at me, staring for an uncomfortably long time as we sped up the narrow city streets.

"It's a long story," she said finally, looking back at the road, jerking the wheel slightly. "I'll tell you when we get there."

We stayed on Eleventh Street, past once-blighted neighborhoods being gentrified by hipsters and young professionals, through Temple University and the newer public housing projects, houses with porches and window boxes where high-rise horrors once stood. And then into a part of North Philadelphia that was as devastated as it had always been, almost reassuring in its dependable decay, unless you had to live or work there. Eleventh Street ended at a chain-link fence and dense brush that obscured one of the train tracks that cut diagonally through North Philly, making literal the dead-endedness of some of the neighborhood's streets.

We turned right, then left, onto Germantown Avenue, a colonial-era highway that cut across the city. It starts almost at the Delaware River and runs through North Philly, then Germantown, Mount Airy, and upscale Chestnut Hill before turning into Germantown Pike at the city limits and eventually ending in Collegeville, fifteen miles away.

Maybe she was taking a back route out of the city, I thought, but we pulled over two blocks later in front of a fenced-in yard with a bored-looking pit bull. There was a school across the street. I wondered if we were just going to park and talk, but Miriam got out, and I followed.

That's when I noticed the blue metal sign rusting in front of the building on the corner. THE LIBERTY MOTEL.

The pit bull followed my gaze. His head swiveled back at me, tilted disapprovingly, as if to say, "You sure you want to do this?"

Miriam glanced quickly around us and bustled forward, head down, clutching her pink, tulip-covered cardigan around her. She was scampering up the steps before I even started moving.

The pit bull looked away, like he'd given up on me.

16

I caught up with Miriam in time to open the door for her. She paused and looked up at me, but I couldn't read her expression.

I followed her into a small lobby or foyer. It was dark and airless, with torn carpet and a vague but insistent mixture of odors—urine, sweat, pot smoke, and fast food.

As if the air weren't full enough, hip-hop blared from a smartphone and dock system behind the desk. The kid bobbing his head in front of the speakers looked up as we walked in. His eyes seemed to recognize Miriam despite her disguise, or maybe because of it. Then they attached to me. It wasn't a hard stare, but his eyes followed us up the steps to the second floor.

The music drowned out whatever noises might have been coming from the other rooms as we walked down the hallway. Miriam took out an old-fashioned room key and opened a door at the end, standing there waiting while I caught up with her.

I slipped inside, and she pulled the door closed behind us, swinging the security latch in place. The hip-hop faded just a bit. So did the reefer smell. The urine odor got stronger, and the rest of it stayed about the same.

The room was almost entirely taken up by a queen-sized bed and a wooden table and chair. She had a bunch of plastic shopping bags piled up on the table. As Miriam slid the room key into her handbag, I glimpsed the edge of a U.S. passport and a cash withdrawal envelope from a bank.

"You going somewhere?" I asked, realizing as I said it how insanely stupid it was.

Before I could apologize, she whipped off her shades and stared more intently at my face, as if maybe I wasn't who she thought I was, maybe this was a big mistake. "No," she said caustically, "I'm settling down here for a while. Seems like a nice place to start a new life, right?"

"Sorry," I said.

She plopped onto the wooden chair and pulled off her wig, draping it across the plastic bags on the table. She ran her fingers through her fine black hair, trying to straighten it out.

I moved to sit on the bed, but she said, "I wouldn't. Bedbugs."

I didn't.

She had a pretty face with delicate features, but the stress was etched deep. She looked ten years older than the woman in the picture, and I wondered if she'd ever recover, or if what she had gone through—was going through—was the kind of thing that just aged you prematurely. Maybe someday she'd catch up with it and once again look her age.

"Yes, I'm out of here," she said wearily. "If they don't catch me first."

She looked at me again, that long, appraising look. Before she could decide whether or not I measured up, I asked, "Why was your husband at my front door? And why were you there, too?"

She looked at her feet. At the mention of her husband, she seemed to lose some of the toughness she'd been trying to exude. She closed her eyes, trying to keep it together.

I felt for her, whatever was going on. It was obvious she was hurting, grieving, and stuck in a situation where she couldn't mourn.

"Did you shoot your husband?" I asked quietly.

She glared at me, bitterness and sarcasm burning through the tears gathering in her eyes. "No, I didn't fucking shoot my husband." She looked away dismissively, as if she couldn't believe I was as stupid and gullible as the rest of them.

"I didn't think so, but I had to ask. Did you see who did?"

She shook her head. "I wasn't supposed to be there. I followed him to make sure he was okay, to see what would happen. I was parked down the block, and this other car drives past, a black SUV, and it parks down the street from your house. It didn't register at first. But as Ron went up the steps, it drives up, and as he's knocking, they . . . they shot him." She looked down for a moment, then she cleared her throat and looked up at me. "I didn't see them."

I paused a second, letting her compose herself.

"I panicked and drove away, terrified, but I came back a few minutes later, drove past . . . Ron was still lying on the steps, surrounded by cops. I knew he was dead for sure."

I gave her a few moments to collect herself.

"They found the murder weapon," I told her. "It has your prints on it."

"What?"

"They found the gun. Ballistics matched it. Your fingerprints were on it."

"That's bullshit." Her tears seemed to evaporate in the heat of her anger. "Your ballistics guy must be in on it."

I shook my head. "He's not. I know him. I trust him."

"You can't trust anyone. Not anymore."

"Bourden said he thought Ron might be involved in corporate espionage."

"That's what I'd say if I were him. I mean, I guess if they saw him skulking around, doing searches and running tests and assays not directly related to his core functions, they might get suspicious about that. But I doubt they really thought that's what was going on."

"What did you do after Ron was shot?"

"When I saw he was dead, I got the hell out of there."

"Where did you go?"

"I don't know. I just drove, for like an hour, terrified they were coming after me. Before I even thought about it, I was headed to Boston, but I realized that just because I don't have anyone there anymore didn't mean they wouldn't look there, anyway."

"Did you go back to your apartment?"

She shook her head. Of course not. And if she had, she wouldn't have stashed the murder weapon there.

"Why'd you come back to Philly?"

She shrugged. "I need to disappear. But first I wanted to tell you what Ron was going to tell you, clear my name with somebody . . . And maybe help you find out who killed Ron."

"You know the only way to clear your name is to stay here and fight the charges."

She shook her head. "They killed Ron. They'll kill me. I'm more worried about my life than my name. Besides, what I'm about to tell you is bigger than one murder."

17

"A couple of weeks ago, Ron and I were in Haiti," she said. "He was part of a team accompanying an aid shipment of Soyagene, Energene's new drought-resistant GMO soybean. It's brand new. The approval doesn't even take effect until next week. You know what GMOs are, right? Genetically modified organisms?"

I smiled. "Yes, I'm familiar with them."

"Right. Of course you are. Anyway, Haiti's had this terrible drought, so someone at Energene thought it would be a good idea to send Soyagene as aid, both seeds to grow and soyflour as food aid. Energene has been outpaced by its larger competitors. There's a lot riding on Soyagene and Early Rise, its new corn variety, to help it catch up. People at Energene are stressed. I'm the office nurse, so I see it, people coming in with stress-related problems, and Ron has been right in the thick of it. Anyway, I thought it would be great to get out of the office. I have a close friend in Haiti from when I was in grad school at Penn, and I wanted to keep an eye on Ron. Make sure he was okay. So I took some vacation time and went with him."

She took a deep breath and let it out. "It was intense. Turned out Soyagene and Early Rise were both controversial in Haiti. Energene was pushing the soyflour as a protein supplement, but soy's not a big part of the local diet in Haiti. And many people—including the president—are opposed to GMOs. There was a lot of political tension and instability, about a number of things, but partly about Energene and the GMO aid shipments, and GMOs in general. Have you been following the political situation there at all?"

I shook my head.

"It's a mess. Last year, near the end of his term, President Abelard banned GMOs. Energene and the other biotech companies put up tons of money to get this guy Martine elected, very pro-GMO, free trade, no regulations. People were shocked, because no one really liked him, but like I said, there was a lot of money behind him. As soon as Martine gets in, he rescinds all the regulations on this stuff. But then he has a heart attack and dies. They have a special election, and one of Abelard's allies is elected, this guy Alain Cardon, and now Cardon is calling for a moratorium on new GMO varieties—including Soyagene and Early Rise. So there's the drought, there's all this political tension, there were also rumblings about some kind of armed rebel faction, and there were criminal gangs adding to the chaos. They stole some of our Soyagene soyflour before it was even cleared for distribution. We were up north, a place called Cap-Haïtien, and the port was crawling with American private security types working for Energene and Stoma, trying to protect assets and keep a lid on things."

"Stoma?"

She nodded. "Stoma's even bigger over there than Energene. Everywhere, really. Especially their GMO corn, Stoma-Grow. It's all over the place. Energene is hoping to make a dent with the new Soyagene soybeans, but they can't get their corn off the ground because Stoma has the corn market locked up. They're pretty aggressive about protecting their market share."

"I know all about that. What does all this have to do with Ron showing up at my house?"

"I'm getting to that. So, while Ron was working, I was spending time with my grad school friend, Regi Baudet, who's a deputy health minister. A few days before we left, there was an outbreak of some kind of respiratory illness in this tiny village called Saint Benezet, out in the countryside. I went with Regi to see if I could help. Some of Energene's security contractors were there when we arrived, skulking around, giving us dirty looks. We had no idea what it was. Regi was stumped, his assistant was stumped, I was stumped. It was bad, too. Everybody had it, but some people were really struggling, wheezing and gasping, especially the little ones and the old people. Luckily, we were able to get some steroid inhalers, because otherwise, some of them wouldn't have made it through the night. Anyway, we got them all stabilized, and we took blood samples and left.

"The next day, everyone was better. But we were curious. Ron studied infectious diseases while getting one of his Ph.D.s, so he and Regi brought some of the samples into a lab there, developed a few theories about it. It gave them a chance to get to know each other, which was nice." She smiled sadly. "Anyway, two days later, the respiratory thing flared up again. We went back to Saint Benezet— this time Ron came with us—and now it was crawling with Energene security teams. We gave out more inhalers and took more samples. That's when the word came down—Energene was sending us back to the States. They said the political situation was too unstable. We barely had time to pack our stuff and say a quick good-bye to Regi. We couldn't take samples with us, so Ron wrote up a list of tests for Regi to conduct in his lab. Then we came home."

She paused, fidgeting, looking around nervously. "The day after we got back, Ron got the lab results from Regi. There was clearly some sort of extreme allergic reaction. It was striking that it was such a distinct geographical area, just this one tiny village, and so pervasive within it. Everyone had it."

She paused again, lowered her voice again. "This was right after the Soyagene shipment was stolen and not too far from where it happened. We realized it could be a reaction to the Soyagene soyflour. The Energene people had said we weren't supposed to tell anyone about the theft, that it was a trade secret or whatever, and that it could compromise their investigation. But if the allergic reaction was because of the Soyagene, something was seriously wrong with it."

"Did you tell anybody?"

She shook her head. "Ron tried to talk to his boss, Vinson, about it, but he couldn't get in to see him. Vinson's useless, anyway, but Ron got the feeling he was avoiding him. He finally got in to see him, and Vinson's got Bradley Bourden there, the CEO, and this guy Royce, one of the security guys we'd seen in Haiti. Ron made up a story about some other project they were working on and got out of there."

"Was this Royce the guy who handles security at the building on Thirtieth Street?"

"Might be. He seems to be everywhere all of the sudden."

"Red-faced guy? No sense of humor?"

"Yeah, that's him." She almost smiled. "Anyway, after that we decided to go to the authorities, the feds. Like, whistle-blowers. We were terrified. I mean, that's hundreds of millions of dollars at stake. Maybe billions. But if it was true, thousands of people could get sick from eating the Soyagene soybeans—people could die."

"What happened?"

"We were freaking out, wondering if Vinson and Bourden already knew about it. We were trying to decide who to go to—USDA, FDA, FTC—we couldn't find anyone who wasn't totally in bed with Energene already. Ron knew them all, because they all worked for Energene at one point or another. They were all good friends of Bradley Bourden."

"What did you do then?"

"Ron was afraid for his professional life, you know. Nobody likes to be the bearer of bad news. But as he kept digging deeper at Energene, he became even more convinced there was a connection between the Soyagene hijacking and the illness at Saint Benezet. He got really scared. He didn't want me helping him, he didn't want me

having anything to do with any of this. He said we were in danger."
She looked over at me, the fear and vulnerability in her eyes accentuated by a tiny flicker of hope. "Then he decided to come see you."

We shared a sad, ironic smile, like, *look how that turned out.*

"Why me?"

She shook her head, as if looking back maybe it hadn't been the smartest idea. "Ron did some work with Energene's insect genetics department. He'd been looking into Stoma's Bee-Plus program when he read about what happened on Martha's Vineyard. He said the official story was guaranteed bullshit, that he couldn't be sure what really happened, but bottom line, you stopped some powerful people from doing some bad things."

Then her eyes sharpened. "While he was digging, he learned some of what went down in Dunston, too. He said in both cases you took on guys like this, you got the feds involved, and you won. So maybe you had connections there that weren't in Energene's pocket. You were local, and he thought he could trust you, so . . ." She shrugged. "I don't know. I guess he didn't know where else to go."

"You said Ron decided to come to me because he learned something else that scared him. What was that?"

As she opened her mouth, the music out in the hallway turned off, accompanied by a loud cracking sound.

I held up my hand.

The place was suddenly silent, like all the other occupants were holding their breath and listening too.

"Is there a back way out?" I whispered.

Her eyes widened, and she shook her head. Then she pointed to a small sliding window set into the wall. I crossed the room and looked out. It was a ten-foot drop to the concrete alley below. Almost directly beneath us was a black Lincoln Navigator. When I put my face up against the window, I could see a heavyset white guy in a brown suit standing next to it.

I ducked back as he looked up. When I turned to look at Miriam, her face crumpled.

I put a finger to my lips, then held it up, telling her to wait for a moment. I crossed the room and stood next to the door, listening. A floorboard squeaked out in the hallway.

I turned and motioned her into the bathroom.

The guy out back didn't look like a cop, but you couldn't always tell. I left my gun in my holster. Then I quietly swung the security latch away from the door. With my back against the wall, I wrapped my left hand around the doorknob and cocked my right fist.

After a few seconds, I caught a strong whiff of cheap men's cologne and felt the knob shifting in my hand. I ripped the door open and whipped my body around, putting everything I had behind my fist, and hoping to God there was some kind of bad guy out there.

18

I've never been a fan of the sucker punch. Kind of lacks class—not that I'm a specialist in that area. The sting of shame is lessened when the sucker you're punching is holding a gun with a silencer—and even more when he's doused with cheap cologne—but there's still something douchey about punching a guy in the face before he has a chance to raise his eyebrows.

Fortunately for this guy, he was shorter than I am and crouching down. I had to adjust my trajectory in midswing, coming down on the side of his head. Fortunately for me, by the time my fist bounced off his temple and he crumpled to the floor, I had gotten over any moral ambivalence. I was hoping pretty hard he wasn't law enforcement of any kind, but cops don't use silencers—and they rarely douse themselves with Axe body spray—so even if he was one, it wasn't my bad.

Axe-Man was down on his hands and knees, his hand still holding that gun. He was wearing a fancy suit—not necessarily a good one, just a flashy one—and a lot of product in his hair. He was young, which could have been why he went to the trouble of using a silencer and then broadcasted his presence with so much body spray.

I stomped hard on his gun hand and slammed my knee into his face. He collapsed to the floor and let go of his gun. I kicked it down the hallway. He was out cold but breathing okay. I cuffed him and went back inside for Miriam. I'd read him his rights later.

She was hiding in the shower, trembling. She almost collapsed when she saw it was me, her eyes pinned to the gun now in my hand.

"It's okay," I said quietly. "Let's go."

I grabbed her by the elbow and guided her toward the door. She pulled back and said, "Can I get my stuff?"

I shook my head. "We'll come back for it."

She grabbed her handbag and her wig from off the chair.

Out in the hallway, she stared in horror at the guy on the floor, trying to get up onto his knees. I thought about grabbing the gun— you never knew when it would come in handy—but I'd sent it pretty far down the hallway, so instead I kicked him in the ribs, twice, then hustled Miriam toward the stairs while he groaned on the floor.

The kid at the front desk was gone. The sound system was shattered, with a bullet hole just to the left of the smartphone and shards of plastic littering the shelf.

Miriam's arm trembled in my grasp as I led her toward the front door. I went out first, gun drawn, but there was no sign of anyone. By the time we were halfway down the path to the street, Miriam was pulling ahead of me, rushing to get to her car. As we reached the sidewalk, we both flinched at a strange popping, cracking noise. Next to us, a six-inch patch of the brown stucco wall exploded into a cloud of white dust.

I turned and saw the guy from the alley, leveling his pistol at us. He was the same age as the other one—young—but his style was more Old Spice than Axe. I brought up my gun, and as he ducked back behind the motel, I pushed Miriam forward. "Get in the car," I said.

I kept my gun pointed toward at the alley. The streets were deserted, but it was a residential neighborhood. There was a school across the street. I didn't know what I was going do if Old Spice started firing, but I didn't want to get into a shootout.

I crouched behind the wall, keeping my gun raised, but he didn't reappear.

I heard Miriam's car snarling behind me, the engine revving.

There was no sign of either of the gunmen, but I could feel eyes on me. Glancing down, I saw the pit bull on the other side of the fence looking up at me, his head at a slight angle. He turned away from me at the sound of Miriam's car speeding away.

We both watched as she disappeared down the block. The dog looked back at me for a moment. Then he left as well, trotting off and disappearing behind the house.

19

I kept my gun raised as I walked back toward the alley. As I'd expected, it was empty. Old Spice was gone, and so was his vehicle. I ran inside and back upstairs. My cuffs were lying empty and open on the ratty carpet. The room was empty, too. All that was left was the smell of cheap body spray.

I was worried about Miriam, hoping she'd gotten away, but there was nothing I could do about that. Part of me thought about just getting the hell out of there, but shots had been fired. At me. And even if none of the neighbors called it in, someone was going to find out. And then they were going to ask why I hadn't called it in.

Besides, I needed a ride. I called it in. Then I called Danny.

The uniforms were there in five minutes—two cars, four officers.

Danny was there in six, pulling in right behind them. He shook his head as he got out of his car. "So which active narcotics case on our docket were you pursuing out here?" He couldn't keep a straight face as he said it.

I flipped him off.

"Seriously. I'm confused," he said. "Suarez tells me you said you were stepping off this case. 'Carrick decided to act like a grown-up for once in his life.'"

He didn't sound anything like Suarez. I told him so.

"Yes, I do," he said. "I've been working on it."

"Well, you'd better keep working."

He looked indignant for a moment, then he gave his head a brisk shake. "Never mind that. I got the call from the task force. I'm out of town for rest of the week. Leaving tonight."

Great.

He leaned closer. "We're having work done on the house. The girls are staying with friends. We'd been planning on staying in a hotel, but now that it's just her, she'd rather not. Nola offered Laura your guest room, but I know how you feel about houseguests. Say the word and I'll quietly make other arrangements."

Even better. "No," I said with a big forced smile. "It will be great having her." I owed Danny favors in the triple digits.

"You're sure?"

"Of course."

"Great. Oh, and Suarez wants to see you ASAP."

It was a perfect day, I thought.

Then Mike Warren arrived.

"So tell me this shit again, Carrick," Warren said for the fifth time, pretending to take notes. "You were just walking along, minding your own business eating a cupcake—"

"A cookie."

"Whatever. And this lady drives up on you, all in disguise, and says, 'Get in the car'?"

"Basically, yes."

We were back in the motel room. Two uniforms were standing by the door, looking awkward but amused at the tension between Warren and me.

I was sitting on the chair, because I got there first. Warren was sitting on the bed, because I hadn't warned him not to. I smiled.

"You think this shit is funny?" Warren scowled. "You had the prime suspect in a murder in custody and you let her escape."

"She didn't escape from me, dumbass. She escaped from the guys who were sent to kill her. Probably the same guys who actually killed her husband."

"Oh, right, I forgot." He hooked his thumb at the empty handcuffs lying on the floor in the hallway next to a folded cardboard evidence marker. "The invisible bad guys who disappeared when she escaped."

"Yeah, that's right, the guys who left the imaginary slugs in the wall outside and the sound system in the lobby. Maybe the kid at the desk got it on sale because it already had a bullet hole in it."

He scribbled in his notebook like he'd thought of something important. Probably a doodle of him shooting me. "So she brought you here to tell you something, right? What did she tell you?"

And there it was. I had a decision to make. If I was walking away from the case, that meant I was hoping Warren would solve it. It meant giving him every bit of information I had. Including what Miriam had told me.

I stalled. "So these two guys come after her, and what, you still think she killed her husband in a domestic dispute?"

He shrugged. "I don't know, man. I figure it's probably the corporate spy angle Bourden was talking about. But who knows, maybe they were coming after you. Someone you locked up—although Lord knows there ain't many of them, am I right? More likely just someone you pissed off."

The uniforms laughed. I did, too. It was a good line, even if it was bullshit—plenty of flaws in my job performance, but none of them was about not locking up enough bad guys. I was too distracted to come back at him. I had to figure out what I was doing here.

If Ron's murder was about something he'd discovered, then Miriam's attempted murder was about the same thing. Probably by the same guys. I'd seen how far these companies could go to protect their interests, their secrets. This stuff was dangerous, and Mike Warren was careless, not just in a case-botching way but in a getting-people-killed way.

I didn't know what to do with what Miriam Hartwell had told me, but I knew what *not* to do, and that was just put it out there without knowing what it meant. So if I was keeping it to myself, I had to figure out what was going on. I had to find Miriam again and find out what else she knew.

Warren was staring at me while I was thinking things through. "Then again, maybe it's about you in a different way." He shrugged again, looking at me sideways. "Like I said before, maybe you're banging the Hartwell woman, her husband comes to confront you about it, maybe tell your girlfriend, and you shoot him. Now she freaks out, she's going to testify against you, you kill her too."

The two uniforms stopped smiling.

20

I laughed, but he'd made it sound plausible. "You think that's how it went down?" I said. "He starts banging on my door while I'm in bed with my girlfriend, then what, maybe I climb out the window and run around the block so I can shoot him from the street, then somehow get back inside in time to close the door so I can open it in front of my girlfriend? I knew you were an idiot, but I didn't know you had this creative side to you. You're like one of these idiot savants. Do you do anything else? Play the piano or math tricks or anything?"

"Fuck you, Carrick. You know it makes more sense than any of the bullshit you're talking about. You can joke all you want, but you'd better be giving me something else to go on, or you move up the suspect list to number one."

He was right; I had to give him something. I turned to the uniforms. "Can you two give us a moment, here?"

One of them moved his hand to his gun, and they both looked to Warren. That alone was scary. Then Warren nodded and waved them out into the hallway.

I leaned forward and lowered my voice. "She said they were whistle-blowers."

"What do you mean?"

"She said she and Ron had discovered some kind of criminal activity, high up at Energene. They were going to blow the whistle."

"What kind of criminal acts?"

I sat back. "She didn't say."

He smirked. "She didn't say, huh?"

"The gunmen showed up before she could tell me."

"So why'd they come to you?"

I thought about it a second. "She said they were scared out of their minds and didn't think they could trust the usual channels. They knew I had some history with this stuff, hoped they could trust me."

He laughed. "They must've been out of their minds, all right. Sounds like bullshit, you know that, right?"

I shrugged. I couldn't argue with that.

"She tell you anything else?"

I'd given him enough to look at Bourden and Energene. I didn't want to get him any closer until I had a better idea of what was going on.

I shook my head. "No."

On my way back to the Roundhouse, I called Nola at work.

"Busy?"

"A little." I could hear people talking in the background. "What's up?"

"Just had a visit from Miriam Hartwell."

"What?! Hold on." The background noise fell away as she moved somewhere quieter. "Are you serious? Did she confess?"

I laughed wearily. "Not exactly."

I told her the highlights of what Miriam had told me, about Ron's suspicions that people were getting sick from Energene's soy.

"So she thinks someone from Energene shot Ron?"

"That's what she thinks. Have you ever heard of anything like that? People having allergic reactions to genetically modified stuff like that?"

"Sure. That was one of the big early concerns about GMOs. Some people worry that if you're allergic to spinach, you could unknowingly eat broccoli spliced with spinach genes and have a reaction. Some people even think there's a link between genetically engineered foods and increases in food allergies overall."

"Really?"

"One of the first GMO crops, StarLink corn, was only approved for animal consumption because there were concerns it might be allergenic. When it got accidently mixed into the human food supply, some people did have reactions. There were huge recalls and lawsuits, and eventually, they pulled it all from the market. It's controversial, though. I don't know if any of it has ever been proven, but there's definitely science to suggest it's possible."

"Huh." Ron's theory was at least plausible.

"Okay, I have to get back to work. So did they charge her? Does she have a lawyer?"

I laughed.

"What?"

"No, they didn't." I didn't want to tell her about the shooting. "She took off again."

21

Lieutenant Suarez looked up when I walked into his office, but he didn't say anything, instead just motioning for me to sit in one of the two chairs facing his desk. He was staring at his computer screen and tapping at the keyboard, but I got the distinct impression that he was doing it randomly. He left me sitting there squirming for two minutes.

His phone buzzed, and he picked it up. "Yes? . . . All right, send them up." He let out a sigh as he put the phone down, waiting a few more moments before looking at me.

"Carrick," he said, as if my name was rich with many meanings, and none of them were good. "Warren got me up to speed. So this is you walking away from it?"

"I did walk away from it. I was literally walking away from it when it drove up next to me and asked me to get in the car. What was I going to do, say no?"

"Well, this might be news to you, but as a police officer, when you see a wanted felon, you should arrest that felon."

"I would have," I said, not sure how boldly I was lying. "But I wanted to hear what she had to say first. Frankly, I wasn't expecting to be ambushed by gunmen. And neither was she."

"Yeah, that's another thing. You're ambushed by gunmen as you say, and you don't return fire? I'm not saying that's a bad move, but very un-Carrick-like."

"We were across the street from a school, and I didn't want to risk endangering the students."

He nodded, hearing me but not accepting it. "Well, you wanted to be involved in the case, you're involved in the case."

He looked over my shoulder and said, "Gentlemen, come on in."

I turned around to see Tom Royce, Bourden's security chief. Next to him was another man whose thin, angular face looked vaguely familiar.

"I believe you know Tom Royce, from Energene," Suarez said without looking at anybody. "This is his assistant, Morris Divock."

Royce gave me a withering stare that said he didn't like this any more than I did. "The good people at Energene have suspicions that Ron and Miriam Hartwell may have been engaged in corporate espionage. They and their friends at the Justice Department have asked for our help determining if that's the case and, if possible, recovering anything that was stolen. As they are cooperating with our investigation, we have been asked to cooperate with theirs."

I gave a polite nod.

Then Suarez said, "That cooperation will take the form of you, Detective Carrick."

My head whipped around.

Suarez was smiling at me. It wasn't a nice smile. "We're fortunate that we have someone so familiar with the case and yet completely nonessential to it. For the next couple of days, I want you to share with these gentlemen all aspects of our official investigation. You can start by taking them back to the Liberty Motel and walking them through what happened."

"Lieutenant—"

He cut me off, cocking an eye at me. "They don't know the city well, so you'll be their official guide. And since I know you haven't had a chance to write up reports on your conversations with Ron Hartwell's mom, his brother, and his building super, you will accompany Mr. Royce and Mr. Divock on follow-up interviews. And then you can write all of it up for the case file. Is that understood?"

"But—"

He held up a hand. "I know how badly you want to help this investigation, Detective Carrick, so I know you will appreciate how important it is that those officially tasked with solving the case can concentrate on the job at hand."

22

I felt better about not telling Warren everything Miriam had said about Energene now that we were sharing everything with Royce and Divock. I wondered how much they knew about what was going on in Haiti. Or about who had killed Ron Hartwell.

"Suarez said you guys weren't from around here," I said from the backseat in a fake cheerful tone. I don't like being in a car that I'm not driving. And I really don't like sitting in the backseat, especially not behind Royce's bright red ears and neck. It helped that every time I asked a question, he got redder. "Where are you from?"

Neither of them moved, but I got the feeling a look had been exchanged.

Royce let out a sigh. "Chicago."

"How long have you been in Philly?"

"Couple weeks."

"They move you around a lot?"

"As much as they need to."

"Must be nice. Traveling around the world all the time."

Divock looked at me in the rearview. Royce didn't respond at all, except for a deepening redness in his neck and ears.

"So what do you think Ron Hartwell might have stolen?" I asked. Divock kept his eyes on the road. Royce turned to look at me, then turned back without a word.

I shrugged. "Be easier to help you if I know what you think he took."

"It's a shame you weren't helping us earlier. It would have been a lot easier if you'd arrested Miriam Hartwell when you had the chance." He took a deep breath and let it out. "We don't know what he took. Information." He turned in his seat to look at me again. "Did she say anything to you about it? Did she tell you anything at all?"

"No." I looked back at him blankly. "She said she didn't kill her husband and she didn't know who did. Or why. Before I could press her on it, the gunmen showed up."

His eyes lingered on me, his sneer letting me know he didn't like me, didn't believe me.

"What kind of stuff was Hartwell working on, anyway?" I asked.

"It's secret."

"Oh, you can tell me. I'm a cop."

"It's technical," he said. "You wouldn't understand."

"Miriam said he was working on some new genetically modified soybean." Seemed pretty straightforward to me.

Royce didn't say anything.

"She said they were in Haiti a few weeks back. You guys ever been there?"

"Once or twice," Royce said without turning around.

"Really? What was going on there?"

He turned his head just enough to see me, but he didn't answer. I understood, too—I was starting to get on my own nerves. We drove the rest of the way in silence.

23

The dog was back at the fence in the lot next to the Liberty Motel. He didn't look at me as we got out of the car, and at first, I took it personally. Then I realized he was probably put off by the assholes I was with. I wanted to explain to him that I had no choice, but he turned and walked away again.

The kid from the front desk was sitting on the front steps, a set of earbuds connecting him to the smartphone that had so narrowly escaped being shot. He plucked one of the buds as we walked up.

"You the police?" he asked as we walked up.

"I am," I said. "These two are just . . . participating in the investigation."

He nodded. "They said I had to wait until you guys were done before I could take down the tape and reopen the motel."

"What's your name?"

"Gerald Toyner."

I inclined my head toward the door behind him. "Anybody still in there?"

"Psh!" He laughed. "You kidding? With these motherfuckers stomping all over? That scared more people away than the bullets did. Folks cleared out before we even asked them. Would've been gone quicker if they didn't have to stop to make up fake names and contact info for Officer Po Po standing by the front door."

"We want to take a look inside," Royce said.

Gerald looked at me, and I nodded. He heaved himself off the steps and got out of our way, then followed behind us.

I pulled down the crime scene tape and let the three of them precede me. Royce and Divock recoiled at the smell of the hallway.

"Jesus," said Royce, turning to glare at Gerald, as if the smell was his fault. The weed part might have been.

I pointed at the ruined sound system behind the desk. "How'd that happen?"

The kid shook his head at the tragedy of it. "I told the other cop about it. Motherfucker comes in, shoots it. No good reason, just that kind of motherfucker, I guess. Then he points the gun at me, big thing with a silencer making it look even bigger. He says, 'Where's the Asian girl in the wig?' I fucking told him, man. He heads up the steps, I took off out the front door."

"What'd he look like?" I said.

"About thirty." He shrugged. "White-guy asshole in a suit." He turned to Royce and Divock. "No offense."

Royce's neck maintained a steady tone, so I don't think he was too offended. Oh, well.

We walked up the steps to the hallway. It seemed longer than before. At the far end, the door to Miriam's room was open. In the light spilling through it, I could see the cuffs lying open on the carpet.

Royce looked at them and then at me, disapprovingly, as we stepped over them and into the room.

It looked the same as before except the table was bare, Miriam Hartwell's shopping bags now locked in an evidence locker.

Royce and Divock looked around the room, then at each other, then at me.

"Okay, so what happened in here?" Royce asked, folding his arms.

I sat in the wooden chair next to the table and waved them toward the bed. "Have a seat," I said, waiting as they slowly settled their butts onto the filthy bed.

I left out more than I kept in. I said she was scared and that she said she was innocent. When I added in that she thought someone was following her, Divock glanced at Royce. "Before she could tell me anything else, company showed up."

"And how did that go down?"

I told them the basics.

"So how did you fuck up with the cuffs?" Divock asked. I think it was the first time he'd spoken. "Forget to click them or something?"

I had no idea how he got out of the cuffs. I was about to tell him there were a variety of ways he could have got out of them, with or without a key. Instead, I said, "Click them? I didn't know you had to click them. What I do is swing them gently almost shut and make him promise to hold his wrists together."

I could hear Gerald snickering down the hallway.

"Don't be an asshole," Royce snapped, although I couldn't be sure if it was directed at me or at Divock. "Obviously you fucked something up. Otherwise he wouldn't have gotten away, right?"

I looked at my watch, thinking I should go before I made the transition from smartass to dumbass and said something I'd regret. "We done here?"

24

Royce and Divock were ready to quit at five o'clock. I was ready, too, but I wasn't done yet. I hadn't learned anything much from them—certainly nothing to make me discount Miriam's suspicions about Energene. I confirmed they were assholes, but I'd known that already.

The plan was to pick Nola's brain a little more about Energene over a quick dinner, then do a little more background work on the case.

But as I pulled up outside the house, I sensed something wrong. The windows were open, and as I walked up the front steps, I heard laughter. Tipsy laughter.

I opened the door and saw Nola sitting on the sofa with Laura Tennison, an almost empty bottle of wine in front of them. That's when I remembered the horrible truth.

We had a houseguest.

My heart sank, but Nola seemed relaxed, like she was having fun.

I said hi and sat across from them. Nola asked me about my day, and I told her a little more about Miriam Hartwell and the Liberty Motel. I played up the part about the dog, added the part about going back there with Royce and Divock, and left out the part about the shooting. I could feel my stress sucking some of the levity out of the room, so I was relieved when Laura launched into a story about something vaguely similar that had happened to Danny. I knew the story, and she left out the funny, relevant, and important parts, but the two of them laughed uproariously at what was left.

They were drunker than I was. Everything was funnier.

They laughed their way through another bottle of wine over dinner, and afterward, I brought the laptop into the bedroom and researched Energene, the drought in Haiti, allergenicity issues with genetically modified food, and which federal agencies could be responsible for whatever vague crime might be related to Ron Hartwell's murder.

When I turned the light out at midnight, Nola and Laura were still laughing in the living room. I was glad Nola was having so much fun, but I wondered if she was going to pay for it in the morning.

25

When I left for work, Nola was snoring hard, and so was Laura in the guest room. When I kissed Nola's forehead, her brows furrowed. She was still asleep, but I was pretty sure her hangover had already gone for a run, showered, and had a full breakfast.

I was feeling almost self-righteous, but as I approached the station, I felt the beginnings of a tiny headache of my own. It grew as I walked into the squad room.

It felt a lot like a hangover, but I hadn't had much to drink. I realized it wasn't from the alcohol. It was from the assholes.

"You're late," Royce said, sitting in my chair, looking at his watch. "Suarez said you're supposed to be in at nine."

Divock was leaning against my desk. He was playing with one of my pencils, wiggling it between his fingers, making it look like it was made of rubber.

I thought briefly about shooting them both. Instead, I turned and walked into Suarez's office. I didn't knock. He was on the phone, but instead of waving me off, he said, "I gotta go."

He put down the phone and motioned for me to close the door behind me.

"What the—"

"I know, I know," he said. "Serious assholes. Maybe even worse than you."

"I can't spend another whole day with them. And I don't know if Warren told you about this, but Miriam Hartwell said she thought there was something going on at Energene."

He shook his head. "Warren thinks that's bullshit."

"He thinks it's bullshit?"

He shrugged. "Evidence points at Hartwell. He likes her for the murder, thinks she's feeding you a line. And it's his investigation."

"Oh, come on—"

"Look, Carrick," he said, cutting me off, pointing at his door, at Royce and Divock waiting outside it. "I know this is bullshit with these two. I don't like it either, but these guys are connected out the wazoo. I got a memo from the chief—'Energene Corporation is to be afforded our absolute cooperation'—saying how much the mayor and the fucking governor appreciate our assistance. I told him two days, yesterday and today. That's it."

I sat back. "It's bullshit."

"You could just shoot them."

"Thought about it."

He shrugged. "With your background, it wouldn't be so out of character. I could get a dozen officers to testify it was temporary insanity. Or just regular insanity."

"Fuck you."

His face hardened. "Watch it, Carrick. I'm still your lieutenant. And I still don't like you. Sorry all this landed on your doorstep, but neither us would be stuck dealing with these pricks if you'd left the case alone." He laughed and sat back. "Think about that, huh? If you'd done what you were told for once, Mike Warren would be stuck with those assholes. You could be out doing police work."

* * *

Royce's list of people he wanted to interview didn't include anyone from Energene. I had been hoping to have another look around, but I guess they didn't need my help to talk to those people.

We started the day in ballistics, Bernie Lawrence looking at me cockeyed as I explained the situation. But he shrugged and answered Royce's questions, repeating everything he had told me the day before, even though it was all in his report.

Royce nodded solemnly and said, "So the gun found in Miriam Hartwell's laundry room is an *exact* match for the bullets that killed Ron Hartwell?"

Bernie looked at me again. "That's what I just said."

Royce sounded like a bad trial lawyer laying out a case, and I looked behind me, half expecting to see someone else standing there that he might be trying to impress. There wasn't.

He turned to me. "And the prints on the gun are definitely Miriam Hartwell's?"

"That's what forensics says."

Royce looked at Divock, and they both nodded this time. Doubly solemn.

Bernie watched us as we left, and I made a mental note to talk to him later and explain why I was bringing these mugs around.

The next stop was the apartment building. Gonzalez, the building super, answered the buzzer with double the exasperation of my previous visit. I told him Royce and Divock were collaborating on the investigation and they wanted to see the laundry room, as well. He gave me this look like, "Really?"

I shrugged and nodded apologetically.

Royce cleared his throat. "Is there a problem?"

Gonzalez looked at me and shook his head, annoyed and disappointed, like he never actually liked me, but he'd thought I at least understood how busy he was.

He led us to the laundry room, fidgeting impatiently by the door while Royce and Divock took turns looking under the change machine.

"And this is where the gun was found, is that it?" Royce asked, pointing.

"Yes."

Royce nodded at that. "And did Miriam Hartwell use these facilities here on a regular basis?"

Gonzalez looked back and forth between the three of us, like he was trying to figure out how this worked. "Well, yeah. I mean, she did her laundry." He looked at his watch.

I was wondering if he was going to ask if she used fabric softener, but we left after that and headed over to my neighborhood to recanvass for witnesses. The first round of interviews hadn't turned up anything, and this round was equally unenlightening—a few people heard the banging on the door. A few more heard the gunshots. No one saw anything.

Several neighbors asked if Nola and I were okay, which was nice. A few asked if we knew who'd done it. The first time, Royce said the victim's wife was the main suspect. After that, I made sure I answered first, saying we didn't know and couldn't comment.

I didn't blame Royce and Divock for wanting to double-check Warren's investigation, but I wasn't crazy about the way they did it—pissing people off, making insinuations about Ron's and Miriam's characters.

I don't think they learned anything new. But I did.

I confirmed that they weren't serious investigators, not even on a par with Mike Warren. It made me wonder what they were really after.

They seemed like they were putting on a show, trying to convince me, or even themselves, that Miriam Hartwell was guilty.

They might also have been trying to gain deeper insights into me, but I was pretty sure that wasn't going to happen. Not until the last stop of the day.

I felt bad about inconveniencing Bernie Lawrence and Gonzalez, even the people who lived on my block. But Dorothy Hartwell had lost her son—and possibly her daughter-in-law, as well. She was hurting. I didn't want to let them hurt her anymore or trick her into saying anything that might make things worse for her or her family.

When she answered the door, I said, "Hello, Mrs. Hartwell. Sorry to bother you, but these gentlemen are from Energene. They think Ron and Miriam may have been engaged in industrial espionage, or spying, and they'd like to ask you a few questions as part of their company's investigation."

Royce, Divock, and Hartwell all dropped their jaws.

Hartwell recovered first. "What do you mean?"

"They think it's possible Ron and Miriam may have been selling company secrets. I am here as a courtesy to them, but the police are not investigating this. It is strictly a private investigation, and you are under no obligation to answer their questions."

Divock's mouth continued to hang open, but Royce's slammed shut, his jaws grinding as he glared at me.

I smiled. "I just wanted to make sure there was no confusion."

Dorothy Hartwell looked at Royce, her expression turning stormy.

He seemed to realize he was on the spot. "We're sorry for your loss, Mrs. Hartwell."

She folded her arms. "Thank you. What would you like to know?"

Royce took out his notebook, keeping his eyes on it and away from her. "Um . . . did Ron or Miriam show any signs of sudden wealth or money concerns in the weeks before Ron's death?"

"No."

"Were they stressed out or otherwise behaving strangely?"

"No."

"Had they expressed any negative feelings about Energene?"

"No."

"Had they made any comments or statements that might lead you to believe they were planning on leaving town anytime soon?"

"No."

"Did their marriage seem in any way troubled?"

"No." Her eye twitched and started to water. "They were both normal, happy, in love, and in no way suspicious until Ron was murdered."

Royce nodded and went quiet. I wondered if he had run out of questions.

"Will that be all?" she asked.

"Um . . . actually, we'd like to talk to your son Brian. Is he available?"

She stared at Royce with such intensity I wondered if she was trying to make his head explode. I took a step away, just in case, but she briefly gave me the same look, letting me know she blamed me for bringing him here.

"He's out of town until late tonight, but he doesn't live here, anyway," she said. "Detective Carrick can give you his contact information."

"Okay. Thank you," he said without looking up. "We appreciate your—"

The door slammed in his face.

To his credit, Royce didn't flinch. But as he turned to walk back to the car, he looked at me and muttered, "Asshole."

"Sorry," I said as we got in the car. "If I'd known you were intending on impersonating a police officer, I would have kept quiet."

"Fuck you, Carrick. You're supposed to be helping us. You didn't have to turn her against us like that."

It was a fun drive back to the Roundhouse. When I saw my car parked on the street, I looked at my watch. It was five o'clock.

"You can let me out here," I said, overwhelmed by the compulsion to get away from them and relief that my two days with them were over.

"Suit yourself," Royce said, pulling over. "We'll see you tomorrow."

I paused, halfway out of the car. "What do you mean?" Suarez had said yesterday and today.

"We need you tomorrow morning, too, when we talk to the brother. Kind of suspicious that he leaves town immediately after the murder, so we want to see him in person. I texted Suarez. He okayed it. We'll pick you up here at nine."

I was stunned and angry. "I'll meet you out there." I wasn't going to get any more information out of them, and I couldn't bear the thought of riding with them again.

Royce turned in his seat, his mouth open as if he was going to argue. But I guess he didn't want to spend any more time with me, either. "All right, whatever. We also need the case file. Warren said we could borrow it tomorrow morning."

"He did?" Cooperation was one thing, but this was a little extreme.

"He did."

Whatever. I opened the door to get out. "I'll bring it."

"Fine. What's Brian Hartwell's address?"

I gave him the address, and as I closed the door, Royce said, "See you there at nine thirty."

As I watched them drive away, my anger slowly cooled. My car was right there, and I was looking forward to getting home—houseguest or not. But I knew I'd regret having to make a special trip in the morning. I turned away from my car and walked up the block, toward the Roundhouse.

Mike Warren was leaning against his desk talking football at Darryl Purcell, who was typing at his computer. Purcell and I didn't know each other well, but he looked up at me, his eyes almost pleading me to distract Warren so he could get his work done.

Through an open door, I could see Myerson, Warren's lieutenant, in his office, looking like he was trying to concentrate on something other than Warren's bullshit. He got up from behind his desk to close the door.

Warren looked up at me and laughed, like he was about to say something funny, but then he didn't have anything, so he just said, "Carrick."

"You told Royce he could borrow the Hartwell case file?" I asked Warren loudly.

Warren shrugged. "The brass said cooperate."

I didn't want to spend any longer with him than I had to, so I didn't tell him how ridiculous it was. "Royce asked me to pick it up for him," I said. "I'm meeting them in the morning, and they want me to bring it."

I was waiting for him to give me shit about bringing the case file home so I could blister him for lending it out to someone who could conceivably be a suspect. But he didn't.

"If you say so." He found it on his desk and handed it over. "Don't lose it."

No surprise, it was kind of thin.

26

The house was quieter than the night before. Nola and Laura were in the kitchen stripping kale and cooking rice. There was a package of tofu on the counter. I don't think they were still in pain, but the memory of the morning was obviously fresh.

Dinner was quiet and healthy and not at all hilarious. I didn't eat much, or at least I didn't feel like I'd eaten much when I was done. Afterward, Nola said there was a documentary on PBS she wanted to watch. Laura said, "That sounds interesting."

It was like we were all on some sort of punishment.

I was more in the mood for a brainless comedy, so I poured myself a scotch and took Mike Warren's case file into the bedroom. Useless, careless, unimaginative. Warren's handwritten notes looked and read like they were written by a child. He had several pages of notes from interviewing me about Miriam Hartwell's flight to avoid prosecution but little about the case itself except for forensics and ballistics. It made me feel even better about holding back on what Miriam had told me.

Around nine thirty, I heard Nola saying good night to Laura. She came to bed, looking exhausted and screwing her face up at my Scotch like she planned on never touching alcohol again.

"How's it going?" I asked her.

She shrugged. "Laura's great. I like her a lot. But I kind of wish it was just you and me."

I patted her on the knee and didn't mention that she had invited her without asking me. Nola was a better person than I was. She might deny it, but we both knew it was true. Sometimes being such a good person had its drawbacks.

"I know," she said, conceding my unspoken points.

"It's just a few days," I said.

She nodded. "What are you working on?"

"Looking over the Hartwell case file."

She raised an eyebrow. "Are you supposed to take case files home?"

"Not really." I told her about my day with Royce and Divock, which led to a conversation about my conversation with Suarez, which led back to what really happened at the Liberty Motel, or at least enough of it that I felt like I was no longer keeping anything important from her.

She chose to focus on the fact that I had been. "Doyle! I can't believe you didn't tell me about that yesterday."

"I didn't have a chance to tell you," I said defensively—and disingenuously. "I didn't want to get into it in front of Laura. And you weren't in any shape for a serious conversation."

She scowled at me, then softened.

"Besides," I added. "You were having fun."

She shook her head at me, then climbed onto the bed and snuggled up. "I guess. But we agreed you'd tell me when anything dangerous like that happens."

"Sorry." I took a deep breath.

"So why did she come to you?"

"Same reason he did, I guess."

"And why's that?"

"Ron thought he was onto something big, something dangerous, and he needed to do something about it. He was a whistle-blower. His bosses seemed like they were in on it. And the relevant authorities were all cozy with his bosses."

"So he came to you?"

"They figured they could trust me because I'd tangled with those types before. They hoped I'd be able to tell them who to go to."

She looked up at me. "And who's that?"

"I'm still trying to figure that out."

She was quiet for a moment. "And Miriam thinks this is why they killed Ron?"

I nodded.

"It would be a lot of money at stake," she said quietly, as if that explained it all. Which it did. "So wait a second. These guys you've been babysitting the last few days, aren't they from Energene, as well?"

"Yup. I was hoping to get some information out of them, but they seem pretty useless."

"You need to be careful, Doyle."

"I'm always careful."

"I mean it."

"I know."

We lay there for a few minutes, and her breathing started to even out. "Don't stay up too late," she mumbled.

I kissed her good night, and then she was asleep.

I was tired too, but I wanted to go over the case file one more time, and I needed to jot down some ideas from what I'd read so far. I also wanted another look at the crime scene. Luckily, it was right out front.

I eased out of bed and went to the front door, out onto the front steps. I tried my best to picture it—Ron banging on the door, where the shooter must have been, Miriam's car when I saw it, where it must have come from. For ten minutes I stood there, figuring the angles. But no matter how I pictured it, I couldn't make it work.

27

I woke up ravenous and tantalized by the smell of bacon. It was early, but I could tell the house was empty. I put on my robe just in case and made my way to the kitchen. There was coffee in the machine and a note from Nola folded on the table.

My eyes were still bleary, but I opened it up. "Laura and I went to yoga," it read. I put it down and laughed. The night of the wine bottles had made a bigger impression that I'd thought—they were in full-on New Year's resolution mode.

A text came in from Royce. "Have to cancel today. Something came up."

"Asshole," I muttered, even as I smiled at the development.

My stomach grumbled as I poured myself a coffee, then I spotted the bacon, a whole plate of it on the counter, and the grumble became a roar.

I folded a piece into my mouth. It was perfect—crisp but not dry, still slightly warm. I sat at the kitchen table and skimmed the case file, then got out my notebook and skimmed that, too.

Ron Hartwell believed I could help him. Maybe I could find his killer and exonerate his wife. That wasn't the help he'd originally had in mind, but it was something.

I ate another piece of bacon, then turned to a clean page and wrote across the top "federal connections" on one side, and "relevant agencies" on the other. In the first column, I listed the federal agencies I'd worked with at one point or another, where I knew at least one person:

DEA
ATF
HOMELAND (?)
FBI (?)

Whatever Ron and Miriam suspected had something to do with food, health, science, maybe trade, so in the second column, I wrote:

USDA
FDA
FTC
CONSUMER PROTECTION
CDC (?)

The lack of any overlap was striking. I'd met a couple of people from CDC back in Dunston, but I didn't know them well enough to trust them with something like this.

FBI was the closest to any relevance, but I had more enemies there than friends and no one I could really trust. Except Danny, and he didn't count.

I ate some more bacon while I tried to coax the lists into overlapping, but it was useless. By the time I gave up, I felt physically sick. At first I thought it was a reaction to the situation. Then I realized I had eaten the entire plate of bacon. As I poured myself another coffee, I saw that Nola's note continued below the fold. Then I felt even sicker.

Laura and I went to yoga
then to get fish for chowder
do not eat the bacon!!

That last line was underlined three times. Beneath it was a pretty decent drawing of a piece of bacon with a circle around it and a line through it.

Crap.

I called Nola, hoping to reach her before she left the market so she could get more bacon, and so she wouldn't still be mad at me by the time she got home. But as I waited for her to pick up, I heard a buzzing sound and saw her phone sitting on the coffee table.

I downed my coffee, grabbed my keys, and hurried out the door. I needed to get some replacement bacon at the deli and cook it before they returned.

I was halfway down the block when a black Dodge Charger pulled up next to me. The driver's window slid down and a guy I didn't know said, "Do you want to talk to Miriam Hartwell?"

If I'd been unsure about getting into Miriam's car, I was even less sure about getting into this guy's. When I paused, instead of threatening to drive off, he said, "She wants to tell you the rest of her story before she disappears."

"Where is she?"

"Someplace safe. But she won't be there long. I can take you there, but we need to go now."

He was in his late thirties, short blond hair. Good-looking, but not so much you'd hold it against him. Hard around the edges, like he'd seen some action, but he didn't scream active military, and he didn't have that douchey, private-army vibe. "Who are you?"

"A friend. A friend without a lot of time to waste."

If he'd wanted to kill me, he could have shot me on my front steps, like someone had shot Ron Hartwell.

For some reason, I trusted him, and not just because he wasn't shooting me. Most people didn't want to shoot me until they'd known me for a little while.

I hooked my thumb toward the front door. "Let me leave a note for my girlfriend."

He shook his head. "You can call her later."

I frowned and raised an eyebrow.

"That's how it has to be."

I looked back at the house one more time. Then I got in the car.

28

For the second time in just a few days I was being driven by someone I didn't know to a place I didn't know. I didn't like it.

"David Sable," he said, reaching out his hand.

"Doyle Carrick," I said, shaking it.

He smiled. "I know."

Okay, maybe a tiny bit douchey. Or maybe I just didn't like him knowing more than I did and not sharing.

I didn't want to keep asking questions and being put off, so I kept them to myself. But my curiosity surged as we turned onto 95 South and even more when we left it, curving between the marshy banks of the Delaware and the back of Philadelphia International Airport.

"The airport?" I laughed as we pulled up to a back gate. "You've got to be kidding me. I need to get to work. I'm late as it is. Where the hell are we going?"

"Can't tell. But we're hoping you'll come. Miriam is hoping you'll come."

"Who's 'we'?"

He smiled. "People who care about the same things you do."

"And what's that?"

"Making sure powerful people don't get away with doing bad things."

"I need to call my girlfriend, tell her where I am."

He shook his head. "Sorry."

"I need to at least let her know I'm okay." And apologize for eating the bacon.

We were driving toward a line of airplanes on the tarmac. He sighed. "Okay," he said, keeping one eye on me as I called Nola.

"Doyle!" she exclaimed. "You ate the bacon!"

"I know. Sorry. I was going to get more, but . . . something came up."

I could hear the beginnings of an exasperated sigh, then it was cut short. "Wait, are you all right?"

"I'm fine. I just . . . something came up, and I have to deal with it. I can't tell you any more than that."

"Are you okay?"

"Yes. Don't be mad about the bacon."

Sable glanced at me and then looked away.

"I'm not," she said. "Keep in touch, okay? Let me know what's going on."

"I will. Love you, babe."

"Love you too. Be careful out there." She already sounded far away.

"Always."

I tucked away my phone as we pulled up to a shiny, twin-engine turboprop, maybe forty feet long. The hatch was open.

I followed Sable up the steps, and as soon as we were inside, the engine started. The interior was plush but tight, filled by four roomy leather seats and a couple of foldout tables.

Sable sat in one of the seats and said, "Buckle up."

"Where are we going?"

"I'll tell you once we're in the air."

29

The plane eased forward and picked up speed. I couldn't help thinking that none of my friends had the kind of money for a private plane.

But my enemies did.

I reminded myself that if Energene or anyone else wanted me dead, there were plenty of ways to kill me that didn't require a private plane.

We climbed steeply for ten minutes, and as we leveled off, Sable turned to me and said, "Florida. That's where we're headed. We have Miriam in a safe place, just for the moment."

"You've got a private plane and a safe house. What do you need with me?"

He smiled, acknowledging the point. "You'll have to ask Miriam."

The door to the cockpit opened, and a guy came out wearing jeans and boots and an open yellow oxford shirt over a white tee. His face looked anywhere from a sprightly mid-sixties to a haggard forty-five. I guessed around fifty, with a medium dose of haggard. His eyes were gray, tired but intense.

He and Sable exchanged a nod, then he turned to me. "You're

Carrick," he said as he walked over to a cooler strapped down behind the seats. He took out a plastic-wrapped sandwich and a bottle of orange juice. "I'm Charlie. The pilot." He clamped the juice against his ribs with his elbow while he opened the sandwich and took a bite.

"Good to meet you," I said.

He nodded and went back into the cockpit.

Sable leaned forward, his eyes serious. "The people after Miriam are probably the same people who killed Ron. We can't risk them finding out where she is or what she's doing. That's why all the secrecy." He sat back. "We won't be gone long. You'll be home in time for dinner."

"Who's paying for all this? Who are you working for?"

He studied my face, like he was trying to decide how much to tell me and how much of it should be the truth. "We know what you did in Dunston. Martha's Vineyard too."

"What are you talking about?"

He smiled. "You made some powerful enemies, right? Well, you made a few friends too. Friends who want the same thing you want."

He kept saying that. "And what is it that you think I want?" I wanted to turn the plane around, go home, and get into bed with Nola. I hoped that wasn't what he meant.

"You want to see that when bad people do bad things, they don't get away with it."

"Everybody wants that."

He laughed. "No, they don't. The bad guys don't. Or the people making money off the bad guys. Or the people who think the bad guys are a necessary evil." He cocked his head. "Do you like being a cop?"

He asked like it was a choice, like it wasn't simply part of me. "It has its moments. I wouldn't mind a slightly lower bullshit-to-accomplishment ratio, but as I understand it, that's a problem with most jobs."

He laughed at that.

"How about you?" I asked. "Do you like being a . . . Actually, what the hell are you?"

He laughed again. "Do you know the name Gregory Mikel, of the Mikel Group?"

It took me a second to realize I did, then another to realize how. "The billionaire?"

He nodded. "I work for him."

"Gun for hire?"

His smile flattened out. "Sort of. Mikel has a vast business empire, but he also underwrites a group called Beta Librae. We work quietly to try to counter some of the damage being done by his fellow billionaires and the corporations they control."

"So he's a good-guy rich guy?"

"Something like that."

"And I'm sure he's never strayed from the straight and narrow while accumulating his billions."

He sat back. "I didn't say that. And he hasn't lost the billions he's made, so I don't think he's undermining his own interests. But he's a good guy. He's uniquely placed and trying to do the right thing. And he's never asked me to do anything I disagreed with."

"Helping Miriam Hartwell flee prosecution is doing the right thing?"

"You tell me. You helped her get away, as well."

I could have given him the same counter I'd given Warren, but I knew it didn't ring true. "What about Ron? Wouldn't it have been the right thing to swoop in before he got killed?"

He gave me a distasteful look, like I was being too glib. "We weren't aware of the situation until it was too late."

"How did you become aware of the situation?"

He smiled. "Kind of a funny story, actually. But I'll have to tell you some other time."

30

Two and a half hours later, we were over the Everglades. The ocean extended to the west as far as I could see. To the east, just as far, were crazy patterns of land and water.

"Time to buckle up," Sable said. "We'll be landing soon." As I did, he added, "It's not an international flight, so it's no big deal, but we're trying to keep a low profile, so we'll be getting off a little early."

An image of parachutes flashed through my brain, but I kept my reaction to a single raised eyebrow.

He shook his head. "Nothing dramatic. Charlie's going to pause as he's turning at the end of the runway. That's when we get off. We'll have to hustle. There's a car waiting for us."

A tiny airport came up at us quick. Beyond it was a tiny town, just a few blocks wide and a mile or two long.

"Everglades City," Sable announced.

I cocked an eyebrow. "Home of the square grouper?" In the seventies and eighties, Everglades City was notorious for the bales of marijuana—nicknamed square grouper—that smugglers would dump in the surrounding waters for locals to retrieve and deliver.

He smiled. "That was a long time ago. Just a small town with an airfield now."

The tires touched down for a smooth landing, then the reverse thrust pushed us against our seat belts.

"You guys ready?" Charlie called over his shoulder as we passed the airport buildings.

Sable called back, "Good to go."

We slowed as we approached the end of the runway and in mid-turn, the plane stopped altogether.

Charlie said, "Go!"

Sable pushed the hatch, and it swung down toward the tarmac, the steps opening out. We hustled down, the air moist and thick around us. As soon as we were on the ground, Sable closed the hatch, and the engines revved again. As the plane continued its turn, we ran, staying low, across the tarmac and the scrubby grass that surrounded it, toward a fence that ended at the water's edge fifty yards away. We swung around the end of the fence, over the water, and found ourselves in a small field. In the middle of it was a nondescript silver sedan.

Sable got in behind the wheel as I got in the other side, and we drove off, not too fast. A gravel road took us onto a small paved road, then we turned onto an avenue with palm trees arcing up out of a broad green median divider.

"Charlie's getting the plane fueled up," Sable said. "He'll pick you up in an hour and a half to take you back to Philly."

"You're staying?"

Sable shook his head. "No, I'll be getting the Helio ready to get Ms. Hartwell the hell out of here."

I assumed he meant a helicopter. "Where?"

He shook his head. "Not my place to tell you. But she seems to trust you, so you can ask her yourself."

We were approaching the middle of town, a courthouse and a church surrounding a small traffic circle with some kind of small communications tower in the middle. To my right and left, I could see the edges of town.

"How long does it take to get the plane ready?"

"Just a few minutes." As we rounded the circle, he pointed down a cross street at a squat, Spanish-looking building with a sign out front: TASTE OF THE EVERGLADES. "After that, he'll be in there fueling himself up on conch fritters and cold beer."

We turned right, into a curved parking lot sandwiched between a U-shaped motel and a standalone central office. A red and white sign said EVERGLADES CITY MOTEL. The place looked neat and almost humble. The office had a small glass vestibule with a simple door on either side, but right between them was an incongruously extravagant concrete fountain, looking totally out of place. Still, it was a lot nicer than the Liberty Motel.

Sable stopped the car and handed me a key. "Room seventeen."

I looked down at it. It had a number seventeen on it. "Okay. Thanks, I guess."

He nodded and put out his hand.

We shook, and as I got out, he said, "I'll see you soon."

Then he drove away.

The breeze picked up, but it was sticky. Sable disappeared around the corner. Then I was alone, except for a few mosquitoes that had already found me. Each room had a door with a number on it, a window, and a pair of cheap white resin chairs facing the parking lot. I found number seventeen and let myself in.

31

The room was sparse: a bed, a table with a couple chairs, and a kitchenette. Miriam was sitting at the table wearing the same shades as before, plus a long, coppery-looking wig. When I closed the door, she took them both off, studying me, searching for something. I don't know if she saw what she was looking for.

"You came," she said.

I nodded.

"I didn't think you would. Sable didn't think so, either."

"How do you know him? Sable, I mean."

She shook her head. "I don't know him, not really. Although I guess he's one of my only friends now. Him and you." She smiled weakly. "Sorry. It's been a rough time."

I sat down across from her. "How's he involved in all this?"

"I was at the airport in Philly, making my big escape. Sable walks up alongside me and says, 'You know they're looking for you, right?' I said, 'Excuse me?' and he says, 'You'll never make it out.' So I had no idea who he was, but I said, 'Then what am I supposed to do?' And he offered to help me. I was terrified. For all I knew, he was some goon from Energene. But I knew he was right—if I went ahead, the police would get me. At least with him I had a chance. So I went with him. Now I'm here, still alive and free, as far as it goes, so . . ." She went quiet for a moment. "I want to thank you. Back at the motel in Philly. If you hadn't been there, they would have killed me."

Her gratitude made me feel guilty. If I'd woken up faster, gotten downstairs faster, reacted faster at the first knock, maybe Ron Hartwell would be alive. Of course, maybe I'd be have been killed alongside him.

"Sorry for all the cloak-and-dagger stuff," she said. "I didn't think they'd find me in North Philly. I needed to be sure they won't find me here."

"What do you know about Beta Librae?"

She shrugged. "Just what Sable told me. An environmental group financed by Gregory Mikel, the investor."

"Have you ever heard of them before?"

"I've heard of Mikel. I knew he was an activist. I'd never heard of Beta Librae."

"Do you trust them?"

She shrugged. "I don't know."

"What do you think they want?"

She let out a bitter laugh. "I don't even know what *I* want, other than Ron being alive and us never to have gone down this road. But that's not really an option."

No, that was not an option.

"I don't know what they want," she said quietly. "But they seem to want me to stay alive, and I guess I want that too."

She didn't seem entirely sure. Her eyes went distant again, and moist. I couldn't imagine what she was going through, but this wasn't the time to dwell on it.

"So," I said, rubbing my hands together. "You said there was something else you wanted to tell me."

She smiled sadly, grateful for the interruption of whatever was going through her head.

"I have Ron's files. The stuff that made him so suspicious in the first place, and some other stuff. I'm not a molecular biologist, so a lot of it I don't understand, but a lot I do. And some of it Ron explained to me before—" Her voice caught, and she took a deep breath. "Anyway, to someone with the right background, it would mean even more. And it would be very incriminating."

"What does it say?"

"There's documents about Soyagene, a report on the stolen shipments, plans for some kind of phase-two rollout starting next week. There's inventories and production memos—some secret and some not. But there's also confidential memos and reports about allergenicity, about different levels and intensities. Ron said he had to dig deep to find it. He printed them out, because he couldn't copy the files electronically. A couple of days later, they were gone. As far as we know, these hard copies are the only ones in existence. He said they prove Energene has known about the allergenicity issues all along. They're planning on releasing it, anyway. If it's true, millions of people could get sick. Thousands could die."

"If it's that unsafe, why would they go ahead with it? Wouldn't they just be sickening their own customers and opening themselves up to massive lawsuits?"

She paused. "I've asked myself that too. I don't know why. I thought maybe the documents referred to earlier versions of Soyagene, before they fixed it. But they're talking about a product they're about to roll out. Maybe they can make their money back before they have to pull it off the market. Maybe they hope to release the next version, the fixed version, before anyone even knows what's going on."

I'd seen companies do that, but not on this scale.

"Energene has pharmaceutical divisions," she said. "They might be hoping to profit from some kind of treatment. I don't know."

"Did you tell Sable?"

She shook her head. "I thought about it. I Googled Mikel, and he seems for real. He might be in a position to do something with it, but Sable . . . I don't know. He just appears out of nowhere. I have no proof of his connection to Mikel. He could be making it all up. I'm trusting him with my life, but this . . . this is too important."

"So what's your plan?"

"I made a copy of the files to give you. I don't know what you did on Martha's Vineyard and in Dunston, but you stopped powerful people from doing bad things, and you got powerful authorities to help you. I need you to do that again."

Oh, that. No problem. I thought back to my mutually exclusive lists and wondered how many friends of friends of friends I'd have to go through to get someone both trustworthy and helpful. Before I could tell them anything, though, I needed to know more about what it all meant. I was still thinking about all that when she continued. "Then I'm out of here."

"Where?"

"Haiti, at first. Cap-Haïtien. I need to get out of the country, and I need to take the files to Regi, my friend at the Health Ministry. We wanted to tell him earlier, but by the time Ron figured out what was going on, we didn't trust the phones or e-mail. Regi will understand what's in those files. He'll figure out what happened to the people in that village, and he'll be able to do something about it. His government isn't crazy about Energene or the other corporations, anyway. They won't be afraid to take them on. Hopefully, once he figures it out, he can get the information out there, to the press, whatever, stop it from happening anywhere else."

"How are you going to get there?"

"Sable."

"And then what?"

"If I'm still wanted for murder, I'll find somewhere nice that doesn't have extradition. Maybe the Maldives if the sea hasn't swallowed them up yet." A flicker of fear passed through her eyes. "And I'll hope whoever killed Ron doesn't track me down."

I put my hand on her shoulder. "I'll find out who killed Ron." I didn't say anything about all the other stuff she hoped for.

"Thanks." She gave me a brave smile, suddenly reminding me of an old lady who's lost her faith but keeps going to church because she doesn't know what else to do. She hoisted her shoulder bag and put on her wig and her shades. "Charlie will come to get you soon. We should get those files so you're ready to go when he gets here."

"Where are they?"

"The motel safe. I didn't know where to keep them."

She turned and put her hand on the doorknob but paused, looking out the window. As she opened the door, I could feel the anxiety coming off her like a charge, like static electricity or lightning about to strike.

32

There were a couple of cars in the parking lot, but no people. The office building was only forty feet away, but it felt like a mile. Miriam looked both ways twice, then hurried across the asphalt. I caught up with her at the steps in time to open the door for her.

The guy behind the desk was barely twenty and gangly enough that I wasn't sure he'd finished growing. He was reading a *V-Wars* comic on his iPad and he seemed reluctant to put it down until he looked up and saw Miriam. "Hi again," he said, smiling. "How can I help you?"

Miriam showed him her room key. "I have some items in the safe."

"Oh right," he said, snapping his finger. "Be right back."

I don't think he was used to anyone using the motel safe. Frankly, I was surprised they had one, and I wondered if it was a real safe or just a closet. As soon as he left, the phone rang once, then started beeping and clicking. I realized it was a fax machine. Then the real phone started ringing, as well. Five times, and then it stopped. *Busy place*, I thought.

A few seconds later, the door to one of the motel units opened, and a man in his fifties stormed out, barefoot and unhappy, with his shirt open and his thinning hair plastered to his scalp with shampoo or conditioner. He left the door open behind him as he stormed across the parking lot.

The kid returned with two manila envelopes and said, "Here you go."

As he handed them to Miriam, the door opened behind us, and the guy with the wet hair said, "Water stopped. *Again.*"

The kid hurried around from behind the desk. "I'm so sorry, Mr. Jenkins. You should have called."

The guy turned and headed back to his room. "I did," he growled, as the kid hurried after him.

Miriam handed me one of the envelopes. "Keep this safe. See what you can do with it. If anything happens to me, or if you run into a dead end, just make sure it gets out before next Tuesday. That's when they're planning to start releasing the Soyagene. That's when more people will start getting sick. Send it to the press, put it out on the Internet, wherever. I'll send it out too, if I'm still . . . If I can." She sighed and shook her head. "I've been terrified someone was going to realize I had this stuff, but I think maybe now the best thing is to just get it out there."

"What about sending it to Mikel?"

She shook her head. "I could give it to Sable, but I don't know for sure that he really works for Mikel."

"Right, but what about sending it directly to him?"

She tilted her head thoughtfully, but then something outside caught my eye. Jenkins and the kid had almost reached Jenkins's open door when the kid stopped. Jenkins turned and glared at him, but the kid was distracted.

Then I saw them, getting out of a black SUV, asking the kid a question. Axe-Man and Old Spice. The gunmen from the Liberty Motel.

33

For an instant, I thought I had gasped, then I realized it was Miriam, following my eyes.

"That's them, isn't it?" she said breathlessly. "No, no, no, no," over and over again, like she was hyperventilating. I put my arm on her shoulder, reassuring, but I was holding my breath, waiting to see if the kid was going to point toward us, if his lips were going to say, "*Yeah, she's in the office.*" His eyes flickered in our direction, but he shrugged and shook his head.

He looked back at us, maybe sensing trouble, wanting to come warn us. But Jenkins snapped at him, and they both went into his room.

"Call Sable," I said. "Do you have his number?"

She nodded, fumbling for her phone. "He said it's just for emergencies." I gave her a look that reflected the urgency of the situation, and she said, "Right," tapping at the phone and putting it to her ear.

Outside, Axe-Man was knocking on the door to room number one, at the end. Old Spice started knocking on room number two, right next to it. Even from a distance, I could see the bulges of the guns under their jackets. Room number one opened, and an older woman looked out at Axe-Man, confused. She shook her head and closed the door. Door number two didn't open, and as Axe-Man walked around to room number three, Old Spice glanced around furtively, then quickly picked the lock and slipped inside. Axe-Man knocked on the door to room number three, and a few seconds later, Old Spice came back out and headed to door number four.

The way they were leapfrogging down the row, we had maybe three or four minutes before they finished checking the units and came to the office. I looked down at the papers in my hand. We had the only two copies. If they got us both, they won.

"Sable!" Miriam hissed into the phone. "They're here. The guys that came after me before." She listened for a second, then looked up at me. "He says he can be here in five minutes."

I took the phone from her. "We have three minutes, tops," I said.

"No way," Sable said. "I can't—"

"There's an open field across the street where you could easily land a helicopter."

"What are you talking about?"

"I'll lead them away from the motel," I told him. "You come and get Miriam in the copter."

"I don't have a copter . . ." He paused, and I could hear a loud engine starting up in the background. "Okay. Three minutes." Then he was gone.

I handed the phone back to Miriam and ducked behind the desk, tearing open the envelope in my hand and pulling out the papers.

"What are you doing?" she whispered, her eyes round with terror.

I grabbed a Sharpie and a sheet of Everglades City Motel stationery from a pile on the desk and wrote on it:

> *Send a copy of this to Gregory Mikel c/o the Mikel Group.*
> *Keep the original somewhere safe, and be careful.*
> *I love you,*
> *Doyle*

I fanned the papers, put them in the fax machine, and punched in Nola's fax number at work—one digit off from the main phone number.

"What are you doing?" Miriam asked again in a strangled high-pitched hiss.

"I'm trying to get this into Mikel's hands. You said if anything happened to you, we needed to get this out, right?"

"Yes," she said, a tight little whisper.

"Just in case." I didn't say it, but there was a good chance something was about to happen to her.

The fax machine dialed and started beeping.

I looked out the door, where Old Spice was knocking on the door next to where Jenkins and the kid were trying to get the shower to work. Axe-Man emerged from the room next to that. Room seventeen, where Miriam had been staying.

She started shaking. They'd already covered half the rooms. A door at the far end of the motel opened, and an old man came out, struggling with a small suitcase. Axe-Man eyeballed him for a moment, then turned so his body shielded the doorknob as he quickly picked the lock.

The older guy tossed his suitcase into the backseat of a dusty Buick. Then he got in and drove around to the office, to the door facing away from Axe Man.

There was no sign of Sable.

Miriam started shaking. She'd been heroic keeping it together as long as she had, but I was afraid she'd used up whatever reserves she was drawing from.

The old guy got out of the car and left the engine running and the door open. The dinging sound followed him as he came up the steps.

The fax machine started pulling the cover sheet through.

I turned to Miriam. "Give me your wig and your shades," I said. "And your cardigan—give me that too."

"What?" She wrapped one arm around her midsection and clamped the other on top of her head.

"Sable will be here in a minute with the copter. He'll touch down in that field across the street. I'm going to draw those two away from here. Once I do and you see that copter coming, you head over there and meet him." It would have been nice if I had my gun.

I took the wig off her head, took the shades off her face, and held out my hand for her cardigan.

She wiggled out of it and handed it over, her face stunned like she was going into shock.

The door opened and the old guy walked in just as the fax machine started sending the second page. I went behind the counter and grabbed the cover page and jammed it into my pocket.

"I just want to check out," the old guy said, holding up his key, impatiently. He wasn't as old as I'd thought, more worn down, like he'd been living so hard he wasn't likely to get legitimately old.

"We'll be with you in one moment," I said.

I squeezed Miriam's shoulder. Then I put on the wig and the shades and stuffed myself into the cardigan as best as I could.

I squeezed past the old man and out the door. Then I got in his car and drove off.

34

I put the car in gear and eased it forward, hoping the car's owner wouldn't realize right away that it was gone. I sank low in my seat, trying to look small as I swung through the parking lot.

Axe-Man was standing twenty feet in front of me. He looked up but didn't seem to recognize me, or rather, didn't seem to recognize Miriam. I stopped, waiting for it. Then he noticed me. And at the same moment, Old Spice stepped out of the door behind him. I eased the car forward as Axe-Man tapped his partner's arm.

I glanced at them, full on, all fake bronze hair and big sunglasses. Then I turned away and hit the gas.

I swerved out of the parking lot, intentionally overcompensating on the turn and grinding over one of the flower beds, so as to give the impression of being in a hurry but not actually moving too fast.

They seemed to buy it.

I fishtailed back and forth onto the street, and behind me the black SUV screamed out of the parking lot, rocketing after me. The old guy ran into the street behind them, chasing after me as well, but he stopped after a few steps.

I felt bad, but I'd leave the car at the airport, and he'd get it back soon enough. Unless these assholes caught up with me. In that case, his car would be the least of my worries.

I didn't know what kind of horsepower either of us had, but I wasn't trying to lose them, just to lead them as far from Miriam as possible before they realized their mistake. Of course, I didn't have a plan for if they actually did catch up with me.

I needed to work on that.

As it turned out, they had more horses than I did. Even with my foot on the floor, they were gaining.

I took a right and then skidded left onto the road with the palm trees lining the median. Up ahead was the traffic circle with the communications tower.

The airport would be just past it.

The SUV was growing in my rearview, and I was starting to wonder if Sable had run into technical difficulties when I saw a small airplane banking from the right and turning in our direction, flying low, straight down the middle of the road. It was a little prop plane, but oddly boxy and square. I didn't know what that was about.

I kept my foot on the gas, and as I approached the traffic circle, the plane roared by, just overhead. Behind me, the SUV stopped growing. Then it started shrinking. By the time I reached the traffic circle, they had stopped completely. The plane slowed down and almost hovered over the motel, then it gently descended onto the road. Like a helicopter. It was the damnedest thing I'd ever seen.

The SUV spun its wheels for a second, its tires screeching as it turned and took off back toward the motel. I continued around the traffic circle and sped back after it, wondering what I was going to do if I caught up with them. The SUV was taking the turns so hard I was hoping they'd roll, but they didn't. Neither did I, but I almost drifted off the road a couple times.

Two blocks up ahead, I could see Miriam running across the street toward the plane idling in the field. The door opened as she reached it, and she clambered aboard without breaking stride.

The SUV was still a block away as the plane rolled forward and miraculously lifted off the ground after just a few feet. I almost relaxed, but then I saw the top half of Axe-Man protruding from the passenger-side of the SUV.

He had a gun, an automatic, and apparently a decent touch with it, because when he let loose, at least three slugs dinged the plane's paint job. I tried to push the pedal harder—maybe I could rear-end the bastards. But I was already going as fast as the car could go, and they were already pulling away from me in pursuit of the plane.

The plane swung around as it rose, and by now the SUV was closing fast. This time, Axe-Man was aiming, squeezing off shots, one, two, three. I was afraid the plane was going to burst into flames. I was close enough that I could see Sable through the window, then the window cracked and I saw a splash of red. The plane wobbled wildly for a moment as it headed off to the north, flying low over the road.

The SUV kept after it, Axe-Man leaning out the passenger side, firing wildly again. I slowed to a stop next to the motel. I didn't know who'd been hit on the plane, or how bad. But there was nothing more I could do for Miriam, or for Sable.

As far as I knew, the fax had gone through by now, so hopefully Nola would get it and send it on to Mikel. I hadn't put her name on it, hoping "*I love you, Doyle*" would be enough to get it to her.

But these guys were ready to shoot down airplanes to keep their secrets from getting out. Suddenly, it sunk in how much I was endangering Nola by sending that fax. I'd told myself no one would ever know a fax had been sent. But if they did, if they looked in the motel office and saw it, it wouldn't take long for them to figure out where it had gone. And who the connection was to me.

I jerked the wheel and swerved into the motel parking lot, leaving the keys in the ignition and the engine running as I ran up the steps and into the office.

The fax had gone through, all the pages lying in the bottom tray. I grabbed them and jammed them into the waistband of my pants. Just as I was turning to run back out, I heard a loud metallic click.

The black circle of a gun barrel appeared at the periphery of my field of vision, inches from my eye. My heart plummeted, not just because now they had me, not just because now they had the files, but because now they'd know where I sent them, and to whom.

Then a voice said, "I don't know what you're playing at, asshole, but this is one crime scene you shouldn't have returned to." He didn't smell of Axe. Inexplicably, he smelled worse, a putrid combination of urine and halitosis.

I turned a little more. When I saw it was the guy whose car I'd stolen, I smiled.

"You think this is funny, asshole?" The gun started wavering, and he adjusted his grip. His grin had meth mouth written all over it. "You picked the wrong motherfucker to mess with, stealing a car I just stole my own self."

Part of me did think it was funny. But I didn't have time to explain to him why.

The gun was a big old thing, a Colt .357 with a six-inch barrel. He was holding it so close to my head I could have just bobbed out of the way and stepped past it to take it from him. Of course, if he pulled the trigger, I'd be deaf for a week.

He must have read my mind, because he stepped back. "Go ahead and make a move. I will open you up."

Axe-Man and Old Spice already knew what the car looked like. They'd be looking for it. I raised my hands, and he laughed. "You're lucky I'm in a hurry to get away from this shithole."

In the background, I could hear the car dinging, with the engine running and the door open, just like before.

He backed out the door, holding the gun on me the whole time. "Drive safe," I said.

"Fuck you," he replied.

As he got in the car, I could see the SUV approaching in the distance.

I hoped Sable and Miriam had gotten away.

The meth head peeled out, and I headed for the other door, pausing to watch as he tore out of the parking lot and screeched into the first left turn. I waited until the SUV went after him, then I slipped out the door and ran the other way.

35

The terrain was distressingly flat and open. I ran full out, the way you do when there's a machine gun involved. I kept the motel between me and whatever was playing out between the SUV and the meth head in the Buick. I'd seen the town from the air, and I knew there wasn't much of it—road out of town to the north and another one to the south. I knew the Buick wasn't going to elude the SUV for long, and however that interaction ended, it wouldn't take Axe-Man and Old Spice long to figure out I wasn't driving.

I had to find Charlie and get out of there the way I came in: by air. And I realized I probably wasn't going to be headed home, either.

I was pausing to catch my breath behind a Dumpster at a Gator Express gas station when I saw Taste of the Everglades, the restaurant, diagonally across the street.

I ran across to the parking lot and hid behind a massive pickup truck with a Confederate flag in the back and huge, coal-roller exhaust pipes sticking up over the bed. When I was sure there was no sign of Axe-Man or his pal, I slipped in the front door.

The hostess seemed startled, and I opened my mouth to describe Charlie, but I knew there wasn't time for that. Instead, I ran past her. The place was sprawling, and I hurried across the deck, through the screened-in porch, into the dining room. There was only a handful of people, and they stared at me like I had two heads. It wasn't until I got to the bar area that I realized I was still wearing my Miriam disguise.

I pulled off the shades and wig as my eyes adjusted to the dim light. The bartender and his lone customer were already staring at me.

"Carrick?" Charlie said, snorting as he looked me up and down and turned back around on his barstool. "Whatever, dude. Don't matter to me what you're into."

The bartender seemed more judgmental, trying hard not to say anything more than "What'll you have?" Even that sounded like he wasn't just asking what I'd like to drink.

I ignored him.

"We need to get out of here," I whispered tersely to Charlie.

The bartender raised an eyebrow and looked at Charlie differently after that.

"Dude," Charlie said, leaning back and waving his hands over the large glass of beer and the platter of fried seafood in front of him. "I'm eating dinner. I'll get you home soon enough."

I grabbed him by the collar, and he turned to me, a look of anger on his face until he saw the look on mine.

The bartender wandered down to the other end of the bar.

"We have to go to Haiti," I said.

He screwed up his face. "Bullshit we do." He leaned forward and lowered his voice. "Sable's taking the girl to Haiti. I'm taking you back to Philly. That's the plan."

"The plan's changed. Sable's hurt."

"What do you mean?"

"The guys after Miriam found her. Sable came in to extract her, in some crazy little plane that dropped out of the sky like a helicopter."

He smiled. "That's the Helio Courier."

"He got away, but they shot him."

The smile disappeared. "How bad?"

"I don't know. But the guys who shot him are about five minutes behind us."

I almost said *me* but figured saying *us* might incentivize him. It did.

"Fuck," he said, sliding off the barstool and tossing two crumpled twenties on the bar. He downed his beer, then we went outside to the giant pickup truck.

"This is you?" I asked as we got inside.

"Don't judge. Belongs to a friend of mine who works at the airport." He looked around as we drove. "I thought you said guys with guns were right behind us."

"They were," I said, looking around myself. "Maybe they left, or maybe they're waiting for us at the airport. I don't know."

"Excellent."

As it turned out, they weren't. Or they weren't fifty yards from the gate. That's where Charlie stopped and said, "Get out here." He pointed at the dirt road where Sable and I had come out. "Go back that way, meet me at the end of the runway. I'll pick you up where I dropped you off, okay?"

I got out and ran past the spot where Sable had picked up the car. I squeezed around the end of the fence and waited in a clump of bushes near the end of the landing strip.

Ten minutes later, I heard the turboprop approaching. As it neared the end of the runway, I ran toward it. The hatch fell open, and I climbed in, pulling it shut behind me. Before I was buckled into my seat, we were rocketing back down the runway, tipping up into the sky.

36

Charlie was worried about Sable—that's the only reason he agreed to take me—but he was worried about himself, too. He was angry about the idea of flying into Haiti on what he considered a whim. He said I hadn't thought it through. It didn't help when he found out I didn't have my passport.

"We'll just do the thing at the end of the runway," I said, "like we did in Everglades City."

He shook his head and let out an exasperated laugh. "Not for international flights, man. And not for international airports. Even in Haiti, there's going to be customs and immigration, cops all over. It's a big airport, with big fences and lots of guards. You're going to get taken in. And I'm going to get into trouble for helping you. Have you thought about this at all? Do speak any Kreyol? Do you even speak French?"

"A little," I said, exaggerating.

The truth was, I was as alarmed as he was. But even after I realized I totally hadn't thought it through, I couldn't think of anything I should have done differently. I needed to follow Miriam and Sable, to make sure they were okay, to help Miriam if Sable wasn't okay, and to help get those files to Regi Baudet.

Ron Hartwell had been convinced that whatever was in those files was explosive, and he had died trying to expose them. I needed to do what I could to help Miriam get them out.

Once we were in the air and I had a moment to think, panic flooded through me once more at the potential danger I had just faxed to Nola.

I glanced out the window, at the land sliding into the distance behind us, and I took out my phone.

Nola answered breathlessly on the first ring. "Doyle! Where are you? What's going on? Are you okay?"

"I'm fine. I'm in Florida." I glanced back out the window. I could still *see* Florida.

"Florida? What are you doing there? How did you get there so fast?"

"It's a long story. I was meeting with Miriam Hartwell. Look, I sent you a fax at work. It's important and it's dangerous. I shouldn't have, but I didn't know what else to do."

"It's okay. What is it?"

"It's what Ron and Miriam uncovered, files and memos. I need you to get it as soon as possible, but you need to be really careful, okay?"

"Sure, okay."

"Make a copy and put it somewhere safe. Send the other copy to Gregory Mikel, urgent, from Miriam Hartwell. Look up Mikel's corporate address in New York—"

"Wait, you mean Gregory Mikel the Beta Librae guy?"

"You know about them?"

"The environmental group? A little. You know Mikel is a billionaire, right?" The signal was starting to break up.

"Yes. Beta Librae—are they for real?"

"Yeah, I think so. What about them?" Her voice cut in and out.

"Look, I'm losing your signal. I shouldn't have sent it to you, I just needed to send it out before—"

"Before what?"

"You need to get out of the house."

"*What?!* Doyle, what are you talking about?" She let out an exasperated sigh. "Laura just left. Can't I just be alone in my home for a moment?"

"The guys who tried to kill Miriam in North Philly found her down here."

"Jesus, is she okay?"

"I think so. She got away. But this is serious."

"You think they could come here?"

"I just want you to be safe."

"Okay, okay. I'll go get the fax. Then I'll . . . go somewhere." I could hear her moving about, grabbing her keys. "When are you coming home?"

"Not just yet."

There was a burst of static, and I thought I'd lost her. "You're staying down there?"

"I think Miriam went to Haiti. I have to go after her, make sure she's okay."

"*Haiti?* Doyle, are you serious? Do you even have your passport?"

"Um . . . No, I just . . ."

"Then how . . . you going . . . into Haiti? How are . . . get back home?"

"I'll figure something out. I'll see you soon. I love you."

"I . . . too, but . . ."

And then she was gone. Outside the window, there was nothing but ocean.

Now that I was off the phone, I could hear Charlie, still muttering obscenities in the cockpit.

I took out the files I had faxed to Nola. There were a dozen pages, three or four of them stamped CONFIDENTIAL. A lot of the pages were almost duplicates, and none of them were all that scintillating to read in the first place, not even the secret ones. I kept reminding myself, *This is what Ron Hartwell was killed over, and he was bringing it to me when he died.*

I pored over each page looking for something, anything that stood out as a clue.

There were several abstracts of scientific reports that were so technical they were indecipherable. There were also a handful of inventory or production reports, lists of quantities of various agricultural products, or forecasts or plans for future production. They included several different varieties of modified corn, sugar beets, alfalfa, soy, and, at the bottom of the page, Soyagene.

There was a distribution memo marked CONFIDENTIAL. It seemed pretty innocuous stuff, talking about the phase-two rollout of Soyagene that Miriam had mentioned, set to start in a couple of days. There was an impressive list of markets, including the United States, broken down into six regions, and two dozen countries around the world, and a calendar of launch dates, stretching over the next six weeks.

There was a sales memo with a list of about a dozen crops, including Soyagene and something called Early Rise corn, as well as a couple of hybrid and genetically engineered sugar beets, two alfalfas, and a bunch of other stuff.

The last item was a production memo, also marked CONFIDENTIAL, that proposed reallocating production resources to accommodate an increase in Early Rise corn production from forty thousand tons to four hundred thousand tons. That was pretty much all it said.

I looked back at the sales memo. The Soyagene was new, so there was no historical data, but all the others, including the Early Rise corn, showed only gradual increases in production over the previous five years. Nothing to suggest an explosion of demand. Seemed like a bold increase in production, but I guessed Energene was an aggressive company.

The thing that stood out most was a secret memo that talked about allergenicity. It was mostly unintelligible, talking about target allergenicity, factor density, and minimum parts per million for symptomology. But it seemed relevant to whatever Miriam and Ron had suspected was happening.

I stared at the documents for the rest of the flight, but I didn't come up with anything remotely like a clue, not even in the high school slang sense of the word.

When I finally put down the files and rubbed my eyes, we were circling in a slow descent over the Haitian coast. Two hours had passed.

We came in over a small mountain. It was peppered with tiny houses, getting denser and denser toward the bottom. Then I saw Cap-Haïtien International Airport. Charlie had said it was much bigger than the airport back in Everglades City, but at first, it looked about the same. As we descended, though, it grew bigger and bigger, and I realized he was right.

The runway was surrounded by a wide, grassy field. A meandering path worn across it continued unimpeded through the surrounding fence and out into the countryside. I tried to memorize its location as the plane descended and the landscape flattened out around us.

I poked my head into the cockpit. "So how long are you going to be here?"

Charlie pulled up one of his headphones, turning to look at me like I was crazy. "Are you kidding me? I'm out of here, man. I'm not hanging out. I'm going to fuel up enough to get home, and then I'm gone."

"What if I need—"

He shook his head. "Unless the Haitians detain me for aiding and abetting an asshole, I'm out of here, man. If Sable needs me, he knows how to reach me. Otherwise, you'll never see me again." He put the headphone back over his ear and went back to landing the plane.

The touchdown was smooth as silk. Things got rougher after that. I could hear Charlie talking to the tower, trying to keep the stress out of his voice. The runway seemed to extend almost to the horizon. What little I knew about turboprops included their efficiency on short runways, their ability to use reverse thrust to stop short. But the plan was for me to slip out at the end of the runway. Charlie had already delayed touchdown until we were a third of the way down the runway, but even so, he had to keep the throttle up, or we would have run out of momentum before the end, even without the reverse thrust.

I couldn't hear what the tower was saying, but I could hear the agitated tone, and Charlie, increasingly defensive as they continued to tell him he was doing it wrong. At one point, he turned and glared at me, furious at having to pretend to be a lesser pilot in order to accommodate my half-baked plan.

Finally, we reached the end of the runway and halfway through the turn, we came to a stop. As Charlie looked at me, I could hear the tinny sound of the tower nattering away at him through the headphones down around his neck.

"Okay," he said to me. "Get the fuck out."

I gave the hatch a push and stepped out before it was fully open.

"And Carrick," he called out after me.

I paused and looked up at him.

"Good luck, man."

37

I closed the hatch and started running. The air was thick and hot, and the land fell away from the tarmac at an excruciatingly gentle slope. Running flat out, I'd almost given up hope of finding the path when I realized I was already on it. Not much of a path.

Up close, the grassy area was vast, probably five times the size of Everglades City Airpark. It was also parched. Behind me, clouds of dust hung in the air, kicked up by my feet. Hope was dimming that I would ever reach the fence, much less get through it, but I kept running and the fence drew slowly closer. And no one stopped me.

I was worn out and starting to wonder if I'd have to take a break along the way, and then I saw a little dip in the dry soil, under the fence.

By the time I reached it, I was so out of breath I would have been on my hands and knees even if I hadn't needed to crawl under the fence. Once on the other side, it took a great effort to get back on my feet.

I looked back through the fence, relieved there was no horde of Haitian police coming after me. Still, I knew I couldn't afford to let up, and I set off at a fast trot.

The path turned into a streambed, dry except for occasional patches of damp soil running down the center. It seemed to be a de facto property line, separating the backs of a series of scraggly, dried-up farm fields. Old tires, plastic bottles, and other debris mixed with the dusty rocks and branches that lined either side of it. I didn't know what I was doing or where I was going, but I knew I needed to put some more distance between me and the airport, so I kept going.

My plan involved relying on my high school French just enough to help me find someone who spoke English. I'd keep asking *"Parlez-vous anglais?"* until someone said "Yes." Then I'd ask for help finding Regi Baudet at the Ministry of Health.

That was my plan.

The streambed had dried up completely by the time it disappeared into a culvert under an actual road. I was pretty dehydrated, as well. A thin coating of dust had stuck to my sweaty skin. Climbing the banks up to a narrow street of tiny stucco homes, I practically bumped into an old man, maybe eighty years old, rail-thin and bent but with a wry sparkle in his eyes. He had on an Old Navy T-shirt.

"Parlez-vous anglais?" I asked him in my clumsy accent.

He shook his head and replied with a burst of Kreyol peppered with words I vaguely recognized but hadn't a hope of understanding. Then he directed another burst over my shoulder.

I turned and saw a starched white shirt and blue pants with a gold stripe. And a badge. The officer's dark skin was shining in the hot sun, but he looked crisp and cool nonetheless.

He looked at me with a gentle smile. His name tag said, BAP-TISTE.

"Bonjou, monsieur," he said.

"Bonjour," I replied with a casual smile. I turned to walk in the other direction. Cops are cops, even when you're a cop. I thought about playing the cop card, but I didn't think it would do me any good. Best thing would be to get far away as fast as possible, try to get my bearings until I could get a line on Regi Baudet.

"Ou pale franse oswa kreyol?" he asked after me. I was pretty sure he was asking if I spoke French or Kreyol.

"Un peu le français," I replied in bad French. A little French. Then I tried once again to walk away casually.

"You seem lost," he said in English.

"Just going for a walk."

"Can I see your passport?"

Crap. "Sorry," I said, patting my pockets. "I left it at the hotel."

He smiled patiently. "And what hotel is that?"

I smiled back. "The Hyatt?"

38

The room they put me in was definitely not at the Hyatt. Turns out, there is no Hyatt Hotel in Haiti. Instead, they put me in a lovely little place sometimes referred to as the Graybar Hotel.

Baptiste had raised an eyebrow when he saw my badge. He was very polite as he put me in handcuffs and led me down the street to a black-and-white SUV with the word POLICE on the side in big red letters. I was pretty sure no one I knew was going to see me, but it was still embarrassing.

It was a short drive to the police station, but enough that I got a quick look at the city. Run-down, for sure, but lovely in places, as well. The streets were narrow, bumpy, and tightly packed with small one- or two-story buildings that sagged wherever there should have been a straight line. They were plain, mostly gray cinder block, although some were brightly painted. Mixed in among them were grander structures, three or four stories, with balconies and architectural flourishes that reminded me of New Orleans.

Automobile traffic was light, motorcycles were plentiful, and pedestrians were everywhere.

The police station was a white stucco building with glass block windows. Baptiste brought me into a dingy squad room that smelled of mildew.

The room had a handful of desks and a row of support columns down the middle, holding up the water-stained ceiling. The cinder block walls were painted a drab, faded green. The floor was almost the same color, linoleum that had molded itself to all the bumps and depressions of the uneven surface beneath it.

Baptiste handcuffed me to a metal chair that was in turn chained to his desk. Once I was secure, he said, "I will return in one minute." And he disappeared.

I thought I was alone, at first. Then I heard laughter. On the other side of the squad room, a door was partially open. The name LT. SIMON was printed across it. Now that I was aware of it, I could hear several voices.

One of them sounded familiar.

Leaning back, I could just see into the office, but I couldn't see who was in there. I tilted the chair and craned my neck, peering around one of the pillars in the middle of the floor.

The voices grew louder, and when the door to the office opened fully, I almost tipped over backward. Throwing myself forward, I righted the chair and shifted to the side so I was hidden behind the support column.

I recognized the voices even before I glimpsed them—Royce and Divock. They were talking to a heavyset Haitian with a leering smile. He looked to be about fifty. Lieutenant Simon, I presumed. I looked at my wrist, at the chain holding me in place, helpless.

I shouldn't have been shocked—Miriam said she had seen them in Cap-Haïtien. I didn't know what kind of relationship they had with the police, but they were sharing a hearty laugh, and I was chained to a chair. I had a strong suspicion things might go rougher for me if they spotted me here.

Their voices dropped to a murmur, then they went silent. I pictured Royce or Divock catching sight of me, coming closer for a better look.

I was squeezing myself behind the column, as tightly as I could, when a voice called out, "Detective Doyle Carrick!"

I thought I was totally busted, but when I looked up, I saw Baptiste staring at me, confused. I peeked around the pillar and saw no sign of the others. The office door was closed. When I turned back to Baptiste, he said, "I should contact the American consulate, yes?"

I smiled and shook my head. "No, thank you." It was important that Miriam's movements couldn't be traced, and her pursuers had already found her twice. It seemed I should be taking similar precautions, especially with Royce and Divock here. "I am here to see Regi Baudet, the deputy health minister."

His eyebrow went up again. "Regi Baudet?"

I nodded.

"And he knows you?"

I shook my head. "Not well. Tell him I know him from the University of Pennsylvania. I came here just to talk to him, and it is very important."

"I see," he said, with a grave nod, pretending to take me seriously. "And you're sure you wouldn't like me to contact the consulate?"

"That's right."

"As you wish. I'll have to lock you up in the meantime."

To their credit, the guards regarded me without open hostility. They confiscated all my possessions, including my wallet and badge, my phone, Ron's files, even my shoes. When I protested, they made it clear that if I caused trouble, things could get worse in a hurry. I had backed up my phone a few days earlier, but not since the interview with Brian Hartwell. Reminding myself the recordings were hosted on a server somewhere, I turned the phone off and handed it over.

The guard who took me from Baptiste was condescendingly dismissive, biting back a smile as he escorted me into the sweltering maze of rank, decrepit cells.

Perhaps the fact that I was a cop meant they were treating me a little more gently than I might otherwise have been. There was a handful of other prisoners, and a few of them called out halfheartedly as we walked passed them, but I couldn't understand the language or decipher the intent, or even if their comments were directed toward me or the guard. I could feel the grit on the floor through my socks.

Halfway down the row, we paused in front of an empty cell. The guard took out a key and opened it, his smile finally breaking out as he extended his arm, welcoming me inside.

It wasn't as bad as I'd feared. A cot in one corner, a seatless toilet in the other. The walls were crumbling, inadequately held together by a thick coat of vivid blue paint. The floor was a mess. When I walked in, I could see I wasn't alone—it was teeming with insect life.

The cot probably was, too, but I willed myself not to look too closely as I sat on it. I thought about Miriam Hartwell's squeamishness in the Liberty Motel, and I hoped she was somewhere better than this.

I barely had time to start a rudimentary inventory of all the day's missteps before a tall, strikingly attractive young woman appeared outside my cell. Her skin was very dark, her shirt bright white, and her sneakers an almost fluorescent yellow. Her eyes smoldered with resentment.

"Who are you?" she demanded when I looked up at her.

"Doyle Carrick. Who are you?"

"I am the assistant to the deputy minister of health. Why do you wish to speak to Regi Baudet?" She seemed impatient, as if she'd been drawn away from something important.

"I have something urgent to tell him."

"He has more important work to do than to play riddle games with you. I doubt very much whatever you have to say is important, but the only way the deputy minister will hear it is if you tell me first."

"It's about Saint Benezet."

Her eyes narrowed but burned brighter, as if some volatile new fuel had been added to the fire. "What about it?"

I stepped closer to the bars, and she stepped back. "Tell Baudet it's also about Miriam Hartwell."

She glared at me for a moment longer, and I sensed that her resentment now was less about being interrupted from her work than about being kept out of the loop. She turned abruptly and strode away, her sneakers slapping against the concrete floor.

As I watched her go, the place suddenly seemed even more drab and depressing than before. My stomach grumbled and I realized I was intensely hungry, although looking around, I couldn't imagine eating in that place. I decided I'd refuse to eat and I'd call it a hunger strike. I was trying to come up with a good cause, when I was startled by a quiet voice asking, "How do you know Miriam Hartwell?"

He was thin and handsome, with dark skin and a gentle, weary face.

I got to my feet. "I don't know her well. She asked me to help her. You're Regi Baudet?"

He nodded and raised a dubious eyebrow, leaning against the bars of the empty cell across from mine. "To help her do what?"

I took a step closer and lowered my voice. "To help her prove she didn't kill her husband. And to tell you what she and Ron had learned about Saint Benezet."

His eyes widened, and he stared at me for a moment. Then he pushed away from the bars and strode off without a word.

39

Ten minutes later, Baudet returned with two annoyed-looking guards. One of them used a large cluster of keys to open my cell.

They all stood back, and Baudet motioned with his head for me to come out of the cell. I resisted the urge to ask what was going on—they would have told me if they'd wanted to. I also resisted the tiny fear that they were going to shoot me in the back and say I was trying to escape.

Flanked by the guards and followed by Baudet, I walked back past the other cells, through a heavy steel door that led to the intake area.

Baudet spoke sharply in Kreyol to the officer behind the window. They went briefly back and forth. Then a nearby door opened, and another guard emerged. He handed me a plastic bag with my belt and shoes, my wallet, and my keys.

I put on my shoes, put my keys in my pocket. I opened my wallet, relieved only the cash was gone. "I need my phone," I said to Baudet. "And my papers."

He turned to look at me, his eyes dropping to the empty wallet in my hands.

"The phone was new," I said. I lowered my voice and stepped closer to Baudet. "The papers were very important."

He closed his eyes and took a deep breath. I couldn't tell if he was irritated at me for my first-world problems or at my jailers for being such thieves.

He snapped a few more words, directing them toward the guard who had given me my belongings as well as the one behind the window. The one behind the window snapped back, shouting now, banging his fist on the ledge below the window, glaring at him menacingly.

Baudet turned and gave me a tiny shake of his head. "It may take some time to get back your phone and your papers." He motioned for me to follow him. We walked through another heavy steel door and a waiting area, a dozen plastic chairs on a concrete floor surrounded by cinder blocks and bathed in the dim glow of near-dead fluorescent lights.

Then we were out on the street, a bustling jumble of cars, motorcycles, bikes, and pedestrians. The sunlight was blinding after the dim light of the jail. It may have been even hotter outside, but the dusty air felt fresh and alive.

Baudet turned up the street without breaking stride, and I fell into step beside him. He gave me a sideways look, studying me as I slid my belt through the loops of my jeans.

I got the sense it wasn't time to talk yet, so I kept quiet.

At the end of the block, he looked back at the police station. "I'm very sad to hear about Ron," he said. "I didn't believe it when you told me, but I looked it up online. It's terrible." His eyes seemed to focus more intently on me, like he was looking inside me. "Do the police really think Miriam killed him?"

"Some of them do. I don't."

"Is she okay?"

"She's devastated."

"How is she physically?"

"Last I saw her, she was fine. Why?"

"I worry about her." There was a break in the traffic, and we crossed. "Please, tell me what happened."

I started from the beginning, with Ron banging on my front door, his murder. Baudet looked back toward the police station. "You saw him die?"

I nodded and told him about Miriam fleeing the scene, becoming a suspect and a fugitive, how she later approached me on the street, took me back to her motel hideaway. We turned down a cross street, a bit less crowded and hectic.

"Why did they come to you?"

"I've been asking myself that same question. Ron suspected Energene was up to something bad. They're powerful and connected, and he didn't know who he could trust. I'm just a cop, but I've been involved in a few cases with these biotech companies, crazy stuff, outside my jurisdiction. Stuff I stumbled across and was too stupid to leave alone."

"I don't understand."

"Because of my involvement in those other cases, he thought he could come to me. After he was . . . gone . . . Miriam felt even more scared and alone. She had no one else to turn to, not even Ron. And it seems she was right to be afraid."

He stopped on the narrow sidewalk and stared at me. "You think someone from Energene killed Ron?"

"Maybe." We started walking again, and I told him about the gunmen arriving at the motel, the shoot-out. I told him about Sable and coming down to Florida, what happened there with the gunmen showing up again, Sable and that crazy plane of his, the Helio Courier, and him being shot.

He stopped again. "*Woy!*" he said, under his breath. This time, he stopped for several seconds. "Where is Miriam now?"

"I don't know. Maybe they just flew someplace safe, but she said she wanted to tell you what she had found, give you copies of Ron's documents, that you'd be able to interpret them. I was pretty sure she'd be coming here. Those are the same documents that your police stole from me, along with my phone. Part of the reason I came here was to make sure you got them."

"Did you look at them?"

I nodded.

"What are they?"

"Shipping documents, memos, lab reports. Some were marked secret. I couldn't understand a lot of it. I don't know if Miriam did, either. I think she's hoping you would."

He sighed. "I'll see what I can do about getting them back."

I nodded. "I don't know for sure that Sable was hit, or if so, how bad. I had hoped Miriam would be here with you. That's the other reason I came here. To make sure she was okay."

He paused to watch as a military transport drove by, POLICE on the side of it in big red letters. A black SUV with tinted windows and a heavy-duty reinforced bumper crossed the other way. I knew it was some kind of private security, and as it passed, I saw a small decal on the side, a black four-pointed star against a charcoal-gray background. Darkstar corporate military contractors.

"I haven't heard from her," he said as he took out his phone. He thumbed through a couple of screens and placed a call. "I have a friend at the airport. If they are flying here, that's where they'd come in."

"That plane they were in, the Helio Courier, it doesn't need an airport. It could land anywhere. And don't use her name. She and Sable took great pains to keep her name out of everything."

Before Baudet could reply, the call was answered, and his face transformed. *"Jean-Pierre, bonjou!"* he said with a smile that looked more like a wince. *"Mwen se* Regi Baudet."

The conversation was brief, and it included the painfully enunciated phrase *Helio Courier.*

Baudet shook his head as he put away his phone. "He couldn't talk. There was some sort of commotion going on. But they have not had any planes like that coming in. He said he would have a list printed up for me of any such arrivals at Haiti's other airports today. I can go pick it up now. Do you want to come along?"

I didn't relish the thought of returning to the airport having so recently escaped it, but it wasn't like I had anywhere else I could go. He raised a key fob and unlocked a dark-green Suzuki SUV across the street. He took two steps toward it, then looked back at me. "Are you coming?"

40

Baudet drove more aggressively than I would have expected, but compared to the other vehicles on the road, he was like an old lady. At one point, a psychedelically decorated minibus almost T-boned us as we went through an intersection.

"What the hell is that?"

Baudet swerved around it. "Tap-tap. Kind of a private bus."

I looked back at it and saw it aggressively pass two police vehicles at once, even though it was jam-packed with riders.

I'd never been to Haiti before, but the police presence on the streets seemed unusual. Tense times indeed. The creases in Baudet's face seemed to deepen with each military or police vehicle we passed. There were a lot of private security vehicles, as well, and I spotted several more with those Darkstar logos. Even covered with dust they were conspicuously shiny and new.

"A lot of military," I said as we swerved around a personnel carrier parked in the middle of the road. "Is everything okay?"

He laughed grimly. "Everything is rarely okay in Haiti. And it's not the military, it's the police. Haiti has no military."

"No military?"

He shook his head. "They were involved in too many coups. We don't have much in the way of external threats. Or at least not military ones. But yes, our interior minister has been warning of narco terrorist activity and possible political instability." He studied me, as if trying to decide what he could tell me. "Frankly, I don't see it, but in Haiti, who knows? Maybe he's right. He's our top cop." He gave me a wry half-smile. "Cops should be trusted, right?"

I laughed at that. "Some of them. Are they expecting trouble?"

"There are many kinds of trouble. Some real, some imaginary. Sometimes the narco gangs fight among themselves, trying to expand into other sectors." He nodded to a commotion up ahead, a cluster of protestors waving signs and chanting. "Sometimes the people protest, the peasant groups, making sure they are heard, that their concerns are on the table."

"Peasant groups?"

"Small farmers."

"You call them peasants?" It seemed antiquated, maybe a little offensive.

"They call themselves peasants. It's an international movement. They are reclaiming the word."

"What do they want?"

He shrugged. "Mostly land, to keep control of it. To be able to do things the way they want to do them instead of the way the United States and the UN tell them, the way the big corporations want."

"Big corporations like Stoma and Energene?"

He nodded. "Among others."

"I thought the way the farmers had been doing things hadn't been working out so well. Especially with the drought and all."

He shrugged. "Some would agree with you. Others would say the old ways have never been given the support the new ways get, because the old ways don't make rich people richer the way the new ways do. They say the new ways aren't about making it easier to grow food; they're about making it easier to grow food on a big industrial scale. It's not so much about old and new as about small and big." He looked at me and shrugged again. "Between you and me, they may have a point. But there are concerns they may disrupt things, try to seize the spotlight. Especially during the trade summit at Labadee."

"What trade summit is that?"

"CASCATA. The Caribbean and South and Central American Trade Association. They're having a big meeting in Labadee, a private resort not far from here. The tourism bureau and one of the cruise lines just built a new hotel there. They want to show it off. CASCATA is voting on a big trade package, including new rules on biotech imports—maybe less, maybe more. The peasant groups are very concerned. So are the biotech companies, Stoma and Energene and the others."

"Speaking of Energene, back at the police station, I saw two of their security agents, guys I met back at their corporate offices in Philadelphia. Royce and Divock. Do you know them?"

He shook his head. "They have a lot of personnel down here these days."

"These two keep popping up. Miriam said she saw them around Saint Benezet. Then they were in Philadelphia looking into Ron's murder. They said they thought he was some kind of corporate spy. When I was arrested just now, they were in the police station. They seemed very friendly with the cop in charge, Lieutenant Simon."

Baudet ground his jaw for a moment, then shrugged, like it didn't mean anything to him. "Those types are friendly with everyone who can help them and who will take their money."

"You think Simon is corrupt?"

"Corrupt?" He laughed, a deep hearty laugh. "It would not be unheard of." His face seemed lighter, as if he'd needed the laugh. As if maybe it had been a while, and it might be a while again.

"Are they down here because of the Soyagene theft?"

"I don't know much about the Soyagene theft. I think they're just down here."

"Miriam said that when she and Ron were working on the Soyagene rollout, a shipment of Soyagene was hijacked, around the same time the people in Saint Benezet got sick, and not too far away. She saw the Energene security agents working nearby and thought maybe the two were related."

He turned to look at me intently but waited for me to continue.

"She said your test results suggested the villagers were suffering from some kind of allergic reaction. Miriam thinks it was a reaction to Energene's new soybeans, the Soyagene that was stolen, and that Energene was trying to hide the fact that their product was so allergenic. That's part of why she's so scared, why she thinks they're after her. If they have to pull the Soyagene from the market, it'll cost them millions."

He nodded, suddenly seeming both sad and haunted. "When I saw the histamine levels, I tested for specific allergens, and when I found out the Soyagene had been stolen, I included that among them, but there was no reaction at all. I sent Ron the results. Yes, the people at Saint Benezet had bought black market Soyagene before the first outbreak, but just that one time. They hadn't eaten any before the second outbreak." He paused. "I did get a positive reaction to Stoma Corporation's GMO corn, the Stoma-Grow, and in Saint Benezet the villagers said they had recently been consuming that. But Stoma-Grow is probably the most common food crop in the world, and this is the first I've heard of anything like this. It wouldn't be the first time genetically modified corn has had unanticipated allergenic issues, but so suddenly, so locally, and so intensely?" He shook his head. "I don't think so. I think Ron and Miriam are wrong about the Soyagene. I wish they were right."

"They seemed pretty sure Soyagene was involved." I realized I had been thinking about who I could give those files to and not enough about what I would tell them when I did. Ron had believed something was in there, and Miriam believed it too, but unless we knew what it was, no one was going to take any of it seriously. It would all be dismissed as vague suspicions and unfounded accusations. "We need to get those files back from the police. Then maybe we can see why."

"We'll get them back." He looked straight ahead, avoiding my gaze as we turned toward the entrance to the airport. "But there is another reason why I know that whatever happened at Saint Benezet was not an allergic reaction to Soyagene."

41

Before I could ask him what he meant, he gasped. Police were everywhere. There was a traffic stop at the entrance to the airport.

"*Mezanmiroo!*" Baudet muttered. "What the hell is this?"

"Do you think it could be Sable and Miriam? A crash or an unauthorized landing?"

"I don't know."

"I don't know if this is a good idea."

"What do you mean?"

"I still don't have a passport or anything. And as brief as it was, I've had my fill of your government's hospitality. Not looking forward to another stay any time soon."

"There should be no problem," he said. "You're with me. They won't ask for your passport unless you are boarding a flight."

These police were not like Baptiste, with his crisp uniform and his wry smile. These guys looked like soldiers, and they looked like they meant business. Several cars ahead of us, I could see they were checking IDs at the gate.

I told Baudet about how I arrived at the airport the first time.

He stared at me with his mouth open. "Are you insane, man? You're lucky they didn't shoot you."

"Well, I got away with it, for a while at least. But I don't know for sure that nobody saw me. Or captured me on video. It's probably best if I don't come inside."

He let out a deep sigh and pulled over to the side of the road.

"Wait here," he said as he got out of the car with his hands raised over his head. "*Bonjou!*" he called out.

The closest officer swiveled his upper body around, so his M16 was now leveled at Baudet's midsection.

The officer barked something in Kreyol. Baudet smiled even wider, hands still up, replying in Kreyol, but in a soothing, friendly tone. He slowly pulled out his wallet and held up his government ID.

I could easily imagine that gun going off, Baudet on the ground bleeding, dying. Looking up with eyes as dead as Ron Hartwell's. I had already developed a fondness for the guy, but before I could shake off the image, my mind was picturing what I would do if he was indeed cut down. Unfortunately, I saw myself bolting from the car, shot in the back, and doing my own rendition of Ron Hartwell's dead stare.

The officer lowered his rifle and examined Baudet's ID, his lips moving as he read it. His chin jutted out, and he spoke briefly, his eyes sullen.

Baudet smiled again and said a few more words. The cop sighed and waved him toward the guard hut. Baudet walked over and picked up a red plastic phone, glancing over at me for a moment before someone apparently picked up on the other end and they started speaking.

While he went back and forth with whoever was on the other end, the other cars inched forward past me. I felt very white and very conspicuous sitting in the passenger seat, parked too far from the curb.

At one point, Baudet was standing with his back to me as he spoke, and he turned, his eyes on me like laser beams as he shook his head. Finally, he hung up and came back toward the car. He thanked the young cop, I guess for not shooting us, then he got in.

"Any word on Miriam or Sable?"

"No." He gave me a withering look as he turned the car around. "The airport is on lockdown. Passengers only. The list was not waiting for me, but I spoke to Jean-Pierre, and he said as far as he could determine, there had been no Helio Couriers or unauthorized or suspicious landings at any Haitian airport in the last forty-eight hours, and no crashes they are aware of." He waved his hands at the cars backed up and waiting. "All this? Extra security because at this time of heightened concerns some crazy *blan* was seen running across the airport grounds."

"Blan?"

"White guy."

"Oh. Just as well I waited here, then, huh?"

"Do you do things like that often?"

I stayed quiet, and he rolled his eyes with an exaggerated sigh.

"Portia said she thought you were trouble."

42

As we drove away from the airport, I kept an eye on the rearview mirror, waiting for the guards to come after us because someone had seen me or recognized me. But they didn't, and I felt great relief as the airport was obscured by the dust rising up from the road behind us.

I turned to Baudet. "What did you mean when you said there was another reason whatever happened at Saint Benezet couldn't have been an allergic reaction to Soyagene?"

His foot eased off the accelerator as he turned to study my face. "Ron and Miriam thought they could trust you. Can I?"

"To do what?"

"To keep a secret."

"Sure."

"This has been declared a state secret. I could go to jail for telling you."

I waited.

He lowered his voice. "Something else hit Saint Benezet. A calamity." He lowered it to a whisper. "Ebola."

"*Ebola?*" I said, struggling to keep my voice down even though we were alone in the car.

He nodded solemnly.

"There's Ebola in Haiti?"

"Just this one outbreak. Apparently a very bad strain. There were no survivors. But it was totally contained. No more cases, and now it is over."

"Jesus. I'm so sorry. How many deaths?"

"Thirty-four. Luckily, Saint Benezet was a tiny village and very isolated. It was a particularly virulent strain. The Interior Ministry, the police, they discovered it and took control immediately. They sealed off the village and sent in their medics, but it was too late to help anyone. All they could do was comfort the sick and . . . contain the outbreak."

"Contain it how?"

"Fire," he said, staring straight ahead as we drove back into the main part of Cap-Haïtien. "After the villagers all died, the police incinerated the village . . . Saint Benezet no longer exists."

"They burned it down? Jesus, is that what you're supposed to do?"

We stopped at an intersection, and he went quiet for a moment, letting the traffic cross in front of us. "It's not what I would have done, no. They said there were no survivors . . ." He looked up at me with haunted eyes. "It is possible they overreacted. But I understand." He took a deep breath and let it out slowly, sadly. A motorcycle came up behind us, honking. It swerved around us and shot through the intersection without slowing down. "Do you know Haiti had been free of cholera for 150 years until just a few years ago?"

I shook my head.

He resumed driving, through the intersection and around an old pickup truck piled high with sacks of some kind of produce. "The UN brought it in. Their soldiers. A tragic mistake, and one we were unprepared for. Nine thousand dead. Seven hundred thousand sick." He sighed again. "Haiti has enough plagues. We do not need Ebola, as well. So I understand." He sounded like he was trying to convince himself as much as me.

"Why was the Interior Ministry in charge? Shouldn't you have been there?"

He nodded but remained quiet for several seconds. "Yes, we should have. Ducroix, the interior minister, he said it was a national security issue, which it was. My boss, Rene Dissette, the minister of health, he is a feeble old man. He didn't want to get into a turf battle. I don't think he wanted to deal with Ebola, either. By the time President Cardon got involved, the village was gone." I could hear the bitterness in his voice, the frustration.

"What about Miriam?" I asked. "What about you? You were both there earlier, right? Shouldn't there be a quarantine? Shouldn't there be announcements, to warn people?"

"The incubation period had passed before I even knew about it. I tried to contact Miriam as soon as I found out. I admit, I was concerned when I couldn't reach her. I am very sorry to hear about Ron, about Miriam's current troubles, but I am relieved her health is okay, as I knew it would be. My people are all fine. The same with the Energene people who were in the village when we were. Everyone is fine—everyone but the villagers. They are all dead." He let out a deep, sad sigh. "So it was not the stolen soybeans that made people sick."

"The entire town had Ebola, and none of it showed up in the blood tests you ran?" It didn't make sense to me.

He shook his head. "The tests we have for Ebola don't work until you are symptomatic for several days. No symptoms, no positive results."

"But there were symptoms, right? That's why you were there. That's why you and Miriam were there, right?"

He looked at me a little longer than I would have liked as we lurched along the fractured road.

"There were respiratory symptoms," he conceded quietly. "But not necessarily Ebola symptoms. Maybe that was something different. I don't know."

I felt something cold, dark, and horrible deep down inside my chest, like something had collapsed and left a tiny black hole in its place.

43

"Ron was pretty sure the Soyagene was causing the allergic reactions, and he even suspected that people at Energene knew it and were hiding it," I told Baudet. "Before the police took them, I read some of those secret memos. There was plenty in there about allergenicity issues."

"And you understood what they were saying? What they meant? Miriam is very smart and a trained nurse, and you tell me she says she didn't understand it."

"Maybe not. But she also said Ron was sure there was a connection between the grain hijacking and the illness at Saint Benezet. And it scared the hell out of him."

"So you think the Soyagene was hijacked and distributed locally, and that's what caused the respiratory distress syndrome?"

I shrugged. "That's what Ron and Miriam thought. Makes sense."

We drove quietly for a minute. "Well, I tested it, and there was virtually no reaction. It's possible perhaps by coincidence some other fate also befell Saint Benezet, something that coincided with the hijacking. Perhaps a pesticide exposure. Something else made them sick, and then they also suffered the Ebola outbreak."

A hell of a coincidence, I thought. I could feel the cold spot in my heart swell. My stomach grumbled loudly, as if in agreement.

"If we could find out if any of the stolen soy ended up anywhere else, we could see how those people were doing, if they were exhibiting any of the same symptoms."

He glanced at me, then thought for a moment. As he turned back to look at the road, he mumbled under his breath, "Toussaint Casson."

"What's that?"

"Toussaint Casson. A local gang leader. If there was a hijacking anywhere near Saint Benezet or Cap-Haïtien, he would be behind it, or at least aware of it. He could tell us if it ended up anywhere else. My nephew Toma, unfortunately, is Toussaint's right-hand man."

Baudet pulled over and took out his phone. Looking out the window, he muttered a staccato stream of Kreyol.

Seeing him on his phone reminded me I needed to call Nola.

"I left Toma a message," he said as he put the phone in his pocket. "Hopefully, he'll call back soon."

My stomach grumbled even louder this time. Baudet raised an eyebrow. "You are hungry?"

I was about to say I was starving, but it struck me that I was in a place where that could be a literal concern. "Very. But I need to call home and let my girlfriend know I'm okay."

Baudet offered to let me use his phone, but we'd passed several places that sold prepaid cell phones, so we stopped in one, a corner store selling a bit of everything: phones, rum, coffee, cigarettes, groceries, even clothing.

I noticed a row of five-pound bags of cornmeal. At the bottom of each bag, tucked into the corner, was the Stoma-Grow logo. Miriam said they were everywhere.

I gestured at the small display of plastic-encased cell phones behind the counter. "Prepaid cell phone?" I asked.

Baudet translated, and the man behind the counter reached back and grabbed one off the rack, putting it on the counter between us.

He scrunched up his face for a moment, then said, "Three thousand five hundred gourde."

The gourde was the Haitian currency. I don't know what it was worth in dollars. The phone was an old-fashioned flip model. It looked like it had just gotten out of some kind of cell phone time machine.

"Can I call the States with this?"

Baudet again translated, and the man sighed and grabbed another one off the rack and switched them. "Four thousand gourde."

I wasn't crazy about using a credit card, especially after having taken such pains not to go through the airport, but I needed a phone, and it was all I had. While I was at it, I got cash at an ATM in the corner. I didn't like being broke, either. Looking at the prices for the soft drinks, I estimated it was 50 gourde to the dollar, so I got 5,000 gourde, a thick sheaf of 250-gourde notes.

Before I left the store, I activated the phone. I paused for a moment, debating the safety of it. I didn't know for sure whether my iPhone was being tapped, but I knew this one wasn't. As we stepped back onto the crowded street, I called Nola.

She answered on the first ring, her voice tentative and suspicious. "Hello?"

"It's me," I said.

"Thank God. Are you back?"

"I'm still in Haiti. They took my phone—"

"Who?"

"It's a long story. Miriam never turned up. We're trying to find out what happened to her. And still trying to figure out what happened to Ron." Baudet was standing by his car, waiting. I turned away from him and lowered my voice. "Did you get the fax?"

"Yes, just a little while ago. The fax machine ran out of ink, and it took me all day to find a cartridge. I have it now, though, and I have the Mikel Group's address in New York. I'll send it out first thing in the morning. What does he have to do with all this, anyway? What's going on?"

"I'm trying to figure that out. Ron and Miriam thought Energene was up to something bad. Mikel's people are trying to help Miriam."

"And now Ron is dead and Miriam has disappeared."

"Tell me what you know about Beta Librae."

"Not much. Mikel's a billionaire, but also an environmentalist. He funds Beta Librae. They're quiet, but they've done some impressive things. They financed an indigenous group in Peru who fought off a logging venture. There was a town in India they helped get restitution when a sugar manufacturer ruined their lake. But like I said, they're pretty quiet. There were rumors they were involved in releasing secret documents exposing an illegal e-waste operation in Nigeria and illegal benzene dumping in Texas. I don't know what else they're up to."

"Do you think I can trust them?"

She laughed weakly. "Doyle, I don't know. They seem well-intentioned, but if you could trust a billionaire, would he be a billionaire?"

"Right. Are you someplace safe? Don't tell me where."

"I'm staying with a friend who I've been really meaning to spend some more time with." She said it with a touch of sarcasm. She was staying with Laura.

"Sorry."

"It's just the two of us, until later." Danny was back in town tonight.

"Okay, good."

"When are you coming home?"

"I don't know. Tomorrow, I hope. I miss you."

"I miss you too. Doyle, I worry about you."

"I'm fine. You stay safe."

"You too."

"Okay. I've got to go. I'll call you soon."

The phone connection had felt like a physical attachment, something concrete connecting me to the woman I love, to my home, to the familiar world. As I watched the connection icon fade, I felt myself snapped back to this alien, unfamiliar world.

When I looked up, Baudet gave me a warm smile. "Everything okay?"

I nodded.

"Good, good. I called someone I know with the local police. He will see what he can do about getting your phone and those files, but it may not be until tomorrow. Best I can do." He gestured to the car. "Let's get you some food while we wait to hear back from Toma."

44

Baudet pulled over two blocks away next to a jumble of plastic tables and chairs out on the sidewalk. Behind them, under a narrow awning, a sign on the wall read BBQ CENTRAL.

"Best food in Cap-Haïtien," he said, adding, with a grin, "plus, my sister works here."

I unfastened my seat belt and reached over to open my car door, but Baudet put his hand on my forearm.

"Wait one moment," he said.

I followed his gaze and saw that there was a lone customer, a man in a military uniform. Then I noticed a sleek black SUV parked out in front.

"What is it?"

He didn't answer at first. A bear of a man wearing a white T-shirt and a nervous smile came out of the restaurant. The man in uniform stood and shook his hand, slapping him on the shoulder. They stood and chatted for a moment.

"Who is that?" I asked.

"That's Marcel, the owner. The other man is Dominique Ducroix, the interior minister." He looked at me and smiled apologetically. "I don't like him very much."

I nodded. My stomach grumbled again.

Marcel and Ducroix shook hands once more, then Ducroix slapped him on the shoulder one last time, put on his shades, and got into the back of the SUV. As soon as the door was closed, the vehicle sped past us down the street.

Baudet watched it in the rearview mirror, and when it turned the corner, he smiled and unfastened his seat belt.

I looked at him as we got out.

"It's nothing," he said. "I just didn't want to talk to him."

We crossed the road, and Baudet gestured for me to take a seat. As we were sitting, a high-pitched squeal made me jump.

"Regi!" said the voice. I turned to see a woman maybe ten years older than Baudet, with glasses and a cloth over her hair. Her face beamed as she closed on him with hugs and kisses.

"*Bonswa*, Elena," Baudet said, grinning. He introduced me to her in Kreyol, and then in English said, "This is my sister, Elena."

She grasped my hand in both of hers and kissed me on the cheek.

"*Bonswa*," she said, then she rattled off something fast in Kreyol. All I understood of Baudet's reply was the last word—"American."

Elena nodded then turned back to me and slowly said, "Nice to meet you."

"Nice to meet you too," I said. "*Bonswa*," I added.

She and Baudet exchanged a few more words, and then she hustled back inside.

Moments later, the bearlike man in the white T-shirt came out, exclaiming, "*Bonswa*, Regi! *Kouman ou ye?*"

Baudet stood and said, "Marcel!" They smiled broadly, and then Baudet held out his arm to me. "*Sa se mesye* Doyle Carrick."

Marcel and I shook hands and bid each other, "*Bonswa*."

"Doyle *se yon Ameriken*," Baudet told him.

Marcel smiled and said, "Good, good. Welcome to Cap-Haïtien."

They bantered back and forth for a few seconds in Kreyol. I heard

Baudet say "Ducroix," and Marcel rolled his eyes. He turned to me and waved his hand in the direction Ducroix's car had gone. "My number-one customer, that guy," he said. "He is a dirty dog and probably a Duvalierist but . . ." He shrugged. Business is business.

Baudet asked him a question in Kreyol.

Marcel shook his head, saying, "No, no, no," and patted him on the shoulder reassuringly. Then he turned to me. "Chicken and fried plantain?"

Baudet said, "*Trè bon*," so I did, too.

When Marcel went back inside, I said, "What's up with that Ducroix guy? Is there a problem?"

"No, not really. He's annoying is all. He loves this place, which is understandable, because the food is so good. But I don't like seeing him here."

Elena brought out two bottles of Prestige beer, dripping with condensation. We thanked her, and she disappeared. Baudet watched her go with a twinkle in his eye, but when he turned back, it faded, like he didn't have the energy to maintain it. He raised his beer and said, "*Santé.*"

We both drank deeply. It was crisp and light, but I knew I had to be careful until I got some food in my stomach.

"So what about Miriam?" I asked. "Where else can we look for her?"

He shook his head. "I don't know. She's not here. The plane didn't land in Haiti. There's no reports of crashes in the area. You said this man Sable was shot?"

"It looked like it, yeah."

He shrugged. "They might have landed somewhere in Florida." He sighed. "Or ditched in the ocean, I guess. I hope not."

I pointed at his phone. "Can you do a search? Google the last twenty-four hours. Plane, crash, and Florida, or plane, wreckage, Florida?"

He picked up his phone and tapped away at it for a moment, then scrolled through the results and shook his head. He repeated the process a few times, then looked up and said, "Nothing. I tried it with 'Caribbean,' 'Bahamas,' and 'Cuba,' as well."

We drank quietly for a few moments. I looked at my watch. It was after six. "Could you try them again? Your friend with the police and your friend at the airport?"

He smiled. "Mr. Carrick, I have done what I can in that regard. These are not close friends of mine. They are acquaintances. Annoying them will be counterproductive. Miriam means very much to me. Her welfare is important to me, too. Perhaps you have a friend you could call at the FAA?"

I shook my head, thinking I'd have to add FAA to the list of relevant agencies where I didn't have any friends. Then I realized I did have one friend with the feds who I had forgotten about.

45

Danny answered on the third ring with a suspicious, "Hello?"

"Hey, partner. How's life with the Federales?" I had gotten up from my chair and was pacing the sidewalk ten feet from where Baudet was sitting.

"Doyle? Where are you calling from? You sound like shit, and your number has like thirty digits."

I laughed. "Yeah, I'm out of town. I need a favor."

"Well, I figured, since it's you."

"A couple favors, actually."

"Goes without saying. Wait, where are you?"

I laughed again. It was kind of ridiculous. "I'm actually in Haiti right now."

"*Haiti?!* What are you talking about?"

"Long story, actually. You probably don't want to know about it."

"Is this about the Hartwell thing? Oh, wait a second—did I hear that you blew off a shift today?"

"*Shit!* I forgot to call out."

"You forgot?" He started laughing. "I leave town for a few days, and you piss off to Haiti and forget to call in?"

He was laughing so hard now that Baudet was smiling at me, thinking something hilarious was going on. I turned to face away from him.

"I need you to keep an eye on Nola, okay?"

That brought him down to Earth. "Sure, of course. Wait, isn't she staying—"

"Yes," I cut him off. I knew they weren't tapping his phone or my burner, but I didn't want to take any chances. "She is."

"What's going on?" Totally serious now. "Is this part of the Hartwell thing, too?"

"Yes, it is. There's guys with guns, and they're not shy about using them." I told him about the Liberty Motel, about Everglades City. "They might be the same guys that shot Ron Hartwell. Look, I'm probably overreacting, but that's why I need you to keep an eye on things." I paused. "How are the kids?"

He paused, too. "They're great," he said quietly. "I guess they can stay with their friends for another day or two."

"That would probably be best. Just a day or two, to be sure."

"Okay. Well, I'll be home in a couple hours."

"Great. I need something else, too." I told him briefly and obliquely some of the details of Miriam and Sable's escape in the Helio Courier. "Anyway, since you're in good with the feds, and since you're not involved in this case, really, I'm wondering if you can use your FBI connections and see if FAA has any reports of planes like that coming down, unauthorized landings, anything suspicious like that, in or around Florida."

"You know I've only been here a couple days. I'm basically on a glorified training assignment."

"I know it's more than that, but I also know I'm asking a lot of you."

"It's not that, it's just . . . Sure, whatever. Yeah, I'll call. I'll just call FAA. Text you back at this number?"

"That'd be great."

"Okay." He took a deep breath. "Look, Doyle, I don't know what you're doing down there, but you know you're not getting away with too many more of these spectacular fuckups in your career, right?"

"Yeah, I know it."

"You want me to talk to Suarez? Tell him where you are? Tell him you're sick or whatever?"

"No, that's okay. I'll deal with it when I get back."

As I got off the phone and returned to the table, Elena came out with two plates of food. Daylight was quickly fading, and she plugged in a set of Christmas lights strung along the awning before she went back inside.

We ate quietly at first. The plantains were okay, but the chicken was amazing—tender and juicy, mild but accompanied by a slaw of spicy pickled hot peppers. There was also a tasty corn porridge, like polenta, with tomatoes and vegetables and spices.

After a few minutes, Baudet put down his beer. "How do you like it?"

"It's delicious."

He nodded in agreement and pointed his fork at the porridge. "My sister is famous for her *mayi moulin*."

"It's very tasty."

After a few more minutes of eating, Baudet put down his fork. "Tell me about this man Sable."

"I barely know him."

"Who does he work for?"

I paused, and we looked at each other, negotiating how much we trusted each other, how much faith we had in Miriam's judgment of each other.

"He said he works for a group called Beta Librae."

He nodded.

"You've heard of them?"

"Vague mentions. Environmental activists, of a sort. Very quiet, eh? Beta Librae is a star in the constellation Libra. It's also called the Northern Claw. That's all I know."

The Northern Claw. That sounded ominous. I ate the last of my food and wiped my hands and mouth on a paper napkin. "So you know Miriam from college?"

"University of Pennsylvania," he said. "I got a scholarship. Premed, before I went into public health. We were quite good friends. She was my first, best, and only remaining college friend." He laughed. "When I returned to Haiti, no one else kept in touch."

"You know her pretty well?"

He gave me a look I couldn't read, then nodded.

I leaned forward, lowering my voice. "Miriam said her next move after coming here was to find someplace without extradition and try to clear her name from there. Do you think it's possible she just fled?"

He picked at the label of his beer bottle, thinking. "It must be a desperate time for her, so yes, anything is possible. But if so, she'll get in touch somehow. She'll let me know. You said she was bringing files, no?"

I nodded.

"If she thinks they're important, she'll make sure I get them."

46

I opened my mouth to tell him about the copy I'd faxed to Nola, that maybe she could fax it back to Baudet. But I didn't. I trusted Baudet a lot, but not with Nola. Not yet. I'd already put her at risk just by sending her that fax. Besides, there was already a copy of those files right here in Cap-Haïtien.

"Earlier, you mentioned a trade summit," I said. "Is that why Energene and Stoma are here?"

He nodded and shrugged at the same time. "As I said, they'd be here anyway, but yes, they're lobbying hard. President Cardon is opposed to allowing the biotech companies to do as they please. His predecessor, Martine, wanted to let them bring in whatever new hybrids and genetically modified seeds they wanted. He wanted to give them long leases for broad swaths of farmland up north so they could grow corn for export, for biofuels instead of food, at a time when we are importing most of our food from the Dominican Republic. Cardon is against all that. He thinks the genetically modified foods need more research to prove their long-term safety, not just health and the environment but also to the economy. President Abelard felt the same way, but when Martine took office last year, he opened our markets to GMOs. The biotech corn has displaced much of the domestic corn. Cardon is against them, and I agree. They need more research, and we need to strengthen our native agricultural sector, so Haiti can be more self-sufficient."

He paused and took a deep breath. "But yes, on Monday, CASCATA will consider a proposal to tighten regulations on biotech imports throughout the entire region. President Cardon will likely cast the deciding vote. Stoma, Energene, and the others are in a tizzy. And the American government, they consider any kind of regulation an affront to democracy."

"Speaking of democracy, it sounds like this is your third president in three years. Is that right?"

He nodded with a sound between a sigh and a laugh. "Cardon was prime minister under President Abelard. In last year's election, Abelard lost to Charles Martine. Martine received massive amounts of outside money to win that election from Energene, Stoma, and the like. It was not something we were used to dealing with."

"And then Martine died?"

"Yes, Martine came in and threw open the gates like they wanted. He invited Stoma to bring in their corn. That *mayi moulin* we just ate was almost certainly Stoma-Grow corn. Then he invited the rest, Energene and the others. Two months later, he died of a heart attack. Dropped dead on the spot." He smiled ruefully. "Some people had conspiracy theories about that, but the way the man ate, I'm surprised his heart lasted as long as it did. Anyway, there was a special election. Martine's backers had spent a fortune to defeat Abelard, sowing misinformation and confusion that peaked right before election. A lot of that came to light after the election, so there was already a backlash against Martine's people. With the special election, the American companies didn't have time to do it again. They barely had time to field a candidate—a man named Dupuis no one had ever heard of. Abelard was too old and tired to run again, so Cardon stepped in and won."

"Is Cardon popular?"

He shrugged. "Cardon is a good man. I don't see him much now that he's such a big shot, but when we were kids, we were like cousins. Many people like him, others don't. Martine was pro-corporate, pro-biotech, pro-GMO, and that was controversial. Cardon is against it, and that is controversial, too. Either way, people are upset. And some feel Haiti shouldn't even be in CASCATA, that it violates our sovereignty. People on both sides get hot about it, which is part of the reason the police are so tense."

"The protests seem pretty peaceful."

"Yes, well, the protests are only part of the reason. The bigger part is Ducroix, the interior minister. He oversees the police. The more he convinces Cardon there is trouble, the more indispensable and powerful he becomes."

As he said it, his face lit up like the clouds had parted to reveal the sun. I thought it was a strange reaction to his last statement.

Then I realized he was looking over my shoulder.

47

"Portia!" he exclaimed as he scrambled to his feet. I turned to see the woman from the jail, his assistant. Her yellow sneakers were glowing in the darkness as she approached the pool of light that surrounded us.

Her smile was only slightly more restrained than his, but whereas Baudet's was a little bit goofy, hers was all-out dazzling. At least, it was until I got to my feet, as well, and she turned to look at me.

I don't know if my presence put her off her stride, but she and Baudet came together awkwardly, clasping each other's hands between them, their bodies maintaining a twelve-inch buffer.

They murmured what sounded like a restrained but intimate greeting. Then Baudet pulled his eyes off her with an effort, like there was Velcro involved.

"I believe you met Doyle Carrick," he said, turning to me. "Doyle, this is Portia Larose, my assistant deputy health minister."

"Detective Carrick," she said coolly, clearly still unswayed by my charms.

Baudet gave me a smile that was bashful, but not apologetic. I understood, too. She was not the kind of woman you would ever make apologies for. "Doyle and I were just having a good talk about politics in Haiti."

Her smile returned in a different form. "Is it possible to have a good talk about this country's politics?" she asked in English.

Elena came out with some sort of fruit drink for Portia. They exchanged kisses and a quick, familiar greeting in Kreyol. Then Elena slipped back inside.

"I don't know," I said. "It sounds like Cardon's not so bad."

She took a sip of her drink, savoring it in a way that strongly suggested it was not just fruit juice. "Cardon seems good," she said, "but it's only been a few months."

"So you must give him a chance," Baudet said. It sounded as though this was a conversation they'd had before.

"Absolutely," she said. "But there is plenty of time for corruption to catch up with him. Either his own or someone else's."

Baudet seemed to be resisting the urge to roll his eyes. He opened his mouth, but before he could speak, the end of the block lit up and an armored police vehicle turned the corner toward us. Its headlights flashed across us as it turned, and a spotlight mounted by the driver's window swept back and forth up the otherwise darkened street. As it rumbled closer, the sound was deafening. It slowed alongside us, the spotlight resting on us. I felt a moment of anxiety, wondering if they were going to harass us.

Baudet and I shielded our eyes, but Portia stared defiantly into the glare, barely squinting, until the truck continued on its way.

"Speaking of someone else," she said, watching the truck disappear around the next corner.

"Who's that?" I asked.

She rolled her eyes.

Baudet leaned forward. "Ducroix's men. The Polis Nasyonal. Portia doesn't trust them."

Her eyes flashed. "And you do?"

Baudet put up his hands like he didn't want to argue.

"So there's no military, and Ducroix controls all the police?" I asked.

"Some more than others," Baudet said.

"The Polis Nasyonal are the worst," Portia said. "They are completely under Ducroix's control."

"I had expected to see more UN troops around. I haven't seen any."

"They're mostly down in Port-au-Prince, anyway, but Ducroix requested even more of them down there. In case there was trouble, which, according to Ducroix, there always is."

"You don't believe him?"

She laughed sadly. "There's always something going on. People are upset. They want to have a voice. They're suspicious of outside interference, and history says they're right to be. This trade summit has people worried we're going to be swamped by biotech corporations, what it could do to the farmers, to the land, to everyone. But there's been no violence. Ducroix makes it sound like they're about to launch a bloody rebellion, but I don't see that at all. So I wonder what he's up to." She shot Baudet a knowing look. "He seems to be overstepping in other areas, as well."

He wrinkled his brow and frowned at her.

"What?" she said, challenging him. Before Baudet could answer, she turned to me. "Cardon kept Ducroix on from Martine's administration. Political expediency, I guess, but he seems too corrupt and ambitious to be given so much power."

Elena came out, holding her apron in one hand and our check in the other. Baudet handed her a handful of bills. I reached for my wallet, but he waved it away. "I insist," he said. He exchanged a few more words with her in Kreyol. She nodded and bent over to kiss his forehead, then mumbled some form of good night, ending with *"Bonswa."*

"Bonswa, Elena," we all said as she turned to walk down the block.

Baudet watched her depart, then shot a glance at me and looked around, as if to see if anyone else was listening. He leaned toward Portia and whispered, "I told Doyle about Saint Benezet."

She shot upright and her eyes went wide, momentarily flickering over at me. "You did what?" Her voice was a hoarse, scratchy cross between a whisper and shriek. "Are you crazy?"

Baudet held up his hands. "It's okay," he said.

She turned to me. "I'm sorry," she said, "but I don't know you. He doesn't know you. He shouldn't have told you."

"We were sharing information," he said calmly. "Doyle has told me some interesting things, as well."

He looked at me and raised his eyebrows. I shrugged and nodded. In for a penny, in for a pound.

He told her about Ron's murder and Miriam's framing and escape, how I had been helping her. Portia put her hand over her mouth and her eyes welled up, but she looked at me with a new appreciation. Then he told her about Ron and Miriam's suspicions about Energene and people getting sick from the Soyagene, but he added that his tests didn't support that. By the time he was done, her eyes had gone from shock and sorrow to anger and stunned fear.

"I told you it was not Ebola," she said quietly when he was done. She turned to me. "In Saint Benezet. It was not Ebola. Regi said they would not lie about something like that. But I think he is wrong. Perhaps it was chikungunya or dengue or maybe even some other hemorrhagic fever, but it was not Ebola. Ducroix's medics had no business diagnosing it or treating it. They don't know how to treat cholera, much less Ebola." Her eyes burned. "If they'd known what they were doing, those people might be alive."

Baudet shook his head. "You can't believe that."

She glared at him. "You are too naïve."

A tense silence stretched on until a phone buzzed. It took me a moment to realize it was mine, a text from Danny reading, "FAA reports no downed planes or unauthorized landings, Helio or otherwise."

I read it to out loud and texted back, "Thanks."

"That's good news, I guess," Baudet said. "Yes?"

"I guess so."

Portia remained quiet, I think annoyed at Baudet for confiding in me and for dismissing her suspicions.

As we sat there in somber silence, the day caught up with me. I'd been outrunning it, holding it at bay, keeping myself ready to move at a moment's notice as soon as I had something to do, somewhere to go. But Danny and the FAA turned up nothing. Suddenly, I was having trouble keeping my eyes open. I turned to Baudet. "No word from Toma?"

He shook his head. "He might not call back until tomorrow."

It occurred to me that if I was going to be any use when he did call, I needed to rest while I could.

As if reading my mind, Baudet said, "I have a very uncomfortable sofa you are welcome to, but Elena has a guesthouse just down the block, a few doors away from me. Basic but clean and comfortable."

I smiled. "Thanks. That sounds great."

48

Portia said a chilly good night to Baudet and a polite one to me. Baudet drove me two blocks through darkened streets, placing a quick call on the way. When we pulled over in front of the guesthouse, Elena was waiting in the doorway. Next to a bare bulb being pelted by a dozen moths and other insects was a tiny plank of wood with hand-painted letters, OTÈL WAYAL. I smiled as I realized it was The Royal Hotel.

She greeted us warmly as we approached and gave us each a kiss on the cheek.

"Welcome," she said.

Baudet and I exchanged phone numbers and agreed to call each other as soon as we heard anything. Then he walked up the street to a small house three doors away.

I followed Elena through the front door and into a small vestibule. To the left was a tiny office, and past the office was a hallway, painted a deep blue, with the steps to the second floor. We climbed the stairs to a second-floor hallway with three doors. She opened one of them and gave me the key, then stepped aside, waving me in.

The room was purple, with bright green furnishings. The colors were an assault, but a cheerful one. I found myself smiling for no reason.

She smiled and closed the door.

I looked at my watch. It said nine thirty. I took out my phone, put in the zero-one-one and started entering Nola's number, but I paused and put in Laura Tennison's instead.

She answered tentatively on the third ring. "Hello?"

"Hi, Laura. It's Doyle."

"Doyle?" she said.

I heard a scuffling sound, and for a moment I thought something terrible had happened. Then Nola's voice said, "You disappear to Haiti, leave me hanging like this, and when you finally call, you call Laura?"

"Nola, sorry, I—"

"Jesus, Doyle, I've been worried sick. What's going on with you?"

"I called Laura's number in case someone was listening in on yours."

"Oh." She paused. "Is that really a concern?"

"I don't know. Just trying to be safe. Especially after the . . . note . . . I sent you earlier. I didn't want to do anything else to draw attention to you. Or to this phone."

"Oh."

I sat back on the bed, feeling the waves of exhaustion wash over me. "Are you okay?"

She sighed. "I'm fine. I'm worried about you, about what you've gotten yourself into this time."

"This one came to me," I said a little defensively.

"Regardless. I don't know if you've spoken to anyone, but apparently you're back on Suarez's shit list."

I smiled, thinking, *There was a time when I wasn't on Suarez's shit list?* Then I said, "I know. I forgot to call out of work."

"Yes, well apparently there's also something about a case file you were supposed to bring in."

I winced. "Crap."

Maybe it was the stress, but for some reason, we shared a good laugh at that.

"I miss you," she said quietly.

"I miss you, too."

"Where are you staying?"

I laughed. "The Royal Hotel." I told her about Baudet and Elena.

"Sounds very nice."

"It is."

"Any news on Miriam?"

"No. Not yet."

"Do you think she's . . ."

"I don't know. I don't think so, but I don't know. Look, I might need you to do something else for me tomorrow. Those pages, the ones you're sending to Mikel, I might need you to fax them back to me tomorrow, from somewhere safe."

"Why? Did you forget to make a copy before you sent them?"

We both laughed. It was an in-joke about a story I'd told her about my mom one time panicking that she had a lost an important document because I hadn't made a copy before faxing it for her.

"Something like that."

"Seriously, though. What happened to the ones you had? The originals?"

I laughed wearily. "The police took them when they took my phone."

"The police?!" She wasn't laughing now.

"It was a minor misunderstanding when I first got here. Because of the passport thing. But it's all straightened out."

"Except they kept the files and your phone."

"Yes, well, we're working on that. Plus, hopefully, Miriam is okay and on her way and bringing them or sending them to Baudet." We fell quiet for a moment after that, because it was very possible Miriam was not okay and not on her way.

"Okay," she said. "Well, let me know where to send them and I will. But then you need to come home. I miss you, and I worry. This isn't your job. It isn't your fight."

I missed her too. More than I would have thought after just one day. And maybe I was scared, too. But I thought about Miriam. About how much she probably missed Ron, about the way someone was setting her up for murder, ruining her life, trying to end it. Maybe they already had.

"But then whose fight is it?" I must have been tired, because I hadn't meant to say it out loud. I expected Nola to get even angrier, but she stayed quiet.

"You'll be okay," I said.

"I'm worried about you," she whispered. "You're in danger. You're not the only one who has seen what these people are capable of. I've been there, too, Doyle. I've seen what can happen."

I didn't know what to say to that, so I didn't say anything. I lay there on the bed, listening to her breathing, letting her listen to me.

After a few minutes, she let out a little snort of a laugh. "How much does it cost to call from Haiti?"

"Ugh," I said. "I hadn't thought about that." I looked at the phone, but the display didn't tell me anything about that. "I guess I should go."

"I guess so. Bring yourself home to me, Doyle. Okay?"

"I will. I love you, Nola."

"I love you, too."

49

I awoke at seven to a sharp knock at the door and a flashback to the night Ron Hartwell was murdered. I felt conspicuously gunless as I pulled on my pants. Then the knock came again and I realized it wasn't the front door, it was the door to my room.

I opened it expecting Elena, but instead it was Portia, carrying a tray with a glass of mango juice and a cup of coffee. She looked even more dazzling than she had the night before, in a crisp blue dress and her canary-yellow sneakers.

I was wearing what I'd been wearing the night before, rumpled and slept in.

"*Bonjou*," she said, offering the tray and biting back a smile as her eyes took in my bed head.

"*Bonjou*," I replied, reaching up to pat down my hair before accepting the tray.

"Regi asked me to make sure you were up. He's been trying to call you."

I looked at the phone. I'd slept through three calls from Regi and a text from ten minutes ago saying he'd be there in fifteen minutes.

"I'll wait for you downstairs," she said.

I dashed into the bathroom, relieved to find a flimsy travel tooth-brush and a tiny tube of toothpaste.

When I was done, I drank half the coffee and cooled my mouth with the juice.

Downstairs, Portia was sitting at the table in the tiny front room. Elena was topping off her coffee as I came down the stairs. She filled mine, as well, without asking.

"*Merci*," I said, earning me a smile as she bustled back toward the kitchen.

"Toma called," Portia said. "Regi is taking you to meet him out-side the city."

Elena stopped in mid-step and spun around. "Toma?"

Portia nodded and pointed at me as she gave some sort of expla-nation.

Elena turned toward me with a stern look and let loose with a stream of Kreyol, turning to Portia and waving her hand toward me.

"She says her nephew Toma is bad news," Portia said, translating. "She says he was a good boy until his mother took him to Miami. She died on the way, and when he came back eight years later, he had learned some bad ways. She says we don't want anything to do with him."

I nodded and said, "Okay," unsure how else to respond.

Elena scowled and continued into the kitchen.

When I looked at Portia, she wore a similar scowl. "She has a point. Toma is a gangster, and Regi is an important man, a busy man with much to do. You should not be distracting him with crazy adventures involving his nephew."

"You don't agree with his concerns about Stoma and the other corporations?"

"Quite the opposite. I think they should be thrown out of the country. After the earthquake, I helped burn the hybrid seeds the biotech corporations tried to donate."

I was surprised. "That seems a little extreme, doesn't it?"

Portia leaned forward. "No, it is not. This isn't just about quaint notions of protecting old ways of doing things. Our farmers can't afford to buy expensive seed each year. They save some of their harvest and plant that. That's the way they've always done it, and they should be free to do so. We've seen it in other places, once the biotech companies get in with their GMOs and expensive hybrids, they push and push until at some point that's all that is available. Then the farmers have no choice." She snapped her fingers. "From that moment on, they can no longer save their seeds. With the hybrids it doesn't work, and with the GMOs it's illegal, even if they try. So each year, they have to borrow money to pay for the seed. It's like an addiction; they can't get off it. Some years the yields are higher and they make a little more money, some years less. But all it takes is one bad year—a year like this year—and they lose everything. There are some who think that's what it's really about, anyway. A big land grab."

"A land grab?" I said. "How do you mean?"

She leaned even closer, warming up. "There's a saying, 'Land is the one thing they're not making any more of,' right? Around the world, people are buying up land. A lot of it. In Africa and South America, investors from the Northern Hemisphere, big corporations, countries like China, they are buying up millions of hectares of farmland, to grow food for export or to convert the land from food crops to biofuels. One company almost succeeded in buying half of all the agricultural land in Madagascar. *Half!* In Haiti, it's different, but not completely so. Our revolution was a slave revolt, but it was also a fight to get our land back, first from the French, then from the Americans. So we're very sensitive to the idea of rich people buying up land and assembling huge plantations."

She sat back and let out a shy smile despite herself, as if she didn't mean to let herself get so worked up. "Of course, buying land isn't easy in Haiti, even for the rich people, and it's highly restricted for foreigners. But I guess that's why they have ninety-nine-year leases and agricultural free-trade zones, where only crops for export can be grown."

"But still you don't want Regi getting involved?"

"Regi is already involved. He has a big job fighting cholera and chikungunya, HIV, and yes, Ebola, too. Minister Dissette is useless, so Regi practically runs that ministry. He can't be distracted getting into trouble with his nephew Toma."

"I don't mean to keep him from his work," I said, sitting across from her. "To be fair, though, he was involved in this before I was. He's Miriam Hartwell's friend. I barely know her."

Her eyes narrowed at the name.

"Do you know her?" I asked.

"We met briefly. At Saint Benezet." She shrugged, unimpressed. I think she was about to say more, but her phone buzzed, and she looked at it. "Regi got stuck behind some protests. He's running late, but he'll be here in a moment."

As she said it, the door opened, and Regi Baudet appeared. *"Bonjou, bonjou,"* he said as he entered, his warm smile fading as he looked back and forth between us and maybe detected some tension. Before he could say anything more, Elena appeared from the kitchen, drying her hands on an old dish towel.

"Regi!" she said sharply, raising a finger at him and following it up with a barrage of Kreyol sprinkled with mentions of Toma.

Regi stepped back and raised his hands defensively, replying in kind. They went back and forth a few times before Elena turned on her heel and stormed back to the kitchen.

"Come on," he said to me with an embarrassed smile. "Let's go before she comes back. We're running late as it is."

He turned to Portia, but once again his smile faltered. "You. Be. Careful," she said to him. Then she gave me a look that made it clear she didn't care if I was careful, but I'd have hell to pay if anything happened to Regi.

50

"We're meeting Toma at the end of Rue Saint Claire," Regi said over the sound of our tires rumbling against the road. "His gang has a place up in the hills overlooking the city."

He seemed nervous about where we were going but relieved to be away from the tense scene at Elena's.

We weaved across the city in Regi's Suzuki, the hills looming higher the closer we got, until we were climbing them.

"I'm surprised they're up so early," I said, looking out the window. I was surprised *I* was up so early. There were already plenty of people on the street, though, most of them coming down the hill with empty water containers to fill. "Toma must be a lot more conscientious than the gangsters in my neighborhood."

Regi gave me a dubious look, and I realized my mistake.

"Still out from last night?"

He nodded.

The yellowed vegetation on the top of the hill looked orange in the rosy glow of the rising sun. As we left the city, the streets switched back and forth up the hill, past houses made of cinder block and corrugated metal. Halfway up, the crumbled asphalt gave way to a leveled but unpaved road, bumpy with rocks and crowded on either side with shacks made of rough-cut wood and scraps of metal. Here and there, small but sturdy cactus plants formed dense hedges between the houses or lining the road, all of it coated with the billowing dust.

It coated the people too. Several of the shacks had laundry hanging out to dry on the cactus fencing. The dust covered that, as well.

The higher we went, the fewer houses we saw, and the fewer people. The spaces between them were wandered by chickens, and here and there a goat was tied by the side of the road.

The Suzuki ground its way uphill, kicking gravel back down the slope behind us and adding to the dust in the air. Finally, what was left of the road curved around and ended. We got out of the car and looked back at the city below us, watching the shadows at the bottom of the hill slowly shrinking as the sun rose over the ocean. We turned back around just as a guy in his late teens emerged from the trees beyond the end of the road.

He was wearing low-slung pants and no shirt, carrying a Steyr machine pistol. The extended magazine sticking out the front gave it an ungainly, lopsided appearance. He was pointing it vaguely in our direction with his finger curled carelessly around the trigger. If it was set to automatic, one hearty sneeze would cut us both in half.

"*Sa ou vlè?*" he said, looking at Regi, his slurring voice and glassy eyes combining to convey a sort of bored, intoxicated menace. His mouth was open, his tongue absentmindedly running back and forth across his bottom teeth.

Regi cleared his throat. "*Mwen se* Regi Baudet. *Mwen ta renmen wè* Toma."

This was not Regi's nephew. He turned to look at me with a sneer. "*Ki moun nèg blan sa ye?*"

Regi looked at me, fear unmistakable in his eyes, then back at the gunman. "*Li se zanmi mwen.* He is my friend."

The kid held the Steyr off to the side, pointed into the air as he stepped up so close to me I could smell the sweat and alcohol coming off him. He stared into my eyes for a moment and said, "Not my friend."

He was licking his bottom teeth again, and as he started to bring the gun down over my head, I couldn't help thinking if he hit me like that, he'd totally jam the magazine. I leaned away from him and jabbed my hand up under his chin, chopping his throat and also snapping his teeth shut on his tongue.

His eyes went wide, and blood sputtered from his mouth. By the time the shock in his eyes had turned to pain, his gun was in my hands. I stepped back so that even with the gun pointed at the ground and my finger safely off the trigger, I'd have time to bring it up if he came at me.

He didn't, concentrating instead on cupping his hand under his mouth and extending his neck away from his body so he didn't bleed on himself. He glared up at me, looking younger now, an angry little boy. He spat out a stream of blood-flecked sibilance. I couldn't tell if it was English or Kreyol.

Regi looked on in horror, and I felt momentarily guilty. "He was going to hit me," I said. Then I realized Regi's gaze of horror was directed over my shoulder.

I turned slowly around.

There were three of them. Bigger and older than the kid with the new lisp.

The biggest of them stared at me through narrowed eyes, then looked past me to Regi, who suddenly looked less scared.

"He was going to hit me," I said again, laying the gun on the ground and straightening with my hands up.

The kid with the bloody mouth went to retrieve his gun but froze when the big guy barked, "Cyrus!"

I almost smiled, thinking if that kid's name was Cyrus, that injured tongue was going to cause him some problems. The big guy gave me a look that helped me not smile.

He turned to Regi. "*Sak pase la a?*"

Regi smiled patiently. "Toma, this is my friend, Doyle. An American."

Toma acknowledged me with a slight nod, then glared at Cyrus and muttered something I didn't catch. Cyrus slunk forward, keeping his eyes away from mine, then grabbed the gun by the muzzle and scurried back toward the trees.

Toma swung a booted foot, connecting with the top of the Cyrus's thigh as he hurried past him. Toma turned and tipped his head, beckoning Regi and me with a nod before he and the other two turned and walked back the way they had come.

We followed them around a stand of trees. The path faded to nothing but reappeared once we rounded the curve.

Regi quickened his pace to walk alongside Toma, leaving me to exchange awkward nods with his two lieutenants.

"He would have totally jammed that magazine," I said, for some reason unable to just stay quiet.

"He's an idiot," said the guy to my right, the bigger guy, in heavily accented English.

The guy to my left nodded and said, *"Depi koulye a sou, li rele 'Thyruth.'"*

They all started laughing, even Toma, who turned around to do it. Before he turned back, though, he said, *"Janjak. Westè. Silans."*

We walked for another ten minutes, Regi and Toma talking quietly in Kreyol, the rest of us quiet. It seemed an almost intimate conversation, but awkward, as well. The sense I got was that they were updating each other on relatives and friends, but that it had been a little too long since they had done so. Of course, they could have been talking about something totally different.

The path widened out into a rutted dirt road, curving around a small hillock. Just past it was a large shack, wood-slat walls under a tar-paper roof. A porch ran along the front, a couple of white plastic chairs at one end.

Behind it was a second building, a barn or a garage.

Between them was a gas-powered generator. One of the two guys who had been walking with me—I think it was Westè, the smaller one—went over and got it started.

A couple of lightbulbs came to life, filling the place with a dim glow.

We followed Toma onto the porch and through the front door. Inside, the hard-packed dirt floor was covered with a filthy rug. The furniture was in better shape, a couple of armchairs and a sectional sofa. The electronics were gleaming—a massive plasma-screen television, a cluster of video and gaming components scattered on the rug in front of it.

Toma tossed his pistol onto the sofa and collapsed next to it. He picked up a game controller, and the television came to life.

"So where is Toussaint?" Regi asked in English.

I could feel Janjak and Westè stiffen. Toma looked at one, then the other and jutted his chin at the door. They went outside, seeming relieved to be excluded from the conversation.

"Why you looking for Toussaint?" Toma asked, idly fiddling with the controller. He sounded like an American.

Regi looked at me and then back at his nephew. "Do you know anything about Saint Benezet?"

He shrugged. "I know the police are all around it, keeping people away from it."

"The people there got sick."

He laughed. "The old ladies say it was Ebola."

Regi shot me an almost imperceptible glance. "Some food shipments were stolen not far from there."

"So what's that have to do with Toussaint?"

"We're trying to figure out if the stolen food made the people sick. I figure nothing like that would go on without Toussaint knowing about it."

He looked at me. "Are you police?"

"Not here," I said.

He laughed.

"We don't care about the theft," Regi said. "We just want to know why people are getting sick. So where's Toussaint?"

Toma tossed the controller aside. "Toussaint's dead. I'm in charge now." He said it casually, but the strain of it was suddenly evident on his face, as if telling us, not having his men around, made him feel he could drop part of his act. "So what do you want to know?"

"How did he die?" I asked.

"Driving back from Port-au-Prince," he said. "Two guns on motorcycles." He looked pointedly at me. "Two *blan* on motorcycles."

"Two white guys?" I asked.

He nodded slowly.

Regi cleared his throat. "Do you know if he stole—"

"Yes." He nodded. "Toussaint stole the food shipments."

Regi shook his head. "You stole *aid shipments?*"

"Not me—Toussaint. And it wasn't aid shipments! It was just sitting there. They weren't distributing it. They weren't doing nothing with it." He shrugged. "People got to eat. Gangsters got to make money."

"What did you do with it?"

"He sold it. Saint Benezet, yes, maybe somewhere else, but I don't know."

51

Driving back to Regi's office, we were both quiet, lost in dark thoughts. I didn't know if Regi was thinking the same thing I was, but judging from the look on his face, it wasn't too far off.

I'd seen powerful people do terrible things for money. My stomach soured as my brain circled a horrible suspicion that it was desperately trying to avoid.

Toussaint had stolen the Soyagene, and someone had killed him. Ron had found evidence suggesting something wrong with the Soyagene, and someone had killed Ron, had tried to kill Miriam. The stolen soy was sold at Saint Benezet, and then something mysterious happened. Something that didn't add up. The police said it was Ebola, but Regi and Miriam hadn't seen any signs of Ebola. The samples hadn't tested positive for Ebola. No one else had contracted it. Portia had serious doubts.

It seemed to me, Regi had accepted that it was Ebola because he couldn't believe anyone would lie about something like that.

He looked at me and opened his mouth as if to speak but didn't. I didn't want to voice my suspicions out loud, either. But as we pulled up in front of a government office building, I turned to him. "We need to talk."

"I know," he said quietly. "Let me check in with my office first, with Portia. Then I'll call Jean-Pierre at the airport, see if there's any word on Miriam."

"I'll see if there's anything new to report at FAA. Might be time to call the Coast Guard." I'd been hoping maybe they'd landed short somewhere, that Sable was on the mend and Miriam was making her way to Cap-Haïtien. I had to concede that was highly unlikely now. I was also thinking it was time to try to reach out to Mikel.

Regi got out of the car. "You coming in, or you waiting here?"

"I'll wait here," I said. "I need to make some calls."

He nodded and walked up the steps.

I leaned against the car and called Nola on Laura's phone.

"Doyle!" Nola said, answering on the first ring. "Are you okay?"

"I'm fine," I told her, smiling at the sound of her voice despite the grim thoughts filling my mind. "Are you okay?"

"Just worried about you. Are you coming home?"

"Not yet," I said. "Miriam hasn't turned up yet, so we're going to get the search started up. Did you send that package?"

"I'm leaving right now."

"Thanks. I'm going to try to call him, as well, but send it whatever way is fastest, okay? It's important that it gets there as soon as possible."

"I'm taking it myself."

"What?"

"It's Saturday, Doyle. His office wouldn't get it until Monday morning. This is urgent, so I'm bringing it myself. To his apartment."

"His apartment?"

"I Googled it. It's on West 58th Street. Apparently, when an apartment sells for thirty million dollars, it's newsworthy."

"Thirty million?"

"I know, right? And part of what made it newsworthy was that it's considered humble for a man like Mikel."

"Jesus. Well look, be careful. I still don't know exactly what's

DUST UP // 197

in those files, but I know it's pretty explosive. Maybe Danny could do it."

"I'm just driving to Manhattan. It's fine. And I don't want to get Danny and Laura any more involved. You're the one down in Haiti without a passport. You be careful, too."

"I will. You keep in touch, all right?"

"You too."

"And thanks. Is Danny there?"

"Yeah, hold on and I'll get him," she said.

A few seconds later, Danny came on the phone. "Hey."

"Hey. There's still no sign of Miriam Hartwell or this Sable guy. Wondering if you could call FAA again, see if they have any news."

"Sure."

"And it might be time to alert the Coast Guard, as well."

"I can do that. You said the plane was a Helio Courier with two people on board flying out of Everglades City, right? And you think the plane had been shot, and possibly the pilot."

"That's right—"

Suddenly, Danny was gone, and Nola was back on the phone. "They shot the plane? Jesus, Doyle, these people are shooting at planes?"

"Yes."

"Why didn't you tell me before?"

"I didn't want you getting upset."

"I *am* upset. Shooting at planes? What kind of maniac shoots at planes?!"

I almost reminded her that I had once, but instead, I just said, "I know. It's messed up."

"Doyle, you need to come home to me."

"I will," I told her. "I'll come home soon."

She took a deep breath and let it out. "Do what you need to do," she said quietly. "Then come home safe."

"Okay."

Just as I got off the phone, Regi burst through the door to the Health Ministry and came down the steps two at a time.

"You okay?" I asked. "What's going on?"

"I need to go," he said, rushing around to the driver's side. "There's been another outbreak of respiratory distress syndrome, another village." He looked up at me, his face stricken. "Portia went to check it out."

52

We sped through the city in silence. We had said we were going to talk, and we hadn't yet, but the things I wanted to say did not bode well for Portia, especially if Saint Benezet was any indication.

As we climbed into the hills outside Cap-Haïtien, Regi said, "We are going to a tiny village called Gaden, no bigger than Saint Benezet, and not far from there." He looked at me, concern etched deep on his face. "It is just on the other side of Toussaint's place in the hills." He held up three fingers, and ticked them off. "Saint Benezet, Toussaint, Gaden, in a line. Very close."

"You think Toussaint might have sold the rest of the shipment to Gaden?"

He shrugged. "Maybe so."

The roads again deteriorated as we climbed into the hills, but instead of slowing down, Regi drove even faster, bouncing and jostling over massive bumps and potholes. I wondered if the vehicle would survive that level of abuse. The tiny shacks on either side became fewer and fewer as the road became little more than a dirt path. They disappeared completely, and I was wondering if we were lost when we rounded a hill and saw a roadblock up ahead. An armored vehicle was parked across the dirt road. The men standing around it wore black T-shirts with POLICE in bold white letters, but otherwise, they looked more like soldiers, wearing camouflage pants and combat boots, each carrying an Uzi.

Regi muttered something to himself. He tapped the brakes but didn't stop.

The officers approached us, one pointing his weapon at the car, the other one waving us off and shaking his head.

"*Vire, vire!*" he shouted at us, making a twirling motion with his hand, like we should turn around and go back.

"*Nou pwal Gaden,*" Regi called out as the officer approached the car.

"*Non,*" he said, shaking his head and pointing back the way we had come. "*Vire, vire.*"

Regi held up his Ministry of Health identification. "*Mwen se Regi Baudet.*"

The officer shook his head and leaned in through the car window, smelling strongly of sweat and rum. His eyes were glassy and blood-shot. He put his face right in Regi's and said slowly, "E-bo-la."

Regi gasped, but I couldn't tell if it was shock or he was simply pulling enough air into his lungs for the frantic barrage of Kreyol that streamed out of his mouth next. The cop was startled, stepping back from the force of it. Then he got angry, maybe embarrassed by his own reaction. He snarled and racked the slide, pointing the gun at Regi—and collaterally at me too—and replying with another stream of Kreyol.

Regi put the car in reverse, swerving and bouncing off the path and onto the scrubby grass as he turned the car around. The cop continued to yell at us as we drove off, his partner laughing at the entire exchange.

Once we had rounded the hill, Regi slowed down and looked over at me. "He says we cannot go into the village because there is Ebola. But Portia is in there."

"You're with the Ministry of Health. Isn't this a health crisis? If there's really Ebola, shouldn't you be in charge?"

"We should, yes, but we have no real power. If the National Police say they're in charge, they're in charge. They've got much more authority. And guns, as you've seen. If there's something like Ebola, they can say it is a national security issue and take over on those grounds."

"But there is no Ebola, is there?"

He sighed and ground his teeth. "I don't know."

"There isn't. It's bullshit. And there wasn't in Saint Benezet, either. Was there?"

"When I went to Benezet, a soldier met me at the perimeter and told me it was Ebola. I said, 'It can't be Ebola,' and he put his gun against my head, and he said, 'You don't think we know Ebola when we see it?' He wasn't like that guy. He wasn't a drunken thug. He looked terrified. Terrified enough that I believed him."

"But you never diagnosed it, did you? You never saw anything to suggest it. Neither did Ron and Miriam. Tell me if I'm wrong, but as far as I can tell, the only indication of Ebola was the statement from the police." I hooked my thumb back at the roadblock. "From them."

"Maybe it was coincidence," he said. "Maybe they had something else, the allergy or whatever, and then they got the Ebola."

"And then the same coincidence happened here? What are the chances of that?"

He took his foot off the gas and turned to look at me as we jostled down the hill.

"Have you ever heard of Ebola wiping out an entire village?" I asked. "One hundred percent fatal?"

He moved his head the slightest bit from side to side.

"Miriam thought whatever was going on at Saint Benezet was a reaction to the Soyagene, right? And Ron thought he'd found proof that Energene knew it and they were covering it up. Maybe the Ebola is a cover story, to help them dispose of the evidence of whatever it was they had done. Maybe Saint Benezet, the people who lived there, maybe *they* were the evidence."

His head whipped around at me, his face horrified at what I was saying out loud, then even more horrified as he looked back toward Gaden. "Portia," he said, turning back to me. "What do we do?"

A part of me kicked myself as I heard my own voice saying, "We need to go in there and see for ourselves."

53

It had taken us forty minutes to get from Regi's office at the Ministry of Health to the roadblock at Gaden. We made it back in twenty.

On the way, I called international directory assistance and got the number for the Mikel Group in New York, the main switchboard.

"I'd like to talk to Gregory Mikel," I said to the woman who answered.

"I see," she said, politely patronizing but not laughing out loud. "That would be our corporate headquarters, and it is Saturday. But I can transfer you if you'd like." I could barely hear her over the sound of the car lurching over a particularly bad stretch of road.

"Yes, thank you."

I was transferred three more times, reminded of what day it was three more times. Each receptionist took me slightly more seriously than the last, but despite their poise and professionalism, I could tell none of them thought there was the remotest possibility that I would ever speak to Mikel.

To be honest, I didn't think so, either. But I had to try.

The fourth receptionist asked me what this was in reference to. I gave her my name and the number of my new cell phone. "If you could tell Mr. Mikel that Sable is hurt and Miriam Hartwell is missing and could he please call me back ASAP."

She didn't miss a beat, pleasantly informing me that she would deliver that message as soon as possible but that it was Saturday and, of course, Mr. Mikel was a very busy man.

By the time I got off the phone, we were just pulling up outside the Ministry of Health offices. A grim resolve had settled over Regi.

I followed him inside. The guard at the front desk smiled and greeted him, as did the handful of other workers we passed. Regi barely acknowledged them as we walked briskly through the building.

We stopped at a door with his name on it, and he opened it to reveal a tiny room, sparse except for a cluttered desk and a window overlooking the street.

On his desk was a small bundle with a rubber band around it and a scrap of paper with REGI BAUDET written on it. My phone, the one that had been confiscated, together with a plastic bag. He removed the rubber band and let the note drop to his desk. He handed me the plastic bag and the phone.

"Are these yours?"

"The phone's mine," I said, taking them both. Inside the plastic bag were the files, filthy and wet with what I hoped was coffee. They looked like they had been rescued from the trash. "This looks like the files. I don't know what good they'll be now."

Regi nodded and frowned as he unlocked one of his desk drawers and took out a single key on a green plastic fob. I powered up the phone as I followed him back the way we had come. The phone didn't log missed calls when it was turned off. The only voice mails were from work. There were four of them. I powered it back off without checking them.

Regi stopped halfway down the hallway and opened a tiny storage room. He started pulling stuff off the half-empty racks and stacking it in my arms: biohazard suits, visors, gloves, tape, several items I didn't recognize.

When he was done, it seemed like we had taken half of what was in there, but it still wasn't a whole lot.

He got a trash bag from somewhere, and we dropped all the protective gear inside. Then he grabbed a couple of gallon jugs of chlorine off a shelf and handed them to me.

As we walked back through the offices, the coworkers who had greeted Regi on the way in kept their distance, as if somehow they knew what was in the bag and where we were headed. As we approached the door, one of the women called out softly, *"Bòn chans,* Regi." Good luck.

He turned and nodded to each of them, like he was thanking them for their concern and for their service, acknowledging that he might not be returning.

I was struck by his bravery. Then I remembered I was going with him, and it scared the hell out of me.

He turned and walked out the door, and I followed.

As we drove back the way we had just come, I opened the plastic bag and pulled out several of the pages.

Regi glanced over. "Is it all there?"

"Hard to say." I could recognize some of the documents from reading them on the plane, but much of it was barely legible now. "I'll have to spread them out, see if I can clean them up. Dry them out."

Between the state of the road and the state of the documents, I hadn't managed to glean anything before we took a right half a mile before where we'd encountered the roadblock. We left the dirt road for whatever you call a road that doesn't quite earn the name "dirt road," and even trying to read became impossible.

I put the pages back into the plastic bag and tucked it into my shirt.

"This will get us close enough to walk," Regi said.

The road faded away to nothing in a few spots, just dirt and rocks going through dirt and rocks, but Regi kept going as the dry grass returned on either side of us and what little road there was became visible again. We were heading around to the other side of the hilltop from the roadblock. After a quarter mile, we stopped. To our left was a raised ridge maybe twelve feet high. On top of it was a stand of small trees. To the right, the land sloped gently down. In the distance, I could see the ocean.

It was a beautiful view, and I was struck by the thought of how many places in the world a view like that would cost a million dollars.

Regi raised the hatch on the back of the vehicle and started laying out the gear. "Have you ever worn this stuff?"

I shook my head. Apart from a few terror drills, all my experiences with this type of gear had involved faceless people inside it protecting themselves from whatever I was doused with. All things equal, I'd rather be on the inside, but I wasn't crazy about it either way.

"They are hot and uncomfortable and hard to move around in. But you must resist the urge to scratch or do anything to breach the containment, do you understand?"

I nodded.

"Good. We'll suit up here except for the gloves and headgear, and when we reach Gaden, we'll put those on, okay?"

Regi walked me through each step of the process. With each layer, I could feel my body temperature rising, the sweat streaming off me, trickling down to my legs. The plastic bag of documents inside my shirt felt like it was glued to my skin. Ten minutes later, we had everything on except for the gloves, hoods, and goggles. Regi put those in a trash bag and handed me one of the jugs of chlorine.

"Let's go," he said, and we set off up the ridge. "Careful not to tear your suit."

I gave him a look I was glad he didn't see and reminded myself that this had been my idea.

Once we got up the ridge, the going was easier. The terrain was level, but the undergrowth was dense. The suits seemed pretty durable, but I was paranoid about getting snagged on thorns or twigs. I kept telling myself there was no Ebola, but it didn't entirely sink in.

Before long, we crossed through a patch of trees. Fifty yards past it was a cluster of small wooden shacks with corrugated metal roofs.

On one side was a vegetable garden surrounded by a fence of plastic netting.

We stopped for a moment and looked. It was utterly still. Regi held up the bag of gear, and I stepped back into the trees, motioning for him to follow. We went in ten feet, just far enough so we wouldn't be easily visible. Regi put his head near mine and whispered, "Just do exactly what I do."

I nodded, and for the next five minutes, we took turns securing our hoods, gloves, and goggles. He would put his on, slowly and deliberately, letting me see how each tie was secured, each flap was affixed down, and then he would watch as I did the same, checking my closures and tightening my ties. Finally, we taped each other's gloves at the wrist and put on our goggles. As we checked each other over, I felt bad that I didn't really know what I was looking for, that I was receiving a level of scrutiny I couldn't provide for Regi. But he seemed satisfied.

When we were done, we exchanged a terse nod and headed into the village.

The mask and goggles heightened my sense of isolation from the world. Instead of reassuring me, they somehow made the threat seem that much more real. Through the goggles, the world seemed scarier, more toxic. There's a big difference between being intellectually confident something is true and testing it by putting on a biohazard suit and stumbling into what is supposed to be a hot zone saturated with one of the deadliest diseases known to man.

As we approached the rear of the closest house, the breeze picked up. I could see the leaves in the trees fluttering, and I could hear it, the hood making an exaggerated crumpling sound in my ear. But all I could feel was heat and dampness. All I could smell was plastic and my own sweat. I had a moment of claustrophobia, a panicky urge to tear it all off. But then it passed.

We walked between two houses and out onto a common area. It was surrounded by half a dozen houses, with a few others farther back.

The breeze disappeared, and again there was no movement, no sign of life, just the two of us there in our space suits. We turned to the right and looked in the first house. Two rooms, sparse and empty except for a couple of chairs, two wooden chests, and a pot rack. There was a rug on the floor and three bedrolls against the wall.

Nothing seemed amiss except that it was unoccupied.

The next hut was in a similar state, empty but unremarkable. Maybe the inhabitants had been evacuated to a hospital, I thought. But if that was the case, Regi's office would have known, would have been involved.

I tapped Regi's arm—time to move on—but he had seen something. He entered the hut and went over to a small wooden table next to a chair. Sitting on it was a rectangular black leather medical bag and a shrink-wrapped brick of a dozen small boxes of steroid inhalers.

He opened the bag and looked inside. In addition to the stethoscope and a few other instruments were several large Ziploc specimen bags, each filled with a dozen blood samples. "This is Portia's bag."

Next to it was a white paper bag, almost empty. The top of it was crumpled over. I unrolled it and looked in. It was filled with white powder.

"Drugs?" I said.

Regi looked at it, then looked at me. "Soy, I think. It looks like the bags that the other Soyagene soyflour came in." He shrugged. "Maybe Miriam was right."

I picked it up and looked at the bottom. It was stamped on the bottom, a barcode and GES-5322x. The code seemed familiar, and I wondered if it matched one of the product codes from Ron's files.

I put it back next to the medical bag.

Regi went outside and paused, looking around the common area as if he thought he'd see Portia if he looked hard enough.

We moved on to the third building. It seemed much like the other two at first. Regi ducked back out, anxious to continue, but something caught my eye.

A wicker chest had been upended, spilling a tangle of brightly colored textiles onto the floor. One of the colors stood out, a deep, vivid red. Moving closer, I saw it wasn't a textile at all. Even in the sweltering heat of the biohazard suit, a chill went through me.

Regi was standing in the doorway looking back in. I beckoned him closer, pointed at the blood on the floor. He looked at it and then up at me, then out the door at the rest of the village. I couldn't see his expression, but I knew that just like me, he was wondering what other horrors we were about to find.

54

"Could it be hemorrhagic?" I whispered. "From the Ebola?" But I knew it wasn't.

He shrugged, then shook his head. "I don't think so."

We hurried to the next house and stopped in the doorway. The walls inside were spattered with blood, three distinct sprays, criss-crossing the walls, as if from an artery.

A table was in splinters. There were bloody footprints on the floor and a red smear that started in the far corner, passed under our feet and extended out the door. We stepped off to either side, our eyes tracing the blood, out the door and across the commons, toward a blue-and-red-painted wooden house, slightly larger than the others.

Regi started running, as fast as his biohazard suit would let him. I ran too, catching up with him at the doorway as he stopped, frozen, his arms braced against the door frame.

Inside was a vision of hell, a tangle of dark-brown limbs drenched in bright red blood. There must have been thirty bodies—men, women, and children—all piled against the rear wall.

Protruding from the middle of the pile was a pair of canary-yellow sneakers, spattered with blood.

Regi let out a wrenching sob and dove at the pile, pushing corpses off to the left and right as he tried to uncover Portia's body.

I stood there, useless, wanting to help him but knowing I would only slow him down. There was no way I'd be able to treat the dead with the single-minded disregard he was showing them right now. Any other time, he'd have been unable to himself.

So I stood back and tried not to get in his way. As he shoved each body off the pile, I saw them individually—an old woman in her seventies, a wiry man of forty, a nine-year-old boy. A pregnant woman.

They didn't look sick. None of them did. They had each been shot in the chest.

When Regi finally uncovered Portia, he sobbed and pulled her to him, resting her back against his legs and cradling her head in his arms. There was a bullet hole between her breasts. Her shirt was soaked in blood.

Even dead, even there, her face was strikingly beautiful.

Regi was oblivious to the other bodies, leaning back against them, surrounded by them. The scene was ghastly and horrific, so tragic and evil and wrenching I looked away to escape it.

The walls were pocked with bullet holes and spattered with blood. The floor was slick with it. A puddle had formed under the bodies. Regi's arms and legs were streaked with it.

A couple of flies appeared, then a few more. I wondered how recently this had happened.

Regi pulled off his goggles and his hood and pressed his face against Portia's, kissed her forehead.

He sobbed uncontrollably, just for a moment. Then he clenched his jaw and stifled it, breathing deeply to get himself under control.

"That's the first time I ever kissed her," he said quietly, his voice tight. "She wanted to, but I said we couldn't. I was her boss." He looked up at me, tears streaming down his face. "I loved her, you know."

I didn't know what to say. I didn't know what to do. I thought about Miriam, about Ron dying on my front steps, at my feet. In front of the woman I loved. Underneath the sorrow and regret, the sympathy I felt for Regi and for Miriam, way down deep I also felt a spark of hatred and fury in my core, tiny but white hot.

He turned away from me. "You can take off that hood," he said. "There's no Ebola here. Not a hint of it. None of these people show any symptoms. There's no sign of medical care or sickness or anything, other than the inhalers and Portia's medical bag."

I pulled off my hood, pulled down my mask, and breathed deeply. The hot, humid air felt cool and refreshing.

"I'm sorry," I said.

The breeze picked up again. Standing in the doorway, I could feel it, hear it. As it subsided, I heard something else, as well.

Trucks.

55

"Regi," I said quietly.

He looked up at me, crushed, devastated.

"Someone's coming," I said. "Trucks. We need to go."

The noise grew louder, closer. There were voices now too, men shouting. His eyes drifted back down.

"Regi."

He looked up at me again, his eyes now vacant.

"We need to go."

That's when we heard another sound—soft but powerful, a low, throaty *whoosh*. Through the door, I saw a wall of flame shooting into the sky at the far end of the village. I felt a wave of heat, although it could have been my imagination.

"They're burning the village."

His eyes stayed on me for a moment as he processed what I was saying. Then he looked down at Portia. Her head fell back, limp. Dead.

I put my arm on his shoulder. "We have to go."

"But . . ." He looked at her with longing and regret and anguish, then up at me, questioningly, beseechingly. His brain was beyond capacity, feeling so much it was unable to think.

"We'll come back for her," I said. It was an outright lie. I knew there was no way, but I needed to get him out of there.

He laid her gently back upon the bodies of the people she had gone there to save. Her arms flopped out, extended at her sides, as if she were protecting the others or leading them or raising them up to heaven.

I let him take one more moment, let him absorb that last look at her. Then I heard another *whoosh,* saw another line of fire, this time closer. This time, the heat was unmistakably real.

I grabbed him by the arm and dragged him out the door and around to the side of the hut. He was in a daze, but when he looked back at the flames engulfing the first row of houses, he seemed to grasp the reality of the situation. A small group of soldiers with flamethrowers was backing toward us, spraying flames at the houses behind them as they approached.

"We have to get out of here," I whispered loudly in Regi's ear.

He nodded, and we slipped around to the rear of the houses and ran along the grassy space that separated the village from the trees that lined the ridge. Up ahead, I saw the jug of chlorine where we had come up through the trees.

We ran up to it, but Regi paused, looking back. "Portia's bag," he said, his eyes momentarily clear. "The samples. We have to get them."

He took off running, between two of the houses. I followed against my better judgment. The air was thick now with the smell of fuel and smoke. When we peered around the front of the houses, we saw the soldiers with the flamethrowers dowsing the blue-and-red house, where the bodies were. Where Portia was.

Regi froze, watching, trembling. I was scared to leave him alone, afraid he might go after them, attack them, try to stop them from incinerating the woman he loved.

But we needed those samples. I didn't quite know why, but I understood that it was true.

I crawled through a window into the house with the bag. It was right there, on the table with the inhalers and the soyflour. As I grabbed it, the bag of flour fell to the floor, sending out a little jet of white powder. I picked it up and jammed it into the medical bag.

As I wheeled around, the doorway erupted in flames. The heat was intense. Instinctively, I raised my arm to shield myself from it and felt the plastic of the biohazard suit melt against my skin. I dove for the window just as another blast of fuel splashed into the hut. As I tumbled onto the ground, a gout of flame followed me through the window.

Regi was standing to my right, near the front of the building, mumbling to himself, his eyes tightly clenched. At first, I thought he was praying, but then I got the impression he was arguing with himself about whether or not to attack the flamethrowers. I grabbed him by the arm and pulled him away, just as the next burst of flame enveloped the entire building, and a cascade of flames came over the roof right where we'd been standing.

Regi was in shock, but once we started running, he kept up. By the time we got back to the tree line, the entire village was in flames. I pulled Regi into the trees, twenty feet, but we could still see the village. Through the gap between the two houses closest to us, we could see the flames rapidly enveloping the big blue-and-red house.

Regi stood there, mesmerized as I opened the jug of chlorine and poured it over his biohazard suit. We both knew the Ebola story was bullshit, but there was so much blood. I didn't want to risk the exposure on the remote chance we were wrong. He moved his head away from the splashes of chlorine, away from the smell of it, all the while watching as the flames engulfed the building where his beloved lay.

I wiped down my own suit with chlorine, as well. Then I tugged at the tabs and zippers and flaps, tearing the plastic as I pulled the thing off me, peeling it away from my skin where it had melted. Then I tore Regi's suit off him.

Once I got him moving again, he seemed to snap out of it, but I could tell he was in a precarious mental state. We scrambled down the incline toward where we'd left the car, but as we drew nearer, I stopped and pulled Regi back.

Inching forward, I peered over the ridge, down at the car. It was surrounded by half a dozen Interior Ministry soldiers. One of them was lying across the hood. A couple of them were smoking. They were laughing, joking, either oblivious to what their comrades were doing or indifferent.

Regi stared down at them, and I could feel his rage. I worried once again that he might plunge forward, engage the overwhelming enemy, and vent his fury before they killed him.

I pulled him farther back from the ridge and gave him a gentle shake. "We need to get out of here," I told him quietly. "So we can take them on another day. So we can stop whatever it is they're doing."

He stared at me for a second, then he nodded and took the lead, grabbing me by the shoulder, pulling me through the trees. We crossed the road around the bend, where it was barely a cow path. Then we plunged into the dense green growth on the other side.

56

The terrain was hard, with lots of up and down, even after we found a semblance of a path. Behind us, black smoke drifted into the sky.

We'd traversed a couple of miles when we came over a slight rise and saw ocean below, maybe two miles away. A small cruise ship was anchored in the bay. A sliver of white sandy beach was dotted with umbrellas, a jumble of low, red-roofed buildings, and in the middle of it, a sleek glass hotel. It looked oddly out of place, more Bahamas than Haiti.

I guess I stopped walking to look at it, because Regi looked over and said, "Labadee."

"What?"

"That's Labadee down there."

"That's it? Where the summit is?" Partly I was curious, but I also wanted to keep him talking, hoping that if I kept him engaged, he wouldn't slip into shock or despair.

He pointed to a little cove off to the left. "Over there is Labadie, ending in *ie*, a very nice but very humble little seaside village. No roads go there because of the terrain, so it's like an island. Very hard to get to except from the water." He pointed at the white beach and the hotel. "Over there is Labadee, with two *e*'s at the end. It was built by a cruise line, a self-contained little bit of manufactured tourist paradise. The cruise ships dock there and drop off a couple thousand tourists at a time, and they play on the beach and in the water for a few hours. Then they would get back on the boat and go off to their next destination because there was no place to stay. The hotel is brand new. The Ministry of Tourism gave them incentives to build it so the tourists will stay a little longer. The whole place is surrounded by a huge wall topped with barbed wire, to keep out the Haitians, so they don't ruin the rich people's vacations."

"Are you serious?"

He nodded.

"Jesus, that's messed up." Something about the cruise ship in the bay looked familiar.

He shrugged. "It is and it isn't. It brings in some foreign investment and spending, employs some Haitians, which is a good thing." He allowed himself a slight smile. "But it is very, very strange."

"I see the cruise ship, but I don't see any people down there."

He squinted. "That's not a cruise ship. The resort is closed to host the summit."

"Why are they having it there?"

Regi shrugged. "To show it off. To attract more foreign investment. But also, if there's instability in the wind, this way they can remain apart from it."

That's when I noticed the helicopter perched on the back of the vessel.

"That's Archie Pearce's yacht," I said, almost to myself.

"Who?"

"Archie Pearce, the head of Stoma Corporation. That's his yacht. I've seen it before. On Martha's Vineyard."

"It's a nice boat. That would make sense. Stoma is very involved in the effort to gain greater access in the region for their biotech products, their genetically modified seeds and such."

I felt a chill as it sunk in that it was Pearce. He'd gotten away with some very shady stuff the last time I'd encountered him. He was very rich and very powerful. And very dangerous.

The path descended into a little hollow, but before the ocean disappeared from sight, I turned back for one last look at Archie Pearce's yacht.

As we continued on, a dozen different types of insects found us. Or at least found me, buzzing around my ears. The heat was getting to me, as well. Once we had put a little more distance between us and Gaden, I sidled close to Regi. "We need to figure out what's next."

He turned to look at me, taken aback, like he wasn't expecting to be making that decision. "What do you mean?"

"I mean we have a lot to do, and I don't know how to go about doing it. I'm not from around here." I barely understood how things worked in my own country. "I guess the first step is testing those samples. We need to figure out where and how."

There was plenty more, as well. I thought about Miriam and wondered once again what had become of her. It was still possible she had landed back in Florida or somewhere else, but hope had been slipping away with each passing hour, and especially after what we had just seen, I had to acknowledge the likelihood that she had been reunited with her husband. I felt rage flaring up in me and shame that I had let this happen to her. She had come to me for help, for protection. Now she was dead. But if I was to keep Regi from losing it over the slaughter of the woman he loved, I couldn't let myself lose it over the death of a woman I barely knew.

Regi took out his phone and tried to place a call. "No signal," he said. "We'll test the samples at my lab at the university, where I tested the others."

"And whatever we find, we have to get word out. Through the media or the Internet; maybe through Mikel. About Saint Benezet and Gaden too. Who do we tell about that here?"

"I must tell Dissette right away," he said, a hint of a sad smile tugging at his mouth. "He is an old fool and a coward. He won't do anything, but I have to tell him, anyway. Then I must tell President Cardon. There is no one else to tell."

57

We made better progress once we found a small dirt road, but the sun was high and beating down hard. As we came over a rocky hill, a cell phone tower rose incongruously out of the scrubby trees. I powered up my iPhone but there were no new messages.

Regi took out his phone and placed a call. He spoke in Kreyol, a dead monotone marred only by a growing sense of exasperation. He shook his head as he lowered his phone. "Dissette is not to be disturbed," he spat. "They say he is in a meeting. More likely taking a nap."

He took a deep breath and placed another call. He was on hold for a moment, then he said, "Chantale!" with a forced cheerfulness. He continued on, this time keeping his voice even and controlled, polished almost. When he finished, the smile disappeared, as if the effort to support it had exhausted him. "My friend Chantale is in the president's scheduling office. I left a message with her asking him to call me," he said when he was done. "I said it was urgent, but I don't know if he'll call."

Next, he called Jean-Pierre at the airport. There was still no sign of Miriam and Sable. He lifted the phone one more time, holding it in front of him. "Portia has a sister," he said distantly. "Studying in Cuba. I must tell her . . ." He cleared his throat and shook his head. "But not now."

We were hiking at a brisk pace, but I think we shared a growing sense of frustration, stuck on foot in the middle of nowhere while we knew something terrible was going down.

I pulled out the plastic bag and looked through the pages as we walked, hoping something would jump out at me. But the terrain was rough. It was hard to get much out of it.

Regi looked over and put out his hand. I handed him the bag, and he started looking through the documents, as well.

"This is useless," he said, squinting and holding a page up in the sunlight. "These are barely legible." As the baking sun dried them out, they got better, but not much.

The road widened, and I heard a vehicle approaching. I tapped Regi on the shoulder, and we clambered into the brush on the side of the road. I stuffed the pages back into the bag and the bag into my shirt.

A Jeep appeared around the curve, slowing as it approached. For a moment, I worried the driver might have seen us. When he pulled off the road and stopped, I recognized him as one of the soldiers from the roadblock. Regi recognized him, too. His eyes flashed with anger.

The driver jumped out and ran into the bushes, leaving an old M16 leaning against the dash. His holster was empty.

As he began peeing against a small tree, I felt Regi tensing up next to me. I put my hand on Regi's arm and shook my head. The guy could still have another sidearm, and even if we killed him, the gunfire would bring his friends. Plus, Regi wasn't a killer. I doubted his soul could handle becoming one, and I hoped he never had to find out.

A thief, though, that wouldn't be so bad.

The Jeep's engine was running. I pointed at it and whispered in Regi's ear, "Let's take it."

I saw a ghost of a smile, and he nodded.

"Quickly." I sprinted out of the bushes and down onto the road. Regi was right behind me. I jumped into the driver's seat and Regi got in the other side.

As soon as I put the Jeep in gear, the guy peeing in the bushes turned and saw us. "Hey!" he called out, grabbing at his empty holster as we drove off. *"Hey!"*

By the time his pants were done up and he had run out on to the road, we were fifty yards away.

Regi smiled briefly, looking back at the soldier, who ran halfheartedly after us. But the smile faded as he turned to face front, and by the time the soldier had disappeared around the curve, Regi's face was stony and grim.

Even in the Jeep, the going was slow, and when the road straightened out, I looked back, worried the guy we'd stolen it from could be gaining on us. Just before the road curved again, he appeared—150 yards back, moving at a cross between a jog and a shuffle. Regi turned to look back as the guy called out weakly and collapsed to his knees.

We left him behind the next curve, but I drove faster, anyway, trying to put more distance between us. I was relieved that he had appeared unarmed, and I found his .45 with a full clip under the seat, along with an unopened bag of fried plantains and a green wool watch cap with OFFICER TURNIER written on the inside in black permanent marker.

I showed Regi the hat and handed him the bag of chips. "Thanks, Officer Turnier."

His mouth twitched in a hint of a smile. He started to wave off the chips but then changed his mind.

"I wonder who'll be angrier at Officer Turnier," I said, "the police for losing his Jeep or his mother for losing his hat."

Regi opened the bag and took a handful of chips and then passed the bag to me.

The road we were on ended up ahead at an intersection with a larger, more defined road.

Regi said, "We should make a right up here, to get us back to Cap-Haïtien. Left will take us toward Labadee."

I nodded, slowing to make the turn. But as we approached the intersection, my heart sank. Another police vehicle pulled across the road right in front of us. Both officers got out and held up their hands for us to stop.

Regi said, "Let me handle this."

I was about to tell him that, in my experience, stealing a police vehicle and stranding an officer might require more than a little bureaucratic finesse. But the officers didn't come any closer. They just stood there with their hands raised, preventing us from going any farther. Another police vehicle went by, followed by two black SUVs with tinted windows, both sporting Darkstar stickers in back. Another police SUV came behind them, and another.

"It's a goddamned motorcade," I muttered. Just my luck to get stuck behind a motorcade out in the remote hills of Haiti.

"They're coming from Labadee."

I looked back the way we had come, searching for any sign of the guy we'd carjacked. Things could go south in a hurry if he showed up and told his buddies about how we'd stolen his Jeep.

Luckily, there was no sign of him. As I turned back around, a massive Hummer limousine slowed and stopped directly in front of us. One of the rear windows slid down, and a face leaned forward.

Archie Pearce. He looked right at me, making eye contact, a vague scowl on his face. Sitting across from him, seemingly unaware of my presence, was Bradley Bourden, the head of Energene.

Pearce didn't break eye contact; he just raised the window as the car eased forward.

"What was that about?" Regi asked as the motorcade drove on.

"That's Archie Pearce, the head of Stoma. I had a run-in with him last spring. Frankly, I'm surprised he recognized me. Last time I saw him, I caused him a substantial inconvenience, but he made it clear he considered me as consequential as a flea."

"That's a powerful man to have as an enemy."

"Don't I know it. The other guy was Bradley Bourden, the head of Energene. I don't think he likes me, either."

Regi smiled again. "I must say I like your taste in enemies."

A couple more vehicles drove by, then the motorcade was over. The two cops got back in their vehicle and followed the others.

I took a last look behind us, then I fell in behind them.

58

I hung as far back as I could, following the motorcade from a safe distance as the road wound down the mountain toward Cap-Haïtien. I was beginning to wonder if they were going to precede us the whole way back, just to aggravate us, but then they slowed to a stop.

Two police vehicles pulled off to the right and waited while everyone else turned left.

I resumed driving slowly, and we passed the entrance to a courtyard flanked by two stone-faced bodyguards. I could see Archie Pearce, slightly stooped but still towering over everyone else. Bradley Bourden seemed tiny next to him. The two CEOs had an entourage of half a dozen men, among them Royce and Divock. They were being greeted by two Haitians. One of them was Ducroix, the interior minister. I recognized him from Marcel's restaurant. He was wearing the same dark aviator shades and military uniform. The other was tall and handsome, wearing an expensive suit and smiling broadly to show off his impressive white teeth.

"Who's the other guy with Ducroix?" I asked Regi.

"I believe that's Vincent Adrien, Cardon's trade minister. Strange that Ducroix is here with them."

"They all seem very friendly." They were shaking hands, smiling and laughing politely. Ducroix held out his arm, gesturing for everyone to go inside. As they turned to follow him, I noticed an odd interaction between Bourden and Pearce, a conspiratorial glance that devolved into utter disdain as soon as each looked away from the other.

The police out front were giving us a hard stare, and I sped off before they could scrutinize the Jeep.

"What do you think that's about?" I asked Regi as we continued down the mountain. "Why would Pearce and Bourden be meeting with Ducroix?"

"There have been protests against them. And the stolen Soyagene," he said quietly. "But I don't like it. I don't trust Ducroix." A furrow formed in the center of his forehead.

Cap-Haïtien spread out in front of us, a handful of dark wisps rising ominously into the sky. I turned to Regi, and he met my gaze with a worried shrug. The furrow deepened.

As we entered the city, an armored police vehicle sped down the road ahead, and a few blocks past it, another one. It struck me that Ducroix was hyping the threat from rebel factions on the one hand, but instead of monitoring the situation on the ground, he was meeting with bigwigs from Energene and Stoma.

Driving through the city, we passed a few more police vehicles and piles of burning tires surrounded by young men who seemed more bored than anything else.

When we reached the Ministry of Health building, a dozen police vehicles were lined up out front, and a cluster of tents had sprung up in the open lot beside it. Officers milled around by the entrance.

Regi held up his hand and said, "Hold on." I was already braking. I did not like the looks of this.

He took out his phone and placed a call. "Dissette," he said to whoever answered. He looked away as a voice came on the other end, and they spoke back and forth in Kreyol, his eyes returning to mine as he ended the call.

"That was Dissette. I told him I thought Ducroix was up to something and that he might have lied about the Ebola outbreaks in Saint Benezet and Gaden, that those people might have been killed— murdered—under false pretenses."

"What did he say?"

"He said those were very serious accusations and that I should come in to the office to discuss them." He looked out the windshield at the police assembling on the front steps. "I asked him if the police were there." He turned to look at me. "He said they were not."

As he said it, a heavyset older man came out the front door in a hurried shamble and approached the officer in charge.

"That's Dissette," Regi said, looking down and covering his face with his hand. "We should go."

I turned the Jeep around and drove down the nearest side street. "Where to?" I asked.

He paused, thinking. "Make a left. We will test the samples at the university, but first we need to stop at my house."

"We need to get rid of this Jeep."

"Elena has a car. She will let me borrow it."

As he directed me through the city, we saw more police and clusters of protestors, more energetic than before. I couldn't read the signs, but many of them had drawings of cornstalks or seedlings.

"They're protesting the proposed trade agreement," Regi says, translating the signs. "'Seed Sovereignty Now' and 'Long live local seeds!'"

"What's that one say?" I pointed at a sign that read SOVE AYITI DE KOLERA AK EBOLA.

Regi cleared his throat. "Save Haiti from cholera and Ebola."

The protests were peaceful, but the police seemed to be preparing for something more. Regi's frown deepened with every police post we passed.

As we approached his house, I slowed to a stop. A police vehicle was parked on the sidewalk midway between Regi's house and his sister's inn.

"You see that?" I asked.

Regi nodded. "I do."

We sat there and stared. "You think they're in your house or my room at the inn?"

"I don't know."

It turned out it wasn't either. A pair of police in dress uniforms exited Elena's front door, got into their vehicle, and drove away. As soon as they turned the corner, we went inside.

She was sitting in a kitchen chair with her hands folded in her lap, her face pinched.

"Elena!" Regi said, running over to her.

She looked up at him, her face blank. She whispered something to him in Kreyol. They went back and forth, quiet but urgent.

"Is she okay?" I asked quietly when they'd stopped.

"I am fine," she said, looking up with an apologetic smile.

"She and Marcel are to cook for the police camped in front of the government services building," Regi said. "She said they have to make enough for thirty men every day. Rice and beans for lunch and *mayi moulin*, cornmeal and stew, for dinner."

"Are they paying her?" I asked.

She looked at me and nodded, her eyebrows inching up in surprise.

"They are," Regi said. "And they are supplying them the food to cook."

"It is not bad," Elena said.

Regi looked unconvinced. "Did they go in Doyle's room?"

She shook her head. "No."

He nodded slowly, then said a few words in Kreyol.

She reached into her apron pocket and handed him a set of car keys.

Regi kissed her on the cheek and took them.

59

From the outside, Regi's house was similar to Elena's—unadorned stucco with a single window and a door with a small step. Inside, it was clean and simple with wood floors and hand-carved wood furniture.

I was surprised by the *Star Wars* memorabilia on the bookshelves, by the picture of Regi shaking hands with Wyclef Jean, and by Miriam Hartwell standing in the corner, pointing a gun at us as we walked in.

She looked like hell—dirty and sunburned and squeezing the gun so tightly in her hands I was afraid it would crumple like tinfoil if it didn't go off. She seemed unable to lower it at first, as if she'd been holding it so long, she'd forgotten how. Then she dropped it and ran to Regi, burying her face against his shoulder. "I'm so glad you're here," she said, crumbling into tears.

"Thank God you're okay," he said, stroking her hair. "We've been so worried about you. I'm so sorry about Ron. So sorry for what you've been through."

When she calmed down, she pulled back from him. "I'm okay,"

she said, maybe a little prematurely. Then she turned and put a hand on my arm. "I didn't expect to see you. Thanks for your help, again."

"Sable?"

Her eyes welled up anew, and she shook her head. "He didn't make it."

"What happened?"

She shook her head. "He was shot as we took off."

"I was afraid of that."

"It looked bad, but he said he was okay. He seemed okay for a while. He got us here, but just barely." She laughed briefly through her tears at the memory of it. "That crazy plane. He put it down in this tiny little clearing. He said we were going to an airstrip, a place called Phaeton, but then he just . . . he said he wasn't going to make it. He said it calmly, and we were going down in this tiny field. I couldn't believe he was doing it. Then I couldn't believe he did it. Then I couldn't believe he was gone." She looked up at me, her eyes streaming. "I think he died before the plane actually touched down."

She took another stab at gathering herself. "Anyway, I didn't know what to do or where to go. I just started walking, until I found a road. I felt terrible leaving him behind, but I didn't know what else to do." She looked down and her voice went quiet. "I barely knew him, but he saved my life."

She cleared her throat and continued. "When I got to the road, I asked some people the way to Cap-Haïtien. After a couple hours, it started getting dark. There were police all over. I don't know which was scarier, them or the groups of young men eying me up, sometimes following me. I had Sable's phone, but it was locked. I found a clump of bushes in an empty field."

"That's where you spent the night?" Regi asked.

She nodded. "It was scary. I don't think I slept more than a few minutes at a time. As soon as it started getting light out, I started walking again. I don't know what it's usually like here, but even at dawn, police were everywhere again. What's going on?"

Regi's eyes went distant for a moment, then he winced.

"What is it?" she asked.

"Portia is dead," he said. He managed two full seconds before the horror of it overcame him and he dissolved into tears.

"What?" She put her arm around him. "What happened?"

He just shook his head, unable to talk.

Watching the two of them comforting each other over their losses made me that much more determined not to suffer a similar fate, or to cause Nola to. But it also reinforced my determination to stop the bastards responsible for it.

I thought about all those bodies in Gaden and the ones in Saint Benezet. Gone without a trace. So many lives lost, so many survivors scarred by sorrow, never to be whole again.

The question of how Portia had died hung in the room, unanswered. Regi wasn't ready to tell her yet.

"I brought your files to show Regi," I said.

Her eyes showed the tiniest flicker of hope as she turned to Regi. "Did you see them?"

He shook his head.

"The police confiscated them from me. We just got them back." I pulled the bag out and showed her. "A little worse for wear."

She unbuttoned the top of her blouse. "I have them, as well," she said, pulling out a sheaf of paper. The pages were crumpled and yellowed, looking almost as rough around the edges as she did.

She gave them to Regi, and he started leafing through them.

"These are better," he said quietly.

"There's more to tell you," I said. "But we need to get going."

"Going where?" Miriam asked.

"We have some samples we need to test. We are going to the university."

"Not your lab?"

Regi shook his head. "The facilities are better at the school. Besides, these are interesting times at work."

60

We took Elena's dented Mitsubishi and left the Jeep parked around the corner—the weapons and the keys stashed under the seats with Officer Turnier's wool cap. Miriam sank down low in the back to avoid being seen. Regi drove, weaving between the cars and trucks and bicycles and pedestrians, his voice oddly detached as he told Miriam what had been going on.

"Ebola?" she exclaimed, sitting up when he told her about Saint Benezet. "That's ridiculous. There were no signs of Ebola when we were there. And there hasn't been Ebola in Haiti. Did people test positive?"

He shook his head. "The Interior Ministry sealed the village," he said quietly. "They claimed authority, and Dissette let them." He wiped his eyes as he drove. "They said there were no survivors."

"There's always survivors," she said, barely a whisper, as if she could see where this was going.

Regi cleared his throat and got himself under control. "They said there were none. And in order to eliminate the possibility of an epidemic, they incinerated the village."

Miriam clamped a hand over her mouth, her eyes wide above it.

"I had already tested the Soyagene for allergenicity against the samples from Saint Benezet, but it was negative. Stoma Grow was positive, but that doesn't quite make sense. Anyway, yesterday, while Doyle and I were trying to find some kind of connection to the Soyagene theft, a call came in. Another outbreak of the same respiratory distress syndrome, this time at Gaden, another tiny village a couple miles away." His voice was steady, but tears began to roll down his face. "Portia went to investigate, to deliver inhalers and take samples, as before. We went after her, but the police had already sealed the village. They wouldn't let us in. They said it too was Ebola."

"It wasn't Ebola," Miriam whispered again.

"We snuck in through the woods," he continued.

We were driving through the eastern outskirts of the city, past the airport. Regi drifted to a stop on the side of the road.

"It wasn't Ebola," Miriam repeated.

Regi shook his head. "No. It wasn't Ebola. They had been shot. The whole village. We found them piled up in one of the houses. Dozens of them." He suppressed a shudder, taking a deep breath before he continued. "Portia was among them."

"Oh, Regi," she said, tears streaming down her dirty face. She leaned forward and wrapped her arms around his neck, squeezing him tight. "I'm so sorry."

"They burned the whole village," he said, holding her arms around him for a moment. Then he patted her arms, and she sat back, wiping the tears from her face.

Regi resumed driving. "Portia took blood samples from the villagers at Gaden," he continued. "So we have to test them, to see if they react to anything. But also we must test it for Ebola."

"There's no Ebola," she whispered, her face turning paler as the news about Gaden and Saint Benezet continued to sink in. She slumped back down in her seat, and this time I don't think it was because she was hiding.

234 // JON MCGORAN

"We have to be sure," Regi said quietly.

"We're all going to die," she said softly. She sounded almost relieved.

"No, we're not," I said.

As we drove in silence for a few minutes, she regained her composure. "So what is this all about?"

"I think Ducroix is planning a coup," Regi said gravely, turning to me as he said it.

"A coup?" Miriam said.

I nodded. "I was wondering if that might be part of it."

"Dominique Ducroix has never been a big supporter of Alain Cardon," Regi said. "He supported Charles Martine in the last election. Cardon kept him on for political reasons. But he is constantly talking about rebel activity when all I see are peaceful protests. He seems to be overstating the threat to justify his increased presence on the street. I warned Cardon not to give him too much power."

I nodded. "I don't know how Gaden and Saint Benezet fit into it, but our friends from Energene and Stoma seemed pretty cozy with Ducroix, and they would surely benefit from a change."

"They could just be here for the trade summit, right?" Miriam asked. "And talking to Ducroix about the Soyagene theft?"

I shrugged. "Possibly, but they seem to be up to something else. We saw them meeting with Ducroix. At his house."

"It would make sense," Regi said, as if talking to himself. "If they want to control Haiti's vote on the trade agreement, guarantee access to the agricultural free-trade zone, they might try to topple Cardon before the vote takes place."

"When is the vote set for?" I asked.

"Monday."

"That's the day after tomorrow."

Miriam looked confused. "But if the Soyagene is not allergenic, how does it fit in? What about Saint Benezet and Gaden?"

"I don't know," Regi said.

"Maybe they somehow got in the way," I said quietly. "Maybe

that's just what they do to people who get in the way." I hadn't meant to say it out loud. When I looked back, Miriam had lost some of her recently regained composure.

"If that is the case," Regi said, "we must make sure they didn't die in vain."

61

The Université Roi Henri Christophe was ten miles outside the city, just past the town of Limonade, on a luxuriously smooth stretch of modern highway. It was less than twenty minutes by car. The campus consisted of a cluster of modern buildings with an enclosed pavilion at the entrance and a large courtyard. It even had ample parking.

We were a quarter mile away from it when I noticed the police, a cluster of cars and a crowd of officers in tactical gear milling around on the edge of the highway by the entrance. As we got closer, I saw the students inside the gate, two hundred of them gathered around a concrete monument, chanting and holding up banners and crudely drawn signs. The signs looked a lot like the ones at the other protests, with plenty of drawings of corn and other plants, and plenty of slogans, some reading AYITI POU AYITI, some with the Stoma logo or the letters GMO with a big red line through them. A handful of them mentioned Ebola and cholera, and I wondered if the fake secret was becoming a fake rumor.

The police looked bored, but there was a definite air of menace about them.

Regi whispered, "Ayayay."

Miriam leaned forward. "What is it?"

His foot came off the gas, but he didn't touch the brakes. Instead, we coasted past the college's main entrance. A few of the police watched us go by.

"Are those rebels?" Miriam asked, looking at the protestors.

Regi shook his head. "There are no rebels. Those are students protesting in support of farmers. Against the agricultural free-trade zone just down the road. Against Stoma and Energene."

Just past the university, Regi turned slowly into a side entrance and followed a driveway around to the back of the campus. The sound of chanting faded behind the buildings.

We parked near a rear door, and Regi swiped his ID to open it. We followed him to a lab on the third floor. The hallways were empty, and the building was silent except for our footsteps and the muffled sound of chanting from outside.

I could see them from the lab window, the protestors inside the gate and the police on the outside.

Regi placed Portia's bag and Miriam's files on the table. As he started pulling lab equipment out of the cabinets, I took the files over to the window and studied them in the daylight, hoping this time something would jump out at me.

"We will be doing ELISA tests for both the Ebola and the allergens," Regi announced. "The Ebola test takes longer, a couple of hours, so we'll start that first."

"I can help," Miriam said.

He looked at her and smiled. "Thank you. We will take proper precautions, but if this is Ebola, there are still risks."

She smiled bitterly and shook her head. "There is no Ebola."

"Even so."

They put on plastic shield masks, yellow plastic gowns, and blue nitrile gloves. I gave them plenty of space. I was confident it wasn't Ebola, too, but it still made me nervous.

"We'll be doing a similar tests for the Ebola and for the allergen. For the Ebola test, we have these well plates, courtesy of the World

Health Organization." He held up a stack of individually wrapped rectangular plastic plates, each covered with rows of dots or indentations. I couldn't tell if the play-by-play was because he was used to teaching there or because he wanted us to understand exactly what he was doing. Whatever the reason, it seemed to have a calming effect on all of us. Maybe that was the point.

"Each well is pre-coated with a monoclonal antibody that binds to a glycoprotein in the Ebola virus. We put the samples in and give them sixty minutes to bind. Then we wash them to remove the material that is not Ebola. Next, we'll apply a second antibody that binds to a different part of the Ebola virus. After a quick rinse, we'll apply a detection molecule followed by a reaction agent. If any of them turn blue, there is Ebola present."

He looked at us as that hung in the air, then he turned to Portia's bag on the table and pulled out the two Ziploc bags with the blood samples. He paused again, looking at them in his hands. They were all that was left of the people of Gaden. Apart from those samples, there was only ash.

"This part takes about an hour," he said quietly, pulling himself out of it as he turned the dial on an old-fashioned kitchen timer. "We do almost the same thing to check for allergen proteins. It is a shorter test, and I have everything we need from the tests I ran on the samples from Saint Benezet. I'll test against Soyagene, regular soyflour, the Stoma-Grow corn, and the Early Rise corn." He looked at Miriam. "Have you ever run assay tests like this?"

"We did them in nursing school."

"Good. Then you can monitor me, to make sure I don't make any errors."

She studied his face. "Are you okay?"

He nodded. "Are you?"

She nodded back.

They stared at each other for a moment, like they both knew the other was lying.

I went back to studying the pages.

62

They worked in silence except for the occasional murmur of direction or reply. Regi laid out three small plastic trays. He mixed something called a coating buffer with each of the corn and soy varieties and put a tiny bit of each into a well on each of the plates. He placed them in the incubator and set a different timer for thirty minutes.

"Now we wait," he said. He raised his visor and motioned Miriam over to the sink, turning on the faucet and washing his gloved hands. When he was done, he stripped off the gloves and the gown and washed his hands again. As he dried them, he stepped aside and gestured for Miriam to do the same.

There had been a glimmer of energy in the room while they had been working, a vague sense of something positive—not quite optimism but something along those lines.

The pause, though, the waiting, it seemed to deflate them both.

Regi walked out into the hallway. Miriam watched him go, her lower lip trembling. She stared at the door as his footsteps receded. Then she silently followed.

Five minutes later, I poked my head out the door and saw them standing by the window at the end of the hallway. Holding each other.

If they had been moving the slightest bit, they would have appeared to be dancing. But they were perfectly still.

They had both been deeply hurt, damaged, and left alone by tragedy. But there was more to it than that. There was intimacy.

I had assumed they'd been friends in college. I realized then they had been more than that. Whatever there was had been awakened, revived by the tragedy and pain, the vulnerability. The need.

I wasn't about to judge.

I ducked silently back into the room and buried myself once again in Miriam's documents. They had to hold the answers. Why else would Ron Hartwell risk his life—sacrifice his life—to bring them to light?

There was something to the allergenicity memo, I was pretty sure of that. But I also knew Regi would be much more likely to figure out what. So I returned to the inventories and production reports.

Why were they there? And why were some secret and some not? They contained similar information, but maybe not identical. The differences would be the key.

I paired off similar documents, the secret and non-secret versions. The formatting was completely different, making side-by-side comparisons difficult. If the answers were in there, I would have to work to find them.

I found a pencil and started with a pair of production reports, a list of hundreds of different seed products. I located Soyagene on the regular inventory sheet and then on the secret version. I discovered a discrepancy right off the bat.

The regular sheet listed forty-six thousand tons of Soyagene GES-5322. The secret list said forty-five thousand tons of Soyagene GES-5322a. Interesting, but probably meaningless.

After that, I started at the top. The first item on the regular sheet was ALFALFA, DRY-RISE—TWELVE THOUSAND TONS. I found it on the other sheet and checked them both off. The next item was SUGAR BEETS, DRY-RISE—THIRTEEN THOUSAND TONS. Check and check. They were listed in a seemingly random order—and not the same random order, either. It was slow going.

I was a quarter of the way down the first sheet when Regi and Miriam walked in with wet eyes and shy, subdued smiles.

"Sorry," Miriam whispered.

I shook my head. "No worries."

Regi sat across from me. He rested his fingertips on one of the papers I wasn't looking at, slid it across the table, and started reading.

I leafed through the pages and handed him the abstracts, thinking that if I were a clue that had not been found yet, that was where I'd be hiding. He read each one slowly before moving on to the next one.

Miriam watched him as he read, her eyes glued to his face, looking for any indication he had found anything noteworthy, anything that could give meaning and purpose to Ron's death. She'd probably been through these documents so many times, trying to read them again would be useless.

Regi read all the abstracts and the memos. Then he started skimming the production reports.

When the timer went off, Regi brought the allergen plates to the sink and dumped the contents of the wells, tapping the excess out onto a paper towel. Using a pipette, he added a few drops from the blood samples to each of the wells. "We'll let these bind for ten minutes. Then we'll rinse it and add the detection antibody."

As we returned to studying the documents, the chants of the students protesting seemed to grow louder in the silence.

After ten minutes, he rinsed the plates and applied the detection antibody, then he sighed and resumed his reading.

"Did you read this allergenicity report?" he asked Miriam, turning his head slightly, speaking to her over his shoulder.

"I did," she said. "I read all of it. But I couldn't make sense of a lot of it. I assumed it referred to the Soyagene, but you said there was no reaction to the Soyagene, right? So that doesn't make sense. Maybe it refers to Stoma's Stoma-Grow corn, since that's what generated the reaction."

He nodded absentmindedly. "We'll see what we get this time."

"Could the memo be from Stoma, then?" she asked. "Maybe someone at Energene stole it—industrial espionage."

They both looked at me. "Could be," I said, shrugging. "But it seems like Energene is behind whatever's going on. Ron was digging around in Energene's secret files, not Stoma's."

"Maybe they're working together," Regi said. "Bourden and Pearce seemed quite cordial."

Miriam looked up. "Archie Pearce, from Stoma?"

I nodded. "We saw them meeting with Ducroix. Any idea why one would help the other conceal product defects?"

She shook her head. "They might be scheming together on some things, but they're still rivals."

Regi sighed and got up. He rinsed the allergen plates and applied another chemical. "In five minutes, we'll add the detection reagent and see what we've got." As he said it, the other timer went off for the Ebola test. "Just enough time to prep the samples for the next stage of the Ebola test."

I nodded.

As they worked with the samples, I continued comparing the two sets of documents. They were almost finished when I spotted another discrepancy—a second Soyagene entry on the secret list: SOY, SOYAGENE GES-5322x, one thousand tons.

Before I could even ponder what that meant, the timer sounded on the allergen test.

We gathered around the plates as Regi added the detection reagent. Nothing happened. "It could take a few minutes for color to develop," he said.

We hovered over them, and after a few minutes, the third well on each of the three trays began to turn a pale blue.

"The Stoma-Grow corn," Regi said softly. "Just like before. The only reaction is to the corn."

After the full five minutes, nothing else had changed.

"So maybe we were wrong," Miriam said. "Maybe Ron was wrong."

"It seems so," he said.

"So what does that mean?" I asked. "If the reaction had nothing to do with the soy, does that mean that the stolen soy could have been a coincidence?"

Regi turned and looked at the Ebola test samples, sitting on the next table. "And if it was a coincidence," I said, "does that mean the Ebola outbreak was real?"

We followed his gaze, but Miriam immediately shook her head. "It couldn't be Ebola."

"The people in Gaden were shot," I said. "We saw them."

Regi shrugged. "Maybe the infection was in the early stages. Maybe only some of them were symptomatic. Maybe Ducroix's men overreacted and killed them all before they even knew who was and wasn't infected."

Miriam's eyes widened a bit, doubt and horror creeping into her mind as the idea that she might have just exposed herself to a deadly disease, might have enabled an outbreak, went from impossible to highly improbable but possible nonetheless.

"No," I said. "I can't believe in a coincidence like that, that the two tiny villages hit by this strange allergic syndrome would coincidentally be hit by Ebola."

Regi shrugged. "They are not far apart."

"Or maybe it wasn't coincidence at all," I heard my voice say quietly. They both looked at me. "Maybe the Ebola was intentionally spread."

It was such a horrible thought, I'd been holding it off, fighting against thinking it. My mind raced to come up with a different answer, any other explanation. Regi and Miriam looked at me in disgust, resisting the notion just as I had, maybe even judging me for having said it out loud.

And then it hit me.

63

I sprang out of my chair, and they both jumped, startled.

"What is it?" Regi asked, alarmed.

I grabbed Portia's bag and opened it. "Which soy did you test?"

"Some regular soyflour and some of the Soyagene. What do you mean?"

"Where did you get the Soyagene?"

Miriam was looking back and forth between us.

"I got it from Energene, when I tested it before."

"Can I see the bag?"

"Of course." As he opened a cabinet and took out a plastic tote, I pulled out the Soyagene from Gaden and looked at the bottom of the bag. It was stamped GES-5322x.

Regi opened the tote and handed me a similar bag, almost full. The bottom was stamped GES-5322a.

Son of a bitch. "They're different," I said.

"What do you mean?" Regi said.

Miriam came over to look. I showed them the two inventory sheets, how the secret one included two different types of Soyagene and the other one just lumped them together.

"So what does that mean?" Miriam asked.

"Maybe nothing. But if we've been testing the 5322a and the 5322x is what's been making people sick, they might be very different." In the back of my mind, I was already coming up with a theory about what was going on, but I needed more information to even consider it.

I held up the bag from Gaden, the 5322x. "Can we run the allergen test again, with this?"

Regi nodded, his face confused but gravely serious. Miriam wore a similar expression. I wondered if they were beginning to suspect the same thing I was.

They suited up and began setting up another three trays. He went through the same process as before, but with the Soyagene-X. Then he set the timer for thirty minutes.

It was a long thirty minutes.

We mostly spent it reading the files, trying to glean anything else from it. I don't know about the others, but I got nothing from it; my mental energy consumed with wondering what the test would reveal. Eventually, I gave up and went to the window. The protestors were getting louder out front. The police across the street seemed more agitated than before.

When the timer finally sounded, Regi added the blood samples from Gaden, following the same process as before, until finally announcing that he was adding the detection reagent. I'd been hanging back, staying out of the way, but I stepped closer to watch. I expected it to take several minutes like it had the first time, but immediately, the Soyagene-X wells turned a deep, vivid blue, much darker than the Stoma-Grow corn had generated even after the full five minutes.

Regi whispered, "That's a very strong reaction."

Staring at those blue dots, Miriam said, "Motherfucker."

She took the word right out of my mouth.

64

For a moment, we stood there, silently processing what we had witnessed. The only sounds were the ticking of the timer for the Ebola test and the chants from outside.

"So what does that even mean?" I asked.

Regi shook his head. "I've never seen a reaction that intense, that immediate. No wonder the villagers were so sick."

Miriam started leafing through Ron's files. "Could it be intentional? There was a report in here . . . This—" She held up one of the abstracts. "It describes target allergenicity and minimum quantities for symptomology."

"Yes," I said, looking over her shoulder. "I didn't understand it when I read it the first time, and I still don't, but I remember thinking 'target allergenicity' sounded more like a minimum than a maximum."

"Exactly," she said.

"But why?" Regi asked. "Why make a product that deliberately makes your customers sick?"

"It doesn't make sense," Miriam said, shaking her head. "The people at Saint Benezet, some of those people would have died if we hadn't been there . . ." Her voice trailed off. All those people she'd helped save were dead now, anyway.

A lot of the pieces had been jamming together in my mind for some time. With this last piece, they all came together, assembling themselves into some kind of crazy whole. The two types of Soyagene, the top-secret memos, even the ramp up in Early Rise corn production.

"It does make sense," I said.

They both looked at me.

"Energene and Stoma are working together to expand the markets for their biotech products, but they're still competitors. Stoma-Grow corn is the most lucrative agricultural product in the world. Energene is trying to replace it."

Miriam gave her head a vigorous shake. "What do you mean? How?"

"The Stoma-Grow also got a positive reaction. It's the most common agricultural product in the world, but the only people to get sick from it were in these two tiny villages—Saint Benezet and Gaden—and only after they were exposed to this secret Soyagene-X." I turned to Regi. "Is it possible that the Soyagene-X doesn't just provoke a reaction on its own but that it makes people who eat it get sick if they eat Stoma-Grow corn, as well?"

Regi was slack-jawed. "Theoretically, yes. They could have engineered the Soyagene to include some version of proteins found only in the Stoma-Grow corn."

Miriam shook her head. "But then why was the Soyagene-X reaction so much stronger?"

"Because that's its purpose. Causing that reaction. That memo about 'target allergenicity' and 'minimum symptomology' or whatever. They weren't documenting an unwanted side effect. They were charting their progress toward a positive goal."

"Jesus," Miriam said. "So you're saying Energene is going to release this stuff so that anyone who eats Stoma-Grow corn will get sick like the people at Saint Benezet?"

248 // Jon McGoran

"Exactly. That's why Ron included that production memo about ramping up production of the Early Rise corn. Energene is going to be ready to cash in when that happens."

Regi slid down into a chair as the rest of his body caught up with the slackness of his jaw. "It's brilliant. It's insidious but brilliant."

"That's insane," Miriam insisted, her voice skittering as if she were on the verge of losing it. "Doyle, you didn't see the reactions to this. It was terrible. Those people were extremely sick. Many of them would have died if we hadn't helped them."

And there it was again. The horror of it. They were all dead now.

Maybe it was because we had gone quiet, but the crowd outside seemed to be getting louder.

"They weren't meant to be exposed to it like that," I said. "It was stolen, remember? Energene is planning to roll it out according to the timeline in that phase-two rollout memo. They'll probably dilute it, mix it with other products, however many parts per million, just enough to cause the reaction to Stoma-Grow corn."

"But then how will people know it's an allergy to Stoma-Grow?" Miriam said. "We were dealing with a very acute reaction, and it still wasn't obvious."

"They'll figure it out," Regi said. "It will just take a while."

"Exactly," I said. "That timeline starts right after the trade vote, so it won't be jeopardized even if someone puts it together right away. But it's supposed to take long enough that by the time anyone figures out people are getting sick from Stoma-Grow, the Soyagene-X will be gone. Everyone will assume it was something to do with the Stoma-Grow itself."

"That rollout schedule covers much of the world," Regi said, looking up. "Apart from the millions of people getting sick, millions more could starve. When people start getting sick from Stoma-Grow, there will be huge disruptions to the food supply. Even if Early Rise is ready to fill the void, people will starve as global production and distribution systems struggle to make the shift."

I nodded. "And it starts on Tuesday. Everywhere they roll it out, people will start getting sick from Stoma-Grow corn."

Miriam shook her head, still trying to grasp it. "Even if the doses are smaller, allergic reactions like that can be wildly unpredictable. If they roll it out around the world like that, people are going to get sick. People are going to die. Children, old people, the infirm."

I put my hands on her shoulders. I didn't want to upset her any more than she already was, but I needed her to understand the reality of the situation. "The people in Saint Benezet and Gaden were a smoking gun. And they were murdered because of it, every last one of them. Obliterated from the face of the earth. Whoever is behind this has already shown they're okay with that."

The room was quiet for a moment. We were all trying to absorb it, even me, trying to decide if I was crazy or if the whole world was. Tears began rolling down Miriam's face. Regi put an arm around her, but he didn't look much better.

I gave them some space, crossing to the window, looking out at the students protesting in the plaza. My brain was grinding its gears, trying to grasp what I had just proposed and at the same time trying to come up with a way to stop it.

Then the timer went off. The Ebola test was done.

65

Regi stared at the plates for several moments. I wondered if he was interpreting the results, double-checking them, or just collecting himself. Then he looked up and said, "There is no Ebola."

We all knew it already, but having it confirmed changed things. It was good news, of course. Nobody wanted an outbreak of something as horrible as Ebola.

But it meant there was an outbreak of greed and evil that in some ways was even worse.

Our most horrible suspicions were confirmed. Bradley Bourden and his friends at Energene were behind all of it, not just killing Ron Hartwell and David Sable and Toussaint Casson, and trying to kill Miriam, but murdering dozens of people in Saint Benezet and Gaden as well. And endangering the lives of thousands of people, and the health of millions more.

It took a few minutes for all that to sink in.

"So what are we going to do?" Miriam asked.

From the moment I opened my front door to find Ron Hartwell dying on my front steps, I'd been trying to get to the bottom of what was going on, so I could figure out what to do about it. Now that the pieces were falling into place, a plan began to take shape.

"This is what Ron died trying to stop," Miriam said. "We need to tell the world. We need to get this story out to the press, to the Internet. People need to know about this so they can stop it." She turned to me, her eyes pleading.

"We'll tell the world, but that's not going to stop it," I said. "Not in time to prevent the coup or the trade vote or the release of the Soyagene-X."

"But you know people, right? In the federal government, from before. You need to call them and tell them."

I thought back to the list I'd made, the people I knew. I shook my head. "The few connections I have are domestic—FBI, ATF, Homeland. This is international. The people I know won't be able to do anything about this. Definitely not in time to stop it."

But I had an idea of someone who maybe could.

Before I could go on, Miriam turned to Regi. "Surely you can use the health ministry to get the word out? This is a health crisis."

"Dissette, my boss, he's in on it. Or at least afraid of it. I need to go around him."

"Yes," I said. "We need to tell Cardon about all this. About Gaden and Saint Benezet. About Ducroix and what he's up to. And if we're not too late, he can stop the coup and tell the world about all this. But we also need to block the release of Soyagene-X. There's only one thing I can think of that can stop a massive multinational corporation like Energene—and that's an even bigger one." They both looked up at me. "We need to tell Archie Pearce he's about to get fucked."

As I said it, something out the window made me pause. The police were slowly advancing on the protestors, and the student with the megaphone was pointing at them. I couldn't have heard what he was saying even if it were in English, but I could hear his voice rising in pitch and volume. And urgency.

There was a noise like a thick branch snapping, and for an instant, everything was quiet and still.

"Oh shit," I said.

"What is it?" Miriam asked.

Regi stepped up beside me.

The megaphone fell to the ground. So did the student who'd been holding it, twisting as he hit the pavement. I saw a brief flash of red on his white T-shirt. Then chaos erupted as the police charged, and the students began running in all directions.

66

"We need to go," I said, scooping up the papers. "Grab everything. Anything we need, anything important."

Out the window, the police were chasing the students, many of whom were running toward the lab building, toward us. The far side of the plaza was almost empty except for the lone student lying on the ground, surrounded by a growing pool of red.

Regi stood there a second longer, his eyes smoldering. He turned to me as if he needed someone to witness his rage.

I clapped him on the shoulder. "We need to go."

He nodded, an icy calm descending over him as he crossed to one of the cabinets. He pulled out a large plastic tote filled with boxes of test tubes, beakers, and other supplies. He took off the lid and flipped it over, gently spilling the contents out onto the floor. Then he went around the room, methodically collecting sample bottles, trays, and the bags of soy and corn.

As he did this, Miriam stared out the window in horror, mesmerized by the sight of the battle down below, the body on the ground. Canisters of tear gas arced through the air, leaving trails behind them, bouncing in the midst of the scrambling protestors.

By the time she turned away from the window, Regi was snapping the lid back onto the tote.

"Let's go," he said, his voice flat.

As we hurried out into the hallway, there was a distant bang and a crash as the front doors of the building slammed open. Miriam jumped at the sound and froze in her tracks. I took the tote from Regi and nodded toward her. He put his arm around her and coaxed her toward the steps.

Sounds of commotion and panic echoed up the stairs as we descended. When we were almost at the bottom, a pair of students burst through the door, their eyes wide with fear.

They stopped and stared at us, probably wondering if we were friend or foe. I figured we could fit two more in the car, and I was about to tell them to come with us, but they dashed around us and ran up the stairs.

None of us said a word. We just hurried down the last few steps to the rear exit.

I pushed the door open. The car was ten feet away. It was a pleasant sunny day.

We stepped outside, and for a moment, everything was calm and peaceful, as if the mayhem we'd seen from the window out in front hadn't actually happened. Then two students rounded the side of the building, running full speed and coughing violently. Their eyes were bright red and their faces streaming wet.

They hopped the little fence at the back of the parking lot and kept running without slowing down, into the sparse brush behind the university.

I turned to Regi. "Give me the keys."

He paused, but I nodded and beckoned with my fingers. He fished them out of his pocket and tossed them to me.

I put the tote in the trunk, and we got in. I took a deep breath and drove off slowly, toward the side entrance where we had come in. To our left, through the fog of tear gas, we could see police in masks chasing down protestors and beating them with truncheons.

Miriam put her hand over her mouth. Regi's eyes narrowed.

I wanted to get us away as quickly as possible, but I kept my foot light on the gas, twenty miles an hour. A couple of the police looked over at us, but then they went back to what they were doing. When we reached the exit, I turned and drove past the police vehicles, keeping it slow but ready to stomp on the gas at any moment. Only a few police remained back with the vehicles. One of them stepped out onto the side of the road, not quite in front of us. He leaned forward squinting, fingering his rifle. I just kept driving, and I guess we looked different enough from the students, because he waved us by impatiently, like he wanted us out of the way.

I gave it some gas, then a little more, watching in my rearview as they receded behind us.

When we were a hundred yards away, Miriam turned in her seat and looked out the back window.

She shook her head, her face regaining some of the same bleak resignation I'd seen earlier. "They're going to kill us all," she said. "And then they're going to do whatever else they want."

"That's not going to happen," I said. "But we need to get you someplace safe." I turned to Regi. "And you have to get word to President Cardon. We have to let him know what's happening."

"I've been trying. I can't get through to him."

We were driving back through Limonade. Police were everywhere.

"You have to try harder. By the looks of it, Ducroix might already be making his move."

He took out his phone and called Chantale again. This time, his voice was sharp, hard. Each time Chantale spoke, he would reply with a sharp "No!" continuing on more insistently than before. They went back and forth four or five times, and then suddenly he stopped. "Allo? Allo? Chantale?" He put the phone down, stunned. "She hung up on me."

"Where are they?"

"She said he was in Plaisance."

"Where is that?"

"It's not too far, maybe an hour. I used to go there in the summer as a child. That's how I know Cardon. But she wouldn't say where in Plaisance he was or why he was there. And she wouldn't even agree to give him my message. She didn't sound right."

"We might have to just go there and find him. Is Plaisance a big city? A little village? Would he be hard to find there?"

He shook his head. "It's a quarter of the size of Cap-Haïtien, not big but not so small, either. Still, he is the president, so unless he is hiding, we should be able to find him. I don't know if he will agree to see me."

"You're going to have to insist. Can Miriam stay at your place while we're gone?"

He looked at her. "Of course."

"I don't need to stay hidden," she protested. "I'm in this at least as much as you two."

We were just entering Cap-Haïtien when Regi's phone rang. He scrambled to get it out of his pocket and answer it, "Allo? . . . Allo, Chantale," a tiny bit of relief softening his face. It didn't last long. As the conversation went briefly back and forth, the life drained from his face. He thanked her quietly and let the phone fall away from his face.

"That was Chantale. Her personal phone. She thinks Cardon is in hiding. Ducroix and his men are searching for him."

"What does that mean?" Miriam asked. "Are we too late? Has there already been a coup?"

He looked at me. "I don't know. If they don't have him, they haven't arrested him. He is still the president. But if he is out of the capital, they might just say he has been deposed."

"The trade vote is tomorrow, right?" I said. "Surely they wouldn't stage a coup right beforehand. The vote would have no legitimacy."

Regi thought for a moment. "It would be brazen. But I don't know if they wouldn't still try it."

I drove faster. "We need to get the word out about all this. We need to tell the world about Energene's plan, and about Ducroix, not just the coup but about Gaden and Saint Benezet. And we need to get word about it to Cardon, as well. It will have more impact coming from him. Maybe enough to get the international community involved. That might be enough to stop it."

As we pulled up in front of his house, Regi snapped his fingers. "I think I know where he is."

67

"There are ruins of an old fort in the mountains not far from Plaisance, near where Cardon used to live. We often went there in the summer, and he would go on and on about the thick walls, the elaborate secret tunnels, how the position was so defensible a small force could hold off a much larger one. Even as an adult, he has mentioned it. If he and his guard were nearby and under siege, I bet that's where he would go." He looked at us both. "I must go there immediately. And I should go alone. I know the area well, and you will just draw attention."

I gestured to the Jeep parked up the street. "There's a rifle in the Jeep, and a pistol. You should take one of them with you."

He shook his head. "I wouldn't know what to do with them. But it's getting dangerous around here, so you should keep them close." He gave me a set of keys. "More important, you should stay out of sight. Take Miriam to Elena's—there's room for both of you. And stay indoors."

"We need to get word out," Miriam said.

"We'll get the word out," I told her as we got out of the car. "But first we need to get off the street. I'm just going to grab the guns from the Jeep."

Guns complicated things, usually more than expected, but Regi was right—it was getting dangerous. I ran up the street to the Jeep, and as I was reaching for the gun under the seat, I heard vehicles approaching. Something about the sound made me pause, made me stay low and dip my head down. Two white police SUVs came around the corner, fast.

Regi and Miriam stepped backward, toward the house, but it was too late. The SUVs pulled up on either side of them. Each had a large red shield insignia on the side, a cheetah underneath the scales of justice and the letters DCPJ. Around the border were the words DIRECTION CENTRALE DE LA POLICE JUDICIAIRE. The Judicial Police. Two pairs of officers jumped out. They were heavily armed but wore crisp white shirts instead of fatigues.

Regi lifted one hand slightly in my direction, patting the air without looking at me, urging me to stay put. Miriam's eyes went wide, and she turned to look at me imploringly.

As the police walked up to them, the tallest one took out a piece of paper, presumably an arrest warrant, and began reading in Kreyol. Regi replied in a calm tone. The cop ignored him, turning to Miriam instead. This time, I heard him: "*Ou se* Miriam Hartwell?"

Regi translated for her—"Are you Miriam Hartwell?"—and she nodded, glancing back at me, worried. I crouched even lower as two officers stepped around behind her and one of them took out handcuffs. Regi stepped in between them, protesting. He held up his government ID, puffing out his chest, and for a moment, it seemed like it might be working. The tall guy with the paper stepped back, and the one with the handcuffs paused. Then the tall one shook his head and held up the second page of the document, which had a photo, presumably of Miriam. He resumed reading. The other one cuffed Miriam, and when Regi protested again, they shoved him out of the way.

Miriam shook as they led her to one of the vehicles. Regi put his hand on her shoulder, speaking into her ear, translating or just reassuring her. As they placed her inside one of the vehicles, she glanced one last time in my direction.

I had the handgun in my hand, but there was nothing I could do. The situation was all wrong. They were too far from me, too close to her, and I couldn't just start shooting police who were executing a legitimate warrant.

As they closed the door, she called out, "Regi?"

"Don't worry, Miriam," he called back. "We'll get you out, okay?"

She gave him a brave nod, then the door closed.

I'd been so busy and distracted by events in Haiti, I hadn't had time to think of Mike Warren, but I felt a surge of anger and disgust. Even from thousands of miles away, he still managed to fuck things up.

The tall cop stepped back in front of Regi, towering over him, and said, "*Èske w konnen ki kote* Doyle Carrick?"

I don't know what it meant, but I recognized my name, and I knew they were looking for me. Regi shook his head.

For a moment, the cops just stood there, then they got into their vehicles and rumbled down the street.

When they turned the corner, I emerged from my hiding place.

Regi didn't move, just stared after them, his eyes burning with anger and frustration.

As Miriam's terrified voice echoed in my mind, I thought about Nola and tried not to picture her in a similar situation. My stomach clenched tighter.

Regi's head finally swiveled in my direction, and we approached each other, meeting in the middle of the street.

"What did they say?" I asked.

"They had a warrant for her arrest. An extradition request from the United States. For murder." He looked up at me. "There was nothing I could do. There was nothing you could do, either."

I knew he was right.

"They asked about you, too," he said.

"I heard my name."

"You need to be careful while I'm gone."

I nodded.

"We'll get her out," he said. "I know people at DCPJ. I'll call them. The Judicial Police is more independent, not so much under Ducroix's control. If she's really wanted for extradition, she'll be okay. They'll take good care of her if they're sending her back to the States."

"Even in the middle of a coup?"

His confidence faltered, but he said, "Yes. Even the bad guys want to stay on the Americans' good side. She might be safer with them than on the street."

Even if that was true, I wasn't crazy about what would happen to her after extradition, either. I'd have to worry about that later.

"I'll call a lawyer too," he said, "see if I can get her released." He took out his car keys. "But right now, I need to go. And you need to get off the street."

"No. I need to take down Energene."

68

Regi had been skeptical when I told him what I had in mind, and even more so when I said I wanted to ask Toma for help. But his resistance softened when I pointed out that Toma might welcome the chance to get back at the guys who killed Toussaint.

He left a message on Toma's voice mail with my phone number, saying it was urgent that he call me. Then he looked up at me. "I can't guarantee he'll get back to you."

I nodded.

"Don't go out on your own," he said. "I mean it. Not now. It's too dangerous."

I said I wouldn't, not sure whether I was lying or not.

He turned to go, then paused. "Thanks for all your help."

"You too."

"You're a good friend to Haiti. And to me. Take care of yourself."

I felt my throat tighten up. "In a few days, we'll be at Marcel's drinking cold beers with Miriam and exaggerating our stories."

He smiled. "I will look forward to that."

We shook hands, and he left, driving away in Elena's car.

As soon as he was gone, I texted Danny. "Do you know anything about an extradition order for Miriam Hartwell?"

"No. I'll look into it."

Then I called Nola on her phone.

"Doyle," she said immediately, like she'd had the phone in her hand already.

"Hi. Are you okay?"

"I'm fine. I'm stuffed. Are you okay?"

"I'm okay. Where are you?"

"The Carnegie Deli."

"What?" Not what I was expecting.

"I've been here all day. Mikel's building is around the corner. I left a note at the front desk asking him to meet me here." She yawned. "I've been here for hours."

"He might not even be in town."

"According to his Twitter feed, he had breakfast here at the deli this morning and gave a talk at a lunch meeting of some green investment group. He's in town."

"How long have you been there?"

"Since noon. The food is really good, but the portions are huge."

"What are you going to do if he doesn't show up?"

"I don't know. I guess leave him another note and get a room nearby. Try again in the morning."

"You have the files with you?"

She yawned again. "Yes."

"Be careful, babe."

"I will. I'll call you when I hear from him."

"Okay. On my cell phone, I guess. I'm getting rid of this one."

"Why?"

"I've learned a lot since this morning."

"What?" She suddenly sounded wide awake. I told her the basics, about Gaden and Saint Benezet, about what was going on with the Soyagene-X, about what Ducroix seemed to be up to. "Jesus, Doyle, that's horrible. This is . . . big."

264 // Jon McGoran

"I know. That's why you need to be careful."

"You need to be careful, Doyle. You're in the middle of all this. You need to get out of there."

"I will. I will soon. I just have a couple of things still to do."

"What's your plan?"

I had told her most of it when the call came in from Toma. I told her I had to go.

"Be careful, Doyle," she said. "I love you."

"You too, babe. We'll talk soon." Then I clicked over, and she was gone. "Hello?" I said, answering the other call.

"This is the *blan*?"

Switching the calls felt like being wrenched from one world into another. "This is Doyle. Is this Toma?"

"What do you want, *blan*?"

I might have overestimated his enthusiasm. It was more like a sullen indifference. But he was nearby, and he agreed to come see me.

As I waited for him, the sunlight dwindled, and the windows darkened. I practiced with two phones, calling the iPhone from the burner, setting up the interview app to record the conversation. I was surprised it actually worked.

When Toma arrived ten minutes later, I realized his attitude on the phone could have been intended to hide the stress now etched on his face even more deeply than the day before.

Heavy is the head that wears the crown, I thought.

"So tell me again what you need from me," he said.

I explained once again what I had in mind, where I needed to go, what I needed in order to do it. He pointed out flaws and suggested fixes.

When we were done, he summed it up, nodding his head gravely. Then his face cracked, and he let out a short laugh. "You crazy, you know that?"

I shrugged. I thought it was a decent plan.

"You have a gun?" he asked.

I raised my shirt to show him the .45 I'd taken from the Jeep and told him about the M16 that was still wedged behind the seat.

He nodded. "I'll get you to the water. You're on your own after that, right?"

I nodded. "When can we go?"

He looked over his shoulder at the window. "It is dark already."

I shrugged.

"You're in a hurry."

I nodded. "That's right, I am."

"It's more dangerous at night."

I shrugged.

He did too, and a few minutes later, we were crossing the street toward the Jeep. He stopped as we approached it.

"Is this a police Jeep?" he asked.

I nodded.

"Where did you get it?"

"We stole it."

"You stole it?" He snorted. "Who's we?"

"Regi and me."

"*Regi?*" He laughed hard at that. "You're a bad influence on my uncle." He got into the Jeep and punched me in the shoulder, hard but playful. "I like it, though. It's good for him."

I drove, and Toma directed me, away from the ocean and toward the hills. He rooted around in the Jeep as we drove, finding binoculars, a canteen, and a flashlight. He tried on Officer Turnier's cap but frowned in the mirror and put it back.

We made a few detours to avoid roadblocks or protests with piles of burning debris in the middle of the intersection. Toma laughed at those, smiling like it was festive.

At the edge of the city, he directed me onto the same road up into the mountains that Regi and I had taken to come meet Toma the first time.

Behind us, the city's meager lights twinkled in the still-growing darkness. Scattered among the streetlights were smudges of flickering, smoking orange from the fires burning in the streets.

It looked like a place teetering on a knife's edge, that could go either way at any moment. We turned another switchback, and the city disappeared behind a row of uneven shacks, the streetlights and bonfires replaced by the occasional light of a candle or the dim glow of small electronics in the otherwise darkened windows.

The solid pavement once again became patched and pockmarked before turning into random chunks of asphalt embedded in hard-packed dirt. The darkness made it even more harrowing as the road dropped any pretense of paving. Before long, we ran out of road entirely.

"Park here," Toma said.

I pulled over to the side of the road, at the same spot where we had encountered Cyrus. The headlights swept out into the dark night over the city before I killed the engine. It crossed my mind that Toma could be luring me to some kind of ambush, but I had called him. I had set this up.

"I need to pick up some supplies," he said, studying my face in the dark. I stared back at him, trying to look inscrutable. The .45 was a heavy and comforting presence against my stomach. I made sure my hand stayed close to it as I followed him through the darkness along the same path we had taken before.

The small cluster of buildings appeared ahead of us, black shapes in the darkness. I could just make out the white chairs on the front porch.

"Wait here," Toma said, barely visible beside me. I saw his form pass in front of the white chairs and then disappear inside. A dim light came on, spilling just enough illumination through the doorway that I could see a pair of eyes glaring at me in the darkness. I might have flinched when I saw them, because a white smile opened up underneath them. Then I made out the barrel of a gun, maybe two feet from my head.

The eyes leaned in closer. "Thcared?" asked a voice in the darkness.

Cyrus, whom I had disarmed last time I was there.

His eyes looked crazy enough that I was thinking he just might shoot me, that I needed to take the threat seriously. Then I heard my own voice saying, "Thcared thtupid."

His eyes hardened, and I thought this was probably the end. Then Toma's silhouette appeared in the doorway with a bag over his shoulder, and his voice hissed, "Cyrus!"

We both turned to look at him.

They snapped at each other in Kreyol until Cyrus tilted his head, waggled the gun pointed at me, and said in English, "And what's the *blan* doing here?"

Toma studied him in the dark for a moment. Then he pulled a pistol out of his waistband.

Cyrus smiled and cocked his gun, still pointed at my head. All in the same instant, Toma smiled too—a tiny, sad, weary smile—and as his hand came up with the gun, Cyrus's smile faltered.

The muzzle flash from Toma's gun was blinding in the darkness. My pupils slammed shut, and by the time they opened up again, Cyrus was missing an eye, and his smile was falling off his face in chunks.

His gun fired too as his fingers responded to his brain's final command, but he was already dead. In that second flash, I could see the red ruin of his face, his remaining eye blank and wide as it rolled up into his head. Then he dropped, swallowed up into the darkness.

I felt a tiny droplet of moisture on my cheek. I wiped it on my shoulder and kept my eyes away from the sky, keeping open the possibility that it could have been rain.

"He's been challenging me since Toussaint died," Toma said, still standing in the doorway. "I didn't ask to be in charge, but I am. It was going to be him or me."

He reached back and turned off the light, then stepped off the porch. "I didn't like him, but I didn't want to kill him," he said as he walked past me. "If one of us had to go, I'm glad it was him."

The clouds parted, and the moon came out, a thin sliver that washed everything with a faint light.

"He could have shot me," I said, sounding shrill in my own ears.

Toma shrugged. "I hardly know you, man." Then he turned and walked away. "Come on if you're coming."

69

We hiked without speaking at first, the birds and crickets making plenty of sounds to fill the void. The moon came and went, lighting our way and then disappearing and leaving us in darkness. Most of the time we walked through low, scrubby brush, but at times, we had to take turns hacking through the trees. Toma had grabbed two machetes, an automatic rifle, and a bag of salty plantain snacks. He shared the machetes and the plantain chips. The rifle he kept for himself.

I didn't know the guy, didn't know how to read him, especially not at night, swinging a machete around. But he seemed upset. I had no idea if Cyrus was the first life he'd taken, and I wasn't ready to concede that he had no choice in doing it, but I understood his predicament. I was heartened that it still wasn't easy for him.

"Fucking Haiti," he said, bitter and weary, fifteen minutes after we'd set out.

I didn't know what to say to that. He had a point. It was not a country without problems. But it had upsides, as well. People like Regi and Marcel and Elena. People like Portia. And it wasn't my country to criticize. How many times a day did I say, "Fucking America"—and with good reason too. But I wasn't Haitian, so I kept my mouth shut.

"The only successful slave rebellion in the history of the world. Did you know that?"

"I might have."

"Yeah, well, you might not have. I never heard it mentioned when I was in the States. Spartacus, sure. There's movies about him. '*I'm Spartacus*'. . . '*No, I'm Spartacus.*' Fuck that—who wants to be fucking Spartacus? I want to be Louverture. At least he *won* his fucking rebellion." He laughed bitterly and hacked at a nearby tree branch, his voice growing louder as he continued.

"This country has such a proud history, and it's such a fucking mess. Don't get me wrong—I know it's not all the Haitians' fault. The Americans and the French and the Dominicans, fucking Dole Fruit and now motherfucking Stoma Corporation, they've been lining up for two hundred years—four hundred years—to rape us and kill us and take our land and our money and our resources. Then they all line up and say, 'Poor fucking Haiti, the poorest country in this hemisphere'—as if it wasn't the most profitable colony in the world before they squeezed it dry. As if they didn't all get together and decide to make Haiti an example, to make sure those black slave-revolting savages would regret the day they dared to take back the land they'd been working themselves to death on, dared to string up the bastards who'd been killing them for generations on it." He sighed, and his voice came down again. "As if they hadn't agreed to make sure the first successful slave revolt was going to be the last one, too."

He kicked a rock in the moonlight, sending it skittering into the brush, causing an indignant squeak and a frantic thrashing in the bushes.

As the silence returned, I wondered if I should chime in, but he was making a lot of sense, and he seemed like he wasn't finished. Plus he was swinging that machete around pretty good. I kept quiet.

"We drove out the French, drove out the Americans, built the citadel—the Eighth Wonder of the World. Sometimes it seems like we can do anything, and sometimes the most basic things other countries do every day, they're just beyond us."

He paused again. Kicked another rock.

"I know what Regi thinks. About Toussaint. About me. But Toussaint was a good guy. He was my friend. Yes, he was a criminal, but he was born into a criminal world. You don't play basketball on a football pitch. You don't play Scrabble on a chessboard. He got himself born into Haiti, the poor bastard, so Haiti was the game he played. And he was good. He wasn't a murderer, he was a thief, in a land where stealing is the national fucking pastime. And nobody cared until he stole food from those rich bastards who weren't even eating it. Who weren't sharing it or selling it or giving it away. They were letting it sit there while people starved. So what if he stole it? He got it into the mouths of the people who were hungry.

"Maybe that's the one crime that can't be forgiven. And when they chase him down and kill him for it, leave me to try to pick up the pieces, within days that asshole Cyrus is making a run at me. Cyrus! He was fucking seventeen years old. He wasn't ready to lead a Cub Scout troop, much less a gang. And you know what?" He turned and looked at me, his eyes gleaming. "If he'd been ready, I'd have let him. Because I never wanted the fucking job."

I was stunned by his eloquence and passion and smarts, and I realized I'd made some assumptions about him. It made me wonder what other assumptions I needed to question.

He sniffled in the darkness. I felt bad for him, and I wanted to reach out, maybe put a hand on his shoulder. But the way he'd been swinging that machete, I couldn't be sure he wouldn't lop it off me.

"That's how it is with Cardon," he said quietly. "He seems like a halfway decent president, but I'm not going to get too attached, because they're turning on him. Fucking Ducroix. Fucking Haiti. Even the cops are gangsters here."

272 // Jon McGoran

He was quiet for a few moments, and he turned to look at me, as if he was wondering how all this was going down. I felt like I had to say something.

"So why did you come back? From the States, I mean."

"Because they kicked me out." He laughed. "But I missed Haiti, too. It's home. I love this country. I really do. But man, sometimes it's exhausting."

70

We came over a slight rise, and there below us was Labadee, the re-sort. The red-roofed cabanas were softly lit, and even the modern hotel rising incongruously from the middle of it seemed somehow subdued.

Out on the ocean was Archie Pearce's megayacht—bright white and bathed in architectural lighting. We stared at it for a moment. Then Toma tapped me on the shoulder and we moved down the slope toward the water.

The incline was steep at first, until we came to a trail that leveled off, winding through the trees toward a set of rough-hewn steps that descended to an open space behind the village of Labadie. A pair of dogs barked at each other in the distance. The pale moonlight showed a small grassy area narrowing into a path that curved through the village toward the water, lapping not far away.

Toma pointed down the path, and as we walked along, the trees and small houses closed in on either side of us. Behind the sounds of crickets and other insects, I could hear the gentle murmur of humans—talking, breathing, eating, the music of women laughing. We passed a couple of narrow paths leading left and right between the jumble of huts.

Toma paused, getting his bearings. Off to the side, I spotted a pair of young boys crouching in the shadows, staring at us. I nodded to them and they ran away. Then we were moving again, down toward the beach.

Fifty feet away, I could see the water sparkling in the moonlight. I heard laughter again, this time men. There was a small fire on the beach, half a dozen men clustered around it, sharing a bottle. They stopped laughing when we walked out from under the trees, but they smiled good-naturedly. From the twinkling in their eyes, I was pretty sure the bottle had made its way around a few times already.

Toma nodded at them and spoke in Kreyol, then pointed at me with his thumb and said in English, "He needs to rent a boat."

The man holding the bottle waved his free hand around in a sweeping gesture and replied in Kreyol. He was thin, maybe seventy, with a scraggly gray beard and mustache. After he spoke, the rest of them laughed.

Toma did, too. Then he turned and looked at me, "He wants to know if you have a date with a mermaid."

I laughed too, and the old man passed the bottle to Toma. He took a drink and passed it to me. Rum, and not bad, either. I took a second sip and passed it back to the old man, who passed it on to the man to his right.

"I wish," I replied.

He laughed. "*Non mwen se Klod,*" he said, then very deliberately to me, "My name is Claude."

"Toma."

"I am Doyle."

Claude nodded and smiled. "We are closed for the night," he said to me in English. "You go where? Do what? What you pay?"

Toma cocked an eyebrow at me, waiting. I didn't feel like I could answer questions one and two, so I took out my wallet and looked inside. "One thousand gourdes. For one hour, probably less."

I held out four 250-gourde notes.

He raised his eyebrows and shrugged, looking me up and down.

He took the money, then said, "You leave deposit," pointing at my wrist. "Your watch."

I paused. The watch had been a gift from Nola. It was inscribed. It was nice. But it was only a deposit. If anything happened to me, I doubted Nola would get the watch back, anyway.

"I want it back," I said.

"You come back, I give it back."

I unfastened it and held it out to the old man. His fingers closed on it, but then he froze as a deep voice behind us said, "*Mwen pral pran ki.*"

Instantly, the men around the fire went quiet. They all stopped smiling.

I turned and saw a mountain of buzzkill stepping out of the shadows. He looked a little more impaired than the gentlemen around the fire. Instead of a sparkle, his eyes had a gleam, and there was nothing friendly about it.

He was alone, just him and the gun he held out in front of him. He walked up and pressed it against Toma's forehead. He took the watch out of the old guy's hand and put it in his pocket. Then he turned to Toma, keeping the gun pressed against his forehead. He took the rifle from Toma and slung it over his shoulder, then did the same with the backpack. I thought about shooting him, taking the same chance Toma had taken with me, but I guess we'd gotten to know each other a little better since then. I didn't want to risk it.

He turned to me, swaying under the influence of whatever he was on and placing the gun against my forehead. "*Ki moun ki fuck ou ye?*"

I only understood the one word, but it said a lot. I was thinking I should have shot him when I had the chance.

Toma translated. "He asks, 'Who the fuck are you?'"

I didn't know what to say, and I was concerned that even if I came up with something clever and hilarious, it would be lost in translation and no one would laugh. The big guy swung the gun away from my face and jammed it back against Toma's head, barking some kind of question. He seemed to be getting angrier. I had a feeling this was going to end badly. But I was also worried that the game was going to go on for longer than I had time to play.

"I'm the one who knocks," I said to distract him, trusting he wouldn't catch the reference.

He looked at me, confused and belligerent. He swung the gun back in my direction, and when it was midway between Toma and me, I decked him.

He was massive, and I knew I wouldn't drop him with one punch, but I figured with three or four, maybe.

The first punch was a right, square in the face. I kept my arm in place, blocking the gun while I followed up with a hard left to his ear that got him staggering. As my right hand wrapped around the gun, it went off, loud and close. I went in fast with the left again, connecting with his jaw and snapping his head around. His grip on the gun loosened enough that I was able to take it away from him. He was already teetering—probably as much from intoxication as anything I had dished out—but he was big, and he hadn't seemed all that nice to start with. I had no desire to see what effect a couple of punches had on his demeanor. I hesitated, just for an instant. Then I brought the butt of the gun down hard against the bridge of his nose. He might have been falling already, but he went down harder after that, hitting the sand with a solid thud.

Toma looked at me with new respect.

After checking to make sure none of my fingers had been shot off, I knelt down and pulled the rifle and the backpack off the big guy on the ground, handed them back to Toma. Then I took the watch out of his pocket. I held it out to the old guy, and he nodded and took it.

He stood and looked at the bills in his hand, then peeled off one of the notes and handed it back to me. He turned to walk down toward the beach and motioned for us to follow, mumbling in Kreyol. As we followed behind, Toma turned to me with a crooked smile. "He says he never liked that guy."

71

Claude led us to the edge of the water and showed me how to operate the boat. It was a low-slung wooden skiff, painted a bright pink that looked muted in the darkness. It was a bit of a mess, cluttered with tools, empty bottles, and other things. The tiny outboard motor looked better suited for beating eggs than a hasty retreat. There was a pair of oars, as well, and I wondered if I'd make better time with them.

Whatever concerns I had were probably mutual, though. As we loaded the tools into the boat, Toma quietly explained our plan. Claude clutched my watch tightly. I got the feeling he was expecting to keep it.

When we were done, though, he clapped a hand on my shoulder and said, "*Fè atansyon. Pote bato mwen tounen.*"

Toma smiled. "He says to be careful and bring his boat back."

I moved a roll of duct tape and a corroded dry-cell battery out of the way so I could sit down in the boat. Toma shook my hand and then gave the boat a decent shove away from the beach. As I placed my hand on the pull cord, I paused and looked out onto the water.

The lights from Pearce's yacht glimmered on the rippling surface. It was a massive boat and probably teeming with hired guns. As I went over the plan one more time in my head, it seemed like there were too many pieces. It came apart in my mind, turning from something solid into sand that slipped through my fingers.

But that wasn't the first time I'd felt that way about a plan. Besides, I told myself as I yanked the cord, I didn't need every part of it to work in order for any of it to work. A partial success could still count as a win.

The engine started right up. It was a dinky little thing, but when I opened the throttle, I felt a slight surge as the boat pushed against the tiny waves.

Making sure I was pointed in the right direction, I took out my phones and erased the call history from the flip phone. Then I set up the interview. I called the burner from my iPhone, and when the call came in, I answered it and put it on speaker. Then I called the number for the interview app and merged the two calls. It was now recording.

Finally, I turned the brightness all the way down on the burner. It wasn't completely off, but even in the darkness, I could barely see it was on. I checked to make sure the iPhone was still connected. Then I pressed the mute button and set it down in the boat.

By the time I had done all that, I was a hundred yards away. I killed the engine, took up the oars, and began to gently row.

Off to my right, the fake resort town of Labadee was bathed in a dim orange glow. It appeared strangely still at first, but as I looked closer, I could see movement in the windows of the hotel, a couple of guards walking around down below on the beach and the otherwise deserted docks.

Straight ahead of me was Archie Pearce's yacht. As I got closer, I could see people moving about inside it. On the upper deck, a guard in tactical garb held an assault rifle. He was standing next to a large searchlight that could make getting away more difficult if it came to that, but it wasn't lit at the moment.

Through the windows, I could see a couple of people moving around on the middle deck, in front of where the helicopter was perched. I couldn't tell if any of them was Pearce.

More people were inside the lower level. That's where Pearce would be. It was open in the back, a deck area just inches above the waterline. That's where I'd have to board.

As I drew nearer, I got a better look at the lower deck. It was set up with lounge chairs on the near side and a café table and chairs on the far side. A single guard was pacing back and forth at regular intervals.

I knew I was going to be apprehended. That was kind of part of the plan. But if possible, I wanted to get inside before it happened.

I stopped rowing forty feet away, slowly bobbing in the water. From this distance, the yacht loomed massive, four or five stories tall. It was covered in lights, but all focused inward and upward. They didn't extend far out onto the water. As long as they didn't turn the searchlight on, I'd be nearly invisible to anyone standing in that light. I spent a minute sizing things up. Then, using one oar, I gently paddled toward the side of the yacht, using a J stroke to stay as silent as possible. I aimed for what looked like a relative blind spot two-thirds of the way toward the front of the boat.

I made it undetected, bracing my hand against the sleek hull so I didn't bang against it. I put down the oar, and placing my bare hands against the side of the yacht, I pulled the boat toward the back, ducking under each porthole I passed.

As I approached the open rear deck, I paused, digging my fingernails into a strip of molding to hold myself in place. After a couple of seconds, the guard walked up to the side, barely six feet away from me. I ducked down as he stood there for a moment, gazing out at the black water. Then he turned and walked to the other side. I counted the seconds until he returned. Twenty between when he left and returned, four seconds standing there looking out onto the water, turn around, pause for a deep breath that seemed full of ennui and self-doubt, and then disappear for another twenty seconds. A part of me actually felt bad for him, for the mistakes he had made that had led him to this place.

Then again, he was working on a billion-dollar yacht, probably making ten times my salary, and I was standing in a leaky wooden dinghy and possibly about to lose my crappy job. But I knew his day was about to take a turn. When he turned and walked over to the other side, I picked up the old dry-cell battery in my right hand and held the oar in my left.

Twenty seconds later, he returned and stared out at the water for four seconds. As he started to turn back, I heaved the battery as hard as I could into the air. As it arced high over the boat, I two-handed the oar and swung it with everything I had. The guard was just finishing his depressing sigh and beginning his trip to the other side of the boat when the oar connected with the back of his head.

My timing was almost perfect. The oar rang with a hollow wooden tone, but a microsecond later there was a loud splash on the other side of the boat, followed by the sound of multiple footsteps and hushed but urgent voices.

I grabbed the railing on the side of the yacht and pulled myself aboard, almost stepping on the guard I had just knocked out. I grabbed a towel the size of a bedspread from one of the lounge chairs and threw it over him.

The decks receded like steps, and at the back of each one, I could see one or two guards peering out at the water on the other side of the vessel. The searchlight came on, knifing out into the darkness on the other side of the boat.

Directly in front of me was an open sliding glass door leading into a wood-paneled room bathed in the bright, warm light of obscene wealth.

I scanned the scene in front of me, but there was no time to pause and figure out what it meant or what I was walking into. I was on the move before I even knew what I was doing.

72

"I thought that was you out on the road," Archie Pearce said, taking the cigar out of his mouth and cackling with something like glee. His other hand held a snifter, the amber liquor sloshing up the sides as he laughed. Even across the room, I could see the liquid coating the inside of the glass. "I had a feeling I hadn't seen the last of you."

He didn't seem the least bit intimidated by the gun I was aiming at his head. I hoped he was faking it. I also hoped I seemed just as unintimidated by the dozen guns now pointed at me.

Bradley Bourden seemed definitely intimidated, and he didn't have any guns pointed at him. Maybe he had some idea of why I was there.

"Carrick?" he said, alarmed, looking around at the men pointing guns at me. "What are you doing here?"

"Yes, tell us, Mr. Carrick," Pearce said, his eyes twinkling with amusement. "Why are you here?"

The room was as solidly luxurious as anything I could have imagined on dry land. Rich wood everywhere, crystal chandelier, oriental rugs. I almost laughed out loud at the stone fireplace.

Pearce and Bourden were sitting across from each other in massive green leather armchairs. Bourden had a snifter and a cigar just like Pearce, but he didn't seem to be enjoying either quite as much, squinting in the smoke.

I could imagine what the room had been like before my arrival— Bourden and Pearce collegially sparring with each other, negotiating the terms of some deal while their men eyed each other up, like an old mob parlay or a presidential summit. I hoped things were about to get a little less friendly.

A quartet of men stood behind each of them. Four more posted in the corners of the room. The ones behind Pearce and those posted in the corners were prime examples of Darkstar private soldiers—solid, chiseled, and handsome, like some kind of genetically enhanced Aryan-dream assholes, complete with the sort of dead lethal eyes that had seen horrible things and wouldn't flinch at seeing them again. And might even look forward to it.

Bourden's men I recognized individually. To his right, Royce and Divock glared at me, Royce's head quickly turning red from the neck upward and the ears inward. To his left were Axe-Man and Old Spice, registering a smoldering recognition, not quite cool enough or dead enough inside to pull off the dead-eye stare.

"I'm just here to talk to Mr. Pearce." I held up my hands, the gun and the burner phone in one hand. "I want to tell him some of the interesting things I've discovered about what's been going on around here these last few days." I made a show of putting the gun and the phone on the table next to me, the phone facedown, disarming myself of both of them as if they were equally dangerous. I pulled the sheaf of papers out of my waistband and held both hands up in the air. "There's something you need to know, Pearce."

"Get rid of him," Bourden snapped. His face was turning red too, although Royce was standing close enough, it could have just been reflecting off him.

Royce smiled thinly and tilted his head at Axe-Man and his pal. They moved toward me, but Pearce held up his hand and said, "Wait."

The Darkstar clones bristled to a higher degree of attention, and the atmosphere in the room changed. The angles of the guns changed, enough that Axe-Man and his sidekick paused, aware that their place in the power dynamic had changed, or at least revealed itself to be different.

"I'd like to hear what he has to say," Pearce said, his eyes once again twinkling with equal parts good humor and malice. He took a sip of brandy and nodded toward one of his men, who stepped forward and patted me down, thoroughly but efficiently. I handed him the papers, and he put them on the side table next to Pearce, who didn't look at them, instead taking a long draw from his cigar. The tip of it glowed red for a moment before he released a dense, languid curl of smoke that unfurled around his head. "Go on."

Bourden's eye twitched as he glanced at the papers, trying to see what they were.

"I know you two are up to something together," I said. "Working together to change the regime down here, get rid of Cardon."

"He knows," Bourden hissed. He turned to Axe-Man. "Shoot him!"

Axe-Man stepped uncertainly toward me but froze when Pearce barked, "No. Shut up, Bradley. I'd like to hear what he has to say."

Bourden paled.

Pearce turned back to me, the veneer of amusement thinning considerably.

"Energene is working on a plan of its own," I said. "Something that will hurt a lot of people, including you and your shareholders."

Pearce raised an eyebrow at that and smiled. "I doubt that very much."

Bourden shook his head and rolled his eyes, like this was nonsense. He took a deep drink, hiding his face in his snifter.

I nodded. "They're coming after you. Coming after your lucrative Stoma-Grow corn market."

Pearce laughed, but Bourden just stared at me.

"Of course he is," Pearce said. "He's just doing his job, Mr. Carrick, the same as countless others. They're all after my market share, and I would be too. But none of them have a hope of succeeding."

"Oh, this time they might. If you look at those papers, you'll see. They're using a specially modified Soyagene—"

Bourden shot a hard, urgent glare and a nod at Axe-Man, who abruptly raised his gun in my direction and even more abruptly staggered sideways with a small, black-red hole in the side of his head.

73

Bourden and his remaining men gasped but didn't move. Neither did Pearce's men, except the one who had shot Axe-Man. Royce, for once, went pale, the redness draining from his face as if someone had flushed his head.

"Jesus, Archie," Bourden exclaimed softly, looking pretty pale himself.

Pearce ignored him, gesturing two of his men toward Axe-Man's body. "Get that off the rug before it stains."

They hustled forward and lifted the body, maneuvering it so that the thin trickle of blood from the hole in Axe-Man's temple came down the front of his shirt and not onto the floor.

They dumped the body onto the deck outside, where any blood could be hosed off. As they came back in, I realized how much things had changed. Two of Pearce's guns were still pointed at me, but the rest were on Bourden and his remaining men.

Pearce turned to me. "Continue." The sparkle in his eyes was gone, replaced by a sharp, black gleam. I was reminded of a predator, its senses sharply accentuated as it closed in on its prey.

For a moment, looking at those eyes, I almost didn't tell him.

286 // J ON M C G ORAN

I thought about all the people who might suffer and die if Bourden's plan succeeded, but I wondered how many more would suffer and die if Pearce and Stoma remained unchallenged at the top of the heap, tightening their control on the world's food supply, up to God knows how many evil plans of their own. It sickened me to be helping him retain his control, but I knew it was what I had to do.

"Energene has a secret version of Soyagene. It contains modified Stoma-Grow corn proteins, making anyone who eats it severely allergic to Stoma-Grow corn. They're releasing it into the food supply. They're going to make Stoma-Grow virtually inedible around the world."

Pearce stared at me expressionlessly for a moment.

Bourden's face was equally still, except for his eyes scanning the place as if he were looking for a way out.

"They're already ramping up production of their Early Rise corn to fill the void. The two of you are trying to topple the Cardon regime, right? Control Haiti's vote in tomorrow's trade vote?"

Pearce stared at me blankly. "Perhaps. Why?"

I pointed at the papers on the table next to him. "As soon as it's a done deal, Energene is going to start releasing their modified Soyagene, bit by bit, all around the world. It will start as a mysterious respiratory disease, first in the world's poorest countries, like Haiti, so no one will care too much about it. But then they'll release it everywhere else. Their secret schedule is right there in those papers. You can see for yourself."

Pearce looked down at the papers, flicking through them one by one as if he understood each of them in an instant. He had a lifetime in this area, and I had told him what to look for, but I was still struck by the strong sense that I was witnessing a truly formidable intellect absorbing everything on each of those dense pages in an instant before moving on to the next. Putting it all together.

"Some of it already got out," I said. "Stolen. Two entire villages were sickened because of it, but Energene and their friends put out a story that it was Ebola, then they wiped out both villages to hide their tracks."

Pearce looked over at Bourden with restrained anger and something else, something I was horrified to recognize as admiration.

The room was silent except for the lapping of the water outside. I heard a faint wooden bounce as the skiff gently connected with the hull of the yacht. I felt an almost irresistible desire to be out there in it, getting away from this place, from these people.

Finally, Pearce put the papers down and smiled. It was a chilling thing to see a smile under those gleaming eyes. I was relieved that they turned to look at Bourden and not me.

"Not bad, Bradley," he said. "I'm impressed. Really. Shame you can't use those smarts for more productive purposes." He laughed. "You too, Carrick, for putting everything together once again. You're smarter than you look. Shame you're wasting your life in civil service."

He turned back to the papers, thinking. "Well," he said finally, folding his hands across his midsection and sitting back in his chair. "Looks like we have a long night ahead of us, rounding up all this"—he looked at the papers again—"'Soyagene GES-5322x.' Making sure no more of it gets out. Ever." He turned to the henchman standing directly beside him. "We'll need to prepare secure quarters for our guests."

I didn't know if he was referring to me as well as Bourden's men, but I couldn't risk staying the night. I'd been dying to ask Pearce how it felt not being the most evil man in the room, but as his men moved to disarm Royce and Divock and Old Spice, I turned and bolted.

That bullet had been let loose pretty casually in there, and I fully expected another one to follow me outside.

But it didn't.

I ran low and aimed for the railing, placing one foot between Axe-Man's body and the guy I had knocked out with the oar. As much as I wanted to keep my head down, as I approached the railing, I looked up and out into the night, trying to spot the skiff before I went over. Luckily, it had only drifted ten feet, and I landed close enough to it that my hand grazed the side as I went under. My head scraped the bottom as I passed underneath and came up the other side. I braced my elbow on the side of the boat and frantically grabbed the pull

288 // Jon McGoran

cord, expecting a hail of bullets to turn both the boat and me into a churning froth of blood and splinters at any moment. As I tensed to pull the cord, the searchlight flashed on and found me immediately.

Just before I pulled the cord, I heard Archie Pearce's voice saying, "Let him go."

The angles and ergonomics were all wrong, but with the help of terror and adrenaline, I ripped the cord as hard as I could. The motor almost came off the boat entirely, but the engine engaged, and the boat slid forward.

I hung on to the side with one hand and rested the other on the tiller, in the back of my mind hoping my iPhone case was still water resistant. The boat was listing at a crazy angle, and water sloshed in as I went, but I was relieved to be shielded from Archie Pearce and his men. At least I wouldn't see it coming.

On the softly lit docks of Labadee, a cluster of guards had assembled to see the commotion. But the action was over, and it hadn't involved them directly. They stood there and watched me put-putting around the spit of land that separated the fake Labadee from the village of Labadie. Soon they were out of sight.

By the time I was halfway back to shore, I realized the searchlight wasn't even on anymore. I made sure the iPhone was secure and hoisted myself into the skiff and then grabbed the oars and started rowing along with the outboard. As I nudged the tiller with my foot to keep us on course, I felt an odd assortment of unfamiliar muscle pains in my core from having pulled the cord in such a contorted position. I couldn't tell if my rowing was making the boat move any faster, but I wanted to do everything I could to get away from there as fast as possible.

A few seconds later, the cabin from which I had just escaped lit up with a muzzle flash. A gunshot rang out over the water, followed by an agonized scream.

I found a little more strength in my arms, rocketing the boat through the water. I didn't stop until the oars dug into the semidry sand on the beach.

74

Toma was waiting for me on the beach, towering over Claude. They each took an arm and helped me out of the boat. My arms were trembling, but I couldn't tell how much of it was from the rowing and how much from the nerves.

"I'm okay," I told them. As soon as I was on dry land, I checked the iPhone. It was still recording.

There were five missed calls—two from Regi, two from work, one from Nola. She'd left a message.

"We heard shots," Toma said. "You okay?"

"I'm okay." I pressed the phone against my ear, trying to listen to what was happening on the boat, what might have been recorded. I could hear voices, but they sounded distant. I hoped it was because they had moved to another room, and that the entire recording wasn't like that.

Claude inspected his boat in the moonlight. He gave me a sad smile as he slid my watch off his wrist and held it out to me. I thought about letting him keep it, my mind making a rough calculation of the odds I was going to get killed down here anyway—I'd hate for the watch to end up on the wrist of some Darkstar asshole—but I shook

that off as negative thinking. It was a gift from Nola. I needed to
bring myself and my watch back to her.

"*Mesi*," I said as I slipped it onto my wrist.

He smiled and patted my arm. "Glad you okay."

"We need to go," Toma said, snapping his fingers in my face to
make sure I was paying attention. "Your large friend woke up unhappy." He pointed over at the giant, man-shaped indentation in the
sand. Claude's drinking friends had left, as well. Toma smiled. "We hid
when he woke up, but he saw you out on the boat. He might be coming
back with friends."

Claude cackled and said something in Kreyol, holding up the remaining gourdes.

Toma smiled. "He says he'd give you back more money if you
knock the big guy out again."

We had a brief laugh. Then Toma said, "Regi called. You need to
call him."

I looked at the display on the iPhone. It was still muted and still
connected to the other phone, still recording whatever was being said
on Archie Pearce's boat. It could be a useless garbled mess, but it
could also be enough to take down two of the worst corporate crimi-
nals on the planet.

Toma followed my gaze, then held up his own phone. "You can
use my phone," he said, looking around to see if anyone was coming.
"But we have to go. Now."

As we ran up the steps, we heard angry voices behind and below us,
but they quickly faded away. When we reached the top, we jogged
along the trail, slowing to a brisk walk as we entered the woods. As
soon as I was confident we were out of earshot, I checked the phone
again. For whatever reason—maybe we were out of range or out of
time, or maybe the phone on the yacht had been discovered—but the
app had stopped recording and the call disconnected.

I stopped walking and went to Nola's voice mail. "Doyle—" she
said, and then the screen went dark except for a little circle spinning
for a second before winking out.

"*Fuck!*" I said. Out of juice. At least it had held out until now.

"What is it?" Toma said.

"I do need to borrow your phone."

He handed it over without question, but I think he might have had one or two when I dialed the thirteen digits of the country code and Nola's number.

The call went straight to voice mail. "It's Doyle," I said. "Call me at this number."

I tried to stay focused and positive, not dwell on the fact that she hadn't answered. I tried to remember the sound of her voice on her message, the tone as she said my name. She hadn't sounded desperate, I told myself, or upset or even urgent. She'd sounded fine. She'd sounded okay.

I took a deep breath and called Regi. He answered almost immediately. "Allo?"

"It's Doyle."

"How did it go?"

"I don't know exactly. Bourden was there, the guy from Energene. He wasn't happy to see me, but I said my piece, told Pearce what Energene was up to, then I got the hell out of there. They're definitely not friends like they used to be."

"How bad?"

"Pearce's men shot one of Bourden's, right there in front of me. There was another shot after I left."

"*Woy!*"

"It might have been Bourden himself, but probably not. Pearce is keeping them on the boat while his men try to prevent the Soyagene rollout." I told him about the phone and how it kept recording, even after I left. "The battery died before I could listen back. But I'm pretty sure we got something."

He laughed. "Doyle, that's great. I didn't think it would work."

"We'll see what it picks up. And I don't know if this will slow down their other plans for the CASCATA vote. Did you talk to Cardon? Is there any word on Miriam?"

"Miriam is okay. I spoke to the DCPJ. They are holding her for extradition, but she is safe and being treated well." He paused. "I found Cardon right where I thought. It's not good. He is holed up in the mountains near Limbe with a few hundred Presidential Guard. Ducroix evacuated him from the capital. He was supposed to meet up with UN troops in Plaisance, but it was a trap. Cardon's men realized it was an ambush and went elsewhere, but they have no communication, no cell service. Even the satellite phone isn't working. As I was sneaking out, I saw Ducroix's troops massing around the mountain. At least a thousand of them. There will be a coup, and it will be soon."

"Do you think the new situation between Stoma and Energene could slow things down?"

"I doubt it matters at this point. Ducroix will just deal with whoever comes out on top. Even if they try to call it off, I don't see him backing away from a shot at power, not when he is this close. And not after he has shown his colors."

"The trade vote is tomorrow."

"Exactly."

"What about the trade minister, the guy we saw at Ducroix's compound? Do you think he's in on it?"

"Vincent Adrien? I believe so, yes."

"So if they control him, do they even need a coup?"

"Not to place the vote but for it to stand. They can't place the vote and then have Cardon disavow it and say it was a dirty trick."

"So they might wait until right after the vote, so there is no question about its legitimacy."

"That's right. The vote will be made during the Cardon regime. Afterward, they can just say they are upholding the will of the previous regime."

"But won't Cardon say otherwise?"

He sighed into the phone. "Not if they kill him."

75

Toma had heard enough of my conversation with Regi to get the gist. I could feel the heat coming off him as it stirred up the anger and frustration he'd expressed on the way out there. His jaw ground in silent fury as we hiked through the night.

When we got back to the gang's hideaway, two of his men were waiting for us, Janjak and Westè, the two who had been making fun of Cyrus before. They looked scared and angry, aiming rifles at us until they saw it was Toma.

The larger of them, Janjak, stepped closer. He leaned forward to speak in a loud whisper. *"Cyrus mouri."*

Toma took a deep breath, puffed out his chest. *"Mwen touye* Cyrus. I killed him."

Janjak and Westè looked at each other, thinking.

Janjak said, *"Poukisa?"*

Toma stepped closer to him, looked him in the eye. "Because he challenged me. So I had to. *Sa se yon pwoblèm?"* I think he was asking if they had a problem with that.

Janjak thought for a moment, then stepped back and shook his head. "No, boss."

"*Bon.*"

Toma spoke to them both in Kreyol. I picked up enough to realize he was leaving Janjak in charge.

As we came around the hilltop to where we had left the Jeep, Cap-Haïtien opened up below us. It looked worse than before—a haze of smoke hanging over twice as many fires, accompanied now by dozens of flashing police and emergency lights.

As we were about to get into the Jeep, Toma paused and sighed, looking out at the city. His eyes looked sad and tired, old beyond their years. "I don't know if Haiti can go through this once again," he said.

I didn't know what to tell him. All the reassurances that came to mind sounded hollow and baseless even before I said them out loud. So I said nothing. I got in the Jeep and waited for him to do the same, wondering what I could do to somehow help make this time different.

Toma got in beside me, and I took off down the hill. The dust rising behind us drifted away, merging with the haze of smoke over the city. We zigzagged through the chaos of Cap-Haïtien, keeping our distance from both police and protestors.

After what felt like hours, we got to Elena's. Toma had a key. He opened the door, and we paused. Lights were on, and we could hear the sound of movement upstairs.

He looked at me. A shrug was the best I could offer.

"*Matant,* Elena?" he called tentatively.

The movement stopped, and for a moment, we all froze—Toma, me, and whoever was upstairs.

Then a thin voice called down the steps, "Toma?"

"*Wi, Matant . . .*"

Elena hurried down the stairs and ran to Toma, kissing his face, caressing it. Her cheeks were wet with tears. I couldn't tell if she was crying from relief that he was safe or if there was something else.

They spoke to each other in Kreyol, both of them upset. I felt like I was intruding, but I also felt like something was going on, and I needed to know what. "Is everything okay?" I asked.

Elena nodded and wiped her eyes.

Toma looked worried. "The men from the Interior Ministry came back, the ones who told them they have to cook for the troops. Now they tell them they have to go to Mouelle and cook there for even more troops."

"Where's that?"

"It's a tiny little village south of Limbe," Toma said, his voice edged with worry and frustration. "It's not right. They shouldn't be able to just tell them they have to." There was a vulnerability in his eyes, and I glimpsed the little boy in him.

Elena reached up and cupped his cheek, reassuringly.

"Did they say why? Why do they have to go there?" I asked.

Toma seemed almost annoyed at the irrelevance of the question, but he translated for me.

She shook her head and replied.

"They wouldn't say," he explained. "But she thinks the troops are gathering there for some big operation. She says she has to meet Marcel in two hours, and then they have to leave in order to get down there in time to have breakfast ready for two thousand men before dawn."

South of Limbe. That's where Cardon and his men were hiding. Elena and Marcel were being forced to feed the men who were going to kill the president.

"Ask her what they have to cook for them."

Toma looked at me sideways, his forehead wrinkled like he thought it an odd question. But he understood I might be onto something. He asked her, and she waved her hand dismissively as she replied.

"Just *mayi moulin*," he said. "It's like a corn porridge, or polenta. She says it's a simple dish but a big job to cook for so many."

Polenta. Corn polenta.

Elena went into the kitchen, and I pulled Toma aside. "You told Regi you weren't there when that food aid was stolen. Is that true?"

He looked at me indignantly. "Of course it's true. If I said it, it's true."

"No, it's not. You're lying. Tell me the truth. You were there, weren't you?"

He glared at me with the familiar smoldering resentment cornered felons reserve for badgering cops who have something on them. He was my only ally, and I didn't want to damage the rapport we'd developed. But I needed to know. "Fuck you. No, and it's none of your business, anyway. I don't need to tell you anything."

"I'm not judging," I told him, and that was true. "I'm not a cop here; I can't arrest you. And frankly, I don't even think what you did was totally wrong, considering. But right now, for the sake of Regi and your aunt and everyone else, you need to tell me if you had any direct involvement with the theft of that aid shipment."

He glared at me another moment, then rolled his eyes and exhaled. "Okay, yes. So what? It was Toussaint's idea, but I was with him when he broke in and stole it. You satisfied?" His eyes were half daring me to do anything about it, half afraid that maybe I would.

"Great," I said, clapping him on the shoulder. "Do you think you could do it again?"

76

A slow grin spread over Toma's face when I told him what I had in mind. It faded when I got to the part his aunt and Marcel would have to play, but he sucked it up and agreed, anyway. It was touch and go as he explained it to Elena, especially when he had to admit why he knew where the Soyagene was. She was a little more judgmental than I had been, and disapproval of what he had done was plain on her face.

When Toma finished explaining to her what I had in mind, I made sure he told her she was under no pressure, that she didn't have to do it if she didn't want to, and that she could be in some danger.

She nodded thoughtfully, and I was relieved she didn't say yes right away. She said she would talk to Marcel about it, and she needed to talk to Regi.

I asked if I could speak to him first, so I could talk him through the plan to make sure it was scientifically and practically sound. I'd feel a lot better about getting Elena and Marcel involved if Regi was behind it, as well. She dialed the phone and handed it to me.

He answered in a hushed voice. "I am halfway home," he said.

"It's Doyle," I said. "There's some new developments. I have a plan."

298 // Jon McGoran

I told him about Elena and Marcel being sent to Mouelle, cooking for two thousand troops. I told him my idea to enlist her help. "So, before anything else, do you think it could work?"

"It's clever," he said begrudgingly. "I'm not crazy about it, but the science is sound." He let out a sigh. "I guess it's a good plan."

"If we're going to try it, we need to do it now, as soon as possible."

"It could be very dangerous."

"I know. And I don't want to push Elena and Marcel into doing it, but it could be our best shot at stopping this." I thought about Nola, about the faxes and the calls, about the risks I had taken, the danger I had put her in. The fact that she wasn't answering her god-damned phone. "It could be our only shot."

I could hear him breathing. "She's my only sister, Doyle. I don't know if I can lose another . . . I can't lose her."

"I understand." I did. And I wondered for a moment if maybe I was somehow becoming obsessed with these guys, chasing them like a white whale. But I hadn't gone looking for them. I hadn't gone looking for Ron Hartwell. I might have gone looking for Miriam, but I hadn't found her. She found me. "Anyway," I said, "Elena wants to talk to you about it, as well. I just wanted you to hear from me what it was I had in mind."

"Let me talk to her. Maybe we have enough there we don't need to do anything else. And Doyle . . . I know this isn't your fight. Thanks for what you have done."

"I'll talk to you soon."

Elena took the phone into the kitchen. As Toma followed, I asked to borrow his phone once more.

He nodded and handed it over without hesitation.

I tried calling Nola. The first time the call didn't even go through. The second try took forever—lots of clicking and hissing. It crossed my mind that maybe the line was tapped, but more likely it was just a bad international connection. When I finally connected, it went straight to voice mail. I took small comfort knowing that the four men I was most afraid might come for her were being held on a boat here in Haiti—and at least one of them was dead. But I still felt the fear and frustration of not being able to reach her.

"Fuck!" I muttered, just as Elena and Toma walked in from the kitchen.

Elena scowled and tutted.

"Sorry," I said.

Toma smirked. "She talked to Regi, and she talked to Marcel," he said, looking down at his aunt.

She nodded. "We do it."

77

When we drove up the alley behind his restaurant, Marcel was loading the back of a battered van with sixty-pound sacks stenciled
CORNMEAL, with the Stoma-Grow logo beneath it. He looked worried but determined. He gave me a curt nod, like he knew that what
we were doing was important but he wasn't crazy about it.

When Elena got out of the Jeep, she went to him and they
hugged. Then he cupped her face and kissed her. It dawned on me
then that their relationship was more than just professional.

It might not have been news to Toma, although he didn't seem
too concerned one way or another. Marcel gave him a nod a few
degrees colder than the one he gave me, no doubt because of the past
worry Toma had put his aunt through.

"We leave in two hours," Marcel said. "If we doing this thing, you
need to go now."

I nodded.

Toma spoke briefly to Marcel. The big man listened and nodded,
then he ducked back into the restaurant, returning moments later
with a coil of rope, a crowbar, and a small rolled-up rug. The rug was

a runner of some kind, long and narrow. It was filthy, and I could smell the mustiness coming off it.

Toma nodded and said, *"Trè byen,"* taking them from him and putting them in the back of the Jeep. As I turned to follow him, Marcel put his massive hand on my shoulder and pulled me close.

"I don't like that thug," he said, tilting his head at Toma. "But Elena loves him. Bring him back safe."

I drove, and Toma directed me across the city and toward the docks. I'd been back and forth through Cap-Haïtien enough times that I was starting to get my bearings. The city and the landscape around it seemed to be shrinking from sheer familiarity. Or maybe it was the fact that the streets were all but deserted.

There were a few fires lingering here and there and police cars speeding back and forth, but it was almost midnight, and things were settling down.

As we approached the water, I could see the cranes on the ships and the docks rising above the buildings. I looked back at the hills looming behind us, south toward Gaden and Saint Benezet, north toward Labadie and Labadee and Archie Pearce's megayacht out in the water.

An hour and a half had passed since I'd told Pearce about Bourden's plan. It would take him some time to determine where the Soyagene-X was located, to put together a plan to intercept it. But he would act fast. In all likelihood, some of his men were already headed to the same place we were.

I drove faster, swerving around a darkened corner on two wheels.

Toma touched my arm. "Slow down," he said quietly. I thought for a moment my driving had made him nervous, but he pointed down the block toward a tall chain-link fence topped with barbed wire. "That's it."

I pulled over and killed the lights.

It was across the street from the dockyard, the gate facing the docks. Inside the fence was a small warehouse, a concrete yard, and two white guys with rifles.

Toma whispered in my ear, "Park over there," pointing at a side street that doglegged from the one we were on and ran behind the warehouse property, uphill from it.

I rolled slowly forward, turned left, then right. When Toma nodded, I put it in reverse and backed right up to the fence.

He leaned his head close to mine and whispered, "The guards weren't here before."

That wasn't his fault, but I was still annoyed. He might have seen it on my face. He shrugged in response.

We got out silently and walked up to the fence. It circled the entire property. The tiny building stood between us and the front gate, effectively hiding us from the guards patrolling it.

Toma had said that the fence was serious but the building itself was flimsy, and that appeared to be the case. It was constructed entirely of corrugated metal.

The fence was ground level where we were standing, but there was a four-foot drop on the inside, so although the fence was eight feet tall, it was a twelve-foot drop on the other side. There was a narrow space maybe two feet wide between the back of the shed and the wall beneath the fence.

Toma pointed out the newly repaired rear corner of the shed, where he and Toussaint had broken in before.

I didn't like it. Not a bit. I didn't even know if the Soyagene-X was still in there, although in that sense the armed guards were an encouraging sign.

"Okay," I whispered to Toma. "You need to go out front and cause a diversion while I break in."

"You kidding me?" He shook his head. "Those guys have guns. Why don't we just shoot them?"

To be honest, the thought had crossed my mind. The rifle was still in the Jeep. Shoot them both, then go in and take it.

Of course, that would be cold-blooded murder.

"No." I shook my head. "Either you cause a diversion and I break in, or I cause a diversion and you break in." There was always a chance it could come to shooting anyway.

He let out a soft, exasperated growl. "What kind of diversion?"

78

I thought for a second. "Pretend you're drunk and you want to fight them. They're professionals, so they won't shoot." I hoped. "Walk up and taunt them, loud. Then give the fence a good long shake, make a lot of noise for a few seconds at least. While you're making noise, I'll pull open the back of the shed."

He thought about it for a moment, thinking about the steps, then nodding to himself. "That might work. Then what?"

"Keep going, circle around the block and come back here. I'll pass the bags of soy up to you, just like we planned. Then be sure you're ready to get the hell out of here."

Standing on the back of the Jeep and keeping our heads down low, we gently unfurled the rug over the barbed wire at the top of the fence. The damp, mildewy smell immediately tickled my nose. I tied the rope to the bumper and draped it over the fence, across the rug.

I gave Toma a nod, and he trotted off around the corner. A few seconds later, I heard him start to sing in a convincingly drunken voice. I smiled and shook my head. Making sure the crowbar and flashlight were secured in the back my waistband, I slowly climbed up onto the fence and used the rope to lower myself down on the other side. I wasn't silent, but I was pretty damn quiet.

The space behind the shed was a pool of depthless black. My foot came down on something soft that screeched and scurried away.

I paused and listened. I could hear Toma, still singing as he rounded the corner, coming closer again.

The guards were speaking to each other in hushed tones. One of them laughed.

As Toma's voice grew louder, I placed the tip of the crowbar under the edge of the newly repaired section of corrugated metal. As soon as I heard Toma yelling and the fence rattling, I popped out two nails across the top, then slid the crowbar down, popping the four nails down the side.

It easily opened enough for me to slip inside. I put my hand over my flashlight and turned it on, letting just enough light filter through so I could see. There were three sets of shelves. Two of them were mostly filled with boxes. The third held a large bundle of five-pound white paper bags wrapped in heavy-duty plastic. I shone the flashlight on it from different angles until I found the stamps on the bottoms of the paper bags. GES-5322x. Soyagene-X.

I wrestled the bundle off the shelf. It was a dozen five-pound bags. Sixty pounds. Manageable but unwieldy. I placed it on the floor and pushed it out through the hole in the back. Then I poked out my head and listened.

I could hear Toma singing again, his voice fading as he continued on his way.

One of the guards called out after him, "Yeah, go on! Get out of here, you crazy drunk voodoo devil!" He had a thick accent that sounded Australian at first. Then I pegged it as South African.

The other one laughed weakly, then muttered, "This fucking place gives me the creeps."

I squeezed out and pulled the bundle of soy farther around the back. As I waited for Toma to return, I tore open the plastic outer wrap.

I heard Toma's footsteps approaching. A second later, he was standing on the back of the Jeep, looking over the top of the fence.

I held up a bag of soyflour, and he nodded, wiggling his fingers like he was ready to catch. I heaved the bag into the air, a smooth arc that crested perfectly over the top of the fence. He caught it easily and put it down in the back of the Jeep. As soon as he straightened up, I threw another one, then another. The first six went quickly and flawlessly. We were working up a sweat, and the cool breeze felt nice coming off the water. But my arms were starting to feel it, and I guess Toma's were too. Number seven had a slight wobble, and Toma bobbled it slightly before securing it.

Our eyes met, and we were more deliberate after that. I removed the rest of the bags from the plastic and started throwing them. Everything went fine until number eleven. The throw was wobbly, but I will forever insist it was catchable. Toma bobbled it badly between his hands, chasing it sideways, away from the rug. He got a grip on it, but only after it snagged on the barbed wire on top of the fence.

Before I could say anything, he yanked it free. The bag tore completely open, releasing a cascade of white powder that coated me from head to toe and billowed out in a cloud around my feet.

I exhaled sharply through my nose and spat in case any of it had gotten in my mouth. The breeze picked up, mercifully clearing the air before I inhaled any of it. I swallowed my annoyance and grabbed the last pack, but as the cloud of white powder slid away on the breeze, so did the plastic overwrap. It skidded along the pavement with a surprisingly loud scraping sound.

Without thinking, I lunged after it, stepping out from behind the cover of the building. I grabbed the plastic and was just turning around when I heard a thick Afrikaner accent say, "Jesus Christ, what the hell are you?"

I froze. Covered from head to toe in white powder, holding the last bag of Soyagene-X in one hand and the plastic wrap in the other.

His rifle was pointed right at my midsection. In the darkness, his eyes looked afraid. I realized he was afraid of me.

"Fuck sake, Jerry, get over here," he said, panic in his voice. "We've got a fucking situation."

"Jesus, I hate this fucking place," replied a different voice with the same accent from the other side of the warehouse. "What is it now?"

I didn't know how I was going to get out of this, but I knew it would be easier to escape one of them than two, and that window that was rapidly closing.

I still couldn't see Jerry, but over the first guy's shoulder, I could see the street on the other side of the front gate. I heard engines roaring, two of them, and saw headlights approaching from the side.

I knew it was Pearce's men, coming for the same thing we were after. More than one window was closing.

The guy in front of me turned his head just a bit and called out, "Just get the fuck over here."

I threw the Soyagene at him, straight at his head. It was a good throw too. I even managed to put a spiral on it. As soon as it left my hand, I dove back behind the warehouse.

I heard a strangled cry and a burst of automatic fire.

As my fingers wrapped around the rope dangling from the top of the fence, I looked back and saw a huge cloud of white powder right where I'd been standing.

I started scrambling up the rope as Jerry's voice said, "What the fuck, Simon?"

Simon said, "He fucking vanished, like some kind of ghost."

And then vanish I did.

There was a roar of engines and a loud crash behind me as Pearce's men barreled through the front gates.

Almost simultaneously, another engine roared in front of me.

I was at the top of the fence—one hand grabbing the rug and the other wrapped around the rope—when the rope jerked forward, and so did I. Luckily, the rug came with us.

Even as I flew through the air, not quite understanding what the hell was going on, part of me hoped Jerry and Simon could see me— white as a ghost, flying across the sky. Hell, I was riding a magic carpet. That would give them something to think about for quite some time.

But then it was time to think about me.

After the initial violent jerk, there was a brief moment of tranquility at the top of my trajectory. Then I started coming down.

The Jeep was tearing ass down the darkened street, pulling me along like a kite. The street was coming up fast, and so was the end of the block. Toma was going to have to turn, one way or the other. In a split second, I was trying to calculate if I would hit the ground first or go into the turn still airborne. Would I splatter against the street or against one of the buildings that crowded either side of it?

I held on tight to the rug, knowing it was my only protection. Maybe in the back of my mind I hoped it actually would start to fly. If ever there was a time for a rug to reveal its powers, that would have been it.

Then I saw twin flashes of red—the Jeep's brake lights—and I said, "Oh shit."

I let go of the rope and tried to roll into the fall but got tangled in the rug. That's probably what saved me.

By the time I hit the pavement, the rug was wrapped around me like a foul-smelling cocoon. The impact still hurt. A lot. But I didn't break anything, I didn't lose all my skin, and I didn't even bang my head.

I hit once, bounced, and then rolled to a stop under the Jeep.

I lay there for a moment, unable to move and terrified that Toma was going to put the Jeep in reverse and back up to look for me. Instead, I felt hands grabbing my feet and dragging me out.

Toma smiled down at me, then started to scoop me up as if he was going to put me in the back of the Jeep like a swaddled baby. I tried to fight him off, but my arms were bound to my sides by the rug.

"No," I barked. "Get me the fuck out of this."

He huffed and glanced back down the block, then found the edge of the rug and pulled violently, spinning me out onto the street. He tossed the rug into the back of the Jeep and grabbed my shirt, pulling me to my feet.

We got into the Jeep and took off. We tore around the corner, then he looked at me and laughed.

"What's so funny?"

He laughed again and pointed at me. *"Blan."*

79

When we got back to BBQ Central, Marcel was pacing in the alley out back. His face when he saw us was a mixture of relief and trepidation. I could understand if there was a part of him that had been hoping we couldn't come back, or at least that we would come back empty-handed.

When I got out, he looked away, almost afraid, muttering an angry stream of Kreyol.

Toma walked up beside me, laughing. "He says you need to wash your face. You look like Baron Samedi, the voodou god."

I walked away from the others and dusted myself off as best I could, trying not to breath in any of the Soyagene-X coming off me, wondering if I'd already ingested, inhaled, or absorbed enough to cause a reaction.

Elena came forward and led me through the back door, tutting and cooing as we passed through the small kitchen and into a tiny bathroom, where she got a damp cloth and wiped off my face and my arms, paying special attention to the scrapes that revealed themselves as she did. She left me in the bathroom to finish. I dunked my head under the faucet a few times, trying to rinse the stuff out of my sweaty hair before it turned to glue.

When I went back outside, Toma was leaning against Marcel's van, looking on while Marcel and Elena mixed the Soyagene-X into the large sacks of Stoma-Grow cornmeal. They had bandannas tied around their faces to keep the dust out of their noses and mouths.

As they finished with each bag, they crumpled the top over, and Marcel put a strip of packing tape across it. I noticed that the rest of the bags were similarly taped and were already in the back of the van. The Soyagene-X bags were gone. Then I spotted them, empty, stuffed into a trash bag.

Marcel looked up at me and nodded.

Toma looked over as I approached. "You okay?"

"I'm fine," I said.

Marcel hoisted the last sack of mixed cornmeal and put it in the back of the van with the others. He slammed the door shut and pulled the bandanna down from his face. "Time to go."

Elena's face was drawn as she got into the van. I felt bad asking them to put themselves in this position.

Toma turned to me. "Let's go."

I grabbed him by the arm. "Ask them one more time—are they sure they want to do this?"

He walked up to the van's driver-side window. Marcel lowered the window, and Toma spoke to them in Kreyol, hooking his thumb back in my direction. Marcel turned to Elena, sitting in the passenger seat. I could see her nodding in the darkness. Marcel turned back to Toma, then looked over at me and nodded too.

Toma turned to look at me. "Okay?"

We got in the Jeep and waited for Marcel to pull out, then followed after him. Toma drove.

The city was largely calm. The fires had mostly burned out, transformed into smoking piles of ash and rubble. The police were noticeably absent. Maybe they were already where we were going.

We made our way southwest through the city, taking a two-lane highway across Plaine-du-Nord, the Northern Plain. The moonlight shone on the scrub brush and farm fields. After a half hour, we passed through the small town of Limbe. It was quiet, and the streets were deserted.

Shortly after, we turned onto a much smaller road and started climbing into the low mountains. We passed a small dirt road that climbed steeply to our left, then we squeezed through a narrow, one-lane pass carved through the rocks.

Just on the other side of it, Marcel pulled off to the side of the road and waved for us to come up next to him.

As we did, we could see a massive encampment stretched out below us—hundreds of tents, dozens of trucks, even a helicopter—all illuminated by the pale moonlight.

Marcel leaned his head out the window. "That's it. We'll be okay. You should turn back."

Toma leaned forward and looked around me at him, shaking his head, speaking in Kreyol. When he was done, he looked up at me and pointed over his shoulder at the hillside to our left. "I know this place. I told them we'll be up on that hill, watching, in case something happens."

I nodded. If something happened, we wouldn't be in much of a position to do anything to help. But we'd try.

Elena leaned forward, talking around Marcel the way Toma had talked around me. She shook her head.

Toma sighed, then got out of the Jeep and ran around to her side of the van. They had a rapid back and forth, a lot of her shaking her head and him nodding. He kissed her on the cheek and ran back and got in the Jeep.

"I told her we'd be watching the entire time, and when they were done, we would follow them back to Cap-Haïtien."

I barely knew the guy, but I felt somehow proud of him. He might have been an outlaw, but he had stepped up, and he was a good nephew. "Sounds good."

Marcel eased forward, and the van disappeared over the rise.

Toma turned the Jeep around and doubled back through the narrow pass, then turned onto the steep dirt road that climbed the hill on the other side of it.

We wound our way up for a half mile or so. Toma killed the headlights and slowed to a crawl, driving by moonlight as the road curved onto a small plateau overlooking the valley below.

Below us, we could see the van's headlights lighting up the road as Marcel and Elena headed toward the camp.

80

Toma raised the binoculars, following the van as it approached the camp. A spotlight lit up the night, and the van stopped in its tracks. I grabbed the binoculars as two soldiers with rifles approached them, one on either side.

Toma grabbed them back, and after a few tense seconds, he let out a loud breath and lowered them. The soldiers waved the van through.

I could kind of see what was going on, but Toma gave me a play-by-play as he watched through the binoculars. Marcel and Elena pulled up behind the tents, next to a clearing with some kind of green tanker trailer. As they unloaded the pots and other supplies from the truck, two sets of construction lights mounted on poles came on, drenching the area in a blue-white glare. Marcel lit a fire and started filling pots with steaming hot water from the tanker trailer. Elena set up the ingredients.

I looked at my watch. It was almost two A.M. I was relieved that I didn't seem to be experiencing any respiratory symptoms from being coated in the Soyagene-X.

"We should each try to get some rest," I said. "Why don't you go first. I'll keep an eye on things and wake you up in an hour."

I wasn't disappointed when he shook his head and said, "You go first. I'll keep watch." I didn't argue, either.

I was exhausted, and I figured an hour of shut-eye would do me good. He gave me two, which was nice of him, but he looked like hell when he woke me up with an elbow and said, "Breakfast time," shoving the binoculars into my hands.

Still half-asleep, I put them to my eyes. It was still dark, and my eyes were a little bleary, but I could see the soldiers lining up. In front of the line, Marcel and Elena stood next to two massive pots. An identical pair of pots sat over wood fires behind them.

Everyone stood motionless, waiting. Then Dominique Ducroix appeared, leading a small group of officers past the waiting soldiers to the front of the line. Marcel and Elena served them bowls of *mayi moulin* porridge.

Ducroix made a big deal of tasting his porridge, nodding and clapping Marcel on the shoulder. Apparently, it had passed the taste test. The officers turned and brought their breakfast back to a large tent in the middle of the camp, probably their command tent. Marcel and Elena began to serve the soldiers waiting in line.

The line of soldiers never seemed to go down. As the ones in front got their breakfast and moved off to eat it, more would appear out of the tent city. Every few minutes, Marcel stirred the pots on the fire behind them. After ten minutes, the first two pots were empty, and together Marcel and Elena switched them for the two that had been over the fires. As Elena started serving up again, Marcel filled the two empty pots with hot water from the tank, stirred in the ingredients, and placed them on the fire. Then he went back to helping Elena serve.

It was an impressive operation.

I turned to Toma. "You should get some sleep."

He shook his head. I probably wouldn't have, either. And I probably would have left me sleeping the way he had done too. I felt guilty about it, but there wasn't much to be done. I offered him the binoculars back, but he shook his head and closed his eyes, resting them at least.

"Let's change places, in case your change your mind." He gave me an annoyed look, but then he let out a massive yawn and nodded his acquiescence.

I got in behind the wheel, and he got in the passenger side. In seconds, his breath was whistling through his nose in a precursor to snoring.

I watched as Marcel and Elena replenished the pots three times. After twenty-five minutes, the line finally started to dwindle. When it was almost down to nothing, the officers returned. I nudged Toma and handed him the binoculars. "Ducroix?"

He blinked a few times, trying to get his eyes to focus, then he looked through the binoculars. "That's him."

"He's back for seconds."

Toma kept the binoculars, and I let him. That was his aunt down there.

"Ducroix is talking to them," he reported. "I don't know what they're saying . . . Now they're walking away. There's no one left in line . . . That's it, then. I think they're done."

He handed me back the binoculars. Marcel and Elena were already breaking things down, rinsing out the pots with hot water from the truck, dumping it onto the ground, loading things into the van.

Behind them, the soldiers milled about in a different fashion than before. They were preparing for something. The first couple of tents started coming down, methodically dismantled. Vehicles were lining up.

I felt a momentary panic. What if the reaction didn't happen in time? Maybe it took longer than I'd thought. Maybe I was still going to develop symptoms. What if it didn't happen at all? What if we were wrong and the reason I wasn't sick wasn't because I'd avoided ingesting any of it but because the stuff wasn't toxic, after all?

They had been serving for half an hour, at least. That meant a thirty-minute difference between when the first soldiers ate the porridge and the last ones.

Marcel and Elena seemed just about ready to go when a trio of soldiers walked up, the one in the middle hailing them. Something about their demeanor made me nervous. They seemed angry.

"There might be trouble."

"What?" Toma asked, reaching for the binoculars. I swatted his hands away. "Hold on."

Marcel shrugged his shoulders and shook his head. He spoke for a moment, pointing back up the road they had driven in on, then shrugged again.

The soldier in front held up his finger, and he and his comrades turned and walked away, back to the large tent in the middle of the camp.

Marcel and Elena stood there obediently for a moment, their hands folded in front of them like chastised schoolchildren. They bent their heads toward each other, like they were whispering to each other. Then they turned and ran to the van. They got in and drove off in a hurry.

"Come on," I said. "We've got trouble."

81

Barreling down the hill as fast as I dared, I explained to Toma what I'd seen. "Hurry up then," he said. "Step on it."

His face was twisted with worry, and I was glad I was driving, because he would have been going faster, and the road was so bumpy and twisted we'd almost rolled over twice as it was. The sky was just beginning to lighten, and I was driving without headlights.

The road straightened as we approached the bottom, enough that we could see Marcel's beat-up van flash by a hundred yards in front of us. We were closing on them fast, and Toma was still urging me to go faster, but I knew that if we were catching up with them, whoever was behind them would be too.

"Hold on," I said to Toma, and as he did, I hit the brakes and screeched onto the road, facing back toward the camp, instead of following Marcel and Elena.

"What are you doing?" Toma demanded.

I gunned the engine, into the narrow pass, then slammed on the brakes, fishtailing so the single lane was completely blocked. I could see headlights coming up the hill toward us, and as soon as we came to a stop, I could hear a vehicle approaching.

"Get out," I told Toma. "Take the rifle, get behind those rocks. If they look like they're going to kill me, take them out if you think you can. Otherwise, just stay back. And if things don't go well, hightail it back to Cap-Haïtien and make sure Marcel and Elena are okay."

He nodded and ran off with the rifle.

I left the headlights on and opened the hood.

The engine sound grew louder, and seconds later, a Jeep just like ours flew over the rise, headlights blazing, skidding to a stop at an parallel angle to my Jeep.

There were three police in it. The two who weren't driving stood and began shouting at me in Kreyol, pointing at my Jeep and at the road that it was blocking.

I held up my hands and smiled, trying to look confused. "Whoa, whoa," I said. "Slow down. I can't understand you. No speaka ze Kreyol, comprende?"

The driver got out and marched toward me, his sidearm raised and pointed at my head. "Move," he said. "Out of the way." I got the impression this was most of the English he knew, but he racked the slide on his gun—the international language.

I raised my hands and smiled, trying to look a little bit scared but not quite as scared as I actually was. "Sorry," I said. "It conked out on me. I'm with Darkstar, I'm on my way to see Ducroix."

He lowered his gun at that. "Ducroix?"

I nodded. "Yes," pointing toward the camp they had just left. "Can you take me to see him?"

I realized almost instantly that might not have been the best tactic, asking them to bring me into the enemy's camp, but at that point, I was just trying to give Marcel and Elena as much time to get away as possible.

He seemed to be thinking about it, like maybe someone coming to see Ducroix was more important than the cooks.

Then one of the other soldiers stepped forward, mumbling.

The others watched him as he walked up to the Jeep, peered inside it, and then walked in a circle around it. When he was done, he said

something to the others, then put his face right in mine. "My Jeep."
He poked his finger in my chest. "You stole!"

I hadn't gotten a great look at him when we'd stolen the Jeep, but
it definitely could have been the same guy. Then I saw his name tag:
Turnier. The name that was on the wool cap we'd found.

His eyes burned with anger. Between losing his hat and his Jeep,
he'd probably been in some pretty deep shit.

I stepped back, put my hand on my chest, and said, "I'm with
Darkstar. If you think *they* stole your Jeep, you can take it up with
them, but we own lots of Jeeps. I think you're mistaken."

The driver laughed and said something in Kreyol. The other one
laughed even louder. I smiled along with them, all friends.

But Turnier was having none of it. "No!" he shouted. "No!" He
stomped in a little circle as he pointed at me and the Jeep. Then
he stopped and dashed straight toward me, past me, reaching into
the Jeep, under the driver's seat, pulling out his cap.

He turned and held it up to the others, showing them his name
written inside. They all stopped smiling. Then he turned to me, his
face practically touching mine, his scratchy breath loud in my ear,
and he said, "Mine."

Off to the side, I sensed motion, and I glanced over to see Toma,
just peeking around the rocks, the rifle barrel aiming at Turnier.
I wondered what kind of skills Toma had with a rifle.

Things were about to go south in a bad way. I shook my head.

Turnier took out his gun, and I was starting to rethink what I
wanted Toma to do. He pointed the gun at me, speaking in rapid
Kreyol to the others, making some kind of a joke. He started laughing. It sounded forced at first, but then he got into it for real. The
others laughed along with him, uncomfortably. His laugh continued
to grow, and soon he was laughing so hard he started coughing, but
he couldn't stop laughing. Then he wasn't laughing anymore, just
coughing. He eyes bugged out a bit, surprised, then worried, then
scared. The other two ran to him, patting him on the back, asking if
he was okay.

One of them started coughing, as well. Then so did the other. In seconds, all three of them were on the ground, wheezing, grabbing their throats, their weapons lying on the road next to them.

Toma popped his head up and looked over at me.

"I guess it worked," I said. In the back of my mind, I felt a wave of relief. If I still hadn't had a reaction to being coated in the stuff, I was pretty sure I wasn't going to.

Toma walked over and looked down at them, frightened by the sight of them rolling around on the ground.

I took their weapons and cuffed them with their own handcuffs. As I was straightening up, the sky beyond them suddenly flashed orange, and I heard a strange but familiar rhythmic sound. I grabbed the binoculars out of the Jeep and ran to the top of the rise.

Toma came up beside me, and I handed him the binoculars. He stared for a moment, then crossed himself and muttered something that sounded like a prayer.

Half a mile below us, the encampment was a mess. Half the tents had fallen down. Soldiers were writhing on the ground. One of the trucks was slowly rolling across the camp in flames, apparently having passed over a campfire.

The helicopter was trying to take off, hovering a few feet up in the air and wobbling unevenly. It started to slowly turn, then listed to one side. For a moment, it looked like it was going to take off in that direction, but then the rotors bit into the dirt, snapping and shattering and sending pieces flying off into the night. It came down on its side, the rotors shearing themselves down to nothing before the engine stalled out and died.

"Come on," I said. "Let's get out of here."

82

As we hurried back to our Jeep, we had to step over the soldiers lying handcuffed on the road. They weren't having fun, but they seemed to have stabilized. Their breathing was loud and labored, but it seemed steady enough.

I reached into their Jeep and took the keys from the ignition. It was blocking the pass as effectively as our Jeep had been.

"What about them?" Toma asked.

I was touched by his concern.

"They'll be okay," I said with unjustified confidence. Miriam had said the symptoms could be life threatening but mostly for children or old people. In a few hours, these guys would probably be breathing fine and once again looking to kill us.

Meanwhile, I got into our Jeep and started it up. Toma got in beside me, and we took off.

We drove in a stunned, exhausted silence. The sky was getting brighter in the east, and in the momentary quiet, I was just starting to think past the immediate crisis. I didn't know what was going to happen with the coup, with the CASCATA vote, or even with

Bourden's plans with the Soyagene-X. Maybe things would turn out okay, and maybe they wouldn't, but I had done what I could.

That left me thinking about other things.

Nola. I took out my phone to call her, but of course it was still dead. I told myself she was fine, that she had probably seen my calls and was now frantically trying to call me back.

I turned to Toma. "Any calls?"

He looked at his phone and shook his head. "My phone's dead, too."

I thought about Miriam. Regi had reassured me that she'd be safe pending her extradition, that she wouldn't just disappear into some Haitian hellhole of a prison. But she was still going to be extradited. Unless I could clear her, she could end up disappearing into some American hellhole of a prison.

However things played out in Haiti or around the world, it was time for me to get home. To be with Nola, to make sure she was okay, to get back to our life together. And to work on clearing Miriam Hartwell of the bogus murder charges, so she could get on with mourning Ron and living her life.

I was thinking about those charges, thinking about Ron Hartwell and how I had ended up here, when I heard the sound of engines getting closer. I looked around, trying to find the source. Toma did too.

The sound was growing unmistakably louder, and it wasn't one vehicle—it was many. I pictured a convoy of Ducroix's men, murderously angry, closing in on us. There was no sign of anyone behind us, but I couldn't tell where they were. I put my foot down, compelled to get the hell out of there. In the growing predawn light, our headlights seemed to be fading, but the road in front of us was suddenly brightly lit.

I hit the brakes as an armored personnel carrier erupted from a tiny dirt road to our left. There was another one behind it.

I threw the Jeep into reverse, thinking we were dead, that Ducroix's men had found us. We'd be disappeared, murdered horribly and never found.

But the vehicles continued on in front of us, headed the same direction we had been. A string of SUVs came next, and one of them slowed as it turned onto the road. It pulled off to the side, then its reverse lights came on, and it backed up directly toward us.

83

Sitting next to me, Toma tightened his grip on the rifle.

"Easy now," I said. The convoy was still moving, showing no inclination to harass us or chase us or shoot us. I didn't want to change their minds about that.

The SUV's rear door opened, and Regi Baudet stepped out. For a moment, I thought maybe Ducroix's men had captured him, and now he was escaping. But they weren't Ducroix's men at all. They were the Presidential Guard.

Cardon had escaped.

Regi ran up to us, smiling wide. "You're okay! Good job, you two!" He clamped a hand on Toma's shoulder and squeezed it hard. He was looking at him totally differently from the day before. He seemed proud.

"Where's Cardon?" I asked. "Is he okay?"

"He's fine." He hooked his thumb at the line of vehicles. "He was two cars in front of us. What about Marcel and Elena?"

"They're fine," Toma told him, obviously proud, as well. "They did it. Fed the whole camp. We watched all of it. Ducroix's men seemed to realize something was up, but Marcel and Elena got out of there."

"One of Cardon's scouts saw the whole thing." Regi nodded. "The entire force is incapacitated."

I told him what had happened with the squad that had been pursuing Marcel and Elena, then the mayhem we had seen at the encampment.

He nodded, looking grave for a moment. "It's a serious business, this stuff."

"What will happen to them?" I asked.

"We'll send medics back for them. They'll be treated, probably released. Ducroix will be arrested. Some others will be detained. They'll be okay."

"What about you?" Toma asked. "Where are you going?"

He grinned. "I am going with them back to Port-au-Prince. Cardon has made me acting health minister, so I'll be quite busy." He looked at me. "But I'll find out where Miriam is, and I'll make sure she is protected." He paused and smiled again. "I must go. I'll call Elena later. And you both, too. Be safe!"

We watched as he got back into the SUV and merged with the rest of the convoy, which was still barreling onto the road in front of us.

"He's a big shot, my uncle," Toma said. "We're all proud of him, you know? I mean, we already were."

"You did good," I told him. "He's proud of you, too."

He opened his mouth to scoff at the notion, but I think it hit him that it might be true. He turned to look back out the window.

We watched in silence for the next few minutes as the convoy rumbled past. By the time the last vehicle disappeared down the road in front of us, it was almost fully light out.

We followed them for ten minutes. When we reached the highway, they went south, and we went north.

The sun was up as we entered the small town of Limbe, and suddenly, so were the townspeople. As we drove down the dusty highway, people began to emerge from almost every building—the tiny wooden shacks, the concrete ones with the metal roofs, the walled-in compounds—all of them. And amid all the dust and poverty, the people were immaculate, dressed in finery, groomed to perfection, all of them looking fresh and shiny and happy and beautiful. Young people and old, entire families walking together, teenagers forming groups, walking arm in arm. For a moment, I thought maybe they were celebrating the defeat of Ducroix's coup.

"Going to church," Toma said.

It was Sunday morning.

By the time we got to Cap-Haïtien, forty minutes later, the streets were bustling with early morning energy.

We, on the other hand, were not. We were dragging.

We had decided on the drive home we would go to Elena's place to figure out what was next.

I don't know if it had anything to do with the events of the night before or if it was just too early on a Sunday morning, but the streets were empty of protestors, police, or Darkstar forces.

Toma had fallen asleep just as we entered the city, but I knew my way now. Just as we were approaching the inn, he started to snore. I pulled over and tapped him on the knee.

He awoke with a start. "What?"

"We're here."

As soon as we walked in the front door, Elena came bustling out of the kitchen carrying a tray with tea and cookies. There were two mugs on it.

I was impressed—and appalled—that after all she'd been through and after having been up all night working, she was already working again. Working still, more likely.

I raised my hand to take one of the cups, and I was about to tell her she shouldn't have, but she swerved and walked around me.

"I have guests," she mumbled. It may have been my imagination, but I caught a distinct impression that there was an implied "*real* guests*,*" as in, not just some friends of Regi.

Well, good for her, I thought, stifling a yawn as I watched her carry the tray past us and into the front room, wondering who these paying guests were.

It was a yawn I never finished.

There, darting around Elena, closing the distance between us in a heartbeat, was Nola.

84

I almost fell back under the force of it as she wrapped her arms around me and peppered my face with kisses. I tried to keep up with her, tried to anticipate her lips, put mine where I thought hers would be, but I couldn't. She was too fast, too thorough, covering every inch of my face, not stopping until she landed on my lips and kissed them deeply.

I wrapped my arms around her and squeezed, holding her to me, lifting her up. I didn't want to put her down. I didn't want to let her go. The reaction I felt at seeing her—the relief, the joy, the love—it bubbled up from somewhere deep with an intensity I didn't want anyone to see. Not even her.

I held her tight and surreptitiously wiped my eyes on her shoulder. I don't know if anyone else saw it, but Nola wasn't fooled. She pulled back and reached up with both hands to cup my face, using her thumbs to wipe away the moisture under my eyes.

I did the same to her.

"Hey," I said, my voice husky and croaking.

"Hey," she said, her voice as soft as the rustle of sheets.

"Hey!" said Toma, stepping up.

Elena was looking on with a broad smile. I got the impression she approved. Toma was looking at Nola with a different kind of smile, and I got the sense that he approved too, in a different kind of way.

"Sorry," I said, clearing my throat. "Nola, these are my friends Toma and Elena. This is my girlfriend, Nola."

They exchanged hellos, and Elena gave Nola a kiss on each cheek.

I looked down at her, grinning, trying to keep my hands off her. "How did you get here?"

"I gave her a lift," said a voice with slight accent that was not Haitian.

Standing in the front room drinking the other cup of tea was a short, dapper-looking man in his late fifties. He had the unmistakable sheen of lots of money.

"Doyle," Nola said, stepping back and holding out her arm, "I'd like you to meet Gregory Mikel."

Mikel put down his tea and came toward me, extending his hand. "It's a pleasure to meet you, Mr. Carrick," he said as we shook. "I've been looking forward to it for some time."

I had no idea what that meant. "Nice to meet you too. This is Toma." They shook hands and exchanged greetings.

"And I guess you both already know Elena."

She was already back in the kitchen. I couldn't help thinking she must be exhausted. I was exhausted.

Mikel nodded and held up his cup of tea as evidence of having met her.

"I brought your passport," Nola said, handing it to me.

"Thanks," I said, smiling down at her sparkling face. I kind of wanted to tear off all her clothes and get back to the kissing, see what came next. She reached out and put her hand on my chest, touching me, but also holding me back. She knew me so well.

"Gregory gave me a lift when I told him I was bringing it to you," she explained.

Gregory. Now she was on first-name basis with a billionaire. I turned to look at him.

"Nola brought me the papers you faxed her," he said. "Very compelling stuff. Things seem to be changing pretty rapidly on the ground here. Is some of that your doing?"

"It was a group effort," I said. "Elena helped. Toma here. And Regi Baudet, who is the new acting minister of health. Most of all, Miriam Hartwell. We could use some of your, um, clout, to help her. They have her in prison here, awaiting extradition."

Mikel held up a hand. "She's fine. I've brought in Fritz Schultzman, one of the best extradition lawyers around. He's with her right now."

"What about when she gets back to the States? The case against her is bogus, but it's pretty strong. Anything you can do about that?"

He reached into his pocket and pulled out a flash drive. "As it turns out, yes."

85

Mikel's computer screen showed a grainy picture of a block of brick row homes at night, looking diagonally across the street. It took me a moment to recognize my own house near the middle.

It seemed far away, a different world from the one in which I'd been living. I felt a sudden yearning to be there, to be home.

In the foreground, a black SUV drove up and stopped at the curb, brightly illuminated from above. The windows were down. It was too dark to see the driver, but I could see the passenger. He turned and looked right at the camera.

Fucking Royce.

In the background, looking small in the distance, a man walked onto the street from the right, crossing toward my house. Ron Hartwell.

A pit opened up in the bottom of my stomach, and I felt like I was falling into it. Hartwell stepped onto the curb, looking around furtively.

From the motions of their heads, the gestures of their hands, it looked like the two men in the SUV were arguing.

Hartwell reached my steps, climbed them. As he banged on my

door—*bang, bang, bang*—the car surged forward. Upstairs, I knew, I was getting out of bed, pulling on my pants, wondering what was going on. Watching the video, I could feel myself urging me to react just a tiny bit faster, unable to resist the feeling that somehow the outcome could be changed, could be different.

Hartwell turned and saw the car, turned back, and banged on the door again, harder, frantic, again and again. The car was speeding almost directly at him. Watching it happen, I couldn't help wondering, where the fuck was I? Why wasn't I there? Why wasn't I opening the door and pulling him inside?

Hartwell kept pounding on the door as he twisted around to look behind him. The SUV didn't skid, didn't shimmy, but it stopped hard in front of my house. There was a flash, and Hartwell jerked and fell back against the door, a dark dot in the middle of his chest. Immediately, there was another flash, another dot, another flash and another dot, grouped within inches of each other, growing and merging.

The SUV was gone before Hartwell's knees even buckled. It drove off and disappeared. As he finally slid to the ground, another car flashed past.

Miriam Hartwell.

My front door opened, and there I was. Standing there, useless, looking down at Ron Hartwell's last breath.

The sight of myself looking down at Ron Hartwell's death sent a chill through me.

Toma had been captivated by the video, gradually leaning closer and closer. He muttered something in Kreyol that sounded like a cross between a curse and a prayer.

Nola looked away for the entire thing, although her hand was wrapped tightly around mine, grasping it, squeezing it, crushing it.

Mikel watched me watching it.

"That's the security footage from Albert's, the deli on my block," I said.

He nodded. "It is."

"Homicide said it never recorded."

"It recorded. Someone erased it. We were able to recover it, but it wasn't easy. I had just gotten it back when I got Nola's message."

"Have you shown it to the police?"

"I'm showing it to you." He let out a sigh. "I don't know who to trust. I'm hoping you do."

"I hope so too."

"Do you recognize the man in the car?"

"His name is Royce. He works for Energene."

Mikel nodded. "His partner's name is Divock."

"They're here now."

That surprised him. "In Haiti?"

I took a deep breath, and I told them everything. By the time I got to the part about Gaden and Saint Benezet, the room was very still, utterly quiet except for the sound of my voice.

Mikel was seething, a quiet rage building up inside him.

"They're monsters," Nola whispered.

Mikel nodded. "That's why we have to stop them."

When I got to the part about my visit to Pearce's boat, Mikel held up a hand. "Have you listened to the recording yet?"

I shook my head. "Not yet. My phone died."

To be fair, I had been kind of busy, but I realized how stupid that sounded. Mikel opened his mouth, possibly to point that out, but we were interrupted by a crash and a squeal coming from the kitchen.

Toma sprang to his feet, but when he got to the doorway, he turned around beaming. "Cardon is on television. Regi is with him!"

86

President Cardon looked somber, dignified, and very much in control. Standing behind him looking equally somber but noticeably more nervous was Regi Baudet. He appeared scrubbed but exhausted, dressed in a nice suit that didn't quite fit him.

We were crowded into the kitchen, watching on a tiny television perched on the counter. Toma translated as Cardon described the nature of Ducroix's coup attempt and the fact that it had been thwarted. He did not say how. As the crowd in Port-au-Prince applauded the news of the coup's defeat, Toma leaned over and kissed Elena on the cheek.

Cardon announced that elements involved in the coup were also involved in the trade ministry, and because of that, the CASCATA trade vote scheduled for later that day had been postponed. He then explained that some public health matters had come to his attention, and he was very pleased to announce the appointment of Monsieur Reginald Baudet as the new acting minister of public health. He said Regi was uniquely suited to usher in a new era of public health in Haiti.

As Regi spoke into the microphone, Toma continued to translate, but his voice sounded tighter, hoarse with emotion.

"He says there is no Ebola in Haiti. He says that was a lie concocted to hide the murders of the people of Saint Benezet and Gaden." Regi's voice seemed to crack when he said it. Toma's voice cracked, as well. "He says President Cardon will bring the murderers to justice but to rest assured—there is no chance of catching Ebola." He paused to wipe his nose. "He says there is a health risk, though. There is soyflour called Soyagene from a company called Energene and Stoma-Grow corn from a company called Stoma, and if you eat the Soyagene or you eat Stoma-Grow corn after eating Soyagene, you could get very, very sick."

He described the symptoms and what steps should be taken by anyone who experienced them. Toma tried to keep up, but he started stumbling before giving up altogether. I made a mental note to tell Regi: brevity is the soul of wit. But even if he wasn't the most riveting public speaker, I was sure he would be an excellent minister of public health.

Toma looked exhausted, his lids heavy. He was standing next to Elena, and he slouched down and let his head rest on her shoulder. He looked for a moment like a little boy.

Elena reached up and patted his cheek, tears starting down her face as she looked back and forth between her brother and her nephew, and the pride overwhelmed her.

The exhaustion was hitting me, as well. As I put my arm around Nola, she whispered in my ear, "It's good to see you, Doyle Carrick."

"It's good to see you too, Nola Watkins," I whispered back.

Even as I looked down at her, I felt another pair of eyes on me. I looked over at Mikel, standing in the doorway staring at me. I felt the unmistakable tension of impatience being resisted and contained. He wanted to give us a moment, but he also wanted something. I was pretty sure he wasn't used to waiting.

I raised an eyebrow at him, and he cocked his head toward the front door.

He wanted a moment alone.

87

The sun was up, people were walking down the narrow sidewalks, cars were going back and forth—and side to side, for that matter. A normal Sunday morning in Haiti, I thought, except for the coup that had just been narrowly averted. Maybe that wasn't too out of the ordinary, either.

"You're to be congratulated," Mikel said, standing on the bottom step. I was standing on the sidewalk so we were roughly the same height.

I shrugged. "Couldn't have done it without a lot of people. Without you, for that matter. Or Sable."

He nodded and sniffed. "He was a good man, Sable. He made the world a better place. Literally, you know? He fought the good fights. He won a lot of them."

I nodded. "So Royce and Divock—we have those guys on video, pretty cut-and-dried. With luck, we'll be able to put them away. The other two, the ones that came after Miriam and shot Sable, one of them is dead. But it looks like the other one got away?"

Mikel thought about it. He took a deep breath and let it out. "Well, I hope not. I hope that with your help, your testimony, maybe we can find him and bring him to justice." He paused, chewing the inside of his lip. "But there's always going to be guys with guns. And there's always going to be other guys waiting to take their place. It's the guys who hire them, who send them to kill Ron Hartwell or Dave Sable, who send troops to wipe out entire villages. I mean, yes, the people who pull the triggers are guilty—I'm not giving them a pass, no way. But the ones directing them, they're even more to blame. They shouldn't get away with it, either. Don't you think?"

"Yes, I do." I looked at him sideways. "Miriam told me that Ron was coming to tell me what he suspected, because they didn't trust anyone else. They wanted to tell me first. How did you know about it ahead of time?"

"We didn't. We were as surprised at what happened as you were, as Miriam was."

"I don't understand."

He smiled. "We weren't surveilling Ron Hartwell, Mr. Carrick. We were surveilling you."

"You were spying on me?"

"We were keeping an eye on you."

"So Sable was there when Ron Hartwell was shot?"

"No. But we became aware of it very soon after."

I stared at him but didn't say anything.

"Have you heard of Beta Librae?"

"The Northern Claw. Yes, it's your shadowy environmental group."

He laughed. "Well, I don't know about shadowy. I'd like to think we've been . . . discreet. And yes, it is a star, and it's sometimes called the Northern Claw, but it's also known as Lanx Borealis, part of the northern scale of Libra, meaning balance. More important, it's the only star in the sky that appears to be green." He paused for a moment, as if he was expecting me to comment on the cleverness of it all.

I was really, really tired.

"Anyway," he continued, "Beta Librae was Sable and me. With a little temporary help now and then, people like Charlie, the pilot. We were a very small operation with a lot of work to do. I thought it was time to expand. I'd heard about what you did in Dunston, then on Martha's Vineyard, as well. I heard some stories about what you had pulled off, fighting against some of the same forces I've been working against. I sent Sable to check you out."

"To check me out?" This time, I laughed.

He folded his arms and looked at me in a way that made me feel smaller than him. I regretted letting him take the higher ground and thought about stepping up next to him. "Do you enjoy your work, Mr. Carrick?"

"I'm a cop."

"I know. It's an important and noble profession. But are you doing what you thought you'd be doing? Making the difference you thought you'd be making?"

I'd become a cop in large part for the dental plan, so in that sense, yes, being a cop had lived up to expectations. But I knew what he meant. "What are you getting at?"

"Mr. Carrick, how would you like to come work for me?"

"What are you talking about?"

"I'm talking about going after the big fish, the ones the cops are too scared to go after, the ones the FBI and the feds are too scared to go after or that are too big for the cops and the feds to even know about. I'm talking about putting together cases against the people who are committing the serious crimes, the big crimes, cases that are so solid and compelling the feds can't ignore them, that the press won't let them ignore. I'm talking about making a bigger difference."

I laughed and shook my head, feeling suddenly light-headed. I didn't know what to say. "I'm a cop," I repeated simply.

"Think about it," he said, clapping his hand on my shoulder. "Dave Sable was a friend of mine, and I'll mourn his death in my own way, on my own time. But he was also an important part of Beta Librae. I was looking to expand this thing because there's so much work we need to do. Now I'm just trying to keep it going."

88

I stayed outside for a moment, wondering what had just happened. When I went back inside a moment later, Mikel was already on his phone, pacing, talking to his lawyer about Miriam Hartwell. Toma and Elena had disappeared. Hopefully, they were finally getting some sleep.

Nola was waiting for me. "What was that about?"

"I'm not sure I really know. I'll tell you about it later."

"You look awful," she said, her blue eyes looking up into mine.

I laughed. "Thanks."

"In a hot kind of way, of course." She laughed, too, but then she turned solemn. "Seriously, though. You look exhausted. The others are getting some sleep. You should, too."

"Absolutely," I said, taking her hand. The thought of sleep was suddenly irresistible. As I pulled Nola to her feet, I eyed the stairs, wondering if I had the energy to climb them. Still, I managed a lascivious smile. "Your room or mine?"

She gave me a sexy smile combined with a dubious raised eyebrow. Before she could answer, Mikel paced back into the room. "Okay," he said crisply. "It's all set up. Schultzman told Miriam Hartwell about the security footage. She's going to allow extradition as long as it's Detective Carrick escorting her. Judge Pauline Greenberg has agreed to an emergency hearing to look at our video evidence as soon as we land in Philadelphia. Schultzman is very confident the murder charges will be dropped." He paused and looked back and forth between us. "What? This is good news." He looked at his watch. "Let's get moving. My jet's here at the airport. We can be in Port-au-Prince in an hour."

I wanted to point out to him that I hadn't said yes, that I wasn't working for him, and that, essentially, he was not the boss of me. But getting Miriam out of a Haitian prison, getting her name cleared and her charges dropped so she could escape this nightmare and get on with the nightmare of mourning her murdered husband, that all seemed more important than a nap.

We woke up Toma and Elena to say good-bye.

Elena kissed each of us and thanked us. Mikel paid for all our rooms and left a big something extra, which Elena tried to refuse until I pulled Toma aside and told him Mikel was filthy rich. He whispered in his aunt's ear, and she relented.

I pulled him aside a second time. "Be cool, and be careful, okay?"

"Always cool," he said, spreading his arms out so I could appreciate the full extent of his coolness.

"That I know. Thanks for all your help out there. You really came through."

He nodded. "Thank you, too. Thank you from Haiti."

I didn't want to ruin the moment with a lecture. But I couldn't not. "You could be doing lots of other things with your life."

He laughed and shook his head, shushing me.

Elena swatted his hand down. "Tell him," she said to me.

"You care about your country," I went on, despite his head shaking and eye rolling. "Maybe you could help Regi. He could get you a job."

"Go on back to America and have a nice trip, okay?" He grinned. "Maybe I'll steal a boat and come visit you."

Mikel had arranged for a car so we wouldn't have to drive to the airport in a stolen National Police Jeep.

Elena and Toma came to the door to see us off. As we were getting into the back of the car, Toma called out, "Carrick!"

I paused, half in the car.

He nodded. "I'll talk to Regi."

I smiled. "Good man."

Then I paused again, shoved my hand in my pocket. "Here," I called out, tossing Toma the keys to the Jeep. "It's up to you what you do with it. There might be some people looking for it, but at the moment, they'll probably be more concerned with other things."

89

The drive to the airport was uneventful. I was nervous, wondering if we would be stopped and harassed, if I'd be arrested for being an outlaw. But I showed my passport, and they let me through with no hassles or questions about entry stamps. I was surprised they didn't pull me aside for questioning just for looking the way I looked. Maybe that was one of the perks of traveling with a rich guy in his private jet.

I was relieved the jet wasn't ridiculously luxurious—I was having a hard enough time trusting Mikel as it was. But it was comfortable. And I was tired.

As I sank into my seat, he asked if he could access the recording, listen to it while we flew. I said sure. I would have agreed to anything if he would just let me catch a few minutes of sleep.

I plugged the phone into his charger, and after a minute or so, it came back to life. I logged in to the plane's Wi-Fi and the interview app. I expected it to take forever, but apparently, billionaires have very fast Internet connections, even on their private jets. Mikel put on a pair of earbuds to listen to the recording. I settled in next to Nola and closed my eyes, but before I could fall asleep, before we were even at our cruising altitude, he gasped.

I opened one eye.

Nola got up and went over to him. He handed her one of the earbuds, and she put it in her ear.

A moment later, they both gasped.

"What?" I asked.

Mikel shook his head. "Bourden just mentioned the fact that they were working with Ducroix to oust Cardon."

I already knew that. I was drifting off again when I heard a tinny pop from the earbuds, and they both gasped again.

Nola's eyes met mine, and she pulled out her earbud. "Someone was just shot."

"I was there for that," I said. "That was one of the guys that came after Miriam. It was right before I left."

By then, I was awake. And they were getting to the part I hadn't already heard. I got up anyway and went over to them.

Mikel unplugged the earbuds, letting the audio come out over the phone's speaker just in time to hear my exit from the boat. I heard the splash, the motor starting, Pearce telling his men to let me go.

After that, it was mostly Pearce and Bourden snapping back and forth, Bourden complaining about Pearce letting me go and about his men killing someone named Jeffries, whom I assumed was Axe-Man. Then Pearce was laughing, telling Bourden he had a lot of nerve to be complaining about anything after the Soyagene stunt he had tried to pull.

"You're lucky I don't have you all shot and fed to the sharks, mate," Pearce said with a snort. "That's what I ought to do, and I have half a mind to at that. Lucky for you, I'm a businessman, and I know this is just business. I'm not going to forget this little dust up, but I'm not going to let it interfere with our plans with Sang Kuu in Southeast Asia or Boku in Central Africa, either." He sounded like a whimsical old man, but then his voice went hard. "So you and your friends, or what's left of them, are going to spend the night here as my guests while my people chase down this poison of yours. And in the morning, we'll pretend it never happened. But you'd better hope we don't miss any, because if I hear about this again, you're all going to wake up dead. Do you understand?"

"Yes," Bourden mumbled, barely audible.

A moment later, there was a gunshot and a scream, "Oh, fuck! My fucking knee!"

That was the shot I'd heard from the water. The three of us looked at each other, stunned, wondering if we'd just heard Bourden being shot. Then Pearce said, "Sorry, mate. I couldn't hear you. I said, 'Do you understand?'"

"Yes," Bourden said, loud and clear over the sound of the man sobbing in the background. "Yes, I understand."

Shortly after that, Pearce had Bourden and his men escorted to their cabins. Pearce must have left the room as well, because the remaining ten minutes was indecipherable mumbling and ambient noise.

When it was over, Mikel spoke first. "Might not be much there from a legal standpoint."

I nodded. "I know."

"What are you talking about?" Nola exclaimed. "They admitted to all sort of things. Criminal things. They call each other by name. They shot someone, for God's sake. How can that not be incriminating?"

"It's plenty incriminating," I said. "It's just not admissible."

"Okay, but it's proof of wrongdoing, isn't it? Couldn't we play it for the authorities so they can look into it, get evidence of their own that is admissible?"

I sighed. "Well, there can be evidentiary problems with that, too, but we could get around them." I looked to Mikel to help me out, but he seemed content to let me handle this. "I mean, the murder is the murder. That's one thing. By now, there's probably no evidence, no body, nothing except for an illegal audio recording, my testimony, several other witnesses who would testify against me, and a Haitian police force in the midst of massive upheaval. As for the other stuff, the international stuff, the people who would prosecute something like this, they almost certainly already know about it. They're just deciding not to go after it."

Nola sighed and shook her head. "Look, I know these people are rich and powerful, and they have rich and powerful friends." She glanced at Mikel, almost accusingly. "And the people in charge of regulating this kind of thing are the same people doing it. But surely we can do something with this."

Mikel cleared his throat, uncomfortable with the guilt by association but not arguing the point. "In order to get something like this taken seriously, you have to put together the entire case. You have to do the regulators' work for them, then leak it to the press, or what's left of the press. You have to embarrass them into it, make it so impossible for them *not* to pursue it that they would lose their jobs or be liable for prosecution if they didn't."

His eyes stayed on me the whole time he spoke, pushing his point from earlier.

Nola looked back and forth between us. "What?" she asked.

"I've asked Doyle to come and help me," Mikel said. "To help me do exactly the type of thing we're talking about."

Nola turned to me with an eyebrow cocked questioningly.

I shook my head. "I can't even think about that right now."

Mikel nodded. "All right. Well, if it's okay with you, one thing we can do is release this. Put it out on whistle-blower channels, give it to the press. Anonymously."

One of the things that had rankled about the way things had turned out was that in order to thwart Bourden's plan, I'd had to help protect Stoma's market share. It bugged me that I was helping Stoma in any way, protecting it, propping up its global dominance.

I looked at Nola, and she nodded just as the seat belt light came on.

I turned back to Mikel. "Do it."

He smiled and said, "Buckle up."

90

Regi was sitting with Miriam in a conference room at the court-house, close but not quite touching. Next to them was a thin man in his sixties wearing a drab but expensive-looking suit. He and Mikel exchanged a nod, and I figured it was Schultzman, the lawyer.

Miriam looked better—clean, fed, and rested—but stressed and a little shell-shocked.

Regi came over to me. I put out my hand to shake it, but he pushed it aside and gave me a big hug. Miriam came over and hugged me, as well. "Thanks," she said, trembling, her eyes wet.

"Sure thing," I said. I introduced her and Nola while Mikel and Schultzman exchanged a few words. Then the judge entered, seeming bored and harried. He asked us all to sit while he looked over the papers, looked at my ID—my passport—signed some documents, stamped some others, and sent the bailiff to process paperwork so they could release Miriam to my custody. Then he was gone.

While we waited, Schultzman studied his papers.

I introduced Regi to Nola and Mikel.

"So nice to meet you, Nola," he began, clasping her hands in his. Then did a double take and looked at Mikel. "Gregory Mikel?"

I gave a quick explanation of how Mikel was involved.

"Thank you for your help," Regi said, gracious but suspicious.

"Happy to help," Mikel said, clapping a hand on Regi's shoulder. "And don't worry," he said, leaning in close and lowering his voice. "If I were you, I wouldn't trust me, either." He displayed a big fake-looking smile. "Anyway, congratulations on your new position. I'll have someone from my charitable foundation contact you and see if there's some way we can help."

Regi nodded, slightly dazed. "Thank you."

Mikel then bent toward Miriam, mumbling reassurances, leading her back across the room toward Schultzman. He kept his hand on her arm, his focus on her and her alone as the three of them spoke quietly. I was just thinking that he reminded me of a politician when Regi said, "Do you trust him?"

I laughed quietly, ruefully. "I believe we're on the same side."

Now Regi laughed. "You be careful around him."

I nodded. "These days, I'm careful around everybody."

The bailiff came back ten minutes later, and then we were done. Miriam was in my custody, and we were headed to the airport.

It occurred to me that billionaire justice was almost as fast as billionaire Wi-Fi.

Before we got on the plane, I called Lieutenant Suarez.

He answered screaming. "Carrick? Where the fuck have you been? You're calling me now? After, what, three days of radio silence? I hope you got a note from a doctor that you've been in a coma, because otherwise, you are in the middle of a shit storm of biblical proportions. I mean it—biblical. You'd better build a fucking ark and start collecting animals, because you will be forever known as the Noah of shit storms."

For a moment, I actually considered asking Regi to write a note—from the minister of health, that ought to be good enough. "Please excuse Doyle Carrick from work these last few days. He has been in a coma."

Instead I said, "I'm in Haiti."

"Haiti? Carrick, what the fuck? Do you know what kind of trouble you're in? You know Mike Warren is trying to get a warrant for you? We're not talking job trouble, we're talking jail trouble. He's talking aiding and abetting a fugitive from justice—"

"I'm bringing her in."

"You're what?"

"I'm bringing in Miriam Hartwell. She turned herself in and is being extradited back to the States. But exculpatory evidence has come to light, so there will be a hearing with Judge Pauline Greenberg to clear her as soon as we return."

"Exculpatory evidence? What are you talking about?"

"Video of the real killers. Video of Ron Hartwell's murder."

He took a long, loud breath. I could feel him seething, now angry that in addition to everything else, I had gone around him. I could have explained I hadn't set it up, but it was a long explanation, and he was not in the mood. Neither was I. "And when is this?"

"We'll be there in about four hours."

"I can't wait. What flight?"

"We're in a private jet."

"Of course you are. Well, get your private-jet ass back here and get me that case file."

The drive to the airport was quiet and awkward, but when it was time to get on the plane, things got sloppy pretty quick. Mostly, it was Regi and Miriam saying good-bye, hugging and crying and saying they'd see each other soon.

I got more misty than sloppy. Mostly saying good-bye to Regi but also saying good-bye to Haiti itself.

I told him I'd be back. And I was pretty sure I meant it.

91

The mood on the plane had been somber even before we landed. There was a bit of a letdown after the initial victories. Then an hour outside of Haiti, Mikel received word that the Helio had been found with Sable inside it, dead. I don't think Mikel really thought Miriam might have been wrong about it, but when we got confirmation, I realized on some level he'd been holding on to a tiny bit of doubt or hope. Now that was gone.

When we landed, Philadelphia seemed like an alien planet. It was cold and wet, and the colors were all wrong. The greens were different. The browns were gray. Everything else was bathed in red and blue lights from the trio of police cars waiting for us on the tarmac. They felt alien, too. They felt like the enemy.

Suarez was standing in front of his black unmarked Impala, its grille lights flashing. Mike Warren and Lieutenant Myerson were next to another unmarked car, its grille lights flashing as well. Two uniforms were there with a patrol car. They were all standing in the cold drizzle watching us with the same pissy expression.

Before we got off the plane, I told Nola what to expect, that I'd be immediately consumed with police business, but that I'd see her at home soon. I kissed her, and she put her arms around me, lingering until I had to peel them off me.

"Don't be long," she said.

I told Miriam what to expect, as well, and that Schultzman and I would be with her the entire time.

I came down the steps with her, and Warren met us at the bottom step, trying not to smile as he held up a pair of cuffs.

He motioned for Miriam to turn around. She looked up at me, and I nodded. We had known this would be part of it.

Warren snapped on the cuffs, looking at me and muttering, "If you'd done this in the first place, we wouldn't have had to chase her halfway around the world."

I hooked my hand on Miriam's arm, staying with her as he led her to his car.

"And if you'd done proper police work," I muttered back, "you'd have known she wasn't the killer, and we wouldn't be cuffing her at all."

We led her to the back door of the patrol car and inserted her inside. The two uniforms got in the front. I went around and to the other side.

"Where are you going?" Suarez asked.

Warren was walking back to his car. He stopped and turned.

"I'm accompanying Ms. Hartwell to the hearing," I said.

He shook his head. "No, you're coming with me to get that goddamn case file and get Warren and Myerson off my ass."

That got a grin from Warren.

I looked back at the plane, at Nola and Mikel standing at the top of the steps. "Afterward," I said as I got in the car.

As we drove off, I could see Warren outside bitching to Suarez. I think the two uniforms realized they were in the middle of something messy, and they just wanted to get the hell out of there.

It was very strange riding in the back of the patrol car instead of the front. I knew the doors wouldn't open from the inside, and I felt claustrophobic. Miriam was trembling, and I put my hand over hers.

We rode in silence to the courtroom, across the street from city hall. We parked in the back and used the rear entrance, getting directly onto the elevator to the seventh floor, where we sat on a bench out in a hallway. Less than a minute later, Warren and Myerson showed up. Warren glared at me as he stepped off the elevator. Myerson looked bored. Mikel and Schultzman arrived just as the bailiff opened the door and led us into the conference room.

Judge Greenberg was already seated at the head of the table, looking at copies of the extradition paperwork. She was a small woman in her fifties with a stern face. I'd seen her before but had never been in court with her. That was probably a good thing.

Schultzman took a seat next to the judge and directed Miriam to the seat on his other side. Warren sat across from Schultzman, looking nervous until Suarez arrived and sat next to him.

It filled me with the warm and fuzzies that my own lieutenant was sitting on the opposite side of the table from me, helping Mike Warren.

Greenberg looked up. "Everybody here?"

Warren and Schultzman murmured, "Yes."

Greenberg recited a bunch of legal boilerplate, explaining why we were there. She asked Miriam if she understood, and at Schultzman's prodding, she said, "Yes."

"Okay," Greenberg said wearily. "Looks like a pretty tight case. But apparently there's exculpatory evidence. Is that correct, Mr. Schultzman?"

"There is, Your Honor."

She waved her fingers. "Let's have it."

As he opened his computer, Schultzman explained that his client had come into possession of previously undiscovered security video.

Greenberg cocked an eyebrow. "How did this come into your possession?"

Schultzman said, "An anonymous tip, Your Honor. And then data recovery to retrieve it."

Her eyebrow retained its position. "Better be good."

Schultzman clicked Play.

By the end of it, Greenberg's eyebrows had relaxed. Suarez and Myerson were scowling at Warren.

"Pretty compelling stuff," Greenberg said. She turned to Warren. "Do you have anything to say, Detective Warren?"

"The defendant's fingerprints are on the murder weapon, which was found on the premises of her home."

She nodded. "That's a good point too. Mr. Schultzman?"

"Your Honor, the video clearly shows the murder and the murderers."

"But if her fingerprints are on the murder weapon, she could be an accessory, couldn't she?"

Schultzman seemed momentarily taken aback that the video was not the slam dunk he had anticipated. I think he was more a paperwork kind of lawyer than a trial lawyer.

I cleared my throat. "Um . . . Your Honor?"

She looked down the table at me. "Who are you?"

"Detective Doyle Carrick, Your Honor."

Suarez leaned forward. "Detective Carrick is not officially involved this case, Your Honor. The murder occurred on his front steps."

"Do you have something to add, Detective Carrick?"

"Yes, just a question for Detective Warren, because I was wondering about the fingerprints too."

Warren's eyes burned as he looked at me.

Greenberg paused for a moment and then said, "What's your question?"

"Miriam Hartwell had no arrest record, so I was wondering where you got the prints to compare to the murder weapon?"

His eye twitched. "Energene had them on file."

I nodded, trying to keep my face as blank and non-gloating as possible. When I was at Energene's offices, they used a palm scanner to access the corporate suite. "The men in the video, the killers, work in the security department at Energene Corporation, where Ron and Miriam Hartwell both worked."

/

"And?" Greenberg asked.

I had been hoping Warren would say it himself, but the way his jaw was clenched, I think his skull would have shattered if he tried to speak.

"They use palm scanners at their corporate offices. If they had Miriam Hartwell's fingerprints on file, they could have easily added them to the weapon and planted it." I shrugged. "Frankly, it seemed odd to me that Miriam Hartwell would have returned to stash the murder weapon on the premises of her own home without stopping in to take any of her personal belongings, prescription medication, or cash before fleeing."

Greenberg swung her head toward Warren, both eyebrows raised. He sat there grinding his teeth.

Greenberg gave him a generous ten count, then turned to Miriam. "Okay. Ms. Hartwell, on behalf of the City of Philadelphia, I apologize for any inconvenience. The bailiff will take you for processing, and then you'll be free to go." She turned to Warren. "Detective Warren, if more evidence comes to light implicating Ms. Hartwell, I'd be happy to consider it, but as of now, the charges are dismissed."

92

The judge left through one door, followed a moment later by Miriam, who was in a daze, being led by the bailiff. Schultzman and Mikel excused themselves and left the same way they had come in.

Then it was just us cops.

"Hey, guys," I said with a big smile.

"Fuck you, Carrick," Warren said, his face caught between a scowl and a pout. "You ain't out of the woods yet, either. You still owe me that case file you took home with you. And you'd better not have lost it."

"He's right, Carrick," Suarez added, standing. "Let's go get it right now. You're on thin ice, and that's mighty close to obstruction of justice. Keep pushing it, and you're bounced."

Myerson looked at his feet.

"Oh, that's right," I said. "I forgot—you needed the case file back so you could hand it over to the actual murderers."

That shut them up. All of them. I kind of liked that, but the silence was getting awkward.

"Hey, I have an idea," I said, just to break the tension. "Instead of giving the murderers the case files, why don't we arrest them? You know, since they're the actual murderers and all."

The three of them stared at me with three different iterations of hatred. I didn't actually care. Fuck 'em. I couldn't believe that these idiots had come so close to such a big screw-up, and they were sitting there trying to tell me I was in trouble.

Almost on a lark, I took out my phone and called Energene, dialed zero, and asked to speak to Bryant at the front desk.

It was Sunday night, so I didn't expect him to be there, but he was. "Front desk. Bryant speaking." I wondered if they ever let him go home.

"Hi, Mr. Bryant. This is Detective Doyle Carrick from the Philly PD. I was there a few days ago."

"Certainly, Detective. How can I help you?"

"Thanks, Mr. Bryant. I don't know if you remember, but I was in there speaking with Tom Royce, helping him with a possible corporate espionage investigation. I may have some information that he would find very interesting. I know he's been out of the country, but I was wondering if you could tell me when you expected him back."

"Sure thing, Detective. He and Mr. Divock are due back this evening. Mr. Royce asked me to stay late for a quick security briefing at seven o'clock. But then they're not due to be in the office for some time after that."

I thanked him and got off the phone, then looked at the others. "Royce and Divock are due back at the office for a meeting at seven o'clock tonight."

They stared back at me blankly, like none of them had an idea what they should do next. I turned to Warren, since he didn't outrank me and technically this was still his case. "Maybe you could call the airlines and see if any of the flights from Haiti have Divock and Royce booked as passengers."

He did, and they did. Ten minutes later, we were driving to the airport. I rode with Suarez. We didn't talk much, but we had fun just being together. Warren and Myerson drove alone in separate cars.

Once we got there, the three of them stood away from me, talking in hushed tones. That was okay. I had no desire to talk with any of them.

Royce and Divock were on an American Airlines flight from Port-au-Prince. We got to the gate just in time to meet them. Suarez had begrudgingly allowed me to be there for the bust—he couldn't say no after I had cracked the case—but only on the condition that immediately afterward I had to get the case file for Warren.

Royce and Divock were among the first ones off the plane. First class. Pricks.

Royce saw me first. His eyes narrowed and his face grew redder. For an instant, he looked around like a trapped animal, then he seemed to accept the situation and tried to regain his cool. Divock didn't notice a thing until Warren was holding up his badge in front of their faces, reading the charges—they were under arrest for the murder of Ron Hartwell—and their Miranda rights.

The other passengers streamed past around them, looking furtively at the commotion and then moving along quickly before any of the trouble rubbed off on them.

Royce stared at my face the whole time, like he was studying it, remembering it, like I should be scared he was going to come after me.

Other than that, they went quietly. Anticlimactically. Maybe even disappointingly.

Yes, it was a victory, and I was glad to see them both arrested, but Mikel was right: they were just assholes for hire, doing what they were told. I wanted the assholes who were giving the orders, assholes like Bourden and Pearce. It wasn't over yet, but I wasn't expecting that they would pay for their crimes the same way their employees would.

By the time we left the airport, it was almost dark again. I'd been awake for a long, long time, but it felt right that it was nighttime again, like the daylight had been some kind of illusion.

I drove with Suarez back to the station. My work was done, even if it didn't feel like it. I was exhausted. I was dying to get home and be with Nola—and Suarez was dying to get that case file back—but I also wanted to see Royce and Divock booked. Suarez bitched— "Come on, Carrick, you've seen that shit a million times. You think it's going to be different somehow this time?"—but I insisted.

Suarez looked at his watch, then he put a finger in my face. "Okay. You see them booked, then we get the case file, or I will fucking arrest you."

I don't know why it seemed so important. Maybe I was hoping it would make the whole thing feel more satisfying.

It didn't. It was the same boring procedure as every time I had done it myself. The same crappy room, the sickly fluorescent light. It was even worse because I was sitting there with Lieutenant Suarez.

My phone buzzed, and I looked at it. Mikel. Definitely not the time to be talking to him.

I was surprised to see Lieutenant Myerson processing Royce and Divock, instead of Warren. Maybe they didn't trust him not to screw it up.

Myerson looked surprised to see me too. He looked at Suarez, and they exchanged a shrug.

I don't know if Royce and Divock were surprised to see me there. They seemed sullen and detached, already gone to whatever neutral mental place would allow them to endure.

Myerson finished processing Royce and Divock, and he led them away. Suarez immediately looked at his watch and stood up. "Okay, come on, Carrick, let's go."

"In a minute," I said.

"No," he said. "Now. It's been a long fucking day. You've been jerking me around for hours. I'm driving you to your house, and you're going to give me that case file—now. Or I'm locking you up." He took a deep breath. "Jesus, don't you want to go home?"

I did want to go home. But I looked at him, studied him. He looked at his watch again. He wasn't just antsy. He was worried. "Come on, goddammit. Let's get the fuck out of here."

And then I knew something was up.

I sat there, unmoving, and he reached down to grab my arm. I don't know if he would have actually laid a hand on me, because just then, the door to the hallway opened, and Mike Warren walked in with a prisoner in handcuffs.

Miriam Hartwell.

93

"Doyle!" she cried out when she saw me. Her face looked as crushed and terrified as it had back in Everglades City, when Axe-Man showed up to kill her.

Warren saw me, and he looked at Suarez. "What the fuck? You said you'd have the file by now."

"Just get on with it," Suarez snapped. Then he turned to me. "And you, come on. No more bullshit. We're going to get that case file, or you're getting locked up too."

"What the hell is going on?" I demanded.

"They arrested me again," Miriam called over her shoulder as Warren steered her away from me. "After they let me go, they re-arrested me for flight from prosecution and resisting arrest."

I turned to Suarez. "You've got to be fucking kidding me. She's innocent!"

"Not of that, she ain't," Warren said with a smile. "Sorry, Carrick. You might have been right about Royce and Divock, but I'm right about this."

"You'll never make it stick. No judge in the city will uphold this."

Warren looked at me, one eyebrow twitching, one corner of his mouth curled up. He knew he wasn't going to get a conviction. He just wanted her in a jail for a few days or a few weeks while she waited for her dismissal. He just wanted her to suffer, wanted me to suffer. Because we'd made him look bad.

"Come on," Suarez said, resting his hand on my arm, almost like he was consoling me, almost like he was admitting how fucked up this was. "We need to go get the case file."

I jerked my arm away from him. "Bullshit. You can't be serious."

"You know what? Fuck you," he said. "Yes, I'm serious. This is Warren's case, Warren's bust, Warren's decision. It's not up to you or me. It's not your case file, and it's not your decision what Warren does with it or what every other cop on the force does when you're not around. It's not about you, Carrick. So I mean it—we're going to get the case file right now, or you're under arrest for obstruction of justice. And if there's anything missing from that file, I swear to God, I will personally drop-kick you off the force."

I wanted to hit him. I wanted to punch him right in the face. I think he would have been fine with that. It would have saved him a lot of trouble.

Instead, I turned to Miriam and said, "Don't worry. This is bullshit. I'll get you out, okay?"

She nodded bravely, trying to keep it together.

Then I turned to Suarez and said, "Okay, let's go."

Suarez was fuming as we drove, his hands squeezing the steering wheel. Maybe I was giving him too much credit, but I think he was as angry at the situation he'd been forced into as he was at me for the usual reasons.

I texted Mikel, "Miriam rearrested. Flight from prosecution. Can you send Schultzman?"

"r u kidding?"

"I wish."

I could see Suarez's eyes drifting over, trying to see what I was texting.

A few seconds later, Mikel texted back. "He's on his way. Have you thought about my offer?"

I didn't reply.

Nola didn't look up when I first walked in. I was surprised, but I was happy to have a moment to take in the sight. She was sitting on the sofa with her feet on the coffee table and her computer on her lap. She looked great. There was a fire crackling in the fireplace across from her—a little early in the season, but it was cold and wet out there. The room was filled with a golden glow that seemed to be emanating from her as much as from anywhere else.

Then I noticed her expression, staring intently at her computer, her face showing a strange combination of emotions.

"Mikel did it," she said, distracted, still not looking up. "He sent it all out there—Ron's files, the recording, all of it."

"What are you talking about?"

"Stoma and Energene are declining comment, but at this moment, shit is hitting the fan." She angled the computer so I could see the screen as I sat down next to her. "Interpol is seeking Bourden and Pearce for questioning. Opposition leaders in half a dozen governments are calling for internal investigations. Trade groups in Southeast Asia and Central Africa are calling for new votes on authorizations of Soyagene and Early Rise. Even Stoma-Grow."

I scrolled down the page. It was big. In addition to all the legal and political repercussions, it looked like shares of Stoma and Energene had both taken a substantial hit.

She looked up at me, smiling wide. "You kind of did it," she said, coming in for a hug, her face buried against my neck. "And now you're home."

I squeezed her, too, but she pulled back and looked up at me, sensing something was wrong.

"What's the matter?" she said. "This is good news, right? Are you okay? Is Miriam okay?"

I let out a short, bitter laugh. "I'm here for the case file," I told her. "Suarez is waiting for it outside. They need it ASAP because they rearrested Miriam. They're booking her for flight from prosecution."

Her smile remained for a moment, like she assumed it was a joke. "They can't do that." But I guess she could see from my expression that they could. "What are you going to do?"

I didn't know. Massive crimes against humanity were going on right under their noses—epic injustices, evil douchebags sickening thousands in order to make billions, wholesale murder—and Suarez, Warren, Myerson, they didn't even want to know. All they cared about were the rules, the turf, saving face, and looking good while doing a half-assed job.

Arresting an innocent woman for fleeing a half-assed prosecution for a crime she hadn't committed was exactly the kind of petty bullshit bust they excelled at.

"I don't know if I can do this anymore," I said. "Being a cop, I mean. The bullshit's getting pretty deep."

We hadn't talked about Mikel's offer, but we both knew it was there.

"He called," she said. "Mikel. He said he'd been trying to reach you."

I nodded.

She reached up and touched my face. "You know I'm behind you whatever you do."

I nodded. "Thanks."

The case file was on the coffee table. She watched me as I opened it and started leafing through the pages, hoping something would come to mind.

Outside, Suarez started honking his horn.

Nola put her hand on my knee. "What are you going to do?"

I didn't have a whole lot of choice. I had to hand it over. Suarez had said he'd arrest me if I didn't, and I believed him. He'd make it stick, too.

He was leaning on his horn.

Looking down, I realized I'd made two piles. The larger pile, the bulk of the pages, were the documents central to Mike Warren's misguided murder investigation: forensics reports, ballistics, photos, witness statements. The smaller pile was just three pages.

My report about meeting with Miriam at the Liberty Motel, Warren's notes about how it proved she was fleeing prosecution. That was the only proof they had that she had fled knowing she was wanted for murder.

As I put the rest of the file back into the folder, Suarez started banging on the door—*bang, bang, bang.* Nola jumped, and so did I. The last time someone banged on our door like that it was Ron Hartwell just before he was killed. That was how this whole thing had started. I thought about the investigation, about how it had been mishandled. It was negligent. Criminal. Maybe even intentional.

Nola squeezed my leg. "Doyle, what's going on?"

I held up the pages I had kept out of the folder. "This is my statement after the incident at the Liberty Motel. This is what Mike Warren needs to prosecute Miriam Hartwell. I was the only one to speak to her before she took off."

"I don't understand."

"Suarez said that if I didn't give him the file I'd be arrested for obstructing justice." I stood up. "He also said if anything was missing from it, he'd have me kicked off the force."

"What are you thinking?"

I dropped those three pages into the fire and watched as the flames enveloped them. "I'm thinking, let him."

ACKNOWLEDGMENTS

This book started, as most of mine do, with a handful of ideas that I found fascinating and compelling. Some were expanded upon and became essential to the finished book, and some did not, but they were all assuredly part of the process, and in that sense, they are in there. I would like to thank Mary Ellen McNish and Idrissa Dicko at The Hunger Project for their invaluable assistance and support and their fascinating insights during the early stages of this book.

Many people were essential to my research into the broader issues at the heart of this book. Bill Freese at the Center for Food Safety and Patty Lovera at Food & Water Watch have been great resources and incredibly generous with their time and expertise. Eric Holt-Jiminez at Food First and Steve Brescia at Groundswell International were invaluable in putting issues surrounding food, agriculture, and land into broader contexts and deepening my understanding of them in ways that go far beyond what is contained in this book.

I took great pains to make sure the science in this book is real and the slight extrapolations are entirely plausible. For that, I thank world-renowned allergist Hugh A. Sampson, M.D., for his incredible expertise and his generosity in sharing it. Thanks to my friend and fellow author Chris Holm for many things: tirelessly sharing his great knowledge of molecular biology and immunology; helping me write lab scenes both accurate and compelling; for "getting it" like a writer—appreciating what I was trying to accomplish, and helping me get there; and for enlisting the help of his colleagues, Jesse S. Buch and Regis Krah. (Thanks, Jesse and Regis!)

As for the technical research, pilots Rick Longlott and Rick Dupont were both hugely helpful with the details of the planes involved, especially the Helio Couriers. I spent considerable time staring openmouthed at film of those crazy little planes taking off and landing, under the guise of "research." Thanks to Neal Griffin for his help with the details of law enforcement. Thanks to my sister Maeve McGoran and my brother-in-law Greg Allen for their help with the Florida scenes. And thanks to Dennis Tafoya for helping me work through countless plot points and details.

When I realized a large portion of this book was going to be set in Haiti, I was both excited and daunted. Early in my research into the ideas behind this book, people began telling me, "You really need to talk to Chavannes Jean Baptiste." Chavannes is the founder of the Papaye Peasant Movement, an organization that for forty years has been supporting land reform and helping Haitians build healthy and fulfilling lives through sustainable small-scale agriculture. I am immensely grateful to Wendy Flick and all the great people at the Unitarian Universalist College of Social Justice, not just for organizing the trip to Haiti, but for making it possible for me to sit down and talk with Chavannes. And I'd like to thank Chavannes Jean Baptiste himself, and all the people at MPP, for their hospitality during our stay, for their knowledge and insights, and for all the great work they are doing for Haiti. Very special thanks to Mayheeda Edwards, translator extraordinaire while we were there, and priceless resource afterward. Thanks also to Marie-Renee Malvoisin, for her help in making sure the Kreyol passages were correct.

One of the great perks of being a writer is getting to hang out with other writers, and I am grateful to the wonderful communities of writers who have made me feel so welcome, to publications like *Crimespree, Spinetingler, Crime Factory,* and *Criminal Element;* conferences like Bouchercon, Thrillerfest, NoirCon, and all the others; and groups like the Mystery Writers of America, the International Thriller Writers, the Writers Coffeehouse, and, most of all, The Liars Club. And especially for my great friend and mentor Jonathan Maberry, for all his support and for all he has done to foster community among the writers of the world.

Finally, I'd like to thank my wonderful editor, Kristin Sevick, as well as Bess Cozby and everyone else at Tor/Forge, Daniel Cullen for consistently excellent cover designs, my incredible agent, Stacia Decker, and everyone else at Donald Maass Literary Agency, and as always, my wife, Elizabeth, and my son, Will, (and Kismet, who is a very good little dog).